My Booty Novel

Published by Wheatmark™
610 East Delano Street, Suite 104, Tucson, Arizona 85705 U.S.A.
www.wheatmark.com

International Standard Book Number: 978-1-58736-637-6
Library of Congress Control Number: 2006924769

"Pavel ... a lonely bachelor, was entering upon that indefinite twilight period of regrets that are akin to hopes, and hopes that are akin to regrets, when youth is over, while old age has not yet come."

—Ivan Turgenev, *Fathers and Sons*

"I'm in some ass right now."

"I'm in some ass right now?"

"Yeah."

That was my boy, Kevin. I hadn't seen him since the Cataclysm and only once since the book tour, which was disastrous in itself. So, it's been about four months and forty pounds since we've really sat down and talked like this.

We did need to have a talk—other than this one. But there are so many things I *don't* want to talk about. This was the least painful—believe it or not.

"And those should be the first words of my next novel?"

"Damn skippy, brother man."

Kev E. Kev's my best friend. We've known each other since college—when I was trying to become a literary genius and he was trying to get everybody to forget about Miles Davis—then John Coltrane—then Charlie Parker—then John Holmes. He was pretty damned successful on that last task at our small, elitist university. Boy, could that boy get laid. While I was always good for a chuckle—I'm mildly humorous—he was wildly erotic. Women would ask me if I'd just awakened from a twenty-year slumber while we all knew Kevin had just stepped out of a magazine. Women—and, well, some men, too—just love the man. I think it's the light-skin'ded brother thang, tall muscular frame, and hazel eyes, or the talented musician thing or his being two points away from Mensa. He's also homoerotically well-groomed (I mean, who the hell trims their beard, anyway?). Of course, it could just be his confidence. Hell, he's one of those narcissistic bastards you'd always suspected of masturbating in a mirror, but he's a'ight. After all, he's never too far from gettin' some, and that knowledge would make anyone bold. When you're like me now, who needs the Hubble telescope to locate a willing partner, you generally skulk off into a corner and lick your wounds with your favorite beer. Kevin? He's hardly ever been scratched.

"Look, Damian," Kevin was continuing over the last of his Red Stripe, "what was your last novel about—in a sentence?"

I shrugged. I was nursing my...beer? Devastated pride? Broken heart?

"No. Really. What?"

"If I could've described it in a sentence, I wouldn't have written a fucking book."

Did I mention how much more successful Kevin was with women in college than I was? It never really bugged me. I was going through a lot of stuff back then. So was he. It's just that I took my stuff out on myself. So did he. He just needed a woman to "exorcise" his demons. And he was a musician. I always think it's easier for them. People get music a lot easier than they do the written word. People aren't tortured with music in high school. If only Thomas Hardy had played guitar. Besides, writers don't really have a stage on which to seduce. Hell, most of us are too shy to even approach one. That's why we're writers. To never have to interact with others. So I never begrudged the brother his success (it's not as though anybody—but myself—has locked me up in a bell tower). But why did his first album have to do *so* much better than my first novel? A damned gold record.

"Damn, you're sensitive."

"Well, I—"

"Two more Red Stripes."

Just then, our waitress plopped two more of my favorite beers on our table. She was a stick figure with hip-hugging, distressed jeans (distressed over the nonexistent hips they could never hug), a concave stomach, a cute blond bob, and an old *Cheers* T-shirt that tapped out where breasts were supposed to be.

"Thanks, Diane," I joked.

"It's Dakota," she huffed.

"Ah ... the shirt."

"Shit, I was like, ten when that went off the air."

She walked off, shaking what a draconian diet would never give her. Kevin laughed, of course.

"Schmoove."

The waitress who used to plop down those Red Stripes was this fine, bi-racial sister, Brianna, with tremendous child-bearers that had not-so-recently (I'd heard) bore two children to her Japanese percussionist husband. I can't believe it's been that long since I'd last stepped into The Scotsman Bar & Grille.

"When was the last time you hit on a woman?"

"Man, that wasn't hitting on a woman."

"No shit."

"I was just *trying* to be clever."

"And when was the last time you were that?"

Like my "line" (which really and truly was not), nothing was quite right tonight. Everything was familiar, yet eerily askew. I was sitting with my best friend in what used to be my favorite bar, drinking my favorite beer, which I hadn't had in a while. Kevin was probably still the same. He always seemed to be. Red Stripe never fails. Lord knows the beer-sticky floor hadn't changed a bit. But me? I'm different. Who wouldn't be after the year I've had? And Brianna hadn't served a drink in this place for some three years, probably on her third child with Junichiro. Lucky bastard. God, I used to love that woman.

I used to love this place. The Scotsman used to be a joint where I could relax, where I didn't have to be beautiful or cool, where I felt I belonged. Because I didn't belong. Nobody did. The Land of Misfit Toys. It was a place where bi-curious babes would make out with bull dykes, get into fist fights with them, and *not* cause a scene; where guys with more tattoos than flesh and more piercings than holes would roam around with their Pabst Blue Ribbons. Where you could hear, "Damn, my dick hurts," and wouldn't bat an eye because you knew some guy had just added another balled rod to his balled rod.

Reformed rockabilly skinheads and black nationalist dreads roamed these sticky floors with A Tribe Called Quest and The Cramps battling it out on the jukebox when there wasn't live music in the house, Johnny Cash and Chuck D, with cheap beer, Rage Against the Machine, and Brianna the common uniters.

But now Brianna was replaced by Diane/Dakota. I guess the dreads and skins have either grown out or cut their hair and go to PTA meetings with Junichiro. The Scotsman's famous concert space is now an arcade and the misfit toys have all been replaced by high tech gadgetry that always confuses me with their acronyms.

"When did this place become a yuppie bar?"

"God, about two years ago," Kevin informed me. "That's why I was surprised you wanted to come here."

"I don't really know anyplace else."

"You still didn't answer my question … or would you rather talk about Samara?"

"That one sentence?!" I yelped.

"Yeah. When someone was looking for that one sentence to describe your book—which is all anyone's really looking for, anyway—what did you say?"

Did I mention that my book tour was disastrous?

"I said, 'If I could've described it in a sentence, I wouldn't have written a book.'"

"That must've gone well."

"Like a lead zeppelin."

On to Beer #2. Maybe it would get the salty taste out of my wounds. "Well," I suddenly piped up, "at least I didn't say 'fucking.'"

"Look, D," Kev started, "I promised not to talk about—well, you know.

I told you all about my *stellar* music career. Do you know that it's lik—ah, skip it. Anyway, you've gotta check out this new singer. She's the real deal, man. Seriously. Making me think about changing directions totally. But other than that, what do we have to talk about? I mean, I haven't seen you in God knows how long."

"My Steelers are doing well."

He gave me that "Bitch" look I've grown to know so well over the years. But what would you expect from a Giants fan?

"All right, all right," I finally conceded, "I told folks that *Winter Soldiers* was a semi-satirical, postmodern science fiction novel about how you can never win a war of occupation."

"Is that one sentence?"

"Yeah. But probably too many syllables."

"You got that right."

"Hell, it's not even what the novel's about. It was just the best I could do."

"I guess that's why it only sold a thousand copies."

"Five hundred."

I mean, *five hundred*! You spend some twenty years wanting to write your first novel and ... and ... Breathe ... Breathe ...

"Damn," Kevin conceded.

His CD went Gold. Oh, I think I already said that.

"That about sums it up."

"Hey, D. Remember in college, how we both wanted to be geniuses?"

"Everybody considered you a genius. I was just that crazy, drunk nigger off in the corner."

"All you had to do was get your hair cut once in a while. That Pirates cap wasn't foolin' anybody."

I chuckled. "Ain't that the truth?"

"Anyway, remember all that crazy reading and studying and writing we did? You with all your existentialist and deconstructionist philosophy."

"Give a brother some credit, I did go through my black nationalist phase. Garvey, Diop—'It's a Black Thing You Wouldn't Understand.' I wonder if I still have that T-shirt."

"Damn, and 'Black to the Future.' Anyway, you had that shit and I was all about studying 'The Greats,' too. Bird, Diz, Armstrong, Miles, Monk, Mingus. I wish I had a damn M in my name. I would've been halfway there. Then there was Ayler and Air. And my classical phase. And who can forget my John Cage fixation?"

"It was a hell of a lot better than when you forced me to listen to *Pet Sounds* for a goddamned month."

"Hey, Brian Wilson's a genius."

"Fuck the Beach Boys."

"Troglodyte."

"Yeah. I'd rather listen to Jimmy Castor any day."

"See, Damian. That's your problem. You're too damned obscure. Nobody knows what the hell you're talking about."

There were too many things I wanted to say to that but not much I really could say. He was right.

"Those were actually fun times, Kevin. The thrill of discovery, and all that."

"I know. I loved them. I wish I still had that thrill. Remember when we were high in Iowa, listening to Mingus, and I couldn't put down my horn?"

"Yeah. You were a real asshole that night."

"Shit, what about your acid trip where you couldn't stop talking about how Bugs Bunny was nothing but Brer Rabbit and how it was yet another example of white people denying and appropriating black genius?"

"Anyway."

"Yeah. Anyway. Do you know what really changed my life, Damian?"

"Dianetics?"

"No. Realizing this poor black son of an Alabama sharecropper—"

"You're from Teaneck, New Jersey, punk."

"Long live the Isley Brothers!"

We clinked beer bottles.

"Realizing that I was never gonna be any of those fools," he informed. "That maybe I'm a genius. Maybe not. But no matter what, I wasn't going to be *that* kind of genius."

"And that's why you came out with a fusion record?"

The Bitch look again. Maybe it was the obvious disdain in my voice. But seriously, Kev's album makes Kenny G. sound like NWA.

"Probably. I don't know. But it was liberating, man. To not have *that* struggle anymore. To not worry about how I stack up against the people I idolize."

"So, I'll never be Toni Morrison?"

"Who knows? Who cares? I mean, you both have dreads. What I do know, though, is that whatever you described to me in that *really* long, polysyllabic sentence won't sell books. And it definitely won't get you on Oprah."

"And 'I'm in some ass right now' will?"

It was Kevin's turn to shrug.

"Hell if I know. But you gotta admit, ass does sell. It sells books, it sells movies, definitely sells music."

"Cars, beer, shampoo…"

"Everything! You'll never see an ugly woman in a tampon commercial.

It's everywhere, D. Hell, we could drive up the block and go buy some right now."

"So, I should write about getting $5 blow jobs from transsexual prostitutes?"

"Hey, gender confusion is no laughing matter. You, of all people, should know that."

"Funny."

"I thought so. But seriously, chuck the sci-fi and write a booty novel."

"A booty novel?"

"Hell yeah. Everybody's got booty. Everybody loves booty. And everybody's always trying to get somebody else's booty. Why not write about it?"

"Because I'm a science-fiction writer."

Kevin smiled. "Look Damian, you might think obscurity's a curse, but the cool thing about it is that you don't have a fan base to piss off when you switch up on them. If Garth Brooks could've been so lucky."

"To have his problems."

"Maybe you could, if you wrote a booty novel."

"But—"

"Well then, hell, D, write a semi-satirical, postmodern booty novel, if it'll make you happy."

It was definitely time for that third beer.

My Booty Novel

Bill Campbell

SUNDAY, SEPTEMBER 23, 20—
9:35 P.M.

Back to blog,
Back to reality…

I know it's been a long time. To all three of my fans who read this damned thing, I apologize. I know how disappointing it must've been for the past four months to not be able to wallow in the shit of my life. But don't worry. The stench is back.

In all honesty, I hate the whole web log thing. As though it's not self-important enough to write a book and expect everybody to read it, we've gone and created the greatest masturbatory scheme for any narcissist who wants to share his most insipid utterance with the entire world … EVERY DAY!!! I am not that fool, but my publisher and agent both think this thing is a good marketing tool. Of course, those are the same jackasses who'd thought *Winter Soldiers* had commercial potential. Who knows? Without this stupid blog I may have only sold *490* copies of the book.

Now, to answer some questions:

No. I ended up not getting married. So, I take back all the nice things I ever said about *her* during the tour.

Yes. I really did enjoy the tour. Sure, I was a leper in Louisville, syphilitic in Cincinnati, and hemorrhagic in Houston. I found out what it must feel like to have a horrific disfigurement. To have people *not* look at you with a quiet desperation in their eyes. Focusing on everything but you. Afraid to look at the freak show standing in the middle of their bookstore. "Really, dear, you'd think they'd do something about that. Cover it up, something." One guy in Memphis actually climbed over me, my table, my books, and the sign announcing my book signing to get to some postcards without ever making eye contact. I was pretty impressed, actually. I mean, what determination. Another guy walked *through* my reading in Charlotte (to my cousin and her roommate) to buy a Grisham novel. And I guided so many people to *The Da Vinci Code,* I wanted a damned paycheck.

But yes. I still had a great time. If it were easy—like cheating on one's partner—everybody would be doing it. It was all forty extra pounds of good eatin' and tons of fun. (If you haven't already, hit the nearest Brazilian barbecue—your arteries will hate it but your taste buds will thank me.) There were a bunch of friends and family I hadn't seen in a long time who were great hosts. I got to party in Malibu and watch Fox News in Boston, two things I'd never done before. The Ethiopian party in Atlanta was a blast. I suffered the worst hangover in Portland and got to eat at Dick's in Spokane. I had great talks in Albany and Birmingham, San Diego and Vegas. And Paul's sneaking me onto Paisley Park to catch a glimpse of His Royal Badness was definitely a highlight. Oh yeah, and that wine-tasting in Sonoma—très chic. Some of the bookstore owners and employees looked at me like a lost cancer patient when nobody showed up, but everybody was really nice. And I guess those doe-eyed looks of sympathy prepared me for the ones I'd get once I got back home.

No. I did not get married after all.

Wait. I said that already.

No. I didn't go to Wales and jack that kid who wrote that horrible review of *Winter Soldiers*. I've decided to try and let it go. Why the hell you'd give a high schooler a satirical postmodern novel is beyond me. And to believe, when I originally came up with the idea, that little blankety-blank was only five! Oh well, you put something out and everybody gets to take their shot. That's what you get for being self-important enough to think that people should read your book.

Anyway, my life has changed a bit in these past few months. I've finally left Satan's lair. It's still hard getting the sulfur stench out of my clothes and hair, but it's good to finally be done with her (who am I kidding?). I now have a tiny room in a rented house with my cousin, Deirdre, and her housemates, Neville and Hep (they're together).

DiDi has saved my ass yet again. She's a year older and has always been a bit of a big sister to me. Those lines were permanently blurred in high school after my parents died and her parents took me in. She stood up for me when some neighborhood kids wanted to see if the black came off my skin by kicking it hard—and often. She tried fixing me up with some of her friends in high school—and then decided tilting at windmills would be more productive (by college, I could fend for myself). She'd used her connections at the battered women's shelter she worked at to get me a job at the Union, a homeless advocacy/service organization, when I first got to town. In short, she's my girl.

The only thing that has ever stood between us was Samara. And DiDi was right about that one. Any woman who's willing to break Luke Sams's nose for you ought to be listened to. But a man has two brains that hardly ever seem to work in conjunction, and, when they do, it's usually trouble for everyone involved. It wasn't until the fifth year of Samara's and my relationship that my cousin and I came to an understanding about the woman I loved. On the seventh, I moved in with cuz.

It's your usual, dilapidated one-story, three-bedroom rental house. Too many wars have passed since its glory days, and it's drafty as hell. There are stains all over the place from when Lizzie Borden whacked her parents, and I sometimes think I smell the Lindbergh baby rotting beneath the kitchen floorboards.

It's cool enough, though. There are a lot of things to get accustomed to. I'm used to living with only one other person—not three. And I'm still trying to get used to listening to guys having sex with each other. Neville's a real screamer, and I sometimes think he and Hep have cockfights over who can be louder. Hep's real cool, though. He does a lot of peace and justice stuff and conflict resolution, which is funny since all he and Neville do are fight and fuck. He's got good taste in music—though he's way too serious about it—about everything—and usually loses out to his lover's milquetoast tastes. Actually, I think he loses out to Neville on just about everything.

And that bastard Neville does not like me. I think he thinks I'm some sort of pot-smoking, loser asshole. Though he does smoke just about as much pot as I do. I'd like to chalk it up to my omnivorous ways. The man's a vegan. Apparently, he'd reigned in this house for a couple years before I arrived. No meat in the abode whatsoever. No eggs. No dairy. A tyranny of tofu. They lived in absolute terror. I think what finally did it for DiDi was when her curves began to plateau. A sister just can't be havin' that.

It was a bloodless coup, relatively speaking. A Velveeta Revolution. DiDi had brought home some ground chuck one night, made spaghetti sauce, loaded her plate with parmesan cheese, and ate dinner in front of the black and white TV. Neville came home, smelled the murder, gawked at the crime scene, and skulked off into his bedroom. Nothing was said. Days later, the carcass parade hit the refrigerator.

That was about two months before I moved in. I didn't know meat had been an issue when I'd first gone grocery shopping, but Hep told me later. I've kind of gotten into cooking recently. To keep my mind off of other things. And I love my meat. I've compromised by buying free range chicken. And while I can't get "Born Free" out of my head while picturing the birds prance to the slaughterhouse, I don't know how it's any better. It still tastes like chicken.

I just think that Neville's taking his frustration with losing his battle to DiDi out on her cousin. He doesn't really say anything. He just looks down his broad, beautiful, black nose at me. When it's not beneath him to talk to a brother, he huffs a lot and gives me that "I'm *trying* to be nice to you" look—as though that, storming Normandy, and curing cancer are the three hardest endeavors ever undertaken in human history.

I pretty much just stick to myself, though, read in my room, *not* write my second novel, and look up recipes on the internet. I do need to get out more (maybe lose this weight), but I don't really know where to start. It's been seven years.

TUESDAY, SEPTEMBER 25, 20—
10:52 P.M.

"Bitch is crazy."

"What?"

"Bitch is crazy."

"What the hell are you talking about, Kev?"

"Well, I realized the other night that I failed you as a friend."

"So, what else is new?"

"Anyway, I'm supposed to be supportive, reassuring, shit like that, make you feel vindicated, right?"

"Sure. I guess."

"All right then. Bitch is crazy."

"Who? Samara?"

"Who else?"

"Good point."

"Well?"

"Yeah … Yeah. You're right. Thanks, bruh."

"No problem."

"Let's go get that beer."

THURSDAY, SEPTEMBER 27, 20—
2:28 P.M.

I think the reason I never got into baking is because you have to follow directions, and I've always had a problem with that. It's been a problem with every job I've had (and yet, not a problem when I'm driving; how weird is that?). I've always had to do things my way, be contrary. Like I was perpetually stuck in a bad Tom Cruise movie. Forever the maverick. Even when I was a kid. Back in Catholic school, I used to wear a Star of David around my neck, and, once in eighth grade, I told Sister Anne de Paul that it would be tragic if *Roe v. Wade* were overturned because we'd lose our right to privacy. That's no way to bake a cake.

I don't actually remember if I knew what I was saying back then. I was a kid. But I don't know what my excuse could possibly be now. I'm thirty-two. I should be able to read a damned recipe and measure out the proper portions of sugar, milk, flour, eggs, whatever the hell goes into baked goods. But I can't. Everything always turns up like the spaghetti sauce I'm making at the moment. I've never read a recipe for it. Hell, I couldn't even tell you if it's a marinara, carbonara, Bolognese, Arrabbiata. I don't even know what those words mean. I've never even bothered to look them up. I just grab my tomatoes, tomato paste and sauce, my truckload of garlic ('cause garlic makes the world a better place), onions, oregano, and basil (if I'm feeling particularly randy). I chop up my hot *and* sweet Italian sausage, throw in some veal, and lightly fry up some ground Angus that can't escape my heavy-handed seasoning before throwing it all into the cauldron and then simmer until I'm sick of the slow burn. If I did that to a cake, it would turn up a pasty, yellow muck covered in chocolate icing with a funny, garlic taste.

I guess that's what happened to my novel. I knew what to do. I knew the rules I had to follow. Character development. Plot points. Arcs. Happy resolve. Believe it or not, I even know proper sentence structure. But I couldn't be bothered. I thought I could create my own recipe. Throw in green peppers, red peppers, olives, mushrooms. That damned good sausage. Hell, make it a paella. Squid, octopus. Always good to have in a novel. I was trying to reinvent marinara when I should've been trying to perfect my profiteroles. But I guess I just can't follow rules.

No. That's not true. With Samara, I didn't break a damned one. Well, OK, I did lust in my heart. But that never became flesh. I was honest with her and true. I wasn't perfect, but I always tried to be the best person I could be. What can I say? She brought it out in me.

Maybe I just didn't give her enough of my time. I was always wanting to write. Maybe I worked too much. Saved the money I should've been spending on her. Maybe I shouldn't have gotten involved with Egon and his stupid theater company. But she was an actress. I thought it would be a good way for us to spend more time together. Be a part of the same community. Then there was the novel. But she'd always known I wanted to be a novelist. That was one of the things she'd *said* drew her to me.

I didn't gain the weight until after the tour. I was never abusive. I never stepped out on her. Sure, I did have my Steelers obsession, but you can't make a man give up his black and gold—why even try? I went out with Kevin every blue moon. The music magazine. Maybe I shouldn't have saved all that money. Gone on vacation more. Gone to clubs more. Less? Started this cooking obsession sooner. Argued less? More? Been a better person, lover, Catholic. Maybe I should've made my marriage proposal a biennial event instead of annual. Bought a ring. But I could've sworn she said she was against "blood diamonds"—would an emerald have worked?—garnet?—what the hell is garnet, anyway? Obsidian's pretty cool, even though I don't know what kind of engagement that would've symbolized.

I don't know why she has me questioning myself so damned much. It's not right. Not fair. Screw her and that damned cake metaphor.

SATURDAY, SEPTEMBER 29, 20—
12:52 A.M.

"When we first moved to Exton, I don't know. I think I was seven, maybe. I don't think I knew what to make of the new home, the new country. I doubt if those people knew what to make of us either. I don't even know if they knew what we were. It didn't really matter. We mainly kept to ourselves. I went to school. Did well. Just like I was supposed to. Little Priti could *not* fail. I don't really think I felt any pressure, though. I never ever came close to failing. It was never an issue.

"But I think around junior high—or maybe fifth or sixth grade, I think—so I guess that's middle school then. Anyway, I don't know. Like, I love my family—for all that's worth—but, well. No man's an island, right? Like, your family can't be your entire life. You can't keep coming home to watch your mother cook and clean and wait for your father to come home from work. That's no life for a kid. I mean, all the other kids were out playing, having fun. And I didn't know how to do any of that. I was different. I knew it. Everybody knew it. Nobody really said anything. Well, one kid, Tommy Connelly, I think. Yeah. He called me a nigger once, but then one of the girls in class, I can't remember who, she told him I was Indian. So, then he started calling me Pocahontas. Then somebody else—or maybe the same girl, God that was so long ago—told him, 'No, Tommy. Like India Indian.' He still called me Pocahontas, anyway.

"But yeah. I wanted friends. It was hard 'cause, like I said, I was different. I was quiet. Scared quiet, but I think everybody thought I was stuck up. I just didn't know how to talk to those *American* kids. Those *white* kids. And it didn't help that I was smart. Straight As, and all that. I don't think many of them liked me. Shit, I think I still 'talked funny' back then. Who knows? That's how I remember it, though.

"So, yeah. It was in fifth grade. There was this new transfer student. Elise Bryan. I think she was from Dover. Her parents had just gotten a divorce—like all those 'decadent Americans,' as my father used to say—and her mother moved her and her two brothers back to Philly. Anyway, this was my big chance, right? Like all the other kids, they all hated the little, stuck-up India Indian. But Elise, she didn't know me.

"I chickened out, though. I didn't know what to talk about. How to talk. After all, I talked funny. But she came to me. You know transfers. Treat them like lepers until they've been properly quarantined and decontaminated. Cleared to walk among the general population. And lepers colonize together, I guess.

"So, anyway, we hung out at recess, talked in the hallway, waited for busses together. In all honesty, she was probably my first crush. She had this fiery red hair. These incredible blue eyes. And dimples. I've always been a sucker for dimples. Probably because of her. Who knows? I wonder whatever happened to Elise Bryan. Maybe I should Google her.

"It was all well and good. Having a sort-of friend. But I wanted a real friend, a best friend. All the other girls seemed to have them. With all their damned cliques. I knew I was never going to get into one of those. But, so what if I were an immigrant? I deserved a best friend.

"I had to act fast. Everybody seemed to start liking Elise. Her nubbins were the first to start turning into breasts, and the boys were noticing. Maybe it was the sixth grade. And some of the other girls were talking to her more and more.

"So I did it. I invited Elise to my house. For a sleepover. I didn't have any Air Supply records. I didn't even have a record player. My father did. But all he listened to was Indian classical and all that damned moaning. I still can't listen to the stuff.

"I was scared. I didn't think my folks liked Americans all that much. I still don't, actually. And I thought Elise would find the whole experience too weird. The food's too hot. It smells weird. We talked funny. But I so desperately wanted the girl to be my friend. Funny how that crap means so much when you're a kid, like, it's so life-and-death.

"Well, my mother seemed receptive. But she always does. That's her little trick. So, I guess it was a Saturday. Elise's mother dropped her off on her way to work. I was on pins and needles and was impaled on the little buggers as soon as she walked in. Like I'm not one of those people who really believes they can point to specific moments, and say, 'That's when everything changed.' Life's not a movie, right? But I swear to God that that was one of those moments for me. My mother was cooking something. I don't remember what. Something Indian. I was trying to convince her to make burgers, but we're Patels. Strictly vegetarian.

"Anyway, the moment Elise walked in, I swear I could see the shock on her face. Like the smell. It overpowered her. It probably didn't help that my father was playing his damned Kishori Amonkar records. She just drones *on* and *on*. Not only that, but Elise's eyes—they seemed transfixed on something. My mother was busy making a big deal about our new guest. Probably something about how good it was to finally meet Elise, how she was so happy that she'd be spending the night, how she'd always been encouraging me to bring my friends over, to have friends, I didn't have many friends, you know. The typical crap parents say to make their kids want to crawl under a rock or immolate themselves. While she was taking Elise's bag and coat, I noticed those blue eyes just not moving from this tiny vase we had.

"When my mother finally left us alone, Elise whispered to me, horrified, 'Are your parents Nazis?' I was like, 'What?' and she pointed to that vase. And there it was. As bright and bold as the sun. A fucking swastika.

I don't think at the time I knew what it meant to Americans. To me, it was just another symbol lying around the house. Another thing about my heritage, history, religion my folks were trying to teach me and I totally tried to ignore.

"I wanted to be American. Not India Indian. So, I didn't care about anybody's goddamned swastika. I wish I did after that, though. Then I could've explained how the Nazis had stolen it from *us*. And that Indians had nothing to do with killing Jews. But it was too late. Elise was lost. We were the Nazis whose house smelled bad and who listened to weird, moaning music that sounded like somebody torturing Jews and whose food was too hot.

"No. I think that moment had definitely changed my life. And I spent too many years trying to erase it from my memory. Because while I was weird, stuck-up, whatever, that was the first time I *really* saw myself, my family, everything, through somebody else's eyes. White eyes. Suddenly, everything about us was wrong. Our speech, clothes, our food. And I no longer wanted to be *wrong*.

"I wanted to be American. More American than George Washington. I scoffed at my father and his cricket obsession. I wanted to be a Phillies fan. What? What's wrong with that, Damian?"

"Oh nothing. The Phillies?"

"What are you? A Pirates fan?"

"Hell yeah."

"Well, I wanted to marry Mike Schmidt—or maybe Bake McBride. Pete Rose was too ugly. I loved the Eagles. What? Are you OK, Damian? Do you need water or something?"

"No. Really. Please. Go ahead."

"And I wanted pizza. With pepperoni and sausage. And I didn't care if I was a Patel or not. I wanted a burger. A big, fat, bloody cow burger—with bacon and ham, and hell, maybe even mutton. I listened to Air Supply. Then Duran Duran and Def Leppard. Absolutely *adored* Michael. Prince was too freaky. I think somewhere in there I masturbated to Madonna. And on the fourth of July, I screamed 'Born in the USA' louder than anybody. And I wasn't even born here.

"I can't really explain what that moment, what that question, did to me. 'Are your parents Nazis?' Can you imagine that? It gave my already upside down world another twirl. I can't believe it's been over twenty years and I still remember it. It still affects me, I guess. It took me so long to get over that. I mean, it's not like I blame Elise. She was just a kid. Hell, she was probably terrified that the little, brown devils were going to throw her in the oven that night. But damn, she fucked me up. I wonder what she's up to these days. Maybe I should Google her."

DATE: Saturday, September 29, 20— 1:43am
FROM: wrinkletime@chimera...
TO: drcross@wintersoldiers....
SUBJECT: Thank you Damian

Damian,

Phil and I were glad to see that you're back to blogging. It's been so long. I guess we're two of your three fans who like your site. We really enjoyed some of your music reviews. We'd never heard of nu jazz before, but, on your recommendation, we checked out Jazzanova and Savath + Savalas and really enjoyed them. DJ Spooky was a little too weird for us, though. But we do look forward to more of your reviews.

We're really sorry that you did not get married. You seemed so much in love. I'm sure, no matter what happened, you'll land on your feet. Also, thank you for mentioning us. We also enjoyed your time in Albany. We look forward to your coming back and, of course, your new book.
Gladys.

PS. Who's this Priti girl? That story was so sad.

SATURDAY, SEPTEMBER 29, 20—
3:12 A.M.

Wow, Fuck Fest Friday Night. My spaghetti sauce really worked. Priti loved it so much she jumped right in the sack—with Deirdre. Then Neville and Hep came home all in love. And you know how those two can go at it. So now, I have two couples on either side of me screaming their heads off. I'm in the middle of my very own horror flick. I'm sure they can hear each other. That's probably why they're all being so loud, the perverse fucks they are.

I need something for my ears. Cotton, an ice pick, a partner of my own? Something to drown out the coital cacophony throbbing in my ears. The Coltrane just ain't working. The saxophone just can't drown out the sap seeping through the walls. There's a vast no man's land between the Maxwell and Al Green they're playing. Maybe it could be filled by Barry White, I don't know, but I just can't do that to myself. Maybe Nina Simone. Nothing can beat her. Maybe Nina and my melancholia can trump their bliss.

Oh well, what can I type about? I mean shit, it's like they're laughing at me. "Ha, ha, you haven't gotten laid in over six months." And it's not like that last time was any fun. More like pathetic.

By the way, I wonder what Samara's up to tonight. Kevin told me she was in Egon's new play. It opened tonight. She's probably riding high atop the male lead right now. Hell, the way tonight's gone, I'm surprised she hasn't called me up to moan and groan in my ear.

Maybe I should listen to Prince.

5:41 P.M.

Last night/this morning was a long one. Funny, when you drown yourself in self-pity, you don't die. You just stay up all night, not read the book in your hand, wish you had a stash, contemplate crying, a heroin habit, calling the ex, moving to another city and starting over, listen to Luther, take a flight to beat the shit out of an uppity eighteen-year-old critic who actually thinks he knows literature, never wanting to write another thing, wonder exactly how much a Russian mail order bride costs, if you could really forego sex and join the priesthood (like you're ever going to have sex again, anyway), at least change your name and rise again like the Phoenix, but you don't die. You never die.

The words on the page were gray soup in my hands when I heard DiDi letting Priti out. I was glad to see that I wasn't the only one to find anti-cuddling women so desirable. I used to think they were the coolest, what was done was done and they let you go on with your life. Of course, I used to like volatile relationships, too. The energy, the passion, the vitality. The utter pain in the ass they are. The constant headache. Like the sex was all that much better. Or better at all.

Anyway, soon after that, there was a knock on my door. DiDi, of course. Hep and Neville were finally doing what I should've been doing: snoring. God, those two are like a Warhol movie: they just go on and on and on and on.

"Come in."

She made her way into my room, which is a mess. It's exactly the place I used to dream of as a kid when I used to dream of being a writer: worn mattress on the floor, books and CDs (well, albums back then) everywhere, papers strewn about, my laptop and stereo at my fingertips, me leaning against the wall reading Ngugi. Of course, when I was a kid, I just *knew* college was going to be filled with sophisticates who could spread erudition like syphilis after the War to End All Wars. And this room was supposed to be in Paris. My living a gauche Left Bank existence, spreading prosaic prose and French women's legs every day while chilling with the ghosts of Baldwin, Wright, Himes, and Hemingway. *Damian's Room*. Oh well.

DiDi retrieved my bong from the closet, plopped down on my mattress beside me, and pulled out a little baggy.

"You ever think about getting a real bed, Damian?"

"Lately."

"Right." She clanked the bowl, filled the bowl, lit that shit. "I can't believe you're still up. Trying to write?'

"I can't seem to get the voices out of my head."

"Is that what it's like?"

"You and Priti, Neville and Hep going at it? Yep. A real fucking nightmare."

"Sorry." She wasn't. I wouldn't be. "Wanna hit?"

"Sure."

"So, what did you think?"

"Think?"

"About Priti?"

Funny. I really couldn't stop thinking about her. Her on top of my cousin. Beneath her. Beside her. Her swinging from the nonexistent chandelier with ecstasy spasming all over her brown face. When people say they don't keep anything from each other, it's a lie. Relationships can't survive total disclosure. "Gee honey, I love you and all, but sometimes, when I look at you, I can't help but feel total disgust." "That reminds me, you know Sandra at work? Yeah. I think she wants to fuck me, and you should see the ass on her." "Well, I'm sure she's had better. I know I have." DiDi and I are really close, but we never share details about our sex lives—and for good reason. Now I can't get her and Priti out of my head. Which is OK, because Neville and Hep are ready to fill that particular vacancy.

"Priti?"

"Yeah, Priti. What did you think about her?"

I have to admit, there was something about that woman that I just couldn't shake. I wouldn't say that she was beautiful or even cute, but she was definitely sexy. Why? I couldn't tell you. At times, I think she looked like Archie Bunker. Her nose a little bulbous—yet hawkish. Her cheeks a bit puffy. And then at other times, she was just so incredibly alluring. Skin, the color of braised wheat. Plump in all the right places. A midnight cascade of hair that flowed to her shoulders, and these haunting, kohl-black eyes that seemed to go right through your soul and straight to your genitals.

I was curious, maybe even fascinated. I couldn't keep my eyes off her. Maybe it was a trick of the lighting. I'd go from my left eye to the right. Archie Bunker, Sophia Lauren. Then back again. Chief Bill Gillespie, Raquel Welch. By the time I was done, I think I was in REM, wanting to devour every inch of her brown body.

"Oh, she's a'ight."

"Yeah." DiDi smiled, leered, sort of like a hunter with a ten-point buck. "You know, I've been pursuing her for months. I think your sauce did the trick."

"How weird is that? Getting laid 'cause your cousin can cook. You did give me credit, right?"

"I had to. Everybody knows I can't cook."

"Neither could Samara. In fact, I can't think of a single woman I know who can."

DiDi shrugged. Took a hit.

"Hey, what was up with that story? About her growing up? A little sad, don't you think?"

My cousin looked at me and chuckled. It was almost four o'clock in the morning. I was getting high. I thought I could finally get to sleep. It's been so long since I've had a good night's sleep. Too many things on my mind. Misery loves company, so it usually just lets itself into my room around two a.m., sits on the bed, and says, "Let's chat, shall we?" It doesn't even have the courtesy to bring a beer or a little baggy like my beautiful cousin here.

"What's so funny, DiDi?"

"Jesus, Damian. She tells that story all the time. I can't believe she got you with it."

"What do you mean?"

"That's like her line. Every conference, every party. Damn, all those bleeding heart, granola white chicks fall for it every time. It's like White Guilt Lite. I guess they're tired of feeling guilty over black folks. Now South Asians, that's something new. Exotic, even. I can't believe you fell for it."

"That's me. Granola white chick."

"Ya know, I thought she was hitting on you. She told me she thought you were kinda cute—even though she asked if you had Tourette's, or something. You kept looking at her funny."

Damn. And I thought I was being slick.

"And you fell for it."

"But I thought—you and her—I mean, she's a lesbian, right?"

"Hey, don't tell anybody I told you this, but it's not like that shit's written in stone. Hell, it took me one small dick too many for me to realize that I didn't really like guys that much. I mean, some people *can* be malleable."

"But *me*?"

"As much as it pains me to say it, you're not totally hideous, Damian Rene Cross. Sure, you need to start going to the gym, but I guess you're not *that* bad-looking. Besides, you can cook—damn, that woman could *not* stop talking about that sauce—and the veal. And you know who the hell Bake McBride is, was, whatever. Not many crunchy white chicks are going to know that."

"So, let me get this straight: ole girl was hitting on me—Tourette's and all—liked my cooking, and ended up sleeping with you?"

DiDi shrugged. "It be's like that sometimes."

"Yeah. No kidding."

***10:17* p.m.**

I feel Priti
Oh so Priti
I feel Priti and witty and bright!

Saturday night. That used to mean something. Partying. Release. A brief reprieve from the bullshit world of work. But I don't punch a clock anymore. So Saturday night doesn't mean anything to me these days. Just another one thousand four hundred forty clicks on the timepiece. I kinda miss it. But I don't miss work. Come to think about it, Saturday night never meant *that* much to me.

Saturday either, for that matter. While my housemates were out all day running errands, etc., I was wondering what it would be like having half-Indian children. How would the two hues mix? The hair? As a true bourgie bastard I'd like the boy to be nappy and the girl to have "good" hair. But the noses? Broad? Hawkish? Both? God, that and some talons, and they could pluck salmon out of the Columbia River.

And names? Krishna Cross? I don't think so. I do like Samina, though. I mean, that Samina Ali's one hot writer. But I don't think that's a Hindu name…

Maybe I should just write that second novel. At least that's what I was thinking when everybody was preparing to leave. Showers, loud music, perfume, colognes, just a general air of excitement. And I hadn't even bathed. The most exciting thing I'd done all day was think that Rani (of Jhansi fame) would be a pretty cool name for Priti and my good-haired daughter. Our little Afro-Indian queen cold kickin' British ass. Hopefully, she'd fare better than her namesake. I'd hate to see her die at twenty-two. All that private school and college tuition out the window.

As you can see, I wasn't accomplishing much. I don't know why I can't just enjoy doing absolutely nothing. It seems like one of life's rights. But I guess I'm just your typical Go! Go! American. I've always got to be doing. No matter what it is. And I was tired of trying to read and trying to write and was trying to watch TV. The old black and white set probably first showed Nixon not giving up Checkers. How many administrations has this set survived? Hell, will it survive this one? Will we? Normal people have plasma screens, flat screens, HDTVs, Tivos, and satellite dishes. But no. Not only do I have to *be* a pseudo-intellectual who disdains popular culture, but I've got to go and *live* with a bunch of the fools. How am I going to be able to drown my miseries in a ten-inch black and white screen? It's just not big enough.

"Damian, Jesus, you're looking pathetic." What an endearing cousin I have.

"I guess I should be wearing Fubu sweatpants."

"Keep it in the community."

DiDi wasn't really dressed-up herself. That wasn't really her thing. Jeans, black blouse, and dreads. Very little make-up, no jewelry. That really hip, self-confident sister thing. It worked for her. Raggedy sweatpants and an old Kordell Stewart jersey was more my steelo.

"Why don't you clean up and go out with me?"

"Uh, I don't know, DiDi. I'm kinda busy here."

"What are you doing? The damn thing only gets the WB."

"I'm thinking."

"Really? It looks more like you're pitying yourself."

"That takes a lot of thought."

"Damian, when was the last time you went out?"

"Shit, I don't know. A week or two ago. With Kevin."

"I'm sure that was fun," she said, sarcastically. I don't think she likes Kev all that much. Sometimes I wonder what self-respecting woman would. But that's a whole other story. "Was he entertaining you with tales of his sexual exploits again? Forget it. Look, Karen's having a party."

"Karen? From the Union?"

"Yeah. Your old bud. You should come along."

By this time Hep and Neville were in the living/dining room. As always, you could smell Neville a mile away. He reeked of expensive tastes and beauty—of being a real, high-maintenance pain in the ass. And Hep was way too cool for that pretty boy. The things he had to put up with. The price of admission, I guess.

They both looked at me. All three were looking at me. Like anything I did was important. Perhaps I was the subject of an experiment I wasn't aware of. But hell, I was feeling too lazy to run through anybody's maze.

"Ah hell," Hep piped up. "You could always come along with me and Neville." He quickly glanced back at his partner. "Couldn't he, Nevi?"

"Uh, yeah. Yeah. Sure," he smiled.

But as soon as his boy looked away, Neville glared. *Don't you dare, you son of a bitch. Don't you know I will* cut *you?* his eyes seemed to be saying. I got the hint.

"Naw, that's OK, Hep. Thanks, anyway."

Neville smiled genuinely this time. "Well, we tried."

"Cousin, you have got to get yourself together. Go out. Enjoy yourself."

"So, I've got to join a gym—"

"Damned right," Neville said, not quite under his breath.

"—and now I have to learn how to enjoy myself?"

"Come on, Dami," DiDi persisted. "Just come to Karen's. A bunch of old Union folks will be there."

"But they'll start asking me about the book and the tour, and I'll have to act like it was all a success. And then they'll start asking about Samara and the wedding, and there's no way to get around that failure."

"Ina will be there."

"Ina? Really?!"

My voice actually cracked.

"How embarrassing. Let's get out of here, Hep."

The boys left.

"And Darnell, I'm sure," I huffed.

"No. They broke up."

"No shit?!"

Damn, it cracked again.

"Have you reverted back to puberty, or what?"

"No. No uncontrollable erections here."

"That's good to hear."

"So when did they break up?"

"About a month, month and a half ago."

"Yeah. But they've been together for years. I thought they were supposed to be getting married soon."

DiDi shrugged. "It must be catching."

"Funny."

"So, you coming?"

God, I used to love Ina. So intelligent. So intense.

"I'm sure Ina would love to see you."

So sexy.

So single!

"Naw. I guess not. I really am busy."

"Thinking."

"Yes. Thinking."

"All right then."

She left.

God, what the hell's wrong with me?

MONDAY, OCTOBER 1, 20—
9:40 A.M.

God, I'm even boring myself.

TUESDAY, OCTOBER 2, 20—
10:17 P.M.

Ina. Ina. Ina. Have ya ever seen the perfect berry? It's skin beautifully shiny, ripe, bursting with juice. You just know the moment you bite into it the incredibly sweet nectar's going to be dribbling down your chin and it's so sweet, so juicy, so perfect, you get sticky with it, licking up every drop.

That's Ina. This beautiful brown berry with reddish hues bubbling up in every pore. High cheekbones, high forehead. A warm, genuine smile with a slightly snaggled tooth. Always so earnest, Ina, you can see the wheels perpetually turning. You can't help being enamored.

And that hyperbolic body of hers…

Not as though you ever really saw it. Just brilliant glimpses of the ecstasy beneath the layers of modest clothing she always wore. There was always something of the sexy librarian fantasy about her. You just knew that once the spectacles came off, you were in for the ride of your life. At least, that was always *my* fantasy. Because Ina's a "good girl," the woman you wanted to take home to your folks, if they hadn't died when you were sixteen. I was trained to love a woman like her. The respectable, middle class, Catholic-school-raised, intact family with 2.3 cars part of me knew that within Ina's womb lay generations of dignified stability and good jobs. The tumultuous aspiring writer who'd seen too many tragic artist movies and liked a little too much booze a little too often needed a hard-drinking tempest of neuroses to be my partner. But that bourgeois side, the side that smashed against my anarchist walls and made me vote Democrat, long for a law degree and the missionary position, write checks to the NAACP, volunteer somewhere, and raise little Jacks and Jills always longed for Ina Yancey.

I had to see her. What the hell was Darnell thinking, letting her go? There's no way in the world I would've. She's been the woman I've always wanted to chase. I've had a crush on her since the first moment I'd seen her at the Union. But things never worked out. Whenever I was single, she wasn't. When she was, I wasn't. Casualties of bad timing. The only time we actually did synchronize our watches was when I got engaged to Samara, she got a ring from Darnell. It's hard to believe that we're both single now. I'd never believe it, but maybe things do happen for a reason.

So, that's right. I showered—finally. I wanted to dress, but I've never been much of a dresser. Jeans and T-shirts. Sweatshirts for special occasions. Like winter. Besides, none of my old clothes fit quite right right now. But at least I smelled human. I was on my way.

"Hey, where you going, Damian?"

"Out."

"Really? That's too bad. Priti's coming over."

"Who? Oh yeah, right. I'll have to pass."

"I was kinda hoping you could whip something up. I've got steak and some garlic."

"What the hell would I make with that?"

"I don't know. You're the MacGyver in the family."

"Sorry to disappoint. Just grab an onion and a button."

"What for?"

"I don't know. Whatever MacGyver would use a button for. Be creative. I'm passing the torch. Gotta go."

"It's about time."

I think my cousin was genuinely happy. Her face was actually beaming. Have I really been that pathetic?

OK, I have.

But not now. Now, I was gone. I revved up the Tercel's massive four-cylinder engine and puttered down the road.

I really didn't want to go down to the Union. It wasn't like I hated the place or the people or the job I had there. The Union's a homeless advocacy group and service provider. Everybody there was mainly nice and mostly earnest. Not all do-gooders greet you with transcendental smiles, patchouli leis, and granola chip cookies. They're not all understanding and conflict resoluting and have tantric sex to Joni Mitchell. They can be ornery and full of shit just like everybody else, and you can't necessarily say that all their hearts are in the right place. There were some real horrible bastards to roll through the Union. I may have been one of them. But it was a good place to work. There were no poverty pimps there working the corner, and you could put up with the bullshit every day knowing that you gave some family temporary shelter.

I was a hotline coordinator. Every morning shelters around town would call and email us with how much space they had available that night. Then, the hotline would light up with calls from homeless folks: single mother with a couple kids, single man, sometimes intact families. And we'd try to find them a place for a night, a week, a month. A temporary reprieve, but it was something. Hell, that revolution we were always talking about in college didn't seem to be coming any time soon. We could usually help. Just hope it wasn't a man with a kid or a woman with a twelve-year-old boy. Then we'd have to let them stay in our lobby because there was no room in the inn for those combinations. There really aren't any facilities for a man with a child. You wouldn't want a little kid in most men's shelters. You wouldn't want yourself there, for that matter. And twelve-year-old boys were treated as men (which, I guess, is how they view themselves), and they weren't allowed to stay in women's shelters for fear of ...?

Those were the moments that broke your heart. When you couldn't help. But it was mostly good at the Union. I really enjoyed the eight years

I was there. I guess you could say I grew up there. I entered a twenty-three-year-old, fresh-faced, idealistic anarchist and left a jaded, hopeless Democrat. But always with a twinkle of hope in my baby browns. Because I know, no matter how bad it gets, there are always good folks like Ruth and Janice and Ina at the Union giving the good fight.

That's part of the reason I didn't want to ever step foot in that place again. That last day, Ruth had gotten everybody together and had thrown me a party. Their faces were so full of pride. They glowed. One of their own had made it. I was a writer going on a book tour. I was their conquering hero.

But I'm not. I'm more like the water boy on the 0-44 Columbia football team. The epitome of failure. I didn't want to return to them and see the carefully camouflaged disappointment on their faces. They were thinking John Grisham. But I'm just Damian Cross. Only five hundred people outside that building know who I am.

Rome wasn't built in a day. You've gotta learn to crawl before you can walk. Well, you've got to start somewhere. They'd place platitudes around my neck like garlands. I've had enough of that. That's why I waited until after five to go down there. Ina was always too dedicated and would probably be there until at least seven. Mostly everybody else would be gone by then.

I pulled into the back first and tried the security code on the back door. I figured they would've changed it in the past seven months, but I had to try. It didn't work. I had to go around front and into the lobby.

There was a bunch of worn-out women sagging there, cramped within the small confines with their children watching television. They always seemed to be the same ones, no matter who they were. Eyes drooping with troubles strangling the life out of them, and here was one more. They had called too late. There was no room for them anywhere. They were going to have to wait and hope for sudden vacancies. Then Norbert would take them in the bus to their new digs. If no one called, then out would come the blankets, cots, and pillows, and they would call the lobby home for the night. Hopefully, they had enough money for the vending machine because their kids were about to become hungry.

Norbert was sitting at the rickety, old reception desk. He was looking bored and geriatric staring at the news. This man was a gen-u-ine success story. A poor man's Horatio Alger tale. Rags-to-better-rags. He's a Vietnam vet, who harbored resentment and a nasty drug habit for years. He was in and out of a few institutions—mental, penal, and marital—until Mohammed and Malcolm told him enough was enough and he permanently quit all three. He cleaned himself up and took on odd jobs. One day he found the Union and volunteered. He wanted to help, give back. A few years ago, he was hired and now does whatever it takes to find someone a home.

The years show on his face. His dark skin has folded in on itself many times over, and there are barriers of bags beneath his eyes. But there's still the fire-next-time in them. His large, gray afro is as wild as ever, and he still looks like he jumped out of bed to put kerosene on his inner blaze. You can still smell the smoke. Kools.

"Look, it's the famous writer."

"Where?"

"It was like *that,* hunh?"

"Worse."

"Fuck 'em."

Did I mention how much I like Norbert?

"So, whatcha know good, Damian?"

"Nothing much, man. What about you?"

"Shit, ain't nothin' good dealin' with these jive-ass muthas."

I mean, ain't he a hoot? So '70s. Like *Shaft in Retirement.*

"Say, Norbert, do you know if Ina's around?"

The old man gave me a wide, missing-tooth grin. "You heard about her and Darnell now?"

"Uhhhh…"

He gave me one of those can't-bullshit-a-bullshitter smiles. "9-5-6-3-2-7."

"Thanks, Norbert."

"No problem, my brother."

I tried to act as cool as possible, but by the time I rushed up the stairs, punched in the code he'd just given me, and entered the second floor, I had to wipe the dew off my brow. I gave myself a couple seconds to catch my breath. I've been smoking way too damned much. God, I'm fat. Fat, out-of-shape, and over thirty. The future is indeed bright!

I made my way to Ina's office and paused at the door. *Holy shit,* I gasped. The librarian had definitely taken off her spectacles. Ms. Yancey was immaculate. I can't remember ever seeing her like this. Ever. Her hair was short and smart. Her lips pouted boldly with fire red lipstick. And a second-skin tight red sweater clung seductively to her twin Olympuses. I was ready to wreck my ship on her shores. I couldn't believe it. I could barely recognize her. What had Darnell done to her? Could I call him up and thank the man?

She was writing furiously at her desk as she always did. Thoroughly engrossed in the task at hand. Her glasses (it was a metaphor, after all) were resting precariously on her nose, and I could see the cutest, little wrinkles dimpling her forehead. I couldn't stop from smiling. Whatever changes she was going through could not alter the core sweetness of this woman. I was hypnotized by the promise of it all.

"Damian?"

"Hunh?"

Smooth, Damian. Courvoisier smooth. Now could you please wipe the damned smirk off your face?

"Hey, what are you doing here?" she smiled.

"Uh well, I was in the neighbor—well, I thought. Well, you know—"

Well. Well. Well. Well. To believe I'm a writer. No wonder nobody bought my damned book.

"You heard, haven't you?"

"Heard? About what?"

No, seriously, at least stop smiling. But then she smiled again, a Cheshire cat expression I didn't know she had.

"Yeah. You have."

Say something, Shakespeare. The quality of mercy is not strained…?!

"Good," she said. "Have a seat."

"Well, you look busy. I don't want t—"

"You know me. I'm always busy. Besides, you came all this way. No, that's right. You were in the neighborhood."

"It's a big neighborhood, Ina."

"With nothing but run-down tenements and a needle park."

"A man without vices is a man without virtue."

"Is eating one of them?"

"You could've acted like you didn't notice."

"But I like it. You look like a teddy bear."

Teddy bear?!

"A twentieth-century symbol of virility if there ever was one," I joked. What else was there to do, really? "No, I picked this up during the tour. Nothing but driving, fast food, and sleeping. Gained forty pounds and lost a fiancée. So, I guess I actually … lost seventy pounds."

"That's definitely a way to look at it."

"Always the optimist."

"Well, I'm sorry to hear it, anyway."

"I'm not. I guess."

Her face turned sour, briefly. "Samara was, well, … Samara."

Was I the only one who liked her? Me and the Seventh Fleet?

"I'm sorry about you and Darnell, too."

"Are you?"

"Well, it's nothing I wish on anybody. Neither one of us is probably enjoying ourselves right now."

She looked at me, into me, through me. Something was happening here. This boob-jutting-fire-red lipstick vixen before me wasn't the demure, little Ina I'd known. There was something in her eyes I couldn't recognize. Something … aggressive? And I was trying not to feel defensive, but something was gnawing at me. I think I started sweating again. I wiped my forehead just in case.

"Yeah. Right," she finally said. "So, when did you find out?"

"Saturday night."

She checked her watch. "You've made good time. I just wish it hadn't taken your cousin so long to tell you."

"Well—" there's that damned word again "—I don't know exactly how to put this—but you know, Ina, you and me, I've always thought—"

"You want to 'hang out?'"

"Do people still do that?"

"I don't know. It's been awhile for me, too."

"Yeah, I guess we're both pretty rusty."

"Maybe we should call Darnell for some pointers."

"Oh. It was like that?"

"No, no. Anyway," she smiled, to get the razor blades out of her teeth. "I mean, this is just a friendly thing. That's what I would want. You understand that."

"Look, in all honesty, I wouldn't even know what to do on a date. The last woman I took out on a date ordered a brontosaurus burger. And that shit ain't cheap."

I got a grin for that one. "Good. Are you busy this weekend?"

"I don't have a job, a social life. I'm never busy. But always preoccupied."

"Are you writing that second novel?"

"Mmmmm."

"Well, what are you doing on Sunday?"

"Sunday?"

THURSDAY, OCTOBER 4, 20—
7:25 P.M.

"Church?! The bitch wants you to go to motherfucking *church*?"

"Hey, come on now. That's uncalled for."

"Since when have you grown so sensitive?"

"Man, I always *been* sensitive. I just hide it behind a smattering of Ebonics, a plethora of profanity, and this patented Ice Cube scowl I bought off of EBay."

We chuckled. Diane/Dakota dropped off our beers. Since when has Dakota become such a cool name? Why those states? Why not Alabama? Vermont? Massachusetts, even? The poor child wouldn't be able to spell her name 'til the sixth grade. I watched her leave. I still don't know why. I'm a guy. Maybe it's a biological imperative.

"Damn, I miss Brianna."

"We all do, Damian. We all do."

"Ya know, she's probably not even named Dakota. It's probably Jane or something, and she just calls herself Dakota for the 'mystery.'"

"So, you gonna go?"

"To church? I don't know."

"Did you explain to her that you're Catholic and, therefore, don't believe in God?"

"It's not that I don't believe in God. It's just that—well, it's complicated."

I took a swig. Kev did the same.

"It might not be that bad, you know."

"What?" I was definitely shocked. This was *not* the Kevin Byrd I knew. Holy water used to burst into flames at his touch. "Ole girl's gonna look at me one day with the Spirit in her eyes, and ask me, 'Do you take Jesus as your own and personal savior?' and I'm gonna be so mesmerized by the Titans in her tube top, I'm gonna dumbly nod, Yes. Next thing you know, I'll be handling snakes, speaking in tongues, saying things like 'Bible-believing church,' reading *Left Behind* and *liking* it, and voting Republican. I'm tellin' ya, man, church is a gateway drug."

"No, seriously. It might not be that bad."

"What kind of woman asks a dude out to church?"

"It's a test, D. You could pass it."

"By lying?"

"Like you've never lied to get laid."

"I may have stretched the truth a little, but … but church. That's serious. I could go to hell for that."

"You don't even believe in hell, Damian."

"Oh yeah. Right. You know, maybe I'm just not ready to date, yet."

"Fair enough. But God, how long has it been, man?"

"I don't know. Six, seven months."

"Look. I promised not to talk about it. I know Samara broke your heart. I don't know how, but knowing her, I'm sure it was fucked-up—"

"Who you tellin'?"

"—but you can't let the woman ruin your life. You can't mourn her forever. Look, I don't know what a seven-year relationship even looks like. Or a seven-month one, for that matter. But you've got to do something. Why not go to church?"

"'Cause it's a little weird. I've dated poets, artists, actresses, and that ex-gymnast—"

"I'm still jealous over that one."

"Yeah. It was cool. But I never once even thought about going out with a holy roller. And with all the women you've been with you're gonna be jealous over one ex-gymnast. One deliciously, inhumanly flexible ex-gymnast."

"Hey, I can begrudge a brother whatever I want to. Anyway, your Ina might not be a holy roller. As I said, it could just be a test. To see if you're the kind of man who'd be comfortable in a church, comfortable with his kids, her kids, *your* kids going to church."

"What's the point in that?"

"What's the point in anything? It's dating."

"I don't know."

"You like the sister, right?"

"Have for eight years now."

"Right. Just remember. Three dates and you're in."

"That shit's real? I thought it was something single guys made up to make us committed ones feel ... well, committed."

"Naw, man," he eschewed. Then he started becoming ... fervent? His voice rising, trying to rally the troops in my testes. "The shit's all too real. So, you go to church. Then go to a movie, then dinner. You survive that then hit that shit like it was 1999!"

I couldn't help myself, I was actually excited. It was a hot August day in the bayou, and I was reveling in a revival tent. I wanted to throw my hands to heaven and praise the Lord.

"Amen, brother!"

SUNDAY, OCTOBER 7, 20—
6:05 P.M.

I've never had bamboos shoved beneath my fingernails. Nobody's ever taken a cat-o-nine tails to my back. I've never even seen a rack. And live wires have never touched my testicles. I have had fire ants crawl all over and bite my flesh, though. That's pretty much why I avoid church.

I couldn't shake that feeling all week—along with the testosterone tingling in my privates. Church, Ina. The carrot, the stick. Whipped cream and horse whip. Her angelic body and eternal damnation. Church seemed like one hell of a desert to cross to get to her Promised Land. Suddenly, milk and honey pot didn't seem all that appetizing. I'd been without Erets Ina for thirty-two years. I could wait another thirty-two ... or catch her in the next life. I just did *not* want to go to church. The last time I'd gone, a smart bomb couldn't find Baghdad on a map.

As an integration baby, I was weaned on two churches: African Methodist Episcopalian and the one holy Roman Catholic Apostolic church. In the AME church, I think I may have been close to believing. Pastor Williams jumping up and down, dancing around the altar, exhorting us with his "Gawd!!!," his Holy Ghost sweat and saliva dousing me in the third row. The choir bringing down the rafters in their rapture. The entire congregation swayed to the rhythm of the Spirit. Big brown mamas in their fancy, blue hats praising Jesus, working their Mahalia Jackson fans like the flames of hell were at their heels. The white gloved ushers with stern, earnest faces, the stoic picture of black manhood. I was carried away. I loved everything about it. The communal wafers. The music. The grape juice blood of Christ. Every week I wanted to go before the entire congregation and be saved.

But I was rescued at mass, and everything religious within me was banished to purgatory. Everything was cold and sterile. The choir was somewhere off in the ether. Removed. Nowhere to be seen. Their crystalline notes shattered hollowly against the whitewashed walls. The crucifix and the stations of the cross oozed all around me. All that blood and no emotion. A somnambulant priest would extol Christ's virtues as though he were snoring. And the automatons in the pews would reply in bloodless kind. Their savior was being massacred before their very eyes, and nobody seemed to care. The Hallelujahs and Amens were so reserved. No one seemed on the verge of passing out or being delivered. Nobody was moved. Sure, they did their calisthenics. Stand, kneel, genuflect, sit, jump down, turn around, pick a bale of cotton. Repeat. All done with cold precision. Everything was rote. The Book told you what to do, what to say, how to be. *And the priest droned on … And the priest droned on.* A couple more deep knee bends and a splash of holy water and you were gone.

The only advantage being that you were home in time for the Steelers' opening kickoff (which is why I ultimately liked mass over chu'ch).

But that was the Reagan era. I haven't been back since. I didn't know how I was going to be able to handle today. That red-ant feeling had been plaguing me for days. And everything seemed wrong when I woke up. It was Sunday morning. *Morning?!* When was the last time I'd seen one of these? I was wearing new clothes, and I could've sworn I was allergic to Indonesian child labor 'cause I felt as though I was breaking out in hives as soon as I put them on. My old stuff no longer fit. I've gone from a 32- to a 38-inch waist. I need to hit that gym. I had decent enough shoes, but I didn't own a tie. I had to borrow one from Hep. He's too tall for me to borrow one of his jackets. I looked like a little boy trying to be a man, which is exactly how I felt. So I bought a damned jacket, and it took me forever to find one that would button up over my gut. I never dressed up, and now I was in this clown suit. Grease paint and a water-fountain carnation, and the effect would've been complete.

You know, if I weren't trying to get laid, there's no way in hell I'd be going through all this.

On my way out, I saw DiDi sitting at the dining room table with her

GRE prep books all spread out. I had no clue she got up this early. How would I?

"Hey, DiDi."

"Dami."

Then I stopped. Something had been bugging me this past week, or so.

"Hey, girl. I've got a question."

"Shoot."

"Remember when you told me that crap about one too many small dicks?"

A mischievous smile played across her baby cheeks. "Yeah. What about it?"

"Was that—? I mean, is that—? Is that really how it happened?"

"Naw. It's just something I say. To make men even more insecure than they already are."

"Is that possible?"

"You're asking, aren't you?"

I must've smiled. Relieved.

"Why? Who was it?"

"Uh, well. You remember that girl I went out with graduation summer? Raina? She went to Dartmouth."

"Yeah."

"Well, she joined GALA as soon as she hit campus."

Deirdre was trying not to laugh. "No shit. Hey, didn't I set you two up?"

"Yes. You did. Another one of your fine choices."

"I knew I liked her for a reason. Hey, wait a second. What are you talking about? I set you up with a lot of great women."

"They might have been great women, but they were fucked-up girls."

"Oh, come on, Damian."

"What about Larissa? That nut tried to cut me."

"I'm sure you did something to deserve it."

"I was fifteen minutes late."

"Right. And you haven't relied on CP Time since. I say she did you a favor."

I jumped in the Tercel, got some plastic courage from an old X-Clan CD, and headed to In His Glory, Ltd. The drive to the church was a lot shorter than I'd hoped. Damnit, I didn't even get lost once. But Ina was there waiting for me. And I was ten minutes early. Blame Larissa.

Now, I don't expect anybody to trust my judgments on beauty. After all, any woman you're trying to sleep with before two a.m. is beautiful (at 2:15, they're absolutely gorgeous!). And absolutely nobody is going to admit that the woman they're chasing is ugly. "Yeah man, ole girl's cross-eyed with these exquisite, green buck teeth. And did I mention the goiter?" Besides, if I'm to be a writer, doesn't everybody have to be beautiful? Isn't that how it works? Like we average people don't deserve love? So yeah, don't trust me when I say that Ina was looking absolutely amazing this morning, but she was.

Her swirling, kaleidoscopic dress was looking straight out of '78. Like an autumnal lava lamp exploded across her body. Warm browns, oranges, and reds. And if I remember correctly, things was *tight* that year, and, on her, I thought they were too revealing for church. (When did I become a prude?) And yet again, totally out of character. Maybe because she used to be so reserved, she somehow brought a touch of class to the whole thing. Aphrodite the aristocrat. And I had to fight the urge to bow—or beg for a shot at that chastity belt. The retro brown leather jacket was pretty cool, too. Pam Grier hip.

"I was afraid you weren't going to come."

No chance of that happening. Well, actually a pretty good one, but these days I'm worshipping a phallocentric god. And if I must sacrifice to satisfy that little bugger, church was just the price I had to pay.

"What? Maybe I reverted back to my Satanic ways?"

Her face told me that wasn't funny. But her frown ends in the cutest, little dimple. It was worth flying that lead balloon.

"Did you want to come in?"

I wanted to say something about her asking me to come *to* church, not *into* church; but I let it go and surrendered unto Ina what was Ina's.

"Swing low, Sweet Cadillac."

Another frown. Note to self: obscure Dizzy Gillespie references will get you nowhere. We entered. *Salt peanuts! Salt peanuts!* I was a bit taken aback. Everything smelled so fresh and floral and new. No fire and brimstone. There was glass everywhere, and the waking autumn sun shone through. People stood and greeted us at the door, passing out programs, smiles, and the friendliest handshakes. People this nice had to be in a cult. Moonies!!! I wanted to break outta there. But Ina put a reassuring hand on my arm and smiled. Damn that smile. I just knew I was about to shave my head and start passing out literature in airports.

But it wasn't like that. It wasn't like anything I'd ever seen before. It was a head trip that (Ina told me later) was being broadcast to over forty markets around the country and twelve Latin American states. I almost tripped on a cable in my confusion. The place was so huge, filled with revelers, television cameras, and projector screens. I didn't really notice when I first drove up. Too busy swatting ants off my ankles. But this glass stadium held close to a thousand people.

My head swirled in the delirium. So many people. So many *happy* people. I was exhausted just responding to all the random "Greetings, friend"s that floated around my dome. Then we sat down, and I swore my skull was about to crack.

It's just no fun knowing you're going to hell if some self-righteous philanderer in a starched collar ain't damning you every step of the way. I wanted that collar and "God" pronounced with at least two syllables. I wanted sweat and spittle and funk. The Holy Ghost strafing us sinners with flaming sulfur. Folks fainting and repenting while Hell's flames licked their lecherous asses.

But In His Name, Ltd.'s heat was set at a very comfortable seventy-two degrees. Nobody was sweating out last night's sin. I didn't even see one Mahalia Jackson fan. The preacher annunciated without denunciating. There wasn't even any Holy Spirit cardio by the altar. And ole boy didn't wear a collar.

Reverend Theophilus Pound-Sterling was a tall, erudite, middle-aged black man with well-tailored good looks. You know him. You must've seen him or his books or his videos, his TV show or at least heard one of his radio programs. He carried himself with such regal, multimedia bearing, you couldn't help but be star struck. But what would you expect from a Harvard Business and Emory University's Candler School of Theology graduate? I'd seen him before on TV, laughed at his name, and quickly changed the channel. I guess I shouldn't have, though, the brother put on a good show.

The choir was massive. At least sixty people. And were quite professional. It wasn't the sweat-dripping gut bucket of Mt. Zion or the castrati soul of St. Thomas More. These people were contemporary. Large screens would roll down all over the place and their original lyrics would flash. Then they'd go into a funk number, then jazz, a little neo-soul and hip-hop with ambiguous enough lyrics to hit the gospel and/or Top 40 charts. There were Patti Labelle acolytes and Kirk Franklin apostates who'd grab center stage and rock the crowd. There were guitar solos, saxophone solos, and one brother with a diamond-studded cross who'd cut and scratch on his Technics turntables. James Brown, Mary J. Blige, Ashanti, and Marvin Gaye were all in the mix. I betcha at Christmas he works in 50 Cent's "It's Your Birthday."

The screens stayed down, and a testimonial parade flashed before my eyes. All done professionally with background music and montages. There was the divorcee who lost everything until she found Rev. Pound-Sterling. Now, she's found a new, Christian husband, has got a new, better job, and finally got her two freaky-looking, tow-headed children back from her alcoholic ex-husband. A different, alcoholic ex-husband who lost his arm in the only steel mill operating on the continent found Rev. Pound-Sterling's broadcasts so inspirational he rehabbed to the tapes and is now, miraculously, a typist in a law firm. A money-grubbing lawyer, with Rev. Pound-Sterling's help, changed his evil ways in corporate America and now does

"The Lord's Work" putting gang members and sexual predators behind bars at the District Attorney's office. There was actually applause for that one.

But the house almost came down for the boxer. That washed-up Olympics wannabe who back-slid his way to a title never mentioned his five drug busts and seven illegitimate kids during his confessional. Nor the guns charge and domestic abuse charges. And I don't want to even get into the night club stabbing. No, he and his childless wife just hugged their way through the montages, talking about how Jesus loves a sinner and how Rev. Pound-Sterling helped him realize this and how he was now doing community service (court-, not God-appointed, no doubt). I wanted to get up and smack the living shit out of the screen. But amidst the thunderous applause, I soon realized that being a heretic was too 1600s, and I didn't really feel like being burned atop a pile of faggots.

The good reverend glowed in everyone's approval. He stood, tall and confident, yet oddly humble. After a good twenty minutes of getting his ego sucked, he stood among us, erect, satisfied. Then he spoke—not preached, not exhorted, never condemned. Someone had taken the hyacinth from his mouth, and he spoke in flowery, relaxing tones. He came off like an ebony Ward Cleaver, patiently leading us all from despair into the welcoming arms of Our Lord. Sin was never mentioned, and the only "damns" I heard were in my own head. *When will this damn thing be over? Why won't these damn ants leave me alone? Damn, Ina looks* fine *today.*

I know that it was the (self) righteous indignation that had originally driven me away from both churches. You get tired, standing in judgment all the time. You just want to lie down every once in awhile. And here was Reverend Pound-Sterling with a pillow for your head. He had taken away the carrot *and* the stick and put you to rest on a beautiful bed with five hundred thread-count sheets. Where were the locusts? The pox? The rivers of blood? Why the hell did Jesus want to be *my* friend? I don't even like myself that much.

"Now that road we're all traveling, that road to change, to revelation, that road isn't easy now. I wish it were. I wish I could tell you that change is no problem. That that road is the smoothest journey you'll ever take, but it's not. I wish it were. God wishes it were. But if it were, would it be worth it? Would it be yet another thing we take for granted? Just another McDonald's stop on the way to salvation?

"My daddy once told me when my first son was born, he said, 'Theophilus, give that boy everything he needs, a lot of what he wants, and make him earn the rest.' My daddy wanted me to raise the best little man I could, and that was his formula. That is God's formula, as well. He has given us life. He has given us the land, the sea, and all the animals within. We *need* nothing. It is all there at our fingertips.

"He has given us what we may ever want. The nice cars and fancy homes and beautiful clothing. We even have our Tivos and satellite dishes and high-speed internet connections and BlackBerrys. They may not be all that easy to get sometimes. But don't be fooled, God wants us to have those nice things. He gave us the ability to invent them, He's given us the faculties to acquire them. He is a good Father, He wants us to be happy. And with a little hard work and determination we can have our Tivos, our children can have their Xboxes, and our wives can have their Manolo Blahniks.

"And with a little harder work, with a bit more determination, we can change our lives, we can travel that road, we can become better sons and fathers, mothers and daughters. But it *is* work. God *will* help us. He'll be there for us. But it's still not going to be easy. Only *easier*.

"God is there for us. He does not always strike us blind like Saul to help us to finally see His truths. He does not always curse us like Job so we can finally realize His glory. Those supreme acts of kindness are rarely duplicated.

"In fact, that road to salvation, to revelation, that road is often hard to find. Revelation—like being struck blind or with the pox—is a gift rarely bestowed. Only the blessed ever receive it. It is there for everyone, as it was for Saul and Job, but only the blessed are open to revelation's glories.

"And once they are seen, it's even harder work for them to be realized. It's not like you wake up one morning, say, 'I think I'll change my life today,' and bam! it's changed. It's not like you can order a life change with fries and have it super-sized. Change takes time, it takes work. Hard work. There will be pain. There will be tears. You *will* backslide. You *will* feel like a failure. 'Cause failure is a part of change. It's built right in. You will fail at times. But you can ultimately succeed. Because God is right there beside you. He is there, urging you on, praying for you. He has given you all you need to succeed. As I said, it won't be easy. Becoming a better person never is. But it will be easier because God is by your side. He is on that road with you, smoothing your path. Sure, there are still potholes, and you may fall in, but God is there with you, ready to pick you up, dust you off, kiss your booboo, and help you continue along your way. God is there for you."

I was definitely confused as the choir did a little reggae number, "Jah Is Jesus," and Ina and I processed out of the church. I was still pondering the ramifications of such an accepting God (there were even gay couples at the church, and the news had me believing that *everybody* hated them) at La Brasserie. My mussels were growing cold.

"So, what did you think?"

"Think? Me?"

"That is what you're doing right now? Thinking, right? You're definitely not eating."

"Yeah, well…" I didn't know what to say. I looked down at those mussels and that white wine cream sauce and knew I was going to enjoy a little sopping later. I looked into Ina's earnest, brown eyes and knew I wa…

"You didn't like it, did you? I'm sorry. I guess it was a bad idea. I really shou—"

"No, no, no," I placated. "It's just been a long time since I've been to church, is all. I think a lot has changed."

"So why did you stop going, Damian?"

She leaned in closer and gave me a look through her glasses that stripped me to the core.

"I don't know. I guess I was sick of the fear and loathing. The guilt. Who wants to be condemned all the time? Just stone me once and get it over with."

"I know. That's why I like this place. It makes me feel good. Like I have a loving relationship with Jesus. Not like He's going to run and get the switch every time I mess up. I've really been messing up a lot lately."

"So, you don't fear God?"

"No. Why should I?"

"Because then all you have left is the government."

She smiled. We picked at our food for a minute. I was using an empty shell to pluck the remaining mussels from their shells. I always think it makes me look "continental," but nobody else ever seems to be impressed. It was just another thing that made me feel this was going badly. I mean, we could've gone to so many things where I could've at least *tried* to be charming. The movies, a play, a football game, a dog show, an autopsy. But church. Why would you invite *me* to church? Besides, what about me screams to be saved?

All right. Stupid question.

"Well, I'm glad you came, anyway."

"I'm just glad I didn't burst into flame upon entry."

She actually tittered. "Were you sweatin' it?"

"It was a concern." I smiled.

"No. I know you hate to dress up. And here you are in a jacket and tie." She was really smiling now. The red began showing in her cheeks. She stabbed a fry (or "pomme frite," when I feel like being "continental"; want me to sing "Le Marseille" or at least "Lady Marmalade"?). "Ya know, most guys wouldn't go on a church date."

"I'm sorry, 'date.' I—well…"

There goes that smile again. How many dimples does this woman have?

"Sure. Why not? And a pleasant one. I've never been here before. I like this place. You've never struck me as a French restaurant type." When was the last time I'd heard anything like that? I didn't think I had it in me to be pleasant. Acerbic, morose, manic-depressive, sure. But "pleasant"?

"Seriously, Damian. I could never get Darnell to go to church with me. Let alone a cute little place like this. I think it was one of *many* problems in our relationship."

I didn't know what to say. But I was done with my mussels and now it was on to the broth-and-bread sopping good time. Things were looking up.

"Yeah, well, Encyclopedia Britannica's still compiling all of Samara's and my problems. I think they're coming out with a leather-bound edition. Three volumes."

"Hey, you know what I haven't done in awhile?"

I know what I haven't done in awhile. What am I? In seventh grade?

"No. What?"

"Dance. I have a desperate need to just dance my ass off. You wanna go next Saturday?"

DATE: Monday, October 8, 20— 12:45 A.M.
FROM: tjacks@leviathan....
TO: drcross@wintersoldiers....
SUBJECT: Finding religion

Was it as bad as all that?

DATE: Monday, October 8, 20— 3:36 A.M.
FROM: drcross@wintersoldiers....
TO: tjacks@leviathan....
SUBJECT: RE: Finding religion

no. it could've been worse. it could've been a rod stewart jazz concert.

MONDAY, OCTOBER 8, 20—
7:41 P.M.

I'm walking on sunshine! Hey! Hey! Hey, what the hell? *And don't it feel good?! Yeah* ... but ... I mean, Katrina and the Waves? C'mon now. My happiness can do better than that. I don't have '80s pop running through my veins ... I have funk. Funk! *Science!* I said, Funk. *Ooh, rock me, Amadeus* ... Aw, Jesus.

I'm trying to tell a story here. Anyway, I know after yesterday I'm giddy as all get out, babbling with pheromone-induced ADD, but my brain has no right becoming an MP3 player on eternal random. It makes for bad blogging.

But yesterday ... Well, I'll never say I enjoyed church. But it wasn't as bad as I thought it was going to be. And I didn't suffer the pox—which is always a plus. And I really did enjoy being with that woman. I could get lost in her *Always—until the dolphin flies and parrots live at sea* ... She's so warm, so genuine. And I'm really digging her wardrobe change. Yet again, thank you Darnell for so thoroughly fucking this woman up. To believe she's been hiding all *that* for all these years. I feel as though I've missed out on so much. But now's my chance.

I want to follow up on that kiss in La Brasserie's parking lot. I just want to be with her. *I wanna sex you up.* Oh ... my ... God! Color Me Badd?! Hell, if I'd been writing about Samara here, BBD would be pumping "Poison."

Oh screw it, Damian. No time to be thinking about *her*. *Love is in the air.* DiDi and Priti seem to be getting along all right. Neville and Hep were all cuddled up last night, listening to jazz ballads. Neville usually screams at such corniness, yet he was all smiles. You actually made a little progress on that second novel of yours today. In an hour you're going out with the boys, which you haven't done in years. Damn, people. Life is good. *I'm on top of the world ... looking down on creation...*

The Carpenters?!

TUESDAY, OCTOBER 9, 20—
11:56 A.M.

"Youghiogheny?"

"Yeah. You ever been? It's right on the Yauk. Actually, there's really no reason to go unless you have family there. There's absolutely nothing there. We don't even have a Wal-Mart. You've got to go all the way to Little Warshington for that.

"I mean, it used to be something. It had a big steel mill, a couple coal mines, and all those barges taking the coal and steel to Lord knows where back in the '50s. Then it started going to shit. And that's where it is now. The only thing we've really got now is Jim Dakota."

"The quarterback?"

"The three-time Super Bowl MVP, Hall of Fame quarterback. You know western Pennsylvania. We breed quarterbacks. Johnny Unitas, Dan Marino, Joe Namath, Jim Dakota. And he's Youghiogheny's own.

"Growing up, when he was winning all those rings with LA, ohmygersh, you couldn't escape him. Everybody had his jersey. Only second to the Stillers. Since he was out on the West Coast, everybody would go down to Chiodo's and watch his game after the Stillers were done. It was Dakota Mania.

"I remember being totally in love with the guy. He was tall and muscular with that long, flowing blond hair and blue eyes. And he had the cutest smile. And besides, he was a winner. Do you know how sexy that is? Especially where I'm from. Since Johnson's mine blew up and closed back in '87, there haven't been that many winners in Youghiogheny, Pennsylvania. The place just reeks of loss. I still hate going back there. I'm trying to convince my mum to move here so I don't have to.

"But yeah, Jim Dakota was the only winner we all had. Unlike all the guys in town, he had a real job, was rich, and probably had his pick of any woman on the continental United States. I know he definitely could've had me and damn near every girl at Bethel High and every woman in the tri-state area.

"My boyfriend, Frankie, just wasn't cutting it. Finger-fucking me in the back of his old Camaro, I could only think of Jim Dakota, being wrapped up in those massive arms that threw for 3,700 yards that year. Frankie Calabrese couldn't do that. No guy around there could. Sure, they tried by bragging about how they used to go to high school with him, how they played on the same little league baseball team, how Jim had stolen the poor jagoff's girlfriend back in tenth grade, how that same jagoff popped Jim Dakota in the eye that very same night. Anything to grab a little of the man's glory. But the only bastard who could was his drunk of a little brother, Steve.

"Back then, Steve was the King of Chiodo's. Getting drunk every night, trying to bang any bimbo who wanted to fuck fame's little brother. Or so I heard, I was still in high school. What did I know? Though I do think Steve trawled Bethel every once in awhile.

"Yeah, '89 was the year that Youghiogheny decided to honor its conquering hero. Hell, nobody had seen him in, like, ten years ... when he'd gone off to Auburn to become a god. I think his parents had even moved out to LA by then. Everybody just left Steve where he was. But yeah, I don't know what they were thinking. Looking back, I don't see how they didn't see that Jim Dakota didn't want to see any of them again. He knew Youghiogheny was a shithole. Hell, I knew it was a shithole back then, and all I'd ever seen were Little Warshington, Pittsburgh once or twice, and Morgantahn.

"But everybody went ahead as planned. I guess people had talked to people who had talked to people, and everybody was sure Jim was coming. We were having a big parade. The Mayor and his wife, the police chief and his family, the Knights of Columbus, everybody was going to be in it. Even Donna Laine, who was on some kids' TV show in the '60s. She was the big-deal celebrity before Jim.

"Me. I was real excited. I was a cheerleader back then. And we were a real big deal. That year we'd won our division in WPIALs and placed third in State. The only thing I liked more than cheering was Jim Dakota—sorry, Frankie, wherever you are—and finally I was going to get to combine the two.

"I think every girl in the area was going crazy with Jim's return. Malls and beauty salons were flooded. Everyone wanted to look their best for the man, hoping to snag him and a one-way ticket out of Depressed Economy, USA. Like any of us could compete with all the silicon and face lifts out in LA.

"But it didn't matter. I'm sure you can figure out what happened. It was too embarrassing, tragic, kinda funny when you look back at it. The one small town's biggest humiliation. They'd built a podium, and everything, and the bastard never showed. People were devastated. But we marched, anyway. The band played. The majorettes twirled their batons, flags were waved, and we tumbled for a few minutes on the stage. To half-hearted cheers, of course. Everybody was crying, ya know. It was the most important day the town had ever had, and now it was going to be remembered for all the wrong reasons.

"I remember the mayor giving this really pathetic speech. Donna Laine was supposed to give Jim the key to the city, but she refused to go on. She was crying loudest and longest, the make-up just streaming down her face, you'd've thought somebody had shot her. Actually, I think she was happy to be the center of attention again.

"So anyway, the mayor had to give the key to somebody. So, he gave it to Steve. Who was *so* drunk, of course. They dragged him away from his 'throne' long enough to get the damned key. But he was crying, too. Somebody had to hold him up to take the key. He was all over the place.

"The stupid bastard went to say something and let out this massive belch. The microphone screamed. Then he wailed something like, 'Why can't you love me?!' and then hurled all over the place. Hit the mayor, the police chief's wife, everybody. It was like watching *The Exorcist*. We were all waiting for his head to do a three-sixty.

"Hey, wait. This isn't supposed to be funny. It's supposed to be, well, sad. Why are you—yeah, actually I do find it a little funny now, too. But I was there. It *was* sad. As though those poor people hadn't been through enough. The mines had left them. The mills, too. Young people were leaving in droves. None of it was ever gonna come back. Just like Jim Dakota. But they soldiered on. Through all that rejection and vomit. They soldiered on. I don't know, now I think it's kinda cool that they did that. Fuck Jim Dakota, right? He wasn't going to ruin their day. Even though he really did.

"The one thing I don't understand, though, is what did those jagoffs ever do to him? I mean, I don't like the place. But I don't hate it either. If they asked me to come back to be honored—though I don't know why they would, I just sell real estate—but I'd come back. Not like my return would mean as much as his did that day. And it really did. It meant the *world* to those people. I'm sure he knew it, too. He had to. And what would it have cost him? One lousy afternoon in the off-season. A plane ticket? It's not like he couldn't have afforded it. What would it really have mattered to him? It would've cost him so little just to humor all those people for a few minutes. I wonder what they all did to deserve that humiliation. What made him hate them so much he refused them just that little bit of happiness?"

I used to dream of returning to high school. The conquering hero. All those bastards would greet me with large smiles and envy in their eyes. I'd pimp-strut down the hallways with my international bestseller in one hand and my international Wolof model with legs up to my ears I'd picked up in Paris on the other. Pimp fedora and platform shoes with goldfish in the heels. A bumpin' funk band playing "Freddie's Dead," thumping that heavy-ass bass line to accentuate my every footfall, because every hero needs theme music.

They would gawk and adore and apologize profusely. I would have finally been vindicated for all the torment, all the anguish I had suffered at St. Thomas More High School. I used to dream of returning to high school, the conquering hero, up until the moment I threw my tasseled mortar board in the air, said a tearful good-bye to Mr. Bercelli, took off the damned gown, and got drunk with Steve and Al, listening to Eazy E and S.O.D. Aside from my sophomoric sense of humor, I haven't been back to high school since. Didn't even bother going to my ten-year reunion.

And yet last night, there I was—back in ninth, tenth, maybe even eleventh grade. Sitting in the Scotsman waiting for my boys to appear with Jenna Mankiewicz, a home girl (though where Youghiogheny is is beyond me), a comely bier frau type, big healthy western Pennsylvanian—eats steel for breakfast and cuds coal for lunch—really thick and solid, bursting beautifully at the seams, she'll be squeezing out future linebackers in no time. Bright blue eyes, blond hair, that cheerleader smile and cheerleader body and cheerleader beauty. The kind of girl you masturbated to in high school, sneered at in your leftist twenties, but are finding quite intriguing right this very minute at thirty-two.

She was Lisa R., Melanie G., Colleen S., Jill L., Jen B. She was all those girls who refused to talk to your black ass back in the alabaster '80s. The ones you never really talked to—because learning trigonometry was all the pointless activity you could handle in a day.

But here's Jenna, the popular girl, the cheerleader with big eyes and even bigger pom poms and a real estate license. Her body still primed for competition. She's sitting next to me. I'm trying to devote myself to my beer, trying not to look at her, think of Ina and the Lord and the salvation I can find between her thighs—but Jenna is here. And hers look pretty glorious, too. What color is Jesus?

A beautiful amber. My beer. Concentrate on the beer. Wow, Red Stripe's distributed by Guinness. Who knew? Do not look, stare at Jenna Mankiewicz. Don't be like the other buzzards circling … circling … getting shot down with a single glare when they get too close. Dead egos are gathering at her feet, and I have no wish to join this orgy of humiliation. One of the carcass munchers, in surprisingly tight jeans, penny loafers, white socks, and an oxford, approached, and rico suavéd, "And you are?" like they were actually having a conversation. Jenna just looked at him, icy blue. "Suitably unimpressed." Pull! Crack! Another clay pigeon shot to shit. *Where are those bastards, anyway?* I wondered. *And I call them my boys …Why did I come so early? Like I ain't never hearda CP Time?*

If I believed in cell phones, I'd have called Kev to curse him out or Ina just to say "Hey"—though I don't know if that's too pathetic. It's been so long. I don't know what to do. I mean, it's not like we've just met. We *have* known each other for eight years. I *could* just call up and say "Hey," right? It's not like I've never said "Hey" to the woman before.

Thank God for ESPN. Football news. Every man's salvation. Yes, God indeed does have testicles … but not a Terrible Towel. The Steelers' big receiver's down *again*. Goddamned Plexiglas.

"Son of a bitch!"

"Asshole!"

I don't remember who said what. But whatever was said by whomever was said simultaneously. Jenna looked at me. I finally allowed myself to look at her.

"I take it you're not a big Plexiglas fan."

"Does he get injured, like, every season?" she asked, a fire in her blue eyes like the Cuyahoga River.

The buzzards gave a collective squawk. All that beauty, all that body, and she knew football. Oh, there were going to be some very busy right hands tonight.

"No. He did have a decent rookie season."

"Oh, you mean when the jagoff spiked the ball in Jacksonville even though he wasn't touched and the Jagwires ran the ball back for a touchdown?"

"Yeah. That was the season. You from Pittsburgh?"

"How'd you know?"

"Ya know, I didn't know that women *didn't* like football until I left Pittsburgh for college."

"Ohmygersh, I don't know what I'd do without my Stillers. I live, eat, and breathe those guys. Thank God for NFL Ticket."

A woman after my own heart. *My* right hand might be busy tonight. She offered hers.

"My name's Jenna Mankiewicz."

Jenna Mankiewicz and Ina Yancey. Oh yeah. Très occupé.

"Damian Cross."

"The writer?"

Syke. She didn't know who I was.

"So, where did you say you were from again?"

"Youghiogheny."

"Youghiogheny?"

"Yeah. You ever been…?"

Damn. I couldn't stop the clarion call. Believe it or not, this blogger is intensely private. I hate people knowing my business, and sometime while Jenna was getting finger-fucked by Frankie Calabrese, I heard the town crier announcing what I was doing to the world. I caught Kev, Bob, and Malik strolling in, catching me red-handed with the tow-headed maiden. I saw them see me, see Jenna, then grab a booth. I could hear derisive choruses of "Jungle Fever" below the tale of Jim Dakota screwing over his hometown.

Fortunately, things were cut short by the arrival of Jenna's friend, Natalie, an attractive, little brunette with big, evil eyes that constantly bore icicles into my skull. The whole time I couldn't figure out why someone like Jenna was talking to me—hell, why she was single—now I wished she'd just shut up. There were too many people looking at us, and I was feeling the church ants returning to torment me. I didn't even like blondes. I'd only ever been with one, and Keisha wasn't natural (though her peroxide pubes were hellafied classy—I wonder whatever happened to her—maybe I should Google her).

"Hey, Nat. This is Damian. He's from Picksburgh."

"Hi," she said, coolly, shooting two stalactites into my frontal lobe.

"Yeah, well, my friends are here," I ventured.

"Oh … well—" was she actually … disappointed? "—here, wait a second." Jenna dug into her purse, produced a business card and a pen. She scribbled furiously. "Here. Email me. We can watch a game, or something."

She handed me her business card. Did I ask? Her hand touched mine. I flinched again. Shit. I really thought I was over that. We shared an awkward moment. Even Natalie noticed—disparagingly, I'm sure.

"Yeah, sure," I fumbled, and handed her one of my cards. I had a thousand printed for the tour. Nine hundred ninety-six to go. "They're actually fun to watch this year."

"As long as Plexiglas doesn't return any time soon."

She really was adorable.

I smiled and left the two to the vultures—though I was sure Natalie had no problem poaching a carrion eater. It was time for me to face the music.

"Ebony and ivory," Bob sang, *"live together in perfect harmony."*

"Wow, I was really expecting 'Jungle Fever,'" I said.

Bob shrugged. "I've mellowed in my old age."

"Shit. Bob Hancock. I haven't seen you in a coon's age."

"Who's the coon?" Bob asked.

Kevin impishly raised a hand.

"It's a Southern saying," I informed. "I've always been afraid to ask."

I can't even remember the last time I'd seen Bob. Or anybody, for that matter. Even before the Cataclysm, I'd become a bit of a hermit—what with the book, work, and Samara and Egon's theater company. I just wasn't going out much. But I didn't even know the brother was in town. The last I'd heard, he was trying to make it in Hollywood—or Holland? Does that even make sense?

It was always hard to keep track. Hancock was always off somewhere, collecting experiences and stories, being the globe-trotting, aspiring writer I'd always wanted to be. One time he'd almost convinced me to go to Senegal with him on his dime (or rather, his father's), but by that time I was with Samara; and she was having none of that. I had love, but Bob had courage. In retrospect, I would've gladly exchanged gifts. Naw, Samaraland's some pretty rough terrain. I wouldn't wish that on the most intrepid of travelers ... but maybe my worst enemy.

Which was close to what Bob had been when we first met. He went to school with Kevin and me. Where Kev had been the mack I could never be, Hancock was the writer I'd never wanted to be. In those angry hip-hop, late '80s where "Prophets of Rage" were battling with "Lyrics of Fury," Bob was the pseudoest pseudo-revolutionary of the lot. All the future buppies with black Africa medallions on their chests and platinum American Express cards in their futures loved speaking in our parents' rage. We were infuriated over the past's and present's atrocities because our own lives were atrociously easy. We couldn't look our own privilege in the eye. So, we looked to the past. Malcolm, Martin, the Black Panthers. The Lost Poets were Bob's favorite. That was all he wrote. "Niggers love ... Niggers love..." He was so full of Nigger Love you'd have thought he was the Negroid Larry Flynt. And when he wasn't lovin' niggers he was worshipping his black sisters, his Nubian queens. The words were everyone's but his. Like MC Hammer, he sampled from the best. Sonia, Amiri, Gwendolyn, Gil Scott. Everybody loved his poetry, his plays, his pissed-off visage.

"Shit, even oil ain't *that* black," Kevin used to say.

And that was it. It was all so damned fake. So many of us were. Trying to be something we never could be or ever really wanted to be. Like we were all lining up to get lynched, or something. Hell, we were a bunch of black kids in a very blue-blood university. The ultimate paradox that would send us into paroxysms of ... rage? For so many, it was simply a costume we tried on freshman year while trying to define our new, adult selves, but for Bob it was something different. Something more desperate. He had something to prove. As though with a good scrubbing he was afraid that his black actually *could* come off. So, every night he smeared gobs and gobs of burnt-cork militancy onto his skin—like it could cover up the Exeter education and millions of dollars his golf phenom father made on the PGA tour. If he could somehow just learn how to properly enunciate "Nigga," none of us would realize just how "white" he really did sound. If he could quote Donald Goines enough, none of us would discover his secret love of Fyodor Dostoevsky.

Hell, so many of us were going through it (though no one would admit it then or now), the guilt, watching the older black folks scrubbing our dorm floors, knowing one day we'd have Salvadoran maids and Filipina nannies ushering our children to Friends Academy. But we were all so busy fooling ourselves that we admired the paragon of MTV blackness. Bob Hancock with his Lost Poets prose was *the* black writer on campus. The Shaka Zulu of pseudo-revolutionary schlock.

I despised him for his lack of craft and hated his self-righteous strut. But then something happened during our senior year. We still don't know what exactly. He's never talked about it. But he changed. Mellowed out.

Afterwards, we started hanging out, drinking, playing chess, and talking literature. Those were the discovery days. Gogol, Achebe, Tanizaki. Octavia Butler and Samuel R. Delany. Good times. Sure, every once in awhile he would still come at us with some black nationalist tract. But it was somehow tempered. More of an intellectual pursuit than an ostentatious parade. And after school, when he started taking advantage of his father's millions and traveling the planet, it all but disappeared (funny what going native in the Netherlands will do to a brother), which is why I was a little taken aback by last night's conversation.

"Still fucking around with the white women, eh Damian?"

"Oh my God, get caught *once* with one on campus, and you're branded for life."

Bob gave me an incredulous look. "Once?"

"Yeah," Kev piped up, "what about that girl from Germany?"

"Steffi?" I asked, disbelieving. "She was a quadroon."

Bob, Kev, *and* Malik all laughed at that one.

"No, seriously," I protested. "Her mom was an occupation baby. Her granddad was a brother from Alabama."

They wouldn't stop laughing.

"I saw *pictures*."

"She had red hair, man," Bob chortled.

"So did Malcolm."

"He's got a point there," Malik volunteered.

"I don't give a shit," Bob responded. "You're takin' that one-drop rule a little too literally, brother man."

They kept laughing.

"Hey Bob, hear from Hilda lately? That was your Dutch girl's name, right? Hilda?" I snickered.

Bob shrugged nonchalantly. "Hey, if you woulda seen ole girl, you woulda stuck your finger in that dike, too."

"He finally admits it," I triumphed, "she was white."

"Naw man, Hilda was one hundred percent, pure mulatto."

We all laughed.

"Jesus," Kev chuckled. "Mulattos, quadroons. It's like we're at a Strom Thurmond family reunion, or some shit. Who here's been with an octoroon?"

Malik kept laughing.

"What the hell are you laughing at, Malik?" I asked. "You were married to a white woman."

"Still am," he claimed, suddenly seriously. "Or well, we remarried."

I tried to hide my shock. Malik and Judy remarried? Who knew nitroglycerine was recyclable?

"Well, I'm not," Bob volunteered, gravely serious this time.

"Oh shit, that reminds me," Kevin erupted. "High and tight, I knew Dwana was gonna be all right."

"And the crow flies at midnight?" Bob asked, sarcastically.

"That's not what I think it is, is it?" I asked, filling with dread. I was really hoping he wasn't actually putting thought into this. I thought he had a music career to pursue.

Kevin had the biggest government-cheese-eating grin I'd seen in awhile. He was actually proud of himself. "Yep."

"So, let me get this straight," I opened. "'I'm in some ass right now. High and tight, I knew Dwana was gonna be all right.'"

"That's it, Negro."

"Jesus, Kevin."

"What?" Bob asked.

"I'm trying to convince Damian here to write a booty novel," Kev volunteered.

"A what?"

"A booty novel."

"Well, at least it rhymes," Malik conceded.

"You mean, like some nig lit bullshit?" Bob asked.

"Nig lit?" we all asked.

"You know, Day, bullshit black romances. Recently divorced sister finally finding a righteous brother. Maybe a 'playa'—or is it 'baller' now?"

"Do people even say that anymore?" I asked.

"I don't know," Bob admitted. "I haven't been relevant since 1997."

"No," I said, "you were still pretty irrelevant back then, too."

"Anyway," Bob continued, "playa, baller, backdoor man, since you want to get all atavistic and shit, the brother's gotta start mending his ways once he finds a righteous sister. I don't know. But somebody's gotta be righteous in the motherfucker. And somebody's gotta be reformed—like fools like that ever change."

"They don't," Kevin informed.

"And religion never hurts," Bob amended.

"Like you and Ina, D," Kev volunteered.

"Shut up."

"And yeah, make sure the brother loves big sisters. That'd be your target audience, after all."

Bob never really minced words to ease digestion.

"And while you're at it, go light on the cursing and *don't* use 'nigger.'"

"Guess I can't base a character on you then."

"Got that right … porch monkey."

"Actually, that sounds pretty good," Kevin agreed. "He needs to write something to get him on Oprah. Maybe something more Boho, though."

"Why?" Bob looked genuinely confused.

"That's how writers make money, Bob," Kevin stated.

"Maybe he should just come out with a fusion album."

Kevin gave Bob a cold stare. Bob chuckled. Malik did, too. And yeah, I snickered.

"So, what would you call this opus, Day?" Hancock asked. "If it were me, I'd call it *Gittin' Some*."

"Hell, why not *My Booty Novel*? No need to be clever."

"So you have been giving it thought?" Kevin was a bit too enthusiastic.

"Man, I thought you were a science fiction writer," Malik countered.

"Fuck that," Kev said. "It's time for ole boy to make some funky dollar bills, y'all."

"He could always do a duet with Kenny G. Look, Damian, I really liked *Winter Soldiers*. If I didn't know you for the bitch you truly are, I'd almost say you have some talent."

Wow, that was a mighty big compliment coming from Hancock. I might have actually started blushing.

"Talent don't pay the rent," Kevin protested. "Ass. Now that sells."

Bob rolled his eyes. "So, what's your next novel about, Damian?"

That was a tough one. I haven't really been able to put it into words—which is why my Word documents have been fairly barren of late. I screwed up my face.

"I've been thinking about property lately. Private property. How, when it really comes down to it, we don't really own anything. And I'm not talking about property tax—which is basically paying rent to the government, right? I'm talking really private. Like even our own bodies.

"For example, right, if you go to a doctor and they take a blood sample and find some rare antigen in your blood, right, they can take that antigen, replicate it, maybe develop a new vaccine, manufacture it, distribute it, make millions of dollars and never tell you—let alone give you a cut. Now, it's not as though you really had anything to do with that antigen. Your body just fought some disease and developed it. But it's still yours and they took it from you. They do it all the time. Exploit people like that. And you're none the wiser. Well, what else can they do to you, take from you, without your ever knowing?

"And well, shit, think about nanotechnology. Soon, there'll be all kinds of man-made activity on a molecular level going on, and we'll have no clue. What will they take from us then? Or worse yet, what will they be doing to us without our having a clue? Wars can be fought, won, and lost without anybody ever really knowing. Diseases spread. Epidemics prevented. An outbreak of Ebola in Switzerland, cholera in Chicago. Ghetto kids being made sterile, Cambodian women having their eggs destroyed. Serious nuclear wars, so to speak, and not one word on CNN."

I ran out of breath and still hadn't given a coherent answer. Silence. Was that a pin dropping? One hand clapping? Finally, Kevin turned to Bob.

"So yeah, I was thinking a booty novel."

"Man, I was with the same woman for seven years," I contested. "What do I know about booty?"

"He's got a point," Malik agreed, "maybe I should write it."

Or Samara, I thought to myself. Besides, Malik taught elementary school and was never the stud he envisioned himself to be.

"Yeah, Day's right, Kev," Bob declared. "A writer should write what he knows."

"Thank you," I said, not sure if I should feel triumphant or not.

"Maybe he should frame it like some nig lit," Bob suggested, "then just talk about his incurable love of white women. He definitely knows about them."

They started laughing again. Of course, that's when Jenna and Natalie walked by, the former waving as they left the Scotsman. My boys spasmed epileptic with laughter. I thought Malik was going to have a seizure. I contemplated putting a spoon in his mouth and my fist down Bob's throat.

"Hell, every sister in the continental United States would hate him," Malik guffawed.

"Oh, they'd hate him in Hawaii, too," Kevin chuckled.

"Samara wasn't white," I informed—like they didn't know. "Wait, why the hell am I defending myself? I've only been with one white woman."

Kevin stared at me.

"OK, two."

"And one quadroon."

"Right. Besides, Kevin Byrd, you've been with divisions of white women."

"Yeah, but I'm a musician. We're *supposed* to screw everybody. Besides, I had that song 'Beautiful Black Sister' on the album. I'm off the hook."

"CYA, nigger."

"Got that right."

Kevin and Bob dapped each other up.

"And as many times as you've lived in Europe, Hancock, I know you've for damned sure been with a whole slew of white women."

"Yeah, but you're so damned sensitive about it."

They laughed again. Bob gave me an incredibly serious look. "Would you really do it, Damian? Write a booty novel just to make some cash?"

I looked at him, at Kev, then caved. "I really don't know. I *am* tired of being broke. There are only so many flavors Ramen can make."

"Thank you," Kev triumphed, raising his hands in Nixonian victory.

"I guess you wouldn't understand."

"No," Billionaire Bob conceded. "I guess I wouldn't."

"But in all honesty, I don't think I could. I mean, I wouldn't even know where to begin. It's not like a writer can just write *anything*. I'm not trained to be a popular writer. My tastes are too obscure. I don't think I *could* write a popular novel. Or, if you believe some critics, even a *good* one."

"You're still on that Welsh kid?" Malik asked.

"To believe that little motherfu—" I had to stop myself. Breathe. "What about you, Bob? Do you think you could?"

He took a swig of beer. "Hell naw. Too much Bukowski and Himes in my blood. I guess I could write a mean, misogynist novel with touches of the absurd."

"What's more absurd than a mean misogynist?"

"Exactly."

"Well then, what about chick lit?" Kev suggested.

"What the hell do I know about being a twenty-eight-year-old white woman?" I countered.

"You sure have screwed enough of them."

"Don't *you* start, Malik."

"Sorry."

"He's got to figure out how to appeal to women," Kev informed.

"Well, I do have a second date with Ina on Saturday."

"Cool, but I was talking literarily. They're the only ones who read."

"Well, there goes my mean misogynist book," Bob said.

"Yeah, bruh," I agreed. "You're about fifty years too late on that one."

"Damn." Bob stared at his beer. You could see the wheels sputtering in his head. He looked intently up at me. "I've got nothing ... wait ... no ... hell, why don't you ... naw ... well, just make sure if you're gonna write about black folks, make sure you have a token white friend. Like on the WB. That way folks won't think you're racist."

WEDNESDAY, OCTOBER 10, 20—
10:55 A.M.

"Hey, jig."

"Yeah, Bob."

"I forgot to mention something."

"Hit me."

"Make sure you have one of them Hollywood endings. Nig or chick, folks *love* a happy ending."

"Whatever, man."

"Naw, seriously, dude. I mean, make the shit *cheeeeesy*. Like folks can see the credits rolling at the end of the book."

"I'm hanging up now, Bob."

"Stay strong, black man."

"You are perpetually stuck in 1988, Hancock."

"It was a good year."

THURSDAY, OCTOBER 11, 20—
8:14 P.M.

I'm not a racist. I have white friends. Hell, some of my best friends are white (irony intended). Or used to be, at any rate. Damn near all my friends growing up were white (I *was* an integration baby, after all). And in college there were Rob, Mike and Mike, and Colin. There was also Tag, a few Joshes, and a handful of Todds.

Here, there was Egon, of course. I wonder what happened to him. We used to be so tight. To believe one argument could separate us like this. Then again, I used to be close to a lot of folks. That was something that really hit home last night. Where had all my friends gone? How had I lost touch with so many people over the years?

I hadn't talked to Bob in years, and to find out that he's been living in town for almost a year was a real shock. And he's not the only one. Of course, I was still around when Chris had decided to move to NYC to become a famous rapper—never to be heard from again. But when had Howard moved to Boston? Three years ago? Where was I? Whatever happened to our token white friend, Simon? Nobody knew. And he'd been gone for years, too. He used to get the best weed. What a tragic loss.

"What about J?"

"That crazy dread from Detroit who spoke patois?"

"Yeah. He was about as Jamaican as Bjork."

"Jamaicaner."

"So, what happened to ole boy?"

"Hell, last I heard he went back to D-Town to spin techno."

"Techno? How sad."

Malik told me that Buu had moved back to Vietnam. We used to love that crazy bastard. We could hardly understand a damned thing the man said, but he was fun to hang with. He always brought the cutest honeys by and was game for anything. One night, drunk off his ass, he decided to body surf off the back of a Nissan. Sparks flying off his belt buckle, the car dragged him for about a block before he let go. Shoes ruined, clothes tattered, and skin flayed, Buu promptly laughed his way back to the Yacht Club and bought us all shots.

Apparently, he now has a wife, two kids, and a bed and breakfast (of all things) back in Ho Chi Minh City. Who woulda thunk? Malik gets the occasional postcard and invitation to check out ole Saigon. And I had no clue Buu had gone.

The entire night was like that, filling up with names I'd thought long forgotten until I started to become claustrophobic. Nicole in Atlanta, Tim Dog in Charlotte, Duane in Miami, Kim in London. Domingo, I knew, was in San Diego. I could hardly believe it. Katina, Carmen, Tonya, Bri. Where had they all gone? Why hadn't I missed them until now? Kev's old flame, Yodit, and her girl, Eden. Boy, I wish I hadn't been with Samara … I mean, when we met them. I could've had a lot of fun with those Eritrean (think Ethiopia and turn north) beauties. But I guess life with Samara really had divorced me from everyone else. And now I was separated from her. What did that leave me?

So, if I were to write a book even remotely based on my life, it'd be hard to write about any friends at all, let alone any token white friends. But if I were to include someone, I guess it'd have to be Mayrav Amou, my insouciant Sephardic sweetheart.

One half of the white women I've ever slept with (a freaky fling in college, Christy, being the other), Mayrav holds a special place in my heart because she's one of the only former lovers I've been able to retain as a friend. I don't know if we've really been through enough for me to say that we're close, but we have known each other for almost nine years. And that says something.

Hell, I remember the first time I saw her. It was when I first rolled into town. Like any good scavenger, I checked out my new, potential hunting grounds. I hit a lot of record and book stores that first month. Those and food are about the only things I ever buy. So it's imperative to quickly find the good spots.

Soul on Wax struck me as a funny ode to Eldridge Cleaver, so I had to try that joint—expecting some kind of Afro hippy haunt with lots of incense and old funk. I wasn't disappointed. There was actual truth in advertising, and the place was dripping with lots of fine wax. You knew this was *the* spot for all the local DJs and connoisseurs. Fortunately, for turntable-less me, the CD collection was enormous, too. Soul on Wax was a huge space with three floors filled with old soul, funk, jazz, electronica, and hip-hop. Perfect. A crate digger's paradise. I knew I was going to be spending a lot of time there.

That day I was feeling funky, rebellious, and *oddly* Nigerian. It had been time to get a fix for my Fela jones. I found *Zombie* and was quite proud of my new acquisition. I turned to make my way to the counter when I saw her. This tiny, little creature with a maelstrom of swirling, raven hair and ecru-olive skin that sucked your eyeballs out of your head. I don't know if Mayrav is beautiful, but there's something so … *intriguing* about her, you can't help but be enamored. She was standing behind the counter inspecting albums and testing them out on a nearby turntable. She was bobbing her head to some early '70s psychedelic funk, eyes closed, deeply entranced by the music. The bass line thumped hypnotically. The Moog synthesizer danced and punched its way through the lava lamp groove. This 5'2" woman grew in the music—as though she were literally being transported to another time and space. I found myself bobbing along, entranced.

Then the singer screeched. He sounded like his throat was being clawed out from the inside. Mayrav stopped. "Ugh." She opened her eyes. Shamrock magnets that somehow latched onto me. Shit. I'd been staring. I'd been caught. I spasmed an awkward smile and rushed to the Jazz section. Shit.

She replaced the LP with some old Isaac Hayes. *Who is the man*? The store throbbed with raw sexuality while I trembled in my embarrassment. I was wondering how long I was going to have to wait until I could approach the counter. Walking out would be too humiliating. Besides, a large part of me (largely my southern hemisphere) wanted to know more about this woman. What did she do here? Where was she from, looking like that? Would she have my first born or just practice conception with yours truly? What was her name? Bob James?! "Take Me to the Mardi Gras?!!!" I'd been looking for that one for years. And it was used, too. Hé toi! I was in heaven.

I immediately rushed to the counter, former embarrassment evaporated in the heat of enthusiasm. I was about to listen to the source of the dopest sample in hip-hop history.

Much to my chagrin, the woman I'd instantly become infatuated with did not wait on me. Instead, I got a bargain basement hipster in clunky, black-rimmed glasses and an auto mechanic's work shirt with a "Joe" name tag.

"Dude, Fela," he trumpeted.

I don't know why I always look for record store employees' approval. After all, it's not like *they* are the musicians. Besides, I know I'm just playing into their hands. And yet, I still smiled. Proud. I too was cool.

"Bob James' *Two*?"

"You're going to regret that one," Green Eyes chimed in, looking up from a warped album.

"But it's got 'Take Me to the Mardi Gras,'" I volunteered.

"Yeah, I know," she said. "'Peter Piper.'"

"Run-DMC. Exactly. The first and coolest sample ever produced."

"OK," she said, and turned back to the black disc in her hand.

I didn't want to let her go. Not that easily. "Hey, what was that crap you were playing just a minute ago? It sounded cool until ole boy started singing."

"It's an old Jan Hammer."

"'Axel F?' Who knew he ever came out with something almost cool?"

"Almost," she concurred, without ever looking up.

She was lost to me. There was no way I could press the matter without looking desperate. I paid and left.

It took a little while to find a job, and if it hadn't been for DiDi and her hook-up at the Union, I don't know how long it would've taken. But once I got that steady paycheck, Soul on Wax became one of my favorite haunts. This was before I became a music critic and could indulge my habit for free. I'd gone several times, trying to wrangle a "casual" conversation with the woman with the wild mane and emerald eyes. All the time wondering what exactly she was. Such an insignificant matter that became a minor obsession.

I don't know how long it took, but at one point when I was checking out, she actually spoke to me.

"You're the Fela guy, aren't you?"

So she had noticed me, and she was interested.

"Yeah. I guess you don't get many of those."

"No. He sells pretty well here," she refuted. At first, I was deflated. I never was as unique as I hoped myself to be. Then I realized that if Fela did sell well and she still remembered me, I did somehow stand out. I could feel my chest puff up a little. "And how was that Bob James?"

"It sucked."

She smiled. "Told you. Maybe you should check out Hugh Masekela."

"Naw, that's all right. I was a DJ at my college radio station—"

"Who wasn't?" the mechanic inserted.

"—and I didn't like his last few albums."

"You've gotta go back," she informed me. She dug around behind the counter, her hair dropping into her eyes. She came out with two CDs, Masekela's *The Boy's Doin' It* and Sons & Daughters of Lite, and handed them to me, blowing the hair from her face. The sexiest thing I'd seen since Christy last handcuffed me to her bed. "If you like Fela, you'll like this Masekela."

"And the other one?"

"Oh, they're a hoot. Some Bay Area Black Panther band from the '70s. I think you'll love 'Operation Feed Yourself.'"

"What about 'Operation Bread Basket' and 'Operation Push'?"

Mechanic groaned. Mayrav smiled.

"Just try them out. Tell me what you think."

I trusted her. Hell, I was so happy that she talked to me, I didn't realize I'd spent $30 more than I'd intended to until I got back to my apartment. And I thought that only happened in strip clubs. But like any other lonely pervert, I kept coming back for more. I'd been pretty knowledgeable before meeting Mayrav, but she introduced me to so much more stuff: Burning Spear, Black Stalin, Weldon Irvine, Marlena Shaw. I'd spent more money than I had any business spending, but I loved music and was intrigued by my new mentor. Some months into this newfound relationship, she had decided to kick it up a notch.

"Were you planning on going to the Black Rock Lockdown on Tuesday?"

Lockdown was an annual concert held by all the local black rock bands, which at the time were numerous. It folded a couple years ago when folks finally conceded that the black band was dead and that black rock had expired in the incubator. I just loved the whole Mother's Finest futility of it all. I mean, hadn't they heard that "Niggaz Can't Sing Rock 'n' Roll"?

"Yeah. Actually, I was," I said, a bit confused with two Nina Simone discs in my hand.

"With anybody?"

"No. I'm still pretty new in town."

"Maybe you should pick me up."

Mechanic looked flabbergasted. *Him?!* he seemed to be thinking. *Me?!* my mind echoed.

"Yeah ... Sure."

And I still didn't know what she was.

I picked her up, anyway. We went. We loved it. The sight was definitely something to behold. The pure energy of it. Brothers and sisters writhing and jumping around on stage. Guitars screeching. Drums pounding. Basses throbbing. The singers' soulful voices rattling the ceiling. Dreads and baldheads jostling each other in the mosh pit. We joined in. The reverie too much to resist. I had to pick a laughing Mayrav off the ground twice. Everybody was so happy, so ecstatic, so optimistic. Nobody knew this was a movement bound to go nowhere. It was an ecstasy that lasted way past my second orgasm ("What? Like five minutes," Samara would've joked). We lay there with sweat and sex drying on our naked bodies and lit a joint. The perfect ending to a perfect evening.

Afterwards, we continued to sleep together. It was more inertia than anything else. Never love. I was just lonely, and Mayrav was the first person in this new town I'd befriended. And she had been fresh off of trying to get over the man she's never gotten over, Stuart.

There was one moment where I almost thought I could love this woman. It was a sticky summer afternoon. I remember it like it was yesterday because I've replayed that scene in my head so many times over the years. She was riding me with an oddly intense nonchalance that only Mayrav has. Intense action with a nonplussed reserve on her face. I was contemplating the spinal ridges along her back, how truly tiny she was, and wondering how flat an ass could be and still be considered an ass. Then watching that plateau sway atop me was getting me a little too carried away. I quickly thought about how in 1956 Don Newcombe hit six homers and batted .356 as a pitcher and how with a power ratio like that, I wondered if they ever contemplated putting him in the everyday lineup when I heard, "Oh my God!"

I smiled and nodded at myself, trying to figure out how to pat myself on the back I was lying on without her noticing, when she jumped straight off me. She made her way to my CD collection. Her ass was *so* flat. Tragic, really.

"You have *Here, My Dear*!" she exclaimed.

"Of course," I said, confused, the latex drying on my penis. "I love Marvin Gaye."

"Do you mind?"

I shrugged. She put the CD in. I love having sex to music, but just instrumentals. I can't sing and hate feeling compelled to do so while riding bareback. She hopped giddily and landed right back on me. I would've given her an 8.9 for technique. She fucked me, working her way down in this beautiful molasses sway of the hips.

"I love this album," she declared. "To think this guy cheats on his wife, leaves *her* for a younger woman, and *he's* bitter."

"Like people have to be right to be righteously indignant."

We continued like that for awhile, talking music and books and movies, changing positions every so often to see just how flexible the other person was. I tried not to sing along until finally the little guy had to speak up.

Afterwards, I thought I could do that forever. Talk, laugh, joke, have sex with this woman, thoroughly enjoying her company. And sex went on like that for a month or so until we found ourselves talking and laughing and joking more than having sex. By the third month, the sex completely disappeared. There was nothing dramatic in its death. It just quietly skulked off into a corner, closed its eyes, and decayed without either of us really minding. She was too busy trying to figure out who Stuart was going to be in her life, and I was occupied with a new job and DiDi introducing me to her social circle and my trying to form one of my own.

But we still hung out, and I do love Mayrav. I will probably love her for the rest of my life. As I said, I don't know exactly how close the two of us really are, but I feel that she will always be a part of me. It's a shame we haven't seen more of each other over the past few years. I take the blame. When Samara and I first started dating and living together, I still saw Mayrav. But one night I let slip that we used to sleep together. After that, she would give me way too much flak every time I saw the woman. She'd say that she didn't trust Ms. Amou. I just knew she didn't trust me (which hurt). Now, I just think she wouldn't have trusted herself in the same situation and projected that mistrust onto me.

But now I'm the freest I've been of Samara in a very long time. I was going on a date with Ina in a couple days. It was past time to see Mayrav.

I walked into her store (she owns Soul on Wax, actually—she comes from money) and didn't see her. Mechanic had been replaced by Punk, who didn't realize that the people who'd originated the turquoise Mohawk and piercings he was sporting now had kids his age. I asked him where Mayrav was, and he pointed me to the back. I went straight to her little office. The door was open. Her back was to me. Her hair was shorter, she seemed somehow wider, but her ass was still slate. I cleared my throat. She turned. There were faint fissures of age showing. She smiled and those green eyes sparkled. I suddenly wanted to talk, laugh, joke, and have sex with this woman all over again.

She approached. "Greetings, my African-American brother," she chuckled, and gave me an exaggerated, sloppily friendly kiss on the mouth. I wondered if I had somehow pissed her off in my absence.

"You're not with that again, are you?"

"Hey, my people came from Africa in 1961. When did yours?"

"Not fair, Mayrav."

One post-coital day I'd finally summoned the courage to ask her what she was. Her paternal grandfather was a Moroccan Jew who survived the Holocaust because the king of Morocco refused to deport the Jews while the Vichy government was sending all the others to concentration camps. He, Mayrav's pops, and his wife joined the mass Sephardic exodus in '56 to Israel to settle in Haifa. Wallowing in utter shit for a few years, he lost his head and joined the big riot in 1959, then decided to emigrate to America—where an African had a shot—in '61. He worked his way up in some furniture store in Rochester until he owned it and several others by 1973.

I got to meet the old guy just before he died at Mayrav's cousin's Bat Mitzvah. I think she wanted to shock the folks by bringing a black guy by. First the WASP, Stuart, then me. I'm sure they thought she was a lost cause. Anyway, I liked him a lot, though he barely spoke to me. He could speak Berber, Arabic, Hebrew, and English. I was jealous.

Her mother's side, with whom she wasn't all that close, came from Armenia. So, she wanted me to decide what she was. A Moroccan Jew and Armenian. While neither one of those had been considered white a hundred years ago, they definitely were now. Funny how things change.

"But you know technically," she had playfully quipped, "I could say I was African-American."

"You know that's not what that means, Mayrav."

"What does any of it mean, Damian?"

She sat down at her eternally cluttered desk. I sat in a chair beside it.

"I guess it would be silly to ask you what you've been up to," she stated. "It *has* been two years."

"Damn. That long?"

"Yes. That long." She didn't look happy. I felt a little singed in her gaze. But then she smiled. "It doesn't matter. I know Samara doesn't like me."

"You don't have to worry about that now."

"I know," she said, not a hint of sadness in her voice. In fact, she might've sounded … happy.

"You do?"

"Kevin told me. He comes in here every once in awhile to see how his CD's doing. It doesn't sell at all here—*my* customers have taste. In fact, I wouldn't even carry it if I didn't know the guy. But I lie and tell him they're doing all right. Just to make him feel better. He's a really good customer."

"Like how you used to fake your orgasms with me."

"Damn. How'd you know?"

Shit.

"Just kidding. Why fake? Then I'd just leave dissatisfied."

"I guess I should stop faking, too, then."

"Oh, congratulations on your book."

"Thanks." Then I asked the question I always try not to ask. "Did you read it?"

"I tried," she confessed. "You really demand a lot from your reader."

Which is why I never ask.

"So, are you working on another one?"

"I'm trying, but I'm a little gun shy. I really got burned on the first one."

"So?" Mayrav said, defiantly. "People used to run screaming from Coltrane concerts."

"That's exactly how I feel … when I'm high." I slumped down in my chair. "I don't know. Kev thinks I should write a booty novel."

"A what?"

"You know, about a guy who's screwing his brains out and screwing women over until he finds Jesus between the thighs of a good woman. You wouldn't understand. You're Jewish."

"No. I get it. Kevin wants you to be a sell-out like him? Misery loves company."

I chuckled, guiltily. "Yeah. I guess so. I don't know. I'm going to have to write something somewhat successful and soon, before my agent and publisher dump my ass."

"Well jeez, Damian. If you're going to sell out why not write chick lit?"

"I keep saying this, but what the hell do I know about being a white woman?"

"You sure have screwed enough of them."

"Where *is* this coming from?"

"I've seen the pictures."

"Yet again, Steffi was quadroon, Keisha wasn't a real blonde, and you said yourself that you're African-American. That only leaves Christy."

She shrugged, mischievously. "If you say so."

"Does it really matter what I say?"

"Not as long as you get so upset. It's cute. Do you think you could really write a booty novel? I thought you wrote sci-fi."

"SF. And I don't know."

"If you do, can I be in it?"

"What? Like a love interest?"

"Sure," she smiled, and I wanted to throw *Here, My Dear* on here in the office and play a little "Let's Get It On."

"Oh hell naw," I chuckled. "A brother in love with a white woman? Only as a morality tale. About how you should stick with your own."

"Hm. Too bad. I think you should go for the chick lit thing, if all you're trying to do is make money. You're so white-identified, anyway."

"Look woman, black people used to like the Doobie Brothers *and* Steely Dan. It's not like I'm a Barry Manilow fan, or something. And I'm telling you I just can't write like that."

"Sure you can. Twenty-eight-year-old, single, professional woman has an affair with a married, rich guy but ends up falling for a guy she hated in the beginning of the book who's not rich now, but clearly will be later in life. Just throw in a bunch of expensive designer names and you've got yourself a novel."

"How the hell do I do that?"

"I don't know. Flip through a *Harper's Bazaar,* or something." She tossed me a CD. "And listen to M.I.A. while you're doing it."

FRIDAY, OCTOBER 12, 20—
3:32 P.M.

Harper's Bazaar
Summer Fashion Issue

Jimmy Choo, Stephanie Hoos, Abaeté
Moschino, DeGrisogono, Chloé
Louis Vuitton, Miu Miu, Roland Mouret

Great Bags! The Season's Best Accessories!
Fendi, $1045
Dior by John Galliano, $1040
Georgio Armani, $1325
Coach, $298
Kate Spade, $245

"Sporting that much python is sure to put a serious dent in your budget."

Max Mara, Juicy Couture, Cesar Paciotti
Donna Karan, Yves Saint Laurent, Emilio Pucci
Burberry Prorsum, Hermès, Givenchy

"Some jewelry speaks louder than words."
"Time flies. Bulova soars."
"Look chic in the heat!"
"Mizensir candles come in dozens of superchic options…"

Sari Gueron, Michael Kors, Oscar de la Renta
Danielle Stevens, Lulu Guinness, Francesca Romana
Malia Mills, Diane von Furstenberg, Marchesa

"Wedges with Everything!"

Marc by Marc Jacobs, Tory by TRB, Little Joe by Gail Elliott

Pale vs. Tan
Karen Elson vs. Paris Hilton
Étrange.

"Everyone is getting it right because everyone is taking chances."

"Say Goodbye to Cellulite?"

Laurence, Lanvin, Yitan, Marni, Tibi, Va-Va Valentino!

"Whether it's a complete makeover or a simple lift or tuck..."
"Is plastic surgery turning us all into clones?"
"Demi Moore in a Roland Mouret dress, fresh off the fall runway."
"Uma Thurman in Dolce & Gabbana."
"Gwyneth Paltrow in Chanel."
"Even Kate Moss prefers to shop with a friend."
"Gwen Stefani in an Anna Molinari dress and a L.A.M.B. Couture jacket..."
"Mutilation is in the eye of the beholder."

Concord watch, $3490
Hermès iPod holder, $325
La Perla Mare bikini, $405
Dolce & Gabanna bag, $1075
Chopard ring, $22,670
Cesar Paciotti sandals, $370
Etro dress, $640

Well, now that we've got our young ad exec heroine, Reid Bentley, properly attired for the beach, how are we going to get her to have an affair with the *very* married Ansleigh Farnsworth IV before she falls in love with aspiring, bohemian businessman, Manny Revel?

Damn. Thank God I'm a guy. I couldn't afford to be a woman.

SATURDAY, OCTOBER 13, 20—
12:21 P.M.

CURRENT CRUSH: M.I.A. (my little Tamil tigress—"There goes the Sri Lankan market," my publisher would say)

RELATIVELY RECENT CRUSHES: Goapele, Samina Ali, "Sophie Okonedo"—because I have, Maureen Dowd, and that freaky, little billionairess, Teresa Heinz Kerry

TRIED & TRUE CRUSHES: Constance Marie, Rachel Weisz, Nia Long, Ming Na, Ziyi Zhang, Zadie Smith, Soledad O'Brien, Thandie Newton, Carla from *Scrubs*, Kate Winslet

THE SEXIEST WOMAN ALIVE WHO CAN ALSO DO SOMERSAULTS: Maurie Daulne of *Zap Mama* fame

TEENAGE CRUSHES: Tootie, Sheila E, Vanity, Lisa Lisa

CHILDHOOD CRUSHES: Mary Ann, Veronica, Lena Horne, Rita Moreno

QUEEN OF MY HEART: Celia Cruz (¡Azúcar, baby!)

QUEEN OF MY SOUL: Sonia Sanchez

QUEEN OF MY ... WELL, YOU KNOW: Angela Bassett

And of course, Queen Noor.

These are the women who I tried to cram into my cranium to crowd out Ina. She was ravaging my brain like a Cossack on crack. I couldn't run away fast enough. Thoughts, musings, fantasies, all about Ms. Yancey. Lisa Lisa's humongous breasts, Goapele's plaintive voice, Sonia Sanchez's amazing poetry. Nothing could distract me from my involuntary obsession. Even the profound lyrics of MC Skat Kat ("You've never seen a kat with so much charisma; Got more moves than a mutant ninja") could preoccupy my mind. Ina and I dancing. Ina and I on that Mexican honeymoon I was supposed to go on with Samara. Ina and I laughing heartily, hugging, sharing a malt at Arnold's. I thought I was going to have to put a bullet in my head when I visualized us running through a field of daisies.

I'd forgotten all about this dating thing. How taxing it could be. When I was still with Samara I couldn't always remember why the grass was greener with her on my arm. Sometimes it looked downright drought-stricken. The movies were always making boy-gets-girl look so fun, so sweet. The anticipation, the fear of rejection, the anxiety. It sucks. Yet another reason to burn Hollywood, burn. Damned liars. I hate this feeling, dangling on tether hooks. And there's no fast forward. I can't skip ahead to the goofy montage. I only have questions to look forward to: What does this woman want from me? When does she want it? Will somebody just tell me? I keep hitting the remote, and nothing's happening. And instead of just chucking the thing through the TV screen, I've got to play along, play it cool.

I've been doing everything within my power this past week (except write that second novel) to avoid the chaos of emotions swirling in my gut, the scenarios exploding in my head. Yeah. I know I could've, should've been writing. It's not like I don't have the time. I really don't know why I can't bring myself to scribble just a few words for this new book.

I also could've been occupying myself with the melodrama shaking our quiet abode. Hep and Neville are rocking the very foundations. They're so loud. Something must've happened. This round of arguments isn't their usual foreplay. This is serious. They are at war. DiDi and Priti have quarantined themselves from this place. I've been trying to leave as soon as they come home. There's a suffocating tension in the house. You find yourself sweating whenever those two are together. Even the silences are unbearable. A lull between the shelling. I remember this all too well.

I could've been cooking, but I no longer really want to eat. My stomach has decided to expand into new markets, and I've finally realized its growth. The other day, I "suddenly" couldn't fit into any of my jeans and had to go buy some new ones. I've gone from a 32" to a 38" waist. While I was shopping, I got myself an X-Large shirt for the first time and thought I was going to cry. Fortunately, I don't do such things, and I guess I won't be doing my basil cream sauce any time soon either (just when I thought I was finally getting it right, too).

Despite the tension and the anxiety and my newfound Orson Welles impersonation, I think this was the best week I've had in recent memory. I've gotten to catch up with some old friends, met a cheerleader/real estate agent I won't be calling. I've got a date with a really impressive woman I've been lusting after for years. Things are looking up. I wouldn't say I've been happy the past few days (Samara's still too much a part of me), but I'm feelin' all right. Too bad I have to go on this date and ruin everything.

But that's why God invented mambo. How can I feel bad listening to this stuff?

Wish me luck.

SUNDAY, OCTOBER 14, 20—
9:41 A.M.

Now here's a little story I'd like to tell
About one bad brother you know so well...

I have to tell you, there was an ice ball in the pit of my stomach that nearly paralyzed me. I was on my way to my first real date in more than half a decade, and I just wasn't liking it. I'm not the kind of person who gets what I want. I'm used to folly, to disaster (just look at the book tour). There was no way this was going to work out. I just knew it.

But I'm not the kind of person who backs down from a challenge (just look at the book tour). I was on my way, listening to Prince for encouragement (which, I admit, is a little perverse). I pulled up to Ina's prefab apartment complex, parked, willed the ice ball into *almost* manageable cubes, and went to face my … destiny? No, that's way too melodramatic.

Ina opened the door. I froze. Damn. Tight jeans and a way-too-tight Pam Grier-as-Coffy T-shirt. Every curve popping out and popping me in the eye. I was a little punch drunk just looking at her. She's been working out. I smiled like a testosterone-addled pre-teen. I wanted to wipe the drool off my chin—but that wouldn't have been cool, either.

"New shirt?" she asked, with that snaggle-toothed smile and dimples.

"Yeah," I managed to say. "You like *Coffy*?"

She looked down at her chest, where our gazes met. "No. Just Pam Grier. One bad-ass sister."

"It's great. Well, I mean, it's horrible. Just an excuse to show as many women's … uh, breasts … as, uh, possible."

"Then I guess it's appropriate, hunh?" she grinned, devilishly.

Damned right about that. I can't wait for the ho smackdown later. Sisters and white chicks giving their all to rip each other's shirts off. Well, I guess the movie *did* have its merits.

"Hold on a second."

I grinned. She grabbed her leather jacket. It was a little chilly and the autumn evening was creeping in on us. I wish we could've had this date in the summer. Ina was really wearing her outfit—and wearing out my optic nerves. The strain not to look was overwhelming. We headed to the Tercel.

"So, where are we eating?"

"Super Fried Rice."

"What?" I think she was a little offended.

"It's the best ghetto Chinese buffet on the planet."

She gave me an incredulous look. "Ghetto Chinese? But I thought…"

"Everything to its own pretensions. As long as it's the best, right? Last time I took you to the best French bistro in town. Now, the best MSG around. Who doesn't like MSG?"

I thought a corpse was rotting in my mouth. Ina's face was *sour*. She used to love ghetto Chinese, thought it was kitschy. I thought it would be fun. I think I was wrong. But I wasn't about to back down now. We reached my G-ride.

"Hey look, Damian. Maybe we should take my car."

"Your Nissan, my Toyota. What do I care?"

She gave another smirk and pressed a button on her keychain. I heard the beep and turned.

"Oh."

A brand new black Escalade flashed its lights. I was stunned. What materialistic, little demon had replaced my little Ina? She had a gleam in her eye I could not, for the life of me, recognize.

"Do you like it?"

"Well, I was contemplating invading Iraq. This could come in handy."

A downward-turned dimple. I just wanted to go home right there and then. Or go find Kevin in a bar or one of his band rehearsals I've been avoiding. Schlocky fusion jazz *had* to be better than this. My adorable bohemian, do-gooding princess has gone Boho. I suddenly realized that she had leapt out of my league. And with the books I write, there was no way I was going to be able to compete with the big leaguers Ina was about to be dating. I guess I was just batting practice.

"C'mon, let's go."

"You need directions?"

"Well, it does have GPS." My shoulders slumped despite themselves. She smiled warmly. "Of course not, Damian. Super Fried Rice is the best ghetto Chinese in town. I love that place."

I chuckled. Relieved. The Pod People have not completely taken over.

We got out our step ladders and grappled up into the Escalade. I instantly got a nose bleed, needed an oxygen tank, and couldn't see the road below. I hated it and fiddled nervously with the radio in order to not deal with my anxiety or find the next Panzer tank we were going to target. Damned Nazis. I hate those guys.

I don't know exactly why I love ghetto Chinese so much, with its Mongolian beef carved out of cow rectum with sludgy gravy, the General Tso testicle chicken, every scrap scooped from the slaughterhouse ceiling, doused with monosodium glutamate, and slung onto your plate. ¡Delicioso! I think it's because I was raised in a *Cosby Show* strait jacket of propriety. My mother, Catholic school, the elitist university, all of them raised me to be an upper middle class prude. Alvin Ailey, Romare Bearden, Toni Morrison, Chopin, Beethoven, Manet, Monet, no Monie Love. I was raised to look up. To admire what Money admired, carve my palette to their tastes, bend my tongue to their dialect. And while, like my Buppy brethren, I've been trained to look back, "give back," serve my community, we all know ... well, you know.

Ghetto Chinese flies in the face of all that. It is not cuisine. It's not a PC appreciation for another culture's culinary capabilities. It is plastic egg rolls and Styrofoam meat. At Super Fried Rice, it's also synthetic sushi and polyurethane pepperoni pizza, fried chicken, French fries, and spaghetti in meat sauce. It's a clearing house for everything bad in the American diet. A stomach ache waiting to happen. I know my mother, who taught me proper fork usage, would be rolling in her grave if she could see me now. Cuban Habanero shirt instead of Savile Row suit, buffalo wings instead of filet mignon. While I do want Moms to be comfortable in her coffin, I do enjoy this little rebellion of mine. I like to sometimes turn my back on the upbringing that keeps rearing its head.

Ina, I thought, felt the same way. But now I wasn't so sure. The new, fashionista clothes and that damned Escalade have really thrown me off. I know this break-up with Darnell has really got her twisted—but one hundred eighty degrees?!

Well, at least ninety. She returned to our table with a plate piled high with utter dietary pollution and a broad smile on her face.

"I love this place," she declared, again, perhaps a little conflicted. "Pizza at a Chinese restaurant. Who woulda thunk?"

"You should check out the taquitos."

"That'll be my next plate."

Ah, who doesn't love a woman who can eat?

Oh yeah. I guess a lot of people, actually. Especially other women. Oh well, screw them. Ina chomping down on some shrimp toast is a beautiful sight.

"Hey look, Ina. I'm sorry for making you drive here. We could've gone some place else. There's a tapas place I've been meaning to check out."

"No, Damian. Don't be silly. I love it. Darnell would never take me to a place like this."

"Dat's 'cause he ain't got no class, dollface," I joked, like I was Luco Brazzi in *The Godfather*.

"He wouldn't have taken me to that bistro, either. It was strictly Cheesecake Factory."

Oh, I guess I wasn't joking.

"I mean, that's what I used to like about going to lunch with you when you still worked at the Union. I never knew where you'd take me. Ethiopian food, that taqueria, Malaysian food, Jamaican. I never knew. It was like a little adventure."

Just call me Marco Polo, baby. Why did the Chinese give that bastard gun powder? Hadn't they heard of colonialism? I'd still be chillin' in Africa, the bastards. But I digress…

"And that Hungarian place. I loved it. Well, not always. But I could never get Darnell to go to any of those places, to try anything new. It was like he didn't want life to be at all interesting. Not like I was talking about climbing Kilimanjaro—but at least try a little Kenyan food—if such a restaurant exists. Or go see a Swedish film. Or one that didn't involve a lot of shooting. But he wouldn't even try. To believe such a chocolate brother could be so vanilla."

"I guess I never had that problem with Samara. She was willing to try anything—or anyone."

Ina gave me a grave look, a little too empathetic for comfort. I squirmed a little. Why were we talking about our exes? She moved her hand across the table. It took everything I had to keep my hand still and let her cover it. She mesmerized me in her earnest gaze.

"I think we've both been through a lot recently."

"Aw, fuck it. It's not important," I shrugged, moving my hand away and grabbing a California roll. "I mean, I can't mourn forever. I'm a thirty-two-year-old black man. I've got at *least* ten years left to live it up. Hell, maybe I'll buy an Escalade."

She blushed. "Oh, that. Yeah. I don't know. I thought I'd give it a try. But damn, it just guzzles gas. I'm not used to spending that much money on a car."

Good. She could be saved. "Welcome to the Church of Consumerism."

"There's only one church I belong to," she stated, *very* seriously.

"Yeah," I chuckled, uneasily, "your Pound-Sterling's a hell of a lot stronger than the almighty dollar."

Her face brightened. "So, you liked him?"

She didn't get my joke. It wasn't really all that good, anyway. "Uh. Yeah. Sure."

"You thinking of coming back?"

And here's where I should've shut up. But what was I gonna do? Point behind her, shout "Look!" and run out of the restaurant?

"Well," I hesitated. "Well look, Ina. I respect you. Respect your faith. I mean, I used to sorta share it."

"But you don't now?" She looked disappointed.

"No. No, I don't. I mean, I don't want to lie to you. I don't want to say, 'Yeah, I'll go again' in the hopes of getting you into bed. That's not me. Neither is church."

"So what? Are you an atheist?"

I think she was getting offended.

"No, no. I don't think so. I mean, some people might think I am. But that's the easy way to look at it. 'Cause I'm really not. I'm just not a Christian … or a Muslim, or Buddhist. And I'm not going to bullshit you and say I'm 'spiritual.' I mean, I'm not some ascetic hiding away in a cave or something until I see the face of God." *Shut up, shut up, shutupshutupshutup!* "I kinda just look at God differently, ya know. Like I don't believe in a benevolent or a malevolent god. No fire and brimstone. No Sermon on the Mount, either. I just, well, I kinda look at God as like, like a parent. You do all you can do, but you've gotta let your kids grow up in their own way. For good or ill or whatever. You can raise a saint or a little shit. My job's not to be too much of a little shit."

She looked at me intently. I could see the wheels turning beneath that high forehead of hers, contemplating whether to break down or just spit me out. I had no clue what to do. I thought about the soft serve ice cream. Or I could just wait for the lightning to strike. Finally, Ina's face lit up.

"Let's go dance, Damian."

The times I feel closest to God, to that higher power, is when I dance. I do it all the time: at work, play, I dance in the shower, cooking in the kitchen, in the middle of the street when I think nobody's looking. That's why music is so central to my existence. While I don't know if I could ever give up books, I *know* I could never forsake music, forsake the dance.

Everybody stop! Damian Time!

The pure ecstasy of it. The pounding rhythm, connecting me to the eternal rhythm of life, the ticking of the clock, the heartbeat, seasons, the tides. Everything is rhythm. It rules us. It makes us a part of the universe. When we dance, we celebrate that rhythm. We are a part of God's universe. The beat, the pounding, the pure sex of it all. Those Christian missionaries, the slave drivers, they wanted to deny us all of that. Believe in a Godhead divorced from life, make us look forward to our own deaths. The slaves never could be denied their dance. They took that God and put a little boogie in His bones. In the black church, even the protestant, puritanical Jesus can do a little soft shoe. Because that God knows what we Africans have been trying to say for almost four hundred years now: dancing tells us we are alive.

And I wanted that with Ina last night. I couldn't wait to take her to WSQ and dance. But I had to wait. It was way too early, and nobody wants to be the first at a party. So I took her to the Scotsman for a couple of drinks.

After my little God speech, I thought our evening was dead. But there's more than one Lazarus in this world. Among the Yuppies in their striped white shirts and Diane/Dakota throwing attitude everywhere her bony hips could jut, Ina and I were determined to have a good time. I don't know, maybe she thought she could save me—like some sexualized missionary. There was something fierce in her eyes. She laughed at all my jokes, and I'm not that funny (*mildly* humorous, as I've said before). She constantly inched closer in conversation until her fingers lightly fox-trotted along my thigh, in my hair, and once on my chest.

Eternally smooth, I was a little freaked out by all the attention. I know I never dated the woman before, but I never imagined it would be like this. But I kept my cool, decided to ride this thing out until the bitter end. It was looking like a good trip. And when we kissed at her Escalade, I was ready to go all the way to Xanadu (Olivia Newton John, bad disco, and roller skates be damned) if I had to.

WSQ is a little hipster joint that Kev, the boys, and I helped open some eight years ago. At the time it was a little hole in the wall in the basement of a cheap, hourly-rate, sperm-splattered motel. It had been a dark, dank underground hip-hop joint with battered furniture, cracked plaster, and water-stained walls. We loved it. We loved George, the owner, a tall Japanese cat with clunky glasses who knew cool before it even knew itself. It was a truly bohemian spot with cheap beer and mad beats. All the best DJs spun there and the sexiest antidisestablishmentarist babes danced on the warped floor. It was a great place to be seen by people too myopic to care about such things. And George had always let me in for free.

But times have changed. George died a few years back. The new management knew the good thing that he had been denying them ever since the place opened. They took the brother's death and flew with it. WSQ moved to a much larger underground place. Now there was a lounge with hip retro furniture (including bean bag chairs), ambient orange lighting, hookahs, Ketel One, and Belgian dessert beers. There was also a spacious dance floor, a custom-made DJ booth, and a disco ball. The nappy-headed bohemians were still there 'cause there was really no place else to go. But their broke asses got even broker paying for the new, imported beers (the new owners didn't even have the decency to keep the Pabst on tap), and they were constantly getting crowded out by the suburbanites who'd read that WSQ topped the "Perfect Dangerous Night in the City" list.

I knew I was a stranger in a strange land as soon as I had to pay a cover. George, may you rest in peace. I was doing my best not to become the armchair, reactionary grandfather. "Boy, you don't know no WSQ. I tell you, when I was young, WSQ was a *club.* Do you know what that is, boy, a *club*?" What did I expect? It had been three years.

Ina and I walked in. The dance floor was dark and dead. There was a gaggle of scrawny dreads doing some capoeira interpretive dance to a banging house beat.

"I'm a tree."

"What was that, Damian?" Ina asked. She was beaming. I think the Brazilian martial arts show on the floor was really impressing her. You woulda thought this was Disney World. "Isn't this place great?"

I looked around. The music was nice. The crowd was gathering with not-quite-beautiful people mellowing in their neat, little cliques. The bar in the round was glowing promisingly. Nobody seemed to be sweatin' too hard—except for the dread dance troupe on the floor. Everybody seemed to be cool with each other. I looked into Ina's glowing face and smiled in the warmth.

"Yeah. It's got a nice vibe."

Your dream's still alive, George me boy.

"Yeah. Darnell would never take me to a place like this."

"Damn, Ina. Did he at least take you out for walks, change your litter box?"

"I should've reported him to the Humane Society."

"Let's go to the lounge. I'm too old to compete with those brothers on the dance floor."

"Yeah. You might break something."

We made our way to the lounge and actually found two seats at the bar. Ina had some neon blue drink while I drank good old Red Stripe. We were having a great time, just shootin' the Shinola. We laughed about old times at the Union, embarrassing stories about our exes, and I gave her my dissertation on the duties of the warm-up DJ.

"See, his job is to simply prep the crowd, establish a cool vibe. The music should be mellower. Not too frenetic. He really shouldn't have people out dancing too soon, or at all, if that can be helped. He's got to get them *ready* to dance. If folks are exhausted by the time the main DJ gets on, everybody—the club, the other DJ, maybe even the customers—everybody will be pissed."

"Why?"

"'Cause folks'll leave early. The club loses money. Like, did you ever notice how sometimes the club'll be banging and then the DJ puts on some fucked-up song and the floor clears out?"

"Sure. I guess."

"Well, he does it so folks stick around, take a break, go to the bathroom, and most importantly, buy more drinks."

"No kidding." I couldn't tell if she were truly interested or just putting me on. I put my money on the latter, but it didn't matter. I'd been drinking.

"Yeah. DJing's not just a matter of spinning records. There are monetary concerns involved as well. Like all art forms."

All the while, Ina's hand danced on my thigh. All the while, I was being watched. It was a burnt gold sister with wavy black hair and a high forehead. She almost looked Asian, and every time I looked at her she was looking at me. She was off in a bean bag corner, chilling with a local DJ, Skip Vindaloo, a scrawny, way-too-pretty Indian kid who'd just signed with Bomb Hip-Hop Records. He was a bit of a local celebrity and one hell of a turntablist, a regular Jack the Ripper on the decks. She was apparently part of ole boy's entourage and was making me uncomfortable.

I'm not one who attracts many women's stares. Of course, how would I know? Women are so much better at visual appraisals than men. They seem to be able to take a quick snapshot of a dude and be able to appreciate the image. We guys, on the other hand, have to take MRIs of some babe, staring hotly at every curve and crevice down to the musculature until women start sweating in the gaze. I was starting to squirm under this woman's scrutiny.

"What is it, Damian?"

"Uh, nothing. Did you want to dance?"

"But I thought this was still the warm-up DJ."

"Yeah. But he's picking up the pace. The main attraction's about to begin."

"Sure. Just give me a couple minutes." She got up and squeezed my leg. I couldn't keep my eyes off of her Pam Grier T-shirt. *Coffy is the color of your skin...* "How did you know I love house music?"

I shrugged, having no clue. Ina left, and my eyes followed.

"Are you Damian Cross?"

"Wha—?!" I started, and turned toward the voice. Staring Girl. *Cool, Damian. Real fucking cool. You should start wearing plastic helmets for your own protection.* "What did you say?"

"Are you Damian Cross? The writer?"

"Uh, yeah. You?"

"A fan."

Hot damn. Somebody who'd actually read *Winter Soldiers*. And *liked* it?! I was dumbfounded. I think I actually blushed. Before I had a chance to respond, ask her what she thought, why she liked it, how the hell she even heard of me, Staring Girl smiled and walked away. My eyes followed. Not a hyperbolic booty like Ina's, but cute and bubbly—like champagne.

"Do you think she's white?"

"What, Ina?" I asked, distracted. "Of course not. I mean, she might be part Asi—"

"No. Not her."

I turned to face Ina. She looked ashen, shocked. Not like Buckwheat after seeing a ghost. But close.

"Who was that?" she finally asked.

"A ... fan?"

"Whatever," she shook. "Her. Do you think she's white?"

She pointed to a woman standing beneath a wrought-iron candle holder. She had tawny skin, black hair with gold highlights, and the cutest, little outfit.

"Is that Juicy Couture? How luxe!"

"What, Damian?"

Damned Harper's Bazaar.

"Nothing. Really. Don't mind me."

"Do you think she's white?" she nearly shrieked.

I shrunk back. "Uh, I don't know, Ina. She could be. Yeah, probably. Italian, or something?"

I was confused ... then enlightened. An incredibly well-manicured, well-coiffed, a real bastard gift-from-God brother with an expensive suit—

"Is that Armani?"

"Will you stop that, Damian?"

—walked up to her with two brimming Martini glasses in his hands. He handed one to the woman with a nearly pornographic kiss.

"Darnell," I gasped.

Ina's face grew dark. Her eyes brimming red. "Let's go."

"Look, Ina, I, well—" I was stammering. The ride back to her place was a silent inferno. I just sat back, waiting for her to explode. I don't know why I agreed to come up to her apartment. I guess I didn't want her to do anything too stupid. Like invite me up to her apartment. "Well, I know—what the—I'm sorry."

She looked into the shiraz I poured for her. Her eyes were red rims, but something was forcing the tears into her gut, where I'm sure they formed jagged barbs.

"Fuck him," she seethed, and put her glass down. She was moving toward me with a determination that, frankly, scared the living shit out of me.

"Well, I—"

Her mouth silenced mine. Her tongue dove between my teeth and made straight for my esophagus. I was stunned. She shoved me against the kitchen counter and became all hands.

I wanted to stop her, to plead reason. But I'd been drinking. Way too damned much. I wanted to tell her to stop. To not do anything she'd regret. To stop unbuttoning my shirt. Kissing my chest. Whoa! Nipple biting. You freaky, little … God, I love this woman! To think of … think of … there are children starving in Africa. In China? In my pants…? Her hands made quick work of my zipper and I could feel the kitchen air, hot breath, her fervent fingers…

I wanted to … she was down … I wanted to … remember what it felt like. The pleasure, the utter content. I leaned back. How long had it been? The hot breath. How long? Months? Years? Centuries? Oh God. Those fingers, that tongue. Mary sweet mother of Jesus! No. Seriously. How … long? Had Dewey defeated Truman? No. I was *not* going to feel guilty about this. Had Lincoln freed my great great grandfather? Had Moses parted the waters? How long? God, that mouth. Swing low, sweet chari … what?!

Sobs?

"Ina?"

I looked down.

Ina was crying.

8:12 P.M.

"HAAAAHHHHHHH!!! Hahahahahahahaha!"

"I don't see what's so damned funny, Kevin. And could you keep it down? My head's killing me."

"Sorry, Damian. It's just that any other nigga woulda got his dick wet last night."

"I guess that just ain't me then. In fact, I doubt if it ever were."

"Riiiiight."

"Naw. Ya know, one of the only pieces of advice Pops ever gave me that was worth a damn was to never sleep with a woman I couldn't see marrying."

"Hahahahaha! ... Wait. You're serious, aren't you?"

"Mostly. Yeah. I mean, it's not like I wasn't out to have some fun, too. But yeah."

"Damn. But it's not li—"

"Look, Kev. I'm hanging up now and going to bed. I think my skull's about to 'splode."

"Did I mention sex? You've got to have lots and lots of sex."

"Man, I hate writing sex scenes."

"Got to give the people—Give the people what they want."

"Damn, Hancock. Anybody ever told you you can *sang*?"

"No."

"There's a reason for that."

"Anyway, lots of sex. And make sure the brother is *very* giving. Like he picks hair out of his teeth for a living."

"Bob. Please stop calling me."

"Hello?"

"Hello, son."

"Aunt Clarissa? You know DiDi has her own line?"

"I know, Damian. Did I wake you? It's almost three o'clock."

"No, ma'am. I mean, yes, Aunt Clarissa. I ... well, I was up late last night."

"Uh-huh."

"So, you didn't want to talk to DiDi?"

"No."

"You wanted to talk to *me*?"

"That is correct, young man. Thanksgiving's right around the corner. Your Uncle Frank and I would love to see you."

"Aw, Jesus … Hello."

"Damian?"

"Shit! Mayrav! What time is it?"

"Six."

"Shit. I'm so sorry."

"Are you hung over?"

"Like you wouldn't believe. I had a really rough night last night. Look, can I … man, I hate to do this, but … damn, I guess you already made dinner, hunh?"

"Yes. I did. Damian."

"I can jump in the shower real quick if you want me to."

"…"

"Look, Mayrav. I'm really sorry. Really. I am."

"…"

"Hey, I'm not Stuart, ya know?"

"Well, I hope you enjoyed yourself last night."

Click!

No. I really didn't.

9:57 p.m.

"I'm so sorry. I really am, Damian. I don't … I don't know what's gotten into me lately. The clothes. That stupid Escalade. I want my old Nissan back. But it's like … it's like I don't even know myself anymore."

"Uh … can I … ya know?"

"Yeah. That's not going to happen."

"I figured."

Zip!

"I'm so sorry. I'm, I'm not ready. I'm sorry I dragged you into this. Went out with you. I'm just not—it's not like I haven't had a good time. I have. And I really like you. I really do. I always have. I thought I was ready. I really did. And you were the first person I thought of. There've been a few guys sniffing around, but I thought … if I were ready, and I really thought I was … I mean, it's been months, months! Like what was I going to do? Mourn Darnell my entire life?! Sit around and become an old maid because of that triflin' bastard? I'm thirty-one! I can't waste my life wondering what would've, could've been. What should've been. He clearly isn't. And I swear she's white."

"She could've been Syrian, or something."

"…"

"Just a suggestion. Sorry."

"Can you believe him? Taking her there?! I'd been begging him for years to take me out to a place like that. I used to love to dance. I used to love doing a lot of things. I remember all those pretentious indy and foreign films I used to go to. The art openings. I used to love just going to the park. Seeing plays. Talking about books. I used to love so many *things*, Damian.

"And then, I don't know. I just stopped doing them. Not immediately. But it's like my interests just withered away. When Darnell and I first started going out, we did some of those things, but I could tell he was always uncomfortable. We didn't share the same interests. It's not like the man's dumb. It's just that … well, I think his mom raised him to be all business. So, he just didn't know what to do with himself, say, at an art opening. And I guess at some point, I just stopped asking him to go. He'd already proved that he loved me enough times. Then later, I stopped going myself. It just seemed wrong to be doing so many things without him. To have him sit at home by himself watching TV while I was out doing things.

"And now look at him. With his *Syrian* girlfriend. At WSQ, of all places. Gloating. Looking so damned good in his Armani suit. And what do I get out of all this? What? I'm thirty-one! I gave up so much for that man. So much! My time, my … my twenties.

"We were supposed to get married. We were supposed to have children. We were supposed to be *together*. I'd waited so long for him. So long for him to ask me to marry him. So long for the dream. We would've had such beautiful children, Damian. Such a beautiful family.

"So I waited—and waited. Because I loved him. I waited by that stupid television while he was movin' on up. My hair started graying a little. I had to start going to the gym because my body started changing on me. Every month I'd have to flush another unfertilized egg down the toilet.

"He moved up, all right. He started making more money. Dressing better. More women started noticing him. And he's a man, right? That's what you men do, right? Other women started sniffing around and you've got to hump the first bitch you see. You've got to … to … home's suddenly not good enough. 'Are you getting gray, Ina? You're getting a little flabby, ain'tcha babe? Wow, look at those arms. You're a regular Arnold Schwarzenegger, eh?'

"Then, while this woman who's stuck by you through mostly thin is sitting at home by the television with her girlfriends mooning over wedding dresses—dresses you told her to moon over because you were finally getting married in six months—you stagger in, smelling of beer and another woman. And you come in in front of her and her friends and flop down in front of them and you confess. Confess?! You tell the whole, fucking world how you love her—LOVE her—but that you can't get married. You can't do it. You've fallen in love with someone else. And she—me, I'm mortified. Rhonda and Sharon are mortified. And he's rolling around in front of *Girlfriends*, gnashing his teeth, wailing, pulling out his hair. Like *he's* the victim. Like I hurt *him*. Like *I* came in smelling like some other woman.

"His world wasn't crashing in around him. He was getting his. *And* taking mine. What does sperm mean to a guy? You produce that crap every day ... for the rest of your lives. And he had the nerve to want to be comforted. He humiliated me in front of my best friends. Every day since then, you can hear the pity in their voices, see it in their eyes, every time they're around me. All my friends do it. Whisper around me, like I've got cancer, or something. They all know what a fool I've been for that man. And he wanted me to go to him that night and pat him on his fucking head, tell *him* that everything was going to be OK.

"Jesus, Damian. Jesus. I'm thirty-one. I used to love the theater, literature, art. I used to love just walking in the park. I used to love Darnell Priestley. Now what do I have to show for it?"

What a difference a day makes
Twenty-four little hours...

Wow, it seems like it was just yesterday when I was sitting on top of the world—I'd reconnected with friends, had a promising date with Ina ... oh yeah, I guess it was. And now I'm plummeting through the layers of Dante's inferno faster than Enron stock.

What the hell just happened here?

Just don't fall into the pit of despair, Damian. Just don't do that.

TUESDAY, OCTOBER 16, 20—
6:12 P.M.

Shit. Too late.

DATE: Tuesday, October 16, 20— 6:33 P.M.
FROM: drcross@wintersoldiers....
TO: inayancey@theunion....
SUBJECT: (no subject)

hey, ina,

i don't know exactly what to say right now, but it would be cool if you wanted to talk.

DATE: Tuesday, October 16, 20— 6:37 P.M.
FROM: drcross@wintersoldiers....
TO: boorman6girl@soulonwax....
SUBJECT: Act of Contrition

mayrav—

contained within attached zip file is a peace offering that hopefully will put a smile on that vicious visage of yours and erase any thoughts of retribution from your mind.
damian

sorry ass mix

1.carol burnett—who's sorry now?
2.john denver—i'm sorry
3.eydie gorme—i'm sorry
4.greg kihn—sorry
5.jimmy cliff—i'm sorry
6.grace jones—sorry
7.justin guarini—sorry
8.serge gainsbourg—sorry angel
9.mary wells—i'm so sorry
10.conway twitty—sorry
11.bo diddley—i'm sorry
12.the impalas—sorry (i ran all the way home)
13.paul zim—i'm sorry (jewish holiday mix)

WEDNESDAY, OCTOBER 17, 20—
6:19 P.M.

DiDi to the rescue. At least that's the way she sees herself. You'd think she has an S on her chest.

"Sorry to hear about you and Ina, Damian."

"News travels fast."

"Faster than a speeding bullet."

Apparently, clairvoyance is one of her super powers.

"So, what are you going to do now?" she asked, concern tensing her facial features. I guess I'm somebody to worry about.

"I don't know. Laugh at my luck, get high, eat some Cool Ranch Doritos."

She looked down at my stomach. "How about some cauliflower?"

"Am I the only one disturbed by white vegetables? It just ain't right. The stuff creeps me out."

"Well, I was thinking," she said, coyly. I knew I was in trouble. "There's this woman I'd like you to meet."

"Deirdre," I said—which meant I was serious, "I thought you promised to give the matchmaking up in high school."

"Well…"

"Well, nothing. You've set me up with future lesbians, future axe murderers, there was that Mensa momma who could only talk about thermonuclear reactors. Do you know what that's like? I don't even know what a thermonuclear reactor is."

"It's a—"

"I know what it is, DiDi. I just couldn't tell you how it works—like the internet. What I don't know is who you gonna set me up with now?"

She was about to say something, but I answered for her.

"Let me see, a pedophile. I never dated one of those before. What about a crack whore? I bet you they're a cheap date. No, no. It's gotta be better than that."

"Larissa was bipolar. How was I supposed to know? I'd only seen her up."

"What about a—"

"A corporate attorney."

"A what?"

"A corporate attorney."

"What about the crack whore? She sounded kinda nice."

"It's commercial sex worker. I thought you were PC."

"Sorry, DiDi. The highly-processed cocaine commercial sex worker," I huffed.

"Thank you." My cousin smiled. "But no, Damian. This woman. You'll love her. She's a corporate attorney, but she does some pro bono work for us down at the shelter. Restraining orders, probation hearings, negotiations with landlords, stuff like that. She's really smart and damned gorgeous. You'll love her, I swear."

"Sounds like you love her."

"She doesn't go that way."

"I thought these things weren't written in stone."

"I can still kick your ass."

I threw my hands up in surrender.

"She's a homegirl," she teased.

I tried not to be interested, but I couldn't help asking. "Where from?"

"Youngstown."

"*Ohio*?" I snarled. "That's Browns territory."

"Don't be so difficult," she admonished. "It's still the Pittsburgh *area*. What do you have to lose?"

I contemplated that for a minute. I knew there was a small piece of my dignity somewhere in the closet I could still cling to.

"I think she's really into music, too," DiDi added. "She always has headphones on. And you can catch her singing, too. When she thinks nobody's noticing."

Whoever she was *was* sounding good. Of course, Larissa sounded good all the way up until she pointed that cleaver at my gut.

"Naw," I finally managed, "I think I'm all right for now. Thanks, though."

My cousin rolled her eyes, and sucked on her teeth. "Suit yourself."

THURSDAY, OCTOBER 18, 20—
5:45 P.M.

I thought it was going to take an act of God to get me out of bed. Tuesday had come and gone and not one word from Mayrav. I can't seem to think of a time she'd been this angry. She was usually a monsoon rain. Short and violent. But nothing lasting more than an hour. Maybe these grudges were something new, or just something I'd never been exposed to before.

Ina, too, was a void of silence. Maybe she was angry with me, too. For what, I couldn't tell you. For not trying something? For just being there in an incredibly vulnerable moment? Seeing her go through all that pain. Maybe she's just embarrassed. Saturday night *was* awkward. I don't know how much I want to see her right now, either. I'm sure she feels the same way—even more so.

And I don't even want to talk about my matchmaking cousin.

So, I've been lying in bed, playing Free Cell and Spider Solitaire. What a waste. I couldn't even bring myself to plug in my game pad and proceed with my Madden Football season. At least my computer Steelers would be going to the Super Bowl (apparently I wasn't the only loser this weekend)—if only I could get up off my lazy ass and *play* the damned game.

I don't know what possessed me to check my email. I haven't the past few days. I was afraid that both Ina and Mayrav would be telling me to take a flying leap. But I did finally check it. No word from either of them. Figures. But I did find an old email from XL Recordings' publicist, telling me M.I.A. (my CURRENT CRUSH) was going to be in town and asking if I wanted to cover the concert and/or interview ole girl.

Hallelujah! Testosterone jolted me out of bed. I made a few calls, but I was too late. I couldn't get my customary complimentary ticket to the concert, and there was no way I was going to get that interview. "You should've called earlier." Yeah, I should've been rolling around in Ina's bed. I should've been planning my wedding to Samara. I should've been celebrating *Winter Soldiers'* twentieth week on the *New York Times* Bestsellers List. I should've been doing a lot of things. But her producer, Diplo, is going to be playing at this club, Jade, is it? after the concert. You should check him out. He's awesome. I'm sure M.I.A.'s gonna be there. I think they're dating.

That almost stopped me. Just like how I fell out of love with Ms. Lopez when she became J. Lo to Combs's P. Diddy. I still lament that Bonnie and Clyde tragedy. But hell, what was the point of having a CURRENT CRUSH if you can't stalk her for a couple hours in a dark, seedy nightclub?

Around ten o'clock I finally got ready. The house is eerily silent these days. Everybody's avoiding each other. People are rarely here—except to annoy me with dreadful, corporate attorney prospects. I'm tempted to do a *Risky Business* and run around naked, but I hate Bob Seger.

Anyway, I made my way to Jade and quickly realized how hip I am *not*. There was a definite moment when time had passed me by and didn't even have the decency to notify me.

Jade's a sushi bar by day and ultra-slick dance club at night. Downstairs, it's incredibly sparse and white. Sterile, almost. With '60s style light fixtures hanging from the ceiling. The chairs are molded plastic. The bar is one long slab of stainless steel, and the bartenders make you impotent in their über beauty. The drinks are all right, but they drain your wallet way before you take your first sip.

Everybody seemed like they were young enough to be my children, and I'm only thirty-two (of course, Ina's got me thinking of my age—making me feel like I'm a lot older than I really think I am). They were dressed to the nines or the 99-cent thrift store chic style that hasn't quite yet died. It didn't matter. They were all young and beautiful and playing with their cell phones—talking into them, transfixed by their LCD glare, texting, or taking pictures of each other.

I went upstairs to check out the dance floor. It was all black and red with leather couches splayed along the walls. Luxe gals in their cute tops and tight hip-huggers sat smoking and drinking fluorescent cocktails, nonchalance oozing from their every pore.

I suddenly felt way too alone. Samara should be here with me. Ina. I think even Mayrav would've dug this scene. It didn't matter. I just didn't want to be by myself. I used to never mind being alone. I guess because I always knew I wasn't. I always used to know *somebody*, no matter where I went. But that's no longer the case. Now, scanning the crowd, all the faces are foreign to me—and way too young. "Shouldn't you be at home, young lady?" I felt like creaking. "Don't you know it's a school night?"

Before I started flashing my AARP card, I decided to just find a nice spot along the wall, sink into my Jack and Coke, and listen to the music. The warm-up DJ was doing a fine job. Getting the crowd riled without making them dance. He, like all the hipster DJs around, was playing a steady string of '90s hip-hop—the stuff I used to listen to in places just like this when I used to roam the streets. Of course back then, it was new—now it's just nostalgia. But everywhere I go, that's all I hear. Like I've never left my twenties.

After about an hour of this and my lonely ass readying itself to go home and play solitaire, Diplo finally came on. A nerdy, little guy from Mississippi, I couldn't wait to hear him. He's all the rage, has even been on NPR (explain that one). I usually don't believe the hype—since I *am* a part of the hype machine and know how full of shit *I* can be—but something told me this guy's for real.

Maybe it was the sexy, brown thing sitting on the VIP couch by his booth. M.I.A., Mathangi "Maya" Arulpragasam (say that five times fast). The tiny Tamil tigress in the flesh. She was so small, so cute. I just wanted to fold her up in my wallet and take her home with me. Nobody noticed her walking in. Yet, everybody noticed her walking in. It was that type of party. If you were gonna be a hipster, you had to be hip. A zoot suit cool was your code of conduct. *¡Wacha!* Black, white, Latino. It doesn't matter. You just can't give a fuck. Even the cool Asian chicas with their clunky glasses, blond streaks, and hyperkinetic hip-hop moves are nonplussed. Even though we were all there for her. Diplo was cool, true, but Maya's the star.

And she knew it. But she's cool, too. Sitting on that VIP couch, not acting like she was just on stage for the past couple hours. Perfectly perfumed, impeccably placid. She out-cooled all of us. Chain-smoking, drinking wine while her friends lavished in their VIP, hangers-on status. The busty brunette showing her wares in tight, white, exoderm clothing. The buzz-cut body builder fresh off a WWII movie set as a Nazi extra guzzling vodka straight from the bottle. A few other groupies in baseball caps or wedges all acting like she *wasn't* the center of attention.

But I wasn't acting. She was the reason I came. No, I would never walk up to her, I would never say a word. If she ever glanced my way, I might nod and smile, show a dimple. But she would never see me, the glare from her spotlight was too bright for her to see beyond her own star. And I was dazzled by it. So dark, so adorable is our Maya, a sweet berry indeed. So talented. I just hoped for a glimmer of recognition. Who knows? Maybe she was one of my *legions* of fans and loved *Winter Soldiers* as much as Staring Girl. How embarrassing. I'm way past fourteen. I needed another drink.

Diplo was dope. He warmed us up with some hip-hop classics, sautéed the crowd in some simmering dancehall, and then really turned up the heat. Before we knew it, the entire club was a disco inferno. Sweaty bodies bumped, grinded, gyrated, wined on the floor. Folks were dancing on the ceiling like an old Lionel Richie video. The Tupelo turntablist was mad, taking us down familiar roads, then jerking us violently off course. But we were so insane, too, we all went along for the ride.

"Walk Like an Egyptian" became a grinding, grimy beat that pounded the walls to dust. Women were squealing in delight, singing along in a charnel house cherubic frenzy. Men were grinding their pelvises until they needed hip replacements. I stood against the wall. Snoop Dogg married The Cure as "Drop It Like It's Hot" popped to "Love Cats." "Sweet Dreams (Are Made of This)" became a pounding house tune.

Diplo mashed up song after song like a monster truck rally. Old songs emitted new sounds. The latest hit was hardly recognizable in his surgical grasp. He cut, he scratched, he excised beats, slapped them onto different songs, put them back in place, and then slashed them into oblivion. And we loved it. Everybody loved it. Drinks disappeared, sweat popped, folks screamed and danced and fucked on the floor. I stood against the wall. Watching. Nodding my head. The bumping, the grinding, the exultation. And Ms. Arulpragasam. Rapidly becoming the center of attention as the sweat-and-alcohol drenched hordes steadily lost their cool. Napoleon Dynamites emerged, spasming their best hip-hop moves. Looking like lepers popping and locking while innocent bystanders were sent to the hospital for being too close to the discombobulated cataclysm. Video cameras, digital cameras, cell phones were flashing all around her. People were cheering her every move. Folks were crowding around her, trying to be a part of her good time, to say that they hung with her. To rub against her star, hoping to bask in the afterglow. I hung against the wall, listening to Diplo dive into Brazilian bass. *Baile!* People were violently thrusting their pelvises at each other. Somebody! Stop them! Somebody's gonna lose a penis out there! It was getting dangerous. And all I kept thinking about was Ina and Samara and how my penis had been lost to me for months. Never … to return … again?

I downed the last of my drink, looked one last time at my CURRENT CRUSH, and sulked on home.

SATURDAY, OCTOBER 20, 20—
12:44 A.M.

"Hello?"
"Hello, Damian."
"Cheryl?"
"Yes, how are you doing, Mr. Cross?"
"Depends. You still my agent?"
"Now that depends on what you tell me."

"The new novel?"

"Of course."

"Well, I don't know. I think it's coming along all right. It's just so complicated. The ideas. I think I might've bitten off more than I can chew."

"Well, maybe you should simplify things a little."

"I can't, Cheryl. I'm a writer. I'm a product of what I read."

"What are you reading now?"

"You'd laugh if I told you."

"Try me."

"*Harper's Bazaar* and the new Jennifer Weiner."

"*Good in Bed*?"

"No. The pregnancy one."

"Can you tell me why you're reading that?"

"I have no idea."

"Now, remember what I told you about new SF writers. Five novels in five years. That way you can hopefully build a steady readership before you kick it into overdrive."

"Well, it can only go up, right?"

"We can only hope. But you're way behind, Damian. You should be on *at least* your third novel by now."

"I know, Cheryl. I know. It's just ... well, I've had a rough year. It's no excuse, but that's all I got."

"Well, when do you think you'll have a new novel ready?"

"Hey, Cheryl. What if I tried going in a different direction? Maybe something a little more ... I don't know, commercially viable."

"Like Jennifer Weiner?!"

"Damn. You sound excited."

"Sorry. I *do* get paid on a percentage basis."

"Yeah. Right. I don't know, maybe not like her. But maybe, something like it. I don't think I could realistically portray white women. But maybe a sister or—no. I don't know, yet. I'm just batting around ideas. This new novel's just not working for me."

"I don't know, Damian. Your publisher will *definitely* drop their option. But if it's a black novel, I do have a few contacts over at Lexington."

"Hm. *Playa Haterz 2: Electric Boogaloo*."

"I hope you don't go that route, but I'm sure we can work something out."

"Thanks, Cheryl."

"No problem, Damian."

"No. Thank you for calling. It means a lot."

"Look, I'm just starting out. Just like you. You've got a modicum of talent, Damian Cross. I know that. I think it's just a matter of time before other people will get to know that, too. Just get to writing."

"Right."

That's it. Stop answering the phone.

"Hello?"

"Hi, Damian."

Shit. Why won't you listen to yourself, Damian Rene Cross?

"Hi, Ina."

"Hey … Damian … look, I—"

"Look, Ina … you don't have to ap—"

"No. No. I think I do. It's just that…"

"Yeah. Uh. No. I know. It's not like—it's not like I don't understand. I mean, Darnell—"

"It hurt, Damian. It really hurt."

"Believe me. I understand. I mean, I'm sure he didn't know you were gonna be there. But, yeah—"

"He *smiled* at me, Damian. The bastard actually *smiled*."

"Damn."

"…"

"…"

"Look, Damian. It's nothing personal…"

"I know."

"It's just that … well … it's just that, I don't think, I don't think I'm ready, yet."

"No, Ina. That's perfectly all right."

"And I think, I think, uh, when I'm ready … when I actually *am* ready to start dating again…"

"Yeah?"

"Well, I think—you know, nothing personal. I love you to death. You're a lot of fun. But … well, it's not like I'm in my twenties anymore. It's not like I want to *just* have fun. I want … I want kids, children. And I want them to have a good, Christian upbringing."

"Oh."

"My folks. My mom, she always took me to church, and my dad always stayed home."

"Right."

"And I don't want that. I want us to go to church as a *family*. I don't think you can do that. Can you, Damian?"

"…"

"Damian?"

"No. I … I guess I can't."

"Right. I'm sorry, Damian. Nothing personal, you understand that. Don't you?"

"Of course. Of course I do, Ina."

I disconnected the phone. I guess it's time to write that novel.

SUNDAY, OCTOBER 21, 20—
11:01 P.M.

And it goes a little something like this...

Reid Bentley, why do you always find yourself in the wrong body? I just landed the Binlan account for the firm, an eight-figure advertising client that has made me the darling-for-the-day at the office. There was to be a nice, little private party at *Breathe* tonight, and I wanted to treat myself to a naughty, little outfit that would catch my new supervisor's, Ansleigh Farnsworth IV, eye. I know I already have his eye, just like that ring on his left hand has mine. But he is one delicious specimen of a man, body trim with loads of muscle, hair graying distinguishingly at the temples, and an infectious smile.

So, I found myself roaming the Burberry aisles, cursing the curves Mother Nature has blessed me with. I couldn't keep my eyes off this sapphire silk blouse. The banded collar perfectly exposes my neckline, and the sheer silk crepe would beautifully highlight my toned flesh. I have the perfect Aubade Bahia tattoo demi bra just for the occasion. Yet, my breasts are the problem. They have been cursing me for over fifteen years now.

I remember when I was twelve, and it seemed that everybody was growing breasts—even some of the boys—except for me. Robin Kelley and Carmen D'Agostino were first, of course, as though they weren't popular enough. It was bad enough that all the boys absolutely adored those two and that they got to date dreamy Jody Bioni and Robbie Gastineau, but they appointed themselves the gatekeepers to womanhood. As more and more girls joined their breasted ranks, they welcomed the cool girls with opened arms, talking cup sizes while I lost out to comparisons to the chalkboard. I couldn't even get my period and would often stare, horrified, at my pristine panties.

Fortunately, by the beginning of eighth grade, I had joined that club, but my breasts were still nonexistent. My mother bought me a couple of training bras to, hopefully, inspire growth. But nothing. The same held true for ninth grade *and* tenth. It wasn't until the winter of my junior year that my breasts started to sprout and grow.

Then, they wouldn't stop. Now, at twenty-eight, I feel like I'm 5'4" x 5'4". My breasts are behemoths. If this incredible growth only would've happened back in the '80s when my heroes were Dolly Parton and Emma Sams and Samantha Fox, then I would've felt good about them. But now the Kate Mosses of the world rule, damned twelve-year-old boys. My monstrous mams have no place in this world. It is all for the small-breasted. Spaghetti straps were an absolute nightmare. And while Burberry is nice enough to have this gorgeous silk top in sizes way too big for my petite form, none of them fit quite right. My breasts are just too big. And I have that perfect Aubade bra. Why does shopping always make me feel so fat? I'm only a size four.

Or...

"Oh no, he di'nt."

"Yes. He did, LeShell."

Bebe poked around her salad nicoise. She was having a bad day, and taking off early from Sweet Berry Cosmetics and the date at the salon and the shopping spree at Prada didn't help matters any. She hoped having an early dinner at The Frog and Peach, her favorite French restaurant, with LeShell, her favorite girlfriend, would help. But what she feared the most was about to happen.

"You need to kick the fool to the curb, girl!" LeShell nearly shrieked.

Bebe Freeman, CFO, started. She looked around to see other people looking at their table. LeShell Watkins had been Bebe's best friend for thirteen years, over half their lives, but darn, that girl was L-O-U-*D*! But she had known that from the first day the two girls had met way back in the sixth grade.

Bebe had been the new girl in Ms. Harris' class at Booker T. Washington Middle School. She was a target. The new girl always was. Eleven-year-old Bebe had been prepared for that. She hadn't been prepared for Tonika Thomas's meaty right hook. It caught her square in the eye and propelled her right into the swings. She tried everything to free herself from the tangle of chain and plastic seat while Tonika rained haymakers on her tiny head. The other girls cheered and hooted and hollered. But Bebe had refused to cry. She wouldn't give those witches the satisfaction. She just kept trying to free herself and her braids from the swing's chains.

"You think you better 'n all us," Tonika was screaming, to the other girls' cheers. "In all them fancy clothes! Like you was Blair or sum'thin'!"

"Tonika!" Bebe had heard over the jeering.

Tonika froze. Bebe looked up. It was LeShell, and she was itchin' for a fight, her little fists balled at her hips.

"This ain't none a your business, LeShell!"

"The hell it ain't! She my cousin!"

It was a lie, but LeShell had flown into Tonika like it was the truth, finishing her off before you could say Ronnie, Bobby, Ricky, and Mike.

The two had been best friends ever since. LeShell's loud voice had saved her then. And though sometimes it embarrassed her now, Bebe knew she'd always love that voice. She just wished it wouldn't be so loud right now. The Frog and Peach was her favorite restaurant. She'd stayed away for a month after the embarrassment LeShell had caused her the last time she'd gotten ethnic up in here.

"I know Darnell's got his problems, but I love him."

"You love the bulge in his back pocket."

"The bulge in the front ain't so bad either, girl," Bebe smiled, devilishly.

That was true. Darnell Priestley *was* well-endowed and one attentive lover. In fact, in the sack was the only place he really paid any attention to Bebe.

"You're not gonna let the brotha get away with this, are you?"

"C'mon now, LeShell. You know me better than that."

"Phew!" LeShell ran a relieved hand through her braids. "I was gettin' worried, Bebe. I know how much that fool's got you twisted."

"Not *that* twisted."

"Good." LeShell moved forward, something on her mind. "Now, I say you take that man's Platinum card and we both go to Burberry or Coach or something. Oooh! What about Louis Vuitton?! No! No! Why don't we just go to Aruba?!"

Bebe smiled. She liked how this woman's mind worked. If only it wasn't so loud. Folks really *were* staring.

"No, no," Bebe smiled again, revealing the cutest dimple in her honey-brown right cheek. "I got something much better in mind."

SATURDAY, OCTOBER 27, 20—
10:26 P.M.

The Saturday night before Halloween, the second biggest party night of the year. I say, let the dead bury the dead. I've had enough of the living for now. Besides, I've been writing and am quite enjoying the company of my own words (even if I'm the only one). But after the past few months, I can understand why my latest holing up in my room was causing some concern. People are thinking that I'm dead to the world. Quite the opposite. While definitely not wanting company, I haven't felt more alive in a long time. Of course, that didn't stop people from wanting a resurrection—or an exorcism.

Right after getting off the phone, convincing Kevin—and then Malik (who seemed a bit too desperate)—that I really did not want to go out, DiDi entered my room. She was dressed as future Hall of Fame Steeler running back Jerome Bettis. She is much too dark and way too light (he is over 250 pounds, for goodness sakes) to look anything like him, but who doesn't love The Bus? The look on her face told me I hadn't showered the past couple days. The curses of "creative genius." Hey, I wasn't about to cut off my ear and I wasn't getting drunk and screwing prostitutes in Paris. Funk was all I had. I turned down the George Clinton as she entered the room.

"Hey, cuz, *your* phone's ringing off the hook."

"Yeah. You'd think I had friends, or something."

Her face lit up. "So, you're going out?"

"Naw."

She darkened.

"I'm writing," I defended.

"C'mon, Dami. It's the second biggest party night of the year. You don't have anything to wear?"

Somewhere in my closet lurked my old cow costume with its "MC" emblem and my plastic meat cleaver. Mad Cow the Avenging Bovine! Making the world safe for veganism! Maybe—like last year—two women dressed as French prostitutes would get on their knees and suck my utters for the camera. God, Samara hated that photo.

"No. I do. Where are you going, anyway?"

"Karen's again."

"Why is she having so many parties?"

"Well, she bought that big house with Clyde and now they're gonna have a baby. It's their last hoorah. You should come."

"Ina's gonna be there, right?"

"Yeah. Probably. But Nandi will be there," she hurried to amend.

"Who?" I asked. "Oh yeah. Right. The 'homegirl' from Youngstown."

I rolled my eyes.

"So, I guess you *definitely* don't want to go then."

"You got that right."

She was a little disappointed in me. So was I. Writing was really just my excuse du jour.

"Mom told me she called you. About Thanksgiving."

"Yeah."

"So, you coming?"

I hated disappointing her twice in two minutes.

"I don't know, DiDi. You know how I feel about that whole thing."

"Yeah, I do," she exhaled. "But things change, Damian."

"Hm."

"No, seriously. I told Dad about Priti. Just came out with it. And he was actually *nice* about the whole thing. Said he wanted to meet her."

I couldn't hide the shock from my face. I couldn't believe that they were serious enough for DiDi to actually tell her parents about her girlfriend. They still weren't too cool about her being a lesbian. Uncle Frank was downright hostile. *Was?!* Now he wanted to meet his daughter's lesbian lover? Uncle Frank? *My* Uncle Frank?! I blinked a couple times and awaited the Apocalypse.

"Exactly," DiDi continued. "I think, well, I think Dad knows ... I think he realizes he's been a real—you know—a real bastard. And I think he's trying to make amends, Damian."

"Funny what three strokes will do," I said, glumly.

"Yeah, I know," she chuckled, nervously. "You should really think about coming back home. Mom would really like to see you."

"Sure, DiDi."

She was looking frustrated. I could tell she wanted to throttle me. I was being a bastard—though I really didn't mean to be. These were her parents, after all, that I didn't want to see. She couldn't help but take it personally.

"Hey!"

Priti suddenly burst into my room, turquoise jewelry jangling. The feather bouncing in her hair. Faux buckskin skirt straight out of…

"Pocahontas?" I ventured.

"Yep," she beamed. "An exercise in irony."

I smiled. I had a sudden desire to become John Rolfe and play Pilgrim with this Indian princess.

"Man, DiDi," I said, "if I would've known that, I would've helped you with a Big Chief Uga Mug outfit."

"Who?" they said, in unison. They really were becoming a couple.

"Oh, it was this real fucked-up *Popeye* cartoon. This Indian chief kidnaps Olive Oyl to mate with."

"Geez," DiDi said.

"Yeah, he even had a song," I declared. "*Me, Big Chief Uga Mug, got to 'em have 'em squaw.*"

"God, Damian, Priti's gonna get enough crap for this. If I dressed up as that fool, they'd lynch my black ass for being culturally insensitive."

"Now *that* would be ironic."

"So, you coming, Damian?" Priti asked.

"Naw, I really have to write this novel."

"The sacrifices this man makes for his art," Priti sighed, haughtily.

"Thank you," I said, not quite vindicated.

Priti bounced out of the room. My eyes bounced with her. Great googelly moogelly. Those hips.

"Look, Dami," my cousin said, choosing to ignore my lascivious leering. "There comes a time, boy, when you've gotta—not forgive—because I don't know how possible that is—but to at least let it go. Just release it. All of it. You just have to. It's wearing you down."

I nodded and watched Deirdre leave for the good time I wasn't going to have tonight.

TUESDAY, NOVEMBER 1, 20—
7:01 P.M.

All Saints' Day, and I had to deal with the Devil. I made some promises. It was the only way I could get out of doing anything last Saturday night. I told everybody I was busy trying to figure out how to write a novel. It was a bold-faced lie, but that was all I had. I don't even know if people believe me anymore when I say it. But I'm sticking to that bit of BS until the lie becomes truth. And they say you can't learn anything from Poli Sci classes. But now I had to at least go see Malik and make things right.

So, I parked the pimped-out Tercel and made my way to Frederick Douglass Elementary. It had been a few years since I'd last stepped into a school. When I was at the Union, I used to liaise (how the hell did that become a word?) on behalf of some of the homeless mothers, trying to keep their kids enrolled in school while they floated around the city. Sometimes, I'd try to keep the mothers themselves enrolled. The experience usually filled me with dread. Combined with the nightmares of my childhood, school was never a delightful experience.

Douglass is intimidating in its dilapidation. Paint peels everywhere. Windows are cracked and barred. The brick looks about to crumble. This is not the best the city has to offer. In fact, Malik had been hired here because it was the worst. The children here know fathers who don't know them. The "strong," black male in this neighborhood is as rare as the dodo—refuging in prison or the grave (but hunting season is open year-round on the angry, black bucks). Teachers like Malik are some of the only male role models the little tykes have. Clearly, he's never told them about his white wife.

The neighborhood's a war zone. Money and poverty duke it out on a daily basis. Gentrifiers have long staked out this fallow territory. Next to the crackhouse lay renovated half-million-dollar homes filling up with families whose children will never step one foot into Frederick Douglass.

The one, untamable beast stands defiantly to the school's right. A roach motel, gated project with only one exit. "Niggers get in, but they can't get out." There are dozens of homicides within its wrought-iron entryway every year. With only the one exit, any target is a sitting duck in there. The employees at the local street pharmacologist jealously stand guard, looking for customers and victims. I shied away as one of them noticed me and made my way to the school's doors.

I pressed the intercom, stated my business, smiled for the security camera, and was allowed in. A disheveled blimp of a woman, the security guard, with missing teeth and donuts in a powder-sugared box looked at me evilly with her cloudy eyes. It seemed like she hadn't seen a good day since Crispus Attucks was shot during the Boston Massacre. She wheezed every syllable as she told me where to find Malik—sorry, Mr. Christiansen.

I walked down the quiet hallway. It was cold, as though there weren't a layer of brick between me and the crisp autumn day outside. The howling wind carried the distant cries of hyperactive children. It was lunch time. Everybody was off at the cafeteria somewhere. I smiled, looking at all the Halloween drawings the kids had made, the gold stars, the *good* memories of Catholic school. And stopped, trying to figure out exactly how to say "Datavises" and why you would name your kid that.

"Masai!"

I turned. A little boy with a huge, bound afro puff was heading straight at me. His limbs a furious whirlpool. A cute, ebony woman was hot on his trail—but quickly losing ground. I dropped my backpack, stepped in front of the boy, and snagged him. When had I started siding with adults?

"Git offa me, nigga!"

The little shit actually started writhing and swinging. I had to wrestle with him—and myself, wanting to get in a couple shots.

"Git offa me! I'ma steal you!"

He kept swinging, a genuine fury in his little eyes. He was screaming bloody murder. For a moment, I didn't know what to do. It passed. I wrapped him up before I had to dot his eye or he busted my lip. The sister walked up to me, catching her breath, spots of perspiration sheening her high forehead. She smiled. Kinda cute.

"Thanks," she exhaled.

"Lemme go!"

"No problem," I said. "Is it OK to let him go?"

Still struggling, Masai seemed to be losing steam. Eight-year-olds have way too much damned energy. I was getting sore. The boy looked like he was about to cry. The woman looked like she was through with the whole business.

"I don't know," she smiled, wearily. "Masai, should this kind gentleman let you go?"

"Uh-huh."

"Do you promise to behave?"

"Uh-huh."

"What was that, Masai?"

"Yes, Miss Withers."

Incredulous, Miss Withers nodded her assent. I could feel Masai's tiny muscles gaining energy as a spark of hope lit his eyes. We all knew what was about to happen. He wasn't fooling anybody. I set the boy down anyway. A devilish smile lit Masai's dark face, and he was gone.

"Bitches!" he laughed, as he darted down the hall.

Miss Withers rolled her eyes. "I need a cigarette," she huffed, and then she was gone. "Masai!"

You couldn't pay me enough. Actually, they'd have to mail my first paycheck to my prison cell. Masai had me at "Nigga." I would've whooped his little ass until the cops stopped whoopin' mine.

I found Malik at his desk. He was eating a packed lunch. A couple of his fourth graders were also in the room, eating their lunches, doing their homework, looking like the victims of the Holocaust, Idi Amin, the Khmer Rouge, Slobadan Milosevic, and every Latin American dictator combined.

"Ah, detention," I smiled, entering. One boy glared at me so hotly I thought he was going to shoot me. *Ha,* I thought at my own apprehension, *nine-year-olds don't carry guns...*

Do they?

"What are you doing, Antwan?"

"Nothin', Mr. Christiansen."

"Then I suggest you do your times tables."

"Hmph." Antwan, my new arch nemesis, threw himself back against his chair. His arms crossed themselves angrily, and his bottom lip jutted out. You could just hear the *Fuck you*s flying across the room.

Malik looked exhausted—like he hadn't slept since the womb. His afro was dented all over, his clothes disheveled, and his eyes were red. Nope. Couldn't pay me enough. I dropped my backpack onto his desk, produced two CDs, and handed them to my boy.

"Goapele? N'Dambi? What are these?"

"You're always complaining about how R&B sucks today. Here's proof that not all of it does."

"Thanks," he yawned.

"Man, these kids are wearing you out, brother man."

"Well—"

"Shut up, faggot."

It was low and angry, almost a growl. But there was no mistaking the words or who said them.

"Did he jus—"

"What did you say, Antwan?" Malik asked, heatedly, without raising his voice. Malik's not a small guy. Quite big, actually. I remember several dudes who backed down in the past when he'd used that voice. Antwan, however, was having none of it.

The boy arched his back defiantly, looking at me with blood in his eyes. No. Really. *Do* nine-year-olds carry guns? "You heard me, Mr. Christiansen," Antwan announced.

Malik huffed hoarsely. He really did look worn down.

Hag—

—gard

Haggard.

He moved to get up. I put out a staying hand and inserted a giant foot into my own mouth.

"So, you think you're grown, young man?"

Antwan shook his head. His fish was hooked.

"Well, a grown-up would say what you just said to my face. If he were a grown-up."

Children ooohed. The boy ... *smiled?* Oh, shit.

"Aw Jesus, Damian," Malik groaned.

Antwan got up. Malik got up. They both moved toward me. The other kids tensed in anticipation. What had I done? There was no escape. I had to stand my ground. That little punk had the scariest look on his face—somewhere between a smirk and a contorted scowl he must've lifted from a 50 Cent video. My hands balled themselves into fists involuntarily. I refused to be punked. If I got one good shot in, I'd have a chance to make my break.

Antwan stood before me and stared up. Did he not see the one hundred sixty pounds I had on him? Did he actually have a gun? All was quiet.

"Antwan," Mr. Christiansen warned.

"Antwan!"

Everybody stopped, turned to the voice. The security guard stood sternly. Her rheumy eyes gave off steam. Her entire body shook violently. She meant business. We were all scared.

"Get your butt over here!"

"Bu—"

"What I say, boy?!"

Antwan's defiant face crumbled into a pout. He was in trouble now. *Oooooooh,* I wanted to say, *you gonna get it.*

"Now!"

He started skulking his way across the room. You could hear the funeral dirge playing in the background. I smiled. Malik just looked relieved.

"You don't understand," he whispered to me. "That little bastard attacked a cop."

I looked, shocked, from Antwan to Malik and back again. The boy reached the security guard.

"Get over here!"

She cuffed him in the back of the head.

"Ow!" he whined.

She quickly grabbed his shirt and swept him down the hall. I suddenly had the feeling that that woman had just saved me from something truly embarrassing.

"And you should see the guy," Malik continued. "He's a good two-eighty, and Antwan just socked him right in the groin."

Ah, to be a kid again.

"Sergeant Dupree almost arrested him."

I suddenly started admiring the brat. Wanted to give him a pound, or something. My hero. Don't get me wrong. I still would've kicked his ass, but I would've admired him the entire time I was doing it.

Malik settled back into his seat and rubbed his eyes. I sat on his desk. The remaining kids gawked.

"All right, back to work," he ordered. The kids feigned work, but we all knew they were trying to listen in. Their little necks craned to the breaking point. To believe I once thought *I* was that slick. Malik leaned in closer. "You know the funny thing, Damian? I've been here long enough I can pretty much tell you who's going to see eighteen and who isn't. Antwan? Not a chance."

"You're kidding me."

"I've been proven right twice already."

Damn. "If the kids are so bad, why don't you leave and do something else?"

Malik hadn't at first planned to be a teacher. I don't know exactly what he'd wanted to do. He didn't either, graduating with an English degree during a recession. The idiot. Nobody had wanted him. He didn't even have enough skills to join the Peace Corps. It was either *Teach for America* or *Espressos for Yuppies*. He was headed for the ghetto.

The man only complains about his job. But he only complains about his wife, too. And every year he seems to be drawn deeper and deeper into both. He and Judy have yo-yoed in and out of each other's arms for years. (I still can't believe they've gotten remarried.) He got his teacher's certificate *and* a Master's in Education. There was just no figuring the boy out.

"Heck, man," he chuckled. "It's not the kids. I love them. I mean—" he leaned in conspiratorially close "—these kids have gone through things most adults couldn't handle. Antwan there, he deals drugs after school because his moms's already got two strikes and they won't touch a kid his age."

"Holy shiooooot. Holy shoot!"

Somewhere, a girl tittered.

"Lexus!"

Acura! Toyota! Yugo! Hyundai! ... Sorry.

She dove back into her book.

"And his story's not the worst. Believe me. And as much of a punk as Antwan just was right then, I bet you Miss Trent has the boy crying in the principal's office as we speak."

I tittered.

"They're always trying to act so tough, always trying to give you trouble, you sometimes forget that they're just little kids, ya know? That's all they are, Damian. Little kids."

Something caught in Malik's throat. He looked out the barred window. *Oh my God, he* does *care,* I thought. I didn't know who to feel sorry for. Him, the kids, the Democratic party, Cubs fans?

"No," Malik continued, composing himself. "It's not the kids at all. It's the adults. The parents, the principal. Some of the teachers. You wouldn't believe some of them."

I would. On one of my school visits once, I was accosted by a frazzled teacher's aide who bemoaned the time she was wasting there. "It doesn't make sense teaching these kids this stuff," she had insisted, hoarsely. "What good does it do to teach kids in *this* neighborhood algebra or how to diagram sentences? What good will it do them? You tell me."

"What? Don't y'all offer a Crackhome Ec course?" I'd said, flippantly.

She'd stormed off. I'd stormed off. Both disgusted.

"Just the other day," he continued, "Miss Withers—"

"Ooooh, he *likes* her," Kia (wait! that's actually a name) piped-up. "They *always* flirtin'."

Yes, kids. They'll sell you down the river faster than a Mississippi slave hunter. The look on Malik's face told me it was true. More fuel to the Judy fire.

"Lexus," Malik admonished. The girl once again quickly got back to "work," her neck giraffing to hear us better. "Anyway," he continued, "she told me that Mr. Blake, this Jheri curl 'pretty boy' from Tuskegee—"

"Is that possible?" I asked, incredulous.

"If I'm lyin', I'm cryin', dyin', deep-fryin'..."

"He soaks his hair in lye then?"

"Seriously. He's right in the cafeteria. You can meet him. Just follow the grease trail. Looks like Bobby Brown before the crack. Anyway, she tells me that he was clowning me the other day in the teachers' lounge, calling me 'the white boy' for the way I talk."

I was about to crack a joke.

"Yeah, I know," he breathed. "But this is a mothe—this is a *school*, Damian. Now I know the bi—boy! I know he doesn't even know the definition of 'contraceptive'—"

"You're making this up, Malik."

"I wish I were. He's an absolute idiot. Why do you think he's teaching here?" He didn't catch the irony of his statement. I didn't want to point it out. "I was tempted to explain to him the role of language within a society. The idea that there's no such thing as a 'proper' form of any language. That any tongue is simply an amalgam of competing dialects and that whatever dialect the moneyed classes speak is the one deemed 'proper.' That our role as educators—one of the roles, at least—is to teach these children *that* dialect so that they may eventually have access to and maybe become part of the moneyed classes. What's so goddamned 'white' about that?"

"Oooooh!"

"Lexus!"

I looked at my boy, all flustered, and the girl, embarrassed, dumbfounded. I couldn't at first figure out the reason behind this Linguistics 101 lecture. And then it hit me. Damned intellectuals.

"You and Judy are on the outs again, aren't you?"

He nodded glumly.

"Wanna talk about it?"

"Naw. Not really."

"You know, the problem is," Malik started vehemently, swigging his beer. It's been a long time since I'd spent a weekday afternoon in a bar. You'd think I'd do it more often. It's not like there's a job standing in my way. But nobody's around at this time of day. Just me, Malik, the bartender, and CNN. Pretty boring. "Ah hell, Damian. I don't know what the problem is."

I didn't know what to say.

"No. That's bullshit. I know exactly what the problem is. Do you know how Judy and I got together?"

After Lucifer and his army were expelled from heaven, he and God had decided to send a representative from each camp to fight the ultimate battle between Good and Evil on Earth. After millennia of this apocalyptic conflagration, the two combatants decided to make it official and get married. Unfortunately for all humanity, none of us can figure out who's on whose side. Malik and Judy have probably forgotten themselves.

Just a guess.

"I dunno."

"It was senior year in college, and we were both in *Themes of Faust Throughout the Ages* together—" See. I was right. "—You know, we made eyes, the usual. Started studying together. We argued a lot. Go figure. Started sleeping together. You know, that really passionate love/hate crap. God, how we *fucked*!"

I tried not to wince at the image. I feel bad saying this, but the problem with Malik and Judy is that they think they're beautiful people, and they just aren't. Whenever they used to get on each other's nerves, they always thought they could do better. They can't. I think deep down they know this. And they resent each other for it. That's why they're always arguing, always breaking up, and always ultimately getting back together.

One time I ran into Judy at a party while she and Malik were having problems. She was drunk. I was nowhere close to drunk enough. She offered me a blow job. I rejected her, of course. I'd just moved in with Samara,

Judy's a bit toothy, and I could never do something like that to one of my boys.

Of course, I've seen Malik humiliate himself like that on more than one occasion—sans blow job offer, of course. At the club, in bars, in line at the grocery store. Then he would abruptly start bad-mouthing his wife and, I'm sure, argue with her later. I never understood why neither of them realized how lucky they were to have found each other.

"Really *fucked*, you know? We went crazy. Did everything. 'Slap it up, flip it, rub it down.' You know what I mean?"

Great, now I had pictures of Judy's gelatinous, pockmarked ass slamming against Malik's hard mound of black belly. *And* that stupid Bell, Biv, Devoe song in my head. *Think happy thoughts, Damian.* Children frolicking in fields of daisies. World peace. A cure for AIDS. Me and Halle Berry frolicking in fields of daisies.

"Everything but invite the Harlem Globetrotters into the fray."

Malik, Judy, Curly Neal, and Meadowlark Lemon frolicking in a field of daisies. When will this nightmare cease?!

"Yeah, I get the picture," I conceded.

"Right," Malik said, maybe detecting the nausea in my voice. "But then she got pregnant. I don't know what we were thinking. I guess we were just young—'cause neither of us is stupid. It was a bad time. Real bad. We didn't know what to do with each other. We didn't argue much—believe it or not—" I don't "—but we definitely didn't get along.

"It was our senior year, ya know? Like our entire lives were in front of us, and we had just ruined it. But you make your bed, right? And Judy didn't want an abortion. So, I asked her to marry me. Then things got a hell of a lot worse. I mean, our families went ape shit. My folks hated her. Her family hated me. Nobody mentioned race, but you knew it was there. Like a five-ton gorilla. I thought my mother's brain was going to explode when I brought ole girl home. Man, I really thought things couldn't get any worse.

"But we got married, anyway. The wedding sucked. It was tense as shit. You woulda thought it was the goddamned Cuban missile crisis. But we got through it. We set up our house, both of us graduated, and we were determined to make it work. That's when I got sent here with Teach for America. I don't know if we were happy, but we got along all right. Then Judy had a miscarriage, and that was the worst of all.

"We were wrecks. I mean, you kinda get used to the idea of having a baby. You get your crib and all these little toys and construct a little nursery and you look forward to, to that idea. Like, how fun it'll be to have this little bundle of humanity in your arms that you get to shape into a person.

"Then you gotta deal with the fact that you're kinda relieved. I mean, we were only what? twenty-two? We were just kids ourselves. We hadn't even got the chance to be adults. It's something you look forward to your entire life, and we weren't going to get that chance. So, yeah, I felt kinda glad that she'd lost the baby and I felt guilty as hell that I felt that way.

"But then we had a decision to make. We'd just gotten married because of the kid. We didn't really know each other. We loved to screw, but we didn't know if we really loved each other. So what do you do? We could just go our separate ways, call it a day. But, I don't know. While there was really no good reason for us to stay together, there really wasn't any reason for us to separate either. We really *did* like to screw and we got along all right and it looked like we were going to survive something that tears a lot of couples apart. And it's worked out all right. We argue too much, God knows."

"And you got divorced once."

"*And* we got divorced once," he admitted, chuckling. "But other than that, Judy and I work. We really do. I know it doesn't look like it—what with us at each other's throats all the time. And I know I could never explain it to someone else—" *You're damned right about that one, son* "—but it really does work. I couldn't think of anybody else's throat I'd rather be at."

I almost choked on my beer.

"You all right, Damian?"

"Yeah. Uh. Sure."

"And well, now I want a baby."

"You do?" My voice cracked.

"Yeah, sure. Why you so shocked? I know I've always said I didn't. But I think it was the miscarriage talking. But God, Damian, it's like the natural progression of life, right? I see all these precious, little kids everyday being ruined by their incredibly fucked-up parents—folks I *swear* are hell bent on fucking up their kids. And then I see these really caring parents, working two, three, four crappy jobs, never making enough, never seeing their kids, and seeing those kids being dragged down by the really bad ones, too. And I want to adopt them all. I want to do it right. I want to continue the line, I want to show that black folks can *indeed* raise their own and have normal, well-adjusted, excellent children. I want the chance to be the father my own refused to be."

That one hit a little too close to home. I gulped down the rest of my beer and looked around for the bartender. I noticed a pause and ventured a glance at Malik. Somebody had put puppy dog eyes in his sockets. Damn.

"So what's wrong?" I finally asked.

He shrugged like one of his admonished students. "It's just that Judy doesn't want to have one. I know it's been almost ten years, but I think she's still smarting over the miscarriage. I mean, if Sarah had lived, I'd be teaching her right now."

His face dropped into his beer. "I just don't think she wants to go through that crap again. I can't say I blame her. I don't really want to, either. But … well, it's not like you can *force* someone to have a baby. But I really want to have one. I really want to have one with Judy. And it's driving a wedge between us. A real big one. We're arguing more than ever—"

Is that possible?

"What?"

"Did I say that out loud? Sorry. Go ahead."

"Yeah. I don't know what to do." He was sounding truly desperate. "And then there's Donna."

"Who?"

"Miss Withers."

"What about her?" I asked, stiffly.

"Well, she's … ya know. She's damned cute."

"Yeah. So?"

"Well, we've gone out a couple times after work, and …"

"You haven't…" I offered.

"No," he jumped—then sank back into his seat. "Not yet. But it's, well, it's kinda hard, Damian. I mean—"

"I don't want to hear this, Malik," I snapped.

"What? I ain't done shit, yet!"

"Yet," I chuckled, bitterly. "Bullshit, motherfucker."

"Hey, what's wi—"

"No, no," I hurried, "let me guess. You're gonna come at me with some crap about how you two really get along and how you can really talk to her and how she really, really *listens* to you."

"Yeah … well … yeah."

"And how she says she can really talk to you and how she really feels comfortable with you. Safe. Not like with all those knuckleheads she's out dating."

"Yeah. She's said that before."

"Of course she has. You're fucking *married,* Malik. You're *supposed* to be safe."

I was really starting to lose it. I knew it. But I couldn't stop.

"It's not like that, Damian. Not at all. It's more like … I don't know … more like—"

"Love?" I scoffed.

"No," he hedged. "Not exactly."

"Fuck that," I fumed. "Either she's playin' you or you're playin' yourself. Shit's real heavy at home and you want a vacation. That happy love like you see in movies, right? Sappy-ass music and plastic tits waving in your face. Fuck the history, the turmoil, all your problems with Judy. You just want to have fun. Be *happy*. Like screwing some kindergarten teacher's gonna get you that."

"Third grade."

"What?" I snapped.

"Donna. She teaches third grade."

I genuinely laughed at that one. I was seeing red and could barely find Malik cowering in his seat. I'd said enough, too much, and it was best that I leave. To believe ole boy would drop this crap on me, *me*, now of all times.

"You know what," I started, standing up and digging for my wallet, "I can't have this conversation right now. I'm out."

I slapped down a twenty and left the bar. I don't think Malik and I will be talking any time soon.

THURSDAY, NOVEMBER 3, 20—

3:12 A.M.

There's a cliché I wanted to use—it's always darkest before the dawn; you've got to learn to kiss before you can fuck; even a dog doesn't shit where he eats? Or are those aphorisms? I can never remember the difference. And now, in the hopes of being clever (hopeless, I know), I've forgotten which cliché, aphorism, platitude, spoonerism I wanted to use.

Hell, go Dylan. *The times, they are a-changin'*. (Don't tell anybody I just did that.) Because I do distinctly remember a time when I used to enjoy hanging out with my friends—going out to bars, chasing tail, drinking, playing video games, smoking, your general pissing around—when they *and* I were fun, and we'd get into all kinds of crap because there was nothing better to do. *Those were the daaaaaaayyyyyssssss!!!*

But now, all of a sudden, they're not so fun. A lot of people are just plain gone. Having families, careers, mortgages, whatever people in their thirties have. Everybody's so busy. Those who are still around…? I don't know. They don't piss around so much, going to bars is steadily losing its appeal, video games are too damned complex, and hangovers just *hurt*. Hanging out feels more and more like work, sometimes even a duty, and I knew the moment I saw Mayrav I was going to have to put in for combat pay.

I was already feeling like crap over going off on Malik. Here he was trying to confide in me, and I went ballistic, more self-righteous than Moses at an NRA rally. But why would he come at me with that crap? I mean, if you're thinking about cheating on your wife, why not confide in Kevin? He'd help you out, cheer you on, make the motel reservations, buy the condoms, and take pictures. He might even join in—hell if I know. But *me*? Didn't he know about Samara and me? How that all went down? And how, if things had gone according to plan, I'd already be sick of wedding

DJs (and how they all suck—if I hear "Celebrate" one more time…) and pure-sugar cake tastings and reception venues and wedding colors and preachers who'd be admonishing me to go to church and explaining how and why Samara would not be taking my name and would have last night been waiting for Kev, Malik, Egon, and him to be taking me to M. Butternut where I could fall in love with a 5'2" dark-skinned Laotian babe with long, raven hair, deep Southern-fried accent, and spherically-fake boobs that *couldn't* shake in my drunk face? How could he have forgotten all that?

Why can't I forget? Why was I still fighting the urge to sob while driving up to Mayrav's place? (Maybe I should've ejected the Luther CD.) Every time I think I'm over it all, something pops up and the bile rises in my throat. *Any love…* I was a little choked up as I parked my Tercel. I mean, I knew this week was going to be rough. I just didn't think it was going to be this rough.

It was a posh, brand-new high-rise condo. It's funny, I kept thinking, when I first met Mayrav I had no clue she came from wealth. She was living in a rental house with one too many roommates. All crammed in like sardines, nobody bathed half as often as they should have. I just assumed nobody could afford a bigger place—or soap. Now, looking upon this crystalline tower, I wonder why she had stayed with those unwashed masses.

Of course, those were the '90s. Starting off the decade in a recession, we all just assumed everybody was poor. Our clothes were tattered, our jobs crap, and our music angry. In retrospect, I guess I should've known better. There was always a sense of cynical accomplishment when folks went dumpster diving for furniture or raided the Salvation Army for kitchenware and clothes. And all those guys with gas station attendant shirts labeled "Chuck" were just too damned ironical to be real. The façade couldn't last. When boy bands and distressed jeans hit, you knew it was over. I'm just pissed that my black ass actually *was* broke back then while folks like Mayrav were just waiting for this condo to be built so they could sell their lofts and move in. I guess money, like water, eventually finds its own level. Hers is on the seventeenth floor.

The lobby was clean and crisp, and the concierge, cordial. He smiled warmly. While I apprehensively moved to the elevator, I smiled nervously, wondering when exactly I had ceased being young and dangerous. There was a time when a guy like that would've been on me like a second skin. Where are you going?! Who are you going to see?! What are you delivering?! There'd have been spittle and anger. Now, all I get is a warm smile and a "Have a nice day." Even cops wave at me now. Damn, I used to like being "dangerous." *I used to be somebody. Instead of middle class, which is what I am, Charlie.* Maybe I should trade in my dreadlocks for cornrows. Dreads are too establishment.

I went up to my girl's floor and rang the bell. I heard a craggy "Come in" and hesitantly entered. Something was not right. I knew as soon as I walked in. The place was cryptically cool and dark. I'd never been here before, but I knew Mayrav liked light. There was none—except the dying twilight sun. Shostakovich was playing on the stereo. The air was dense with depression.

"Mayrav?" I offered, over the mournful violins.

"Damian."

My eyes slowly adjusted, and I found her sitting under a Billie Holiday poster at her dining room table. A cigarette smoldered in one hand, a glass of wine teetered in the other. Her clothes were disheveled. Her hair, a black storm. Her eyes glowed green in the dark. Screw the combat pay, I wanted to call Saddam to see if he had any room for a brother in his spider hole.

I moved slowly to the table. There was a bottle of red wine drained to the tannins and another one sitting in waiting.

"Uh," I said, "I thought you quit smoking."

"I did," she said coldly, and inhaled. "Get a glass. Open the bottle. I have white in the fridge, and there's always Johnny Walker."

I didn't really feel like drinking. I'm just not liking it as much as I used to. But there was no option in her voice. I moved to the kitchen, fumbled around awhile, and found a glass. I returned and grabbed the wine key, ready to do what I was told. *And* ask a stupid question.

"So, how's it going, Mayrav?"

She looked at me, way too long for my comfort. I swallowed hard and popped the cork. I just don't remember her ever being as angry as she's been with me these past few weeks.

"I talked to him today."

"Him? Who?"

Clear tears started creeping out of the red in her eyes.

"Stuart."

Damn. I suddenly realized that this was going to be a long night. One I wasn't going to want to talk about for a long time.

FRIDAY, NOVEMBER 4, 20—
5:26 A.M.

Make it sloppy.

The command reverberated in his cranium. *Make it sloppy.* His Aero shot through the night traffic. Cars, people movers, police pods, skyscrapers, holo boards, the air was choking with obstacles. He was in a hurry. He had no need for laws. He downshifted and tilted the nose of his car. He slammed down on the accelerator, and the Aero plummeted. Floor after lighted floor sped by. Before leveling, the congestion was one hundred feet overhead. He hit the accelerator and moved smoothly toward his target.

Make it sloppy.

He had no problem with killing. No guilt, no pain of conscience. It was his job. It was something he did. He never spent nights talking to skulls. The blood on his hands washed cleanly down the bathroom sink. There were no palpitating hearts underneath his floorboards. But there was no thrill in it either. No thrill, no joy, no adrenaline rush. Just a job. That was why they called him "Ice."

And he had no problem with tonight's directive. He could make it sloppy. He had done it before. He would do it tonight. He would probably spend the rest of his life making it sloppy.

People had to be taught a lesson. ChicaCorp was his town, his turf. He had grown up here. After the war, he had spent seven years protecting this place. He had lost his original leg doing just that. When the Mayor had first approached him for a special assignment, he gladly took it. He did so well—eliminating a burgeoning Yakuza threat—that he was put on the Mayor's permanent payroll. And he'd been earning a steady check ever since. He was cold. He was efficient. He was Ice.

A large black man with lightning reflexes, a scar down his right cheek, and dreadlocks down to the small of his back, Ice was too recognizable for this task. Sometimes, this was exactly what was needed. Message sent. But today was different. The Mayor's office didn't want the Slovaks knowing who hit them. Just that they were hit. Maybe that would convince them not to muscle in on ChicaCorp's X market.

As the Aero darted toward Peachy Restaurant, Ice concentrated on his face. Nanoengines all over his body started to tingle. His skin started melting from brown to ecru. His hair began to shrivel and straighten. Soon it was bright red. His eyes were turning in upon themselves. Molecules around his eyes began to harden into metallic rings and soon pierced his brows. A stud appeared in his right cheek where his scar had been. Soon, he was no longer a black man. He was jaPunk—like those Yakuza bastards he had chilled to get this job in the first place. A smile creased his new face.

He shook out his right arm. Two automatic pistols jutted out of the flesh of his forearm. A large blade sprang from the top of his hand, and a ring of spikes sprouted around his wrist. He knew the same would happen on his left arm, and upon command, automatic weapons could pop out of his back on a thought's notice if the need arose. His tech was that good. The Mayor made certain of it.

His Aero pulled up to Peachy's air port. An officious-looking valet rushed to his door. The assassin quickly ordered his armory back into his flesh. Ice stepped out, much shorter and more sinewy than his original, massive frame. There were going to be a lot of people, a lot of blood, here. He needed the extra dexterity this body would provide.

Ice stepped steadily onto the platform. He looked down at the abyss below. Two hundred feet of sheer blackness loomed down there and a sure blood-and-pulverized-bone splat if he lost his footing. He looked back up as the valet held up a palm. The iris scan was quick. It told the valet everything this identity had to offer: birth date, height, weight, religion, occupation, address, and credit balance. Peachy was very selective in its clientele.

Ice watched the valet's eyes scan the info that was running through the man's head. He waited. Soon, concentration turned into a smile, *this* client was *very* important indeed, and the valet put a reassuring hand on Ice's slender shoulder.

"Welcome, Mr. Edo. Please enjoy your time at Peachy."

"Thank you," Ice said, with a slight Okinawan accent. As he moved along the platform, his weaponry started to sprout all over his body. He kicked open the door.

"Welcome to ChicaCorp, motherfuckers!"

He would definitely make it sloppy, he thought over the screams and bullets.

3:39 P.M.

Funny, after two showers and thousands of typed words, I still can't remove Mayrav's scent from my fingers.

TUESDAY, NOVEMBER 8, 20—
8:30 P.M.

"Xanadu Travels."

"Hello, Gene? Is Olivia there?"

"Yes. One moment please."

...

"Olivia."

"Yes, Olivia. Damian Cross here."

"Ah, Damian. Are you packed and ready to go?"

"Yeah. That's what I was calling about."

"Really?"

"Yeah, well ... you see. I don't want a refund!"

"Good. Because you know our policy."

"Well, it's just that, just that—you see I ... well ... I was, uh, sorta hoping that I could postpone—"

"Postpone?!"

"Yes. Uh. Postpone the trip."

"But it's a honeymoon package."

"I know. I know. I mean, I know it's sorta short notice—I mean, this

Sunday, jeez—but well, there's not going to be a honeymoon. There were … there were complications, I guess you could say. Yeah, complications! And I'm not getting married! I just wan—"

"OK, OK, Damian. I'm really sorry. I'll see what I can do. No promises."

"Those are the last things I need right now."

"Right. Well, let me call you back."

"…"

"Damian?"

"Yeah, yeah."

"I really am sorry."

THURSDAY, NOVEMBER 10, 20—
3:19 P.M.

Ya know, I was perfectly content, wallowing in my own self-pity (why hasn't Mayrav called?), when something truly tragic happened: I couldn't find my penis. I could've sworn it was there yesterday. But this afternoon in the shower, when I looked down at my ever-expanding belly, it wasn't there. Gone. My penis just up and disappeared. I almost cried.

There just aren't that many options open to a man whose penis has disappeared. It's time to take the bull by the horn, so to speak. Time to hit the gym.

SUNDAY, NOVEMBER 13, 20—
1:01 P.M.

[**Author's Note**: Due to the author's misadventures last night and subsequent hangover, the account of said misadventures will be postponed until tomorrow when the author, hopefully, is no longer drunk. Now, if you will excuse me, I think I may have to vomit once again. **The Author.**]

MONDAY, NOVEMBER 14, 20—
5:08 P.M.

Saturday night, I lay awake in bed, reading my Mahfouz, trying my damnedest not to move. Every time I did, I found myself moaning a mournful duet with Coltrane's wailing horn. I'd been to the gym for the first time since college, and lactic acid was screaming in my every joint and sinew. I kept trying to think of *My Favorite Things*, but all I could think of was Icy Hot, Ben Gay, heating pads, and Ace bandages. And Samara, of course. I was in *pain*.

A phone rang somewhere in Midaq Alley. I put away dreams of Salma Hayek to answer it, hoping it was Mayrav. It was.

"Hi, Damian," she croaked.

"Mayrav?!" Why *does* my voice keep cracking? It's like I'm trapped in a bad *Brady Bunch* rerun. "Uh, how you doing?"

"I've been better."

"Tell me about it," I murmured.

"Tell me something, Damian…"

"Yeah?"

"Have you ever been at a party, really enjoying yourself? Everything's just really good, really right. The music's good, the food, the company. Even the night's perfect. Like you go outside and it's seventy-five degrees, a little chilly, but with a nice humid breeze—"

It was hard enough following Mayrav—I mean, was she tripping (the white, drug-taking sense of the word—not the black, triflin' sense)? Was she about to go all Marlon Brando, *Apocalypse Now* on me? "The horror, the horror." And talk about cutting off little kids' inoculated arms? But there was something going on outside my door. Like glasses clanging, or something. I wondered if Neville and Hep were having yet another knockdown/drag-out. Of course, they've been pretty quiet lately. I wonder if they've even been around.

"And then something happens," Mayrav continued. "While you were chatting everybody up and getting a little buzzed, people were leaving."

Yes, definitely clanging glasses.

"And before you know it, you're the last person standing at the party. It's still pretty early, but everybody else is gone. You're standing in the kitchen, trying to figure out a way to extricate yourself from the situation. Your hosts are staring at you with disappointed looks on their faces. You're trying to gulp down your wine without gulping and being rude, cursing yourself for being the last one left. How did *you* get stuck? I hope they don't want me to help clean up."

What's with those stupid glasses?

"Daaaayyy—meeeee—aaaaannnnn," came the screechy voice outside my door, "come out and plaaaa—yeeeee—aaaayyyy!"

Kevin.

"Yeah," I said into the phone, distracted.

"That's me and being single," she confessed.

"Daaaayyy—meeeee—aaaaannnnn, come out and plaaaa—yeeeee—aaaayyyy!!!"

"That party was over years ago. Everybody's gone and had kids, my hosts have cleaned up and gone to bed, the lights are out, and I'm still standing in the kitchen with the damned wine glass in my hand."

"Daaaayyy—meeeee—" Smash! "Ah, shit!"

"Kevin!" I shouted.

"Yeah!"

"Hey, Mayrav, could you hold on a second? I think there's been an accident."

"Tell me about it."

I paused, furrowed my brow, and put down the phone. I opened the door to find Kevin standing over broken glass, staring at his hands, relieved. No cuts.

"What the hell you doing, man?"

He shrugged. "I looked at the calendar. Thought you might need a friend."

I smiled—despite myself. "The broom and dustpan are in the kitchen closet. I'll get off the phone in a second." I jumped back to the phone. "Mayra—?" Dial tone. Oh well. I didn't feel like thinking about it.

Rollin' in my Six-Fo'…

Actually, Kevin's Nissan Altima. Not exactly a G-Ride, but we ain't Gs.

"So, here's the plan," Kevin announced. "I'm getting you as drunk as humanly possible. And there's someone I want you to see."

"I'm not exactly feeling sociable tonight."

Kev threw in a disc. Vaguely familiar horns started blaring. Tons of brass, a nice break beat.

"You never feel sociable, Damian."

"True dat," I confessed, glumly. "I'm going through some changes."

"Who ain't?" he said, pensively. "Look, I was supposed to be your best man, and it's my duty to make your wedding night something you won't forget—or need to forget."

Something strange started happening. I felt the need to cry. I *desperately* needed to change the subject. I pointed to the stereo. "Youngblood Brass Band?"

"Yeah," Kev said, enthusiastically. I think he needed to change the subject, too. Kevin Byrd is not the type of man who talks about his feelings. Absolutely hates talking about others'. That's why we're best friends. Leave the talk for Oprah. "I remember your talking about them before. I decided to check them out."

"I'm impressed you actually listened to me. You're probably the only person who does."

He shrugged.

"So, what do you think?" I asked.

"I don't know. Brass band hip hop. It's definitely intriguing. That guy on sousaphone, makes it sound like scratching?"

"Yeah?"

"I tried it out. I think I got it down."

"How long did that take?"

"'Bout fifteen minutes, or so."

"Très formidable."

"Damian." He looked at me. "Only the truly pretentious speak French, dude."

"C'est vrai," I affirmed. "C'est vrai."

Make my pain Jamaican. A bottle of Red Stripe and a shot of Myers rum. Even in Mojito, a Cuban restaurant/dance club, it just seemed right. Of course, by the time Kev and I got there, the restaurant part was closed, which was too bad. Ropa vieja and platanos also seemed right. But hell, when you can't go Beny Moré, Bob Marley will do the trick. I downed my second shot, forgetting about that damned woman who was almost my wife tonight.

Of course, she was always on my lips while I endlessly babbled about everything else.

"You remember Grady?" I asked.

Kevin was looking around for something/one. I was trying to stick to the task at hand. There were too many attractive women to be a fool in front of for me to look beyond the rum and beer. He turned to me, distracted. "From *Sanford & Son*?"

"No, ya big dummy," I Redd Foxxed. "The Communist."

"Oh yeah, tall, bald guy. I remember that bitch. Wonder whatever happened to him."

"Don't know. Maybe you should Google him." I drained my beer. I was already starting to feel as good as could be expected. I had to be careful—pace my happiness before I started crying. "Anyway, remember how he used to say that the '90s were the decade of the mindfuck?"

"Yeah. Vaguely."

"Well, I keep trying to think of what this decade is, and I just can't figure it out. I just have no damn clue. I keep thinking that people should be up in arms, screaming in the streets, crap like that. But it seems like nobody wants to say nothin'. All I keep hearing about is who J. Lo's screwing."

"Marissa!" Kevin summoned.

A caramel-cocoa cutie with the bubbliest booty turned, looked at my boy, screwed up her face, and came our way anyway.

"Marissa, Damian. Damian, Marissa," he introduced. "Damian's that writer I told you about."

Marissa was *not* impressed. She turned to Kevin. "I thought you said you were gonna call."

"I thought I did," he bullshitted.

"No. You didn't."

"I'll call Monday. Promise."

There are definitely things to believe in: the Easter Bunny, leprechauns, weapons of mass destruction. Kevin's promises to a woman ...? Marissa knew the deal.

"Mm-hm."

She rolled her eyes and started to walk away.

"Marissa," Kevin harkened, again. She gave a contemptuous half-turn. Kev smiled. "Show my boy your tattoo."

Her face contorted, she exhaled dramatically, but she complied. She wriggled her tight jeans down her beautifully-molded ass. In cholo calligraphy, "Faster" was etched across the small of her back.

"Damn," I gasped.

She slid her pants back up and looked at Kevin. "And don't you forget it."

His hazel eyes sparkled. "Now woman, how the hell could I forget *that*?"

"Hm." She sauntered away.

"Now, instead of worrying about what to call this decade, you need to figure out how to call Marissa."

"Hell Kevin, what the hell is she? Twenty-one? Twenty-two?"

"Twenty-three, I think. Like I know."

"Man, what the hell do I have to say to a twenty-three-year-old?"

"Hammer! Don't hurt me!"

We laughed.

"No, seriously," Kevin continued. "You know what kind of pressure a tattoo like that puts on a brother? Am I going fast enough? Should I go faster? *Can* I go faster? Is this too fast? *Can* I go too fast? Shit, man, I pulled my damned groin."

I laughed some more. The bartender put down another shot and beer. This night wasn't so bad after all. At least in a hip club like Mojito, I wouldn't have to hear "Celebrate."

I held up my glass admiringly.

"Black man, love your black rum."

It burned a little going down but felt oh-so good. "No, it's relevance," I said. "It's like these teeny boppers hoppin' around here. What could I possibly say to them that would be in the least bit interesting? I mean, didn't they grow up listening to New Kids on the Block?"

"More like Hootie and the Blowfish."

"Oh my God. I'm old. Geez, what do you talk about with them?"

"I don't know. Mainly myself. That usually keeps my audiences *riveted*."

That's what you think, bruh.

"What was that?"

God, I need to stop doing that.

"So yeah, anyway. Relevance. That's my problem. I don't think I'm in the least bit relevant. I've got three books going, and I don't have a damned thing to say in any one of them. Maybe I should go back to writing plays."

I started in on the beer. Kev gave me another one of his looks. Not quite the "Bitch" look—but close.

"How many times do I have to tell you, Damian? Booty novel. What could be more irrelevant than that?"

"True. But not only do I not have the desire, I wouldn't even know where to start."

"Start with your own life."

"What? I was with the same woman for the past seven years. I know nothing about dating. Ina proved that."

He chuckled. "Well, it sounded kinda funny."

"Tragicomic's more like it." I started drifting off into thought.

"Hell man, you could write about my life."

"*How to Catch Every Disease Known to Man in Five Easy Lessons.*"

"Hey, I haven't even had a cold sore."

"Lucky you," I said, grimly. "Nope. Unless you count messing around with Mayrav, I've really got nothing."

"Mayrav? When?"

"Just the other night."

"Damn. I've always wanted to hit that."

"You've always wanted to hit Mother Theresa."

"Not since she died."

"Still."

"What can I say? It's a pathology. So did you?"

"Hit it? No."

"God, Damian. What do I have to do? Buy the condoms? Get the room? Hell, do you need me to join in? Show you what to do?"

"Don't do me any favors. It's just that, well, we both knew it was a mistake before it even got started. I went to her place. She was already drunk. Grumbling about bitch-ass Stuart and what a bitch-ass his bitch-ass is. She wanted me to catch up. And she was playing Shostakovich."

"Jesus."

"That's what I'm saying. Shostakovich! I was feeling sorry for her, sorry for myself. It's wedding week, ya know? I had to postpone that honeymoon trip—"

"Postpone?"

"I'm going, damnit! I haven't been out of this country yet and I've always wanted to see Mexico." I took a breath. "Anyway, we knew what was gonna happen. That was why we were so determined to have me catch up. So I did. We rolled around for awhile. It was cool. But … I don't know. Somewhere along the way my tongue started getting sore, and I just got up and left. Neither one of us said a word. I just left. It was kinda fucked-up, really."

"And yet you keep going back for more."

"What does that mean?"

"Nothing, D."

"Anyway, I hadn't talked to her again until tonight. She was on the phone when you were doing your *Warriors* routine. And I have no clue what in the world she was talking about."

Kevin looked pensive for a minute. His eyes burning. "I don't know. I'd start with that. Better, of course. Some artistic flourishes, and all that. But yeah, why not start with that? Can't make her white, though."

"Technically, she's African-American."

"Anyway," he said, incredulously, "why not make her Latina? Brothers are always hookin' up with Latinas in the movies lately."

"Why not Asian?" I joked along. "Brothers who are in the movies are always hookin' up with Asian chicks."

"The new white meat," Kev guffawed.

"I got it. I'll make her half-Asian/half-Mexican."

"Better yet, half-Asian/half-Moroccan Jew."

"No, my brother. To keep it real, I'll make her half-Asian/half-*black*."

"What? A Thai coon?" came a third, husky, feminine voice. Kevin and I looked up, confused. "That's what I call myself, anyway," this woman said. "I simply refuse to be Cablanasian. Besides, where did the Caucasian part come in?"

"There's a little Caucasian in all of us," Kevin said, mock-gravely, "yearning to breathe free. Here, sit down."

She must be special, I thought, Kev never gives up his seat. I guess he doesn't have to. Yodit was the only other woman I'd ever seen him be chivalrous to. The Negro must be in love.

"Nandi," Kev opened, "this is Damian."

"The writer," she said. Screw Kevin. I'm in love.

"Yeah," he said. "The one I've been telling you about."

"He's the talk of the town," she said, cryptically, confusing everybody but herself. "Anyway, we've met before."

"We have?"

She gave me a look like I should've remembered. I looked at her. The edges of my world were starting to fray and blur, but I gave it my best shot. The almond eyes, that silky, black "good" hair generations of my people have made such a big deal about, an eerie perfection to her golden skin I would've found intimidating if I hadn't been so drunk.

"Sorry," I shrugged.

"Damian's a little drunk," my boy offered. "It's his birthday."

"That's OK," she said, giving a look that said it wasn't. "Happy birthday, anyway."

"It's in May."

"But it's still a special day, man."

"I'll never forget it."

Nandi wanted to get past her confusion. "Nice to meet you, anyway." She offered her hand. Long, slender sienna fingers. The tips calloused—but very pleasant. "So what are you two talking about?" she asked. "By the way, my Dad's Chinese, Jamaican Chinese. I just think 'Thai coon' sounds better than anything else I could come up with."

The rum was getting to me. I didn't know if she were talking too fast or if I just couldn't keep up. I was slowing down. The world was starting to tilt. I wanted to hold onto something for a little stability.

"I'm trying to convince Damian here that the future is ass."

"I thought it was plastic," she stated, simply.

I chuckled. *The Graduate*. I liked this woman already. If Kev actually were falling in love, I was ready to applaud his choice. She was definitely not a silly, little twenty-three-year-old with "Faster" tattooed on her ass. Though …

"No," I said. "Kev wants me to write a booty novel."

"I keep telling him that ass sells."

"But you're an SF writer, Damian."

SF. Not "sci-fi." Impressive.

"That's what *I* keep telling him."

"Well, that *Convicta et Combusta* was a bit absurdist, but—"

"You saw that?!" Yep, you guessed it. My voice cracked.

She gave a sly smile. A dimple. You know I'm a sucker for dimples. I took a swig of my beer to dampen the warm spot growing in my … let's say, heart.

"Yeah," she said. "Egon Troyer put it on at Laughing Stock—what?—a year ago. I always see his stuff. I'm friends with his fiancée. I think Samara Herndon was the lead. She was really good."

"That woman *can* act," Kev smiled.

"Tell me about it," I swallowed.

"Sounds like you've got a fan, Damian," Kevin said, the devil in his eyes.

Then it hit me. Staring Girl.

"Holy shit," I said. "You were at WSQ a few weeks ago."

She smiled again, satisfied. The woman looked like she was about to say something, I edged forward involuntarily and was left dangling, as she turned to Kevin. "So, why do you want him to write a booty novel?"

"To make money."

She rolled her eyes. "Hell, I'll give him money." Somebody needed to. "Look, Vikram's about done setting up. We should get closer."

"Sure, I just need to settle up here."

Nandi shrugged, slid off the stool, and walked off. My eyes instantly became plastered to her slender back and pert ass. She moves with mesmerizing grace—like she was the African queen she was named after—or a gymnast. I tried—but I couldn't keep my eyes off her. Kev laughed.

"I knew it."

"What?"

"I knew you'd like her, nigger."

She disappeared into the gathering throng by the DJ booth, and I was finally able to look at my best friend. "Her thighs touch."

"What?"

"Her thighs touch. A woman's thighs should touch. At least a little. Samara, her thighs never touched."

"Far from it."

"Hey."

He shrugged.

"I just like it when thighs touch. Who is she, anyway?"

"She's my new singer who you've *refused* to see no matter how many times I've asked. Feel stupid now, don't you?"

I didn't answer.

"Won't miss our next practice, will you?"

Yet again. Silence. I refused to prove him right.

"You two aren't—" I gave vague gestures "—are you?"

He laughed, wholeheartedly—bitterly? "Oh hell no. Could you imagine it? She's a singer, dude. She needs to be *loved*, adored. Just like my pathetic ass. We'd just sit around all day waitin' to be loved by the other. Besides, even a dog doesn't shit where he eats."

He *wasn't* trying to hit that? She must be really talented. Or else she was another Yodit in the making.

"She isn't the someone you wanted me to see, is she?" I asked.

"Naw, man. But that will be coming up soon."

He settled our tab after getting us another round. I skipped on the rum but was more than happy with a fresh beer. I wobbled a little to my feet. I needed to but refused to slow down. I took another swig. A tiny, bronzed whirl spun past me into Kevin's arm. "Kevin!"

Kevin chuckled and ended the friendly hug. I couldn't make out the face, but this was a woman who carried the weight of the world on her ass. Very heavy. Very nice. Big booties are best. I was in my own fog enumerating the reasons I preferred fat asses over flat, wondering if this were indeed a false dichotomy—like King vs. X; Booker T. vs. the MGs—because there are millions of glutei that are both, when Kevin and his new honey turned to look at me. *God, I'm drunk*, I thought, as Kevin introduced us.

"Damian, this is Yanely. Yanely, Damian."

She was short and plump, with cinnamon skin and the biggest eyes. And really, really young. Her smile was warm. Or maybe it was just me. I had been drinking way too much. I knew at that moment that I was going to have the worst hangover in my life in the morning. Good. She reached unsteadily for my hair. She seemed a bit drunk, too.

"God, I just love your dreads," she slurred, slightly. "They're so long. How long have you been growing them?"

I looked up, thinking, to see Kevin slinking off into the crowd. He threw me one, last diabolical grin before disappearing amongst all the flesh.

Don Newcombe, "Nuke" (where colossal sax man, Sonny Rollins, got his nickname), 1955. Hitting something like .360 with 7 homers and 23 RBI. All that in only a little over 100 ABs. Not bad for a pitcher (going 20-5 with a 3.20 ERA and striking out 140 bastards ain't chopped liver, either). The 1955 Brooklyn Dodgers. Jackie Robinson, Roy Campanella, Gil Hodges, Carl Furillo, Duke Snider, Pee Wee Reese… Damn. My 1960 Pirates? Roberto Clemente was their *only bat. But Maz gave us that home run (take* that, *punk-ass Yankees).* We are family… *No, that was '79. Willie "Papa" Stargell, Dave "Cocaine" Parker, Bill "Mad Dog" Madlock, Tim Foli, Phil Garner.* Wu-Tang Killer Bees—*Bonds and Bonilla! Why did you let them go? Why?! How? How the hell did gimp-ass Sid Bream with his Frankenstein-reconstructed knees score all the way from second?! Think happy thoughts, Damian. Like my Steel Curtain Stillers.* Gerela's Gorillas are here for the show/And so is Franco's Army! *Naw, c'mon, Damian. Concentrate. Keep it baseball, homes. Yankees suck! Remind yourself to buy that vintage Clemente jersey…*

(Yes, ladies, I am the stereotypical male who thinks about baseball while having sex.)

Sex as conversation. Yanely and I. We know what's going to happen. Or at least have a pretty good idea. We'd be stupid if we didn't. Leering at each other the way we do. Fondling. But we have to be legit. We're not *animals*. So we talk. And talk. And talk. Filling the air with nothing. The music blares. Vindaloo mixes. And we talk. But we don't. There's nothing to talk about. Music she's never listened to. Music I haven't heard. Books she's never read. Books I refuse to read. Movies? TV? "Ever been to Pittsburgh?" "No." "Ever been to Houston?" "No." I don't even have cable. Besides, I only like movies that English speakers who roll their Rs care about. There's a decade between us. I've already been where she's going. Those tracks have long since dusted over. She couldn't follow in my footsteps even if she wanted to. But somehow, we've met here. Mojito. The music explodes. Pheromones ignite. Our tongues wag. Our fingers explore. There's way too much testosterone between us. Finally, she says, "Let's go."

Sex as song. She's been here before. I've been here before. Maybe I was wrong about that footstep thing. The world's not flat. I've circumnavigated the globe to land in Yanely's apartment seven years later. She turns the TV on Mute. She darkens that apartment. Her roommate, Irene, a little Asian powder puff of a girl's still at the club. She knows not to come home for awhile. Hopefully, she'll go get high with a little help from her friends. 'Cause we're about to hit her stash. Yanely hands me the papers and the baggie. I begin to roll. She turns on the stereo. Carlos Santana and Buddy Miles. "Free Form Funkafide Filth." Hell yeah. She knows her stuff. She knows how to be hip. Cool. Retro. Obscure. She knows this black-and-bronze fantasy and turns on the soundtrack. Will War be next? Azteca? El Chicano? Will she put on Willie Bobo and we boogaloo our booties across the apartment? I lick. I light. We smoke. *To Sir with Love* is on the set. Ah, Sidney, my ace boon coon. Buzz heaps upon buzz. My fingers dance along the folds of her plump, brown flesh. So soft, so firm. So *female*. We babble, but nobody's listening. Prince is on the stereo. "Adore." "How Come You Don't Call Me Anymore?" "Scandalous." Yeah, she's a pro. I don't give a *damn* about all the jockeys that were here before me. Oh shit, it is Saturday night! How cool is that? I focus on those pouting, raspberry lips of hers and dive in.

Sex as cinema. Intermission. She pulls away. Stands. I reach for her. "Insatiable." A finger to the lips, a smile. I sit back and watch. In the TV glow, a familiar scene unfolds. *Insatiable's my name when it comes to you...* She squirms, she writhes. Cine-seductive. A little high, a lot drunk, a mile off beat. The light bounces off her slow-grind hips. Her eyes are supposed to be siren slits. Her hand creeps through her long, black hair, tumbling into her face. I'm supposed to be seduced, I'm supposed to be beside myself with lust. I'm not supposed to be laughing—which is what I really want to do. Sharon Stone? Kim Basinger? Which anorexic vixen first vamped this idea of seduction? Why is Yanely not the first woman who's pulled this Esterhaus vaudeville act before me? Just because a punk-ass Baldwin brother is paid to be excited by this act on film doesn't mean I'd like it in the flesh. I'm gonna have to bust ole girl back down to the minors. But she's only twenty-two. She'll be back in the big leagues soon enough. I swallow hard on laughter, leer like the script says to, and move toward her again.

Sex as Olympic event. We're on the couch. We're against the wall. She's on the coffee table. I'm on the floor. We're both on the floor. Yes, the floor routine. Ribbons, hoops, balls. Stretch, contort, curl. Repeat. Half-twist, single Lutz, double axle, triple Lindy. My body's working on muscle memory. How long has it been exactly? Creaking, groaning, moaning. Pain, pleasure. Sheer exhaustion. Just keep up, Damian. She's so damned young. At thirty-two, I'm way past retirement age. But I'm young at heart, right? Sure, whatever. I see lots of aspirin, gallons of caffeine, Ben Gay, and a big greasy burger in my immediate future.

Sex as baseball. Well, you've read that one already.

Sex as memory. Yanely is adorable. Everything about her I like. I'm captivated by her every curve. How her rolls—when she's bent—deliciously cascade into the others. My tongue explores every crevice, every inch. The forehead. The lids that capture her wonderful, wide eyes. Her glowing cheeks and pouting lips. Her breasts—heavy yet light—and firm. Her hips and thighs. Round marble. Her cute, little mound of belly that shimmies down into a delicious glen. Everything's so soft. Everything screams, moans, coos woman. This woman, every woman. I find myself thinking of Samara and Mayrav and Keisha, Christy, and Steffi and every woman I've ever slept with and a few I simply messed around with and how they moved and moaned and cooed. I think of Ina and wonder how she'd look nude in the cathode blue of the television screen. And … Nandi? Where the hell did she come from? Priti?! And I force myself to think of Yanely, this adorable, young woman above, below, and beside me. We all deserve that much.

Sex as comedy. Sidney's kicking Cockney ass on screen, Prince is wishing me heaven, Gerela's got his gorillas, and Franco, his army. I don't remember how I ended up dangling upside down off the couch and how she's riding me like Catherine the Great on the Pony Express. But somehow, we tumble off. I hit my head. Groan. But we're still attached. And we laugh. We pulsate and we laugh. She digs in her heels and gallops all the way to Santa Fe. *La la la la la la la la la.*

Sex as tragedy. The sun's turning the night sky blue. And in the emerging light, when everything is done, I can see Yanely's eyes glistening with tears.

Sex as LL Cool J song. *Don't call it a comeback, I've been here for years…*

Sex as vomit. Yep. Twice. Not exactly the *coolest* exit, but I'm able to stumble home with a smile on my face, and a song in my heart.

WEDNESDAY, NOVEMBER 16, 20—
9:53 p.m.

Those schoolgirl days
Of telling tales and biting nails are gone…

"Damian!"

"Yeah. Hey, Kev."

"So, did a brutha do his job, or what?"

"Sure, man. It was the best wedding night I've ever had."

"You hit it?"

"Man, you know I don't talk about that crap."

"Ahhhhh, Lil Miss Manners got laid. I knew it."

"Anyway, what's her story?"

"I don't know. I think she's from Texas or Arizona, or something. Hangs out in the musician crowd. Likes dudes with dreads. Figured she'd like your Rapunzel ass."

"Wait a second. She wasn't the 'someone' you wanted me to meet, was she?"

"Naw, D. I wanted you to check out Vindaloo. But I guess you were a *little* preoccupied."

"Yeah. I guess I was. Why'd you want me to see him?"

"He's joining the band."

"Really?"

"Yeah, man. I'm tellin' you, I'm makin' moves. Flippin' the script. All those new millennium Negro catchphrases. You need to check us out before we go on tour."

"Sure, man. Next week."

"'Cause a Nandi, right?"

"Naw. You're my boy. You know I'll always support you."

"Riiiiiight."

"Should I call her?"

"Nandi?"

"Relax. Naw. Yanely."

"Aw, Jesus. Fucking Catholics. You're feeling guilty, aren't you?"

"I wouldn't say that. It's just that it's been a couple days. I ain't called, and I haven't heard from her. I don't know the proper etiquette in these situations. It's been so long."

"Like I'd fucking know."

"You got a point there. But should I?"

"Look, Damian. Don't go making something it's not."

"Yeah. Right. Right."

A friend who taught me right from wrong
And weak from strong
That's a lot to learn

"Hello?"

"Yes, uh ... Yanely?"

"Yeah?"

"It's Damian. From the other night."

"Oh. Hi."

"Just callin' to see what's up."

"Nothin'. Just looking for a job."

Oh yeah. She did mention something about temping or something, didn't she?

"Will you shut up?!"

"Uh, who was that? A kid?"

"Yeah. My daughter. Siobhan. I'm on the phone! Put that remote down!"

Hang up, Damian! Hang up, Damian! Hanguphanguphangup!

"Really? How old is she?"

"Four. And a little terror. But my mom refuses to take care of her anymore. So she shipped her ass up here with me. What can you do?"

Hang up.

"Are you there?"

"Yeah. I'm here."

I'm sorry. Did someone hear a train wreck?

"I thought I heard a noise. Anyway, yeah, well, I was wondering if you'd like to go out some time."

"Well, I'm kinda busy, ya know? The kid, the job search."

There's your out, dumb ass.

"Nothing serious. Coffee or something. My treat."

You IDIOT!!!

"Yanely?"

"Yeah. I'd have to bring Siobhan, though."

"Sure, why not? I love kids."

Now, why would you go and say something like that? Really, I think I'm just about through with you.

"Maybe I'll leave you with her then."

"Say, day after tomorrow."

"Put! That! Down! Yeah yeah, sure, Damian."

"See you then."

If you wanted the moon I would try to make a start
But I would rather you let me give my heart
To Sir with love!!!

FRIDAY, NOVEMBER 18, 20—
6:20 P.M.

Oh my God. I can't believe it. My sociological clock is ticking. I want a baby. Now, I've always liked kids (OK, when I was a kid, they were pretty shitty), but I'd always said that it was because they weren't mine. But I was just trying to be funny. I just love children. I don't know if it's that perpetuating the circle of life thing or their innocence or the sense of wonder they possess. I just love the little buggers.

I just hadn't realized the urge to have one of my own was so strong. It was always "a couple years from now" with Samara. I agreed. We couldn't afford one. She had her acting. I had my writing. We just didn't have the time nor the means. Now I don't care. Siobhan made me realize that. She's such an adorable, little thing. You can't help but fall in love. Her moms on the other hand…

Yanely's red Mini Cooper pulled up around noon. *Run, nigger, run* was echoing in my brain. But I stayed put and opened the door. Kevin was right. I am Catholic. I'd never really had a one-night stand. It wasn't like I've been willing to marry every woman I've ever slept with—like Pops had advised. I've just had to always wear a sports coat or tie with my casual sex. I could never hit it and quit it, like Kev. Or graze on chickenheads. That kind of conduct was more for the dog species of the male kingdom.

Something I never wanted to be. My dad was a dog, and I knew what kind of pain that could cause. The humiliation. And I never wanted to be the source of so much hurt. But looking back on it and on the horrible afternoon I'd just had with Yanely, I realize now that I'd been fooling myself. Granted, I'd never had a one-nighter. But how much better was the two-night, three-night, or four-week stand? Or just because I'd stay a little while, did it make it any better? And what the hell were fuck buddies like Mayrav? Just another way to have fun and not commit and to sit imperiously in the amen corner when my women friends would testify to the sins of my brothers. *I* was never like that.

I mean hell, I knew from the moment I met Yanely I didn't want a future with her. She's too young. We have nothing in common. But it was my wedding night, I was drunk and depressed, and I just wanted to have a little fun. I'm pretty sure she didn't want a future with me, either. It was just a good time to have. There was no way it could be more. Why couldn't I just let it be that? There were no professions of love. No deception on anybody's part. There was absolutely no reason for me to feel guilty. Yet, I did. I probably always will. And sleeping with Yanely one more time wouldn't change that.

But a brother had to try, right? :-)

My heart wasn't in it, though. It's just that the world is so different sober. My vision was no longer blurry and frayed. She wasn't as attractive as I'd remembered. Not Strobe Light Honey territory, but still … Not like I minded so much, though. It's not like anybody has ever confused *me* for a *Playgirl* model. And I would never cringe with having her on my arm.

Besides, I always hated it when guys dissected women into meat like they were Kobe steak. Like that three hundred-pound slob who's not on anybody's offensive line, talking about, "Yeah, she'd be kinda cute if she lost a coupla pounds." Yanely, though, had a layer of frost on her that chilled me to the bone. It was probably the stench from the rotted cheese that was apparently my face to her. She was probably thinking, *Damn, I was trying to hook up with Kevin and I got* this, *instead. I need to stop drinking.*

Her daughter, on the other hand, was all warmth. All smiles. She was a lot lighter than her mother with incredibly blue eyes. I was taken aback.

"Her father's Irish," Yanely said icily, pulling on a Marlboro Light. "So, where did you want to go again? Coffee, right?"

"Actually, I was thinking about the zoo."

"Ooooh, Mommy, could we?!"

Youbastardsonofabitchcocksucker, Yanely's eyes said to me. *Damian, fake a headache, heart attack, gunshot wound, and let's get outta here,* my head said to me. But where was I going to go?

"The zoo's open? It's like, November."

"That's the advantage of living down here. It's warm enough to stay open 'til December."

"Oh, great."

"So, can we go, Mommy?"

Infinity ticked by as Yanely and I looked at each other. Finally, she looked down at Siobhan with a smile. "Sure we can, sweetie."

"I'll drive," I volunteered.

"No, I got it."

Siobhan squealed in delight and grabbed my hand to lead me to Lord knows where. Yanely grabbed her jean jacket tighter to her voluptuous frame and trudged forward.

Lions and tigers and bears. Siobhan loved them all. She looked at everything with wide-eyed wonder. She was so full of exuberance and curiosity. *I* was actually excited, and I hate zoos. I had no clue animals could be so fascinating—outside of being medium rare on my dinner plate. "What's that?!" "A porcupine." "What's that?!" "A lemur." "What's that?!" "A red panda." "Pandas aren't red. They're black and white." "Well, it's not really a panda. They just call it that." "That's stupid." "Tell me about it." But she didn't like elephants.

"I don't like elephants."

"Why's that, Siobhan?"

"They smell."

"They probably think you smell, too."

"Nuh-uh. I took my bath today."

One of the elephants seemed to trumpet in dissent. It looked like she wanted her kid off her teats. Yanely gave a look of sympathy.

"See. You know what it said?" I asked Siobhan.

"No. What?"

"It said, 'Get that smelly Siobhan away from me. She *stiiiinks*."

"It did not."

"I'm telling you. That's what it said. I know. I speak Elephant."

"You do not," she gasped.

I stepped back and gave the best elephant call I could, spraying spit to the four winds. Siobhan laughed. Even Yanely smirked. Mama elephant seemed to shake her head in reply.

"See?"

Siobhan was all laughs. "You're silly."

If this girl was a terror, she definitely left the horror flick at home. She grabbed my and her mother's hands, and we walked on through the bright, autumn day. Yanely was warming up, smoking less and less, and really seemed to be enjoying herself. We found ourselves smiling more and more at each other. We were looking like one, big, happy, blended family. Onlookers were probably baffled about how the brown Mexican and black black dude had a virtually white kid. But we didn't seem to be minding. We were just basking in Siobhan's joy, and I was wondering if it made any sense to date a woman out of affection for her daughter.

"Wow! Look at those!"

"The flamingoes?"

"They're so pink! Why isn't that one pink?!"

"She's too young. See, flamingoes eat stuff with things called car-o-te-noids that make them turn pink. When that one grows up, eating that stuff, she'll be pink, too."

"If I eat car-car-car-noids, will I grow up and be pink, too?"

"Sure. You can be Pink Siobhan, Super Hero. You can fly through the air and beat up bad guys."

"I *hate* bad guys."

"Me, too. Let's go get 'em." I picked her up and flew her through the air. She giggled all the way to the car, where she promptly fell asleep.

We drove back—mainly in silence—with Maná playing in the background. The sheen of the day quickly lost its luster, and a tension settled in the Mini. Conversation spasmed for a few minutes and quickly died. Yanely pulled up to my place with a deep exhalation.

"Well, thanks for a really cool day, Damian," she finally said. "I really enjoyed myself."

"Yeah. Me, too. Siobhan's a great kid."

"I see she's got you fooled."

I don't know. She *is* the girl's mother. Clearly, she knows the child better than I do. But I found it hard to believe that that little darling was *Bad Seed* material.

"Well, yeah," I hedged. "Let's do it again some time."

Yanely's bronze face darkened. "Yeah, well…"

"Yeah?"

"Her father's back in the picture," she confessed, in one, quick breath.

"Oh."

"Well, he's always been in the picture. I moved up here 'cause a him. But he'd moved out on Friday."

Wow, you don't waste any time.

"But he came back this morning. Said he wants to work things out. He's a real prick, you know. I don't even know if I want him in our lives. But what can I do? He *is* Siobhan's father. You … you understand, don't you?"

I tried to hide my glee under a show of disappointment. This was *really* a situation I wanted no parts of. "Yeah. Of course, I do, Yanely," I said, chin dramatically low on my chest.

"Good," she exhaled deeply, and offered up a tearful smile.

"Well, good luck with that."

I gave her a peck on the cheek and bound out the car. My steps were really too light on the way to the porch. I heard her annoying, little horn, and turned. Yanely was vigorously puffing on a cigarette. The car whipped around. Little Siobhan whipped around with it, waving enthusiastically until they were out of sight.

Damn, I'm gonna miss that kid.

SATURDAY, NOVEMBER 19, 20—

12:22 A.M.

"I'm tellin' y'all, you need to go," Bob [If you do not remember this punk, please refer to the **TUESDAY, OCTOBER 9, 20—** entry; I hate constantly dropping narrative hints to remind the reader] was pontificating about his latest trip. "Kuala Lumpur is the bomb."

"Do people say that, anymore?" I asked.

"Who cares?" he continued. "The place is cool as hell. Modern, colonial, tropical, and Third World—"

"Do people say *that*?"

"No, they're 'developing nations' now. Damn, Day. Will you let a brother speak?"

"Be my guest. But I thought we were African-Americans now."

"It may have gone back to 'black,'" Malik suggested.

"Like you'd know," Kevin interjected.

"Well, how the hell do you say 'beat down' these days?" Bob threatened.

I threw my hands up in surrender.

"The food's great. And cheap. Four bucks for an entire meal." I didn't dare ask why a spoiled, rich kid would care about cost. "I had the best fried chicken in my life at this Indian joint."

"Fried chicken?" Kevin asked, incredulously.

"Yeah. And collard greens and chitterlings, too."

We were dumbfounded.

"OK, that last part was bullshit. But yes, fried chicken. You can seriously grub in KL. And they got these really cool clubs, and shit. I mean, it's a real hip Muslim place. No Kanduhar, that's for sure. Only the Arabs wear burqas, or whatever they're called. And the women. Shit."

Kevin, Bob, this drummer Raheem from Kev's new band, Malik, and I were there. It was awkward at first with Malik—especially since nobody else knew what had happened between us. But ole boy had wanted to have it out before things got too freaky deaky. Why he chose the bathroom as confessional, I'll never know. I mean, who wants to have a heart-to-heart with your dick in your hands? But there we were, dueling urinals, straight talking. Well, he was talking. I was a little distracted, having a little urethral problem.

"Hey, Damian," he'd started. "I just wanted you to know there's no bad blood."

"Uh-huh."

"I mean, we're cool, right?"

"Yeah. Of course."

"You sure?"

"Yeah, Malik. Damn. We boys. You know that."

"Cool. 'Cause I wasn't mad at what you said. Seriously. I needed to hear that shit. I mean, it seems like there are two kindsa people these days, know what I'm sayin'?"

"Uh..."

"Like there are people who are purposely assholes. Ya know, like those women who proudly call themselves 'bitches,' thinking it gives them license to be pricks. Folks who are always out to offend. Like a bullshit, reactionary response to all things PC."

"Right." I was really having a tough time.

"Then, there are folks who *never* want to offend. Who *never* want to ruffle feathers. They think that they're being a bad friend if they hurt somebody else's feelings. But ya know, sometimes people need their feelings hurt. Sometimes, it's the best medicine.

"I mean, shit, Damian. With Miss Withers. Donna. I was fucking up. I mean I hadn't done anything. But I was going to. I knew I was. I guess that's why I went to you instead of Kevin. I needed a coach, not a cheerleader. I needed someone to tell me I was fucking up before I threw away ten years of my life. And you did that. You told me I was fucking up. You're a real friend, man. Hey, are you OK?"

"Yeah. I guess," I said, wiping sweat from my brow. "I don't know. I think something might be wrong with me."

"And women," Bob continued, back at our booth. "Damn, fellas. So many, so fine. Well, the Chinese. Some a them are cute, but they're really, really tiny. Like sticks. No, twigs. And shit, I've been a twelve-year-old boy, not like I wanna screw one. Besides, everybody considers them white over there, and y'all know how I feel about that."

"Naw, maybe I should ask Hilda."

"Fuck you, Damian," he said, over our laughter. Bob's one spook who refuses to give up the ghost. "But the Malays got a little booty on 'em. And the Indian babes. I mean, daaaamn. First off, they are b-l-a-c-k. Not like your monkey-ass, Day. But Crayola black. And they are just *stacked*. Hips and ass all over the place. I was in African-American heaven, y'all. And some a them, like remember that fine, black Barbie doll babe, Natalie, from school?"

"Ahhhh, Natalie," Kev and I both said, dreamily, in unison.

"Yeah. I thought I saw a woman who looked just like her. I almost got run over gawking at her."

"Damn." Kev and me again.

"And remember that one a year below us, uh Nicole, Nicole…?"

"Robinson?"

"No."

"Thomas?"

"No."

"Thompson?"

"Johnson?"

"James?"

"Walker?"

"No."

"How many Nicoles did you guys go to school with?" Raheem asked.

"That's nothing," Kevin said, "there were three Jennifer Joneses in our year alone."

"Damn."

"Well," Kev continued, "like you want black folks being but so creative when naming their kids."

We all laughed.

"That reminds me, Malik," I said. He was all ears, still trying to prove there was no bad blood. "I saw a name at your school, D-a-t-a-v-i-s-e-s. How do you say that?"

"Dah-tay-vee-us."

"Geez."

"Yeah. And if you mispronounce it, he's likely to cut you."

"Now see," Bob chimed in, "why should the child have to pay for his parents' illiteracy? Simpson. Yeah, Nicole Simpson."

"Oh yeah," Kev agreed, grimly. "So fucked up what happened to her."

"Hey, Byrd, didn't you…?" I asked.

"Four times," he beamed. "She was damned nice."

"Yes, she was," Bob affirmed.

"Hancock, you too? Am I the only fool who didn't…"

"You may very well have been," Bob chuckled. "But it's not too late. She's got a twin in Malaysia. The damned thing was, though, every time I hit the clubs, there wasn't an Indian babe to be found. They were all over the place during the day, but nowhere to be found at night."

"Well, it sounds like they were camouflaged," Raheem quipped.

"Yeah, maybe," Bob continued. "There were Malays all over the place, though. And to be honest, Sukiyaki was *all right*."

"Was that her name?" I asked, knowing the answer.

"That's what I called her."

"That's fucked up, Hancock."

Bob shrugged.

"And racist," Malik added.

"You know what," Bob started, the high horse waiting for him to mount, "I'm on a mission."

"What? To screw a woman in every country you go to?"

"Naw, I stopped that nonsense in Djibouti." (A reference to one of Bob's old comedy routines: "Where were you last night?" "In Djibouti." "Oh really. Did you like it?" "It's pretty hot and humid. But it's nice. I'd definitely come again." You get the idea.) "Naw, man. I'm on a mission to bring back racism."

"You trippin'," Raheem said. We all agreed.

"Naw, y'all. Think about it. Back when there was good, old-fashioned racism, we had strong brothers and sisters, I mean real superhero-type motherfuckers. Like Harriet Tubman and Sojourner Truth. Frederick Douglass, Charles Drew, Dubois, Booker T. Washington, Ida B. Wells, Marcus Garvey, Rosa Parks, Paul Robeson."

"Preach, brother! Preach!"

"Coltrane, Miles, Louis Armstrong, Joe Louis, Jackie Robinson, Muhammad Ali, Sidney Poitier, MLK, Malcolm X, Angela Davis, Ellison, Wright, Thurgood Marshall."

"Can I get a witness?!"

"That brother who helped pioneer open-heart surgery, the gas mask, Benjamin Banneker. The list goes on and on. Richard Pryor, for fucksakes. Folks that really made you proud to be black." He stopped to take a breath.

"But now, when they tell us racism is over, all we get is Poof Daddy, Clarence Thomas, and Will Smith. Shit ain't right, y'all."

No comment.

"I just think it's time to bring back some *Birth of a Nation*-type racism. Light a fire under some folks' asses."

"And a noose around our necks," I said, standing up.

I had to get out of there. Go to the bathroom, something. I went to the internet jukebox instead. Bob's little harangue was making me feel a little nostalgic. I suddenly wanted an Afro and a Black Power pick. And some funk. While making my selections, another memory popped into my head. I finished up and turned.

There was a little commotion going on. Kevin had gotten up and was scrambling for an extra chair. Nandi had arrived. He moved the chair next to his and offered it to her. He was acting so chivalrously around her, I was surprised he wasn't wearing armor.

I sat down. Nandi was looking good, in a retro pink velour sweat suit and "dissent is patriotic" T-shirt, hair pulled back in a ponytail. You know you're fine when you can look beautiful in a sweat suit. Of course, having lived with a woman for seven years, I know how much effort can go into a devil-may-care look.

"You throw on some tejano, D?" Kevin asked me, with a deceptive smile.

"What?"

"Or a good, old bolero? Maybe some mariachi?" he continued.

"What are you gettin' at, Kev?"

He kept that smile and looked to Nandi. Was I being sabotaged? "D here's got a sudden taste for Mexican." Yep. He turned back to me. "How *is* Yanely, anyway?"

"Uh, she's fine," I hesitated, and looked around. Bob and Malik perked up. I'm pretty sure they knew what was going on. Raheem looked oblivious. Nandi gave me an uncomfortable smile. I think she knew, too. "Met her little daughter today. What a sweetheart. We went to the zoo."

"That musta been … nice."

Should I get up and slap the motherfucker?

"Yeah," I conceded. "Actually it was. That little girl is so cute. So light. I thought you said she liked bruthas with dreads." Might as well own it, right?

"No," he corrected. "I said *dudes* with dreads. Remember that bassist, Rory, from Bomb-Sniffing Dogs?"

"That little Mick bastard who always liked getting drunk and fighting?" Bob asked, trying to prove a point.

"Will you stop?" Malik asked.

"Nope."

"No," Kevin answered. "The WASPafarian with dreads down to his ass."

"He's the daddy?" I asked.

"Damn skippy."

Those schoolgirl days…

"'To Sir with Love'?'" Nandi chimed in. "You picked this, Damian?"

"Yeah," I smiled. "I love this song. Well, actually the movie, but Lulu's cool, too. I mean, Sidney was so bad-ass, makin' those British bastards call him 'Sir.' Or like when he busted that 'They call me Mr. Tibbs' line on Rod Steiger's cracker ass in *In the Heat of the Night*."

Did I just say "cracker"? Bob is truly insidious.

"I thought that was Carroll O'Connor," Malik volunteered.

"No," she corrected. "That was the TV show."

"Right," I continued. "I mean, Sidney Poitier always demanded dignity. The first proud black man on film, really. Sure, you got the Panthers and Melvin Van Peebles, but Poitier was the first, truly bad-ass brother in my life."

"Exactly," Bob piped up. "And when did all that happen? When America was officially racist. Now, it'd be like, 'Boy, what do they call you up there in that fancy, northern city?' And Will Smith would go, 'Like, they call me the Fresh Prince of Bel Air,' and go do the Running Man off-stage."

"Jesus, Bob, you're incorrigible."

I stood up again.

"Don't go throwin' those SAT words at me, boy. You know I'm right," he chuckled.

"Burn, baby, burn," I said, raising a sarcastic fist. Speaking of which…

I was trying hard to act like I wasn't irritated at the whole scene and tried not to run to the bathroom. I really tried not to scream when I pissed in pain or shriek when I saw the pus. I tried my damnedest to act cool when I rushed back to the table and slapped some money down on the table. I did say, "Damn," when I heard the Isleys singing "Fight the Power." And I nearly failed in my attempt to not turn around and slug Kev when he said, "Tell Yanely I said, 'Hey.'" I mean, exactly what the fuck was his deal? But I was in a hurry. I had a lot of pissing and screaming to do, and I wanted to be alone.

6:37 P.M.

Oh, Doctor, doctor, can't you see I'm burning, burning
Oh, Doctor, doctor, is this love I'm feeling?

Dr. Katrina Jenkins. A fine sister with a close-cropped natural and a splash of gray. High forehead and intelligent eyes. I'd say mid- to late-thirties. I think under different circumstances I could've really developed a crush on her. But I was really hoping to never see her again. Who needs the humiliation?

In all honesty, when I revisited this doc-in-a-box this morning, I really had no expectations of seeing Dr. Jenkins. I just assumed that the physicians in these places just picked up extra shifts here or were on some sort of rotation. What were the odds, right? Well, whatever they were, they were definitely against me.

And boy, I was feeling like a hard-luck case, if there ever was one. Having to come here twice in a year—after having nothing even resembling a cold sore for the first thirty-one years of my life. The last time, in May, I was itching madly and was buckling under the humiliations being heaped upon me at the time. The tour had been a wreck, and Samara and I were falling to pieces. The last chunk of dread being my coming to this place.

Dr. Jenkins had looked down her nose at me. I looked up at her with a pair of doe eyes I normally don't possess. "Syphilis," she had diagnosed, I think a bit disdainfully.

I'd groaned. How could Samara have done this to me? I had known things weren't going well at all. I think that was why we were planning to get married. A life preserver in the tsunami of our relationship. Stupid, I know. But when do people think rationally? But Samara ultimately had said "Fuck it" and swam for a lifeboat of her own. That would've been fine (no, it wouldn't have been—I still would've been devastated), but why did she have to strap me with the syphilis rock, pulling me under, before dipping herself? I was near tears.

"You know," Dr. Jenkins had continued, "if you are to have unprotected sex, against which I strongly advise, you should be in a long-term, *monogamous* relationship."

It had been a nightmare. I was going mad like Edgar Allen Poe. I thought I was going to shatter right there on the examination table. I'd gathered the robe around myself and swallowed hard. "I am," I'd finally gasped. "For seven years now."

Her stern face had suddenly melted. It had sympathy written all over it. It just made me feel even more pathetic than I'd already felt. She also swallowed hard on something, and said, "Damn."

Exactly. But this scene was completely different. There was no sympathy in Dr. Jenkins' voice or face. I don't blame her. I'm a two-time loser. And I should know better, especially after what Samara had pulled on me. And I do know better. I know I don't even know *half* the shit that's out there. I knew the risks going in, so to speak. I just didn't care. I have excuses (wedding week, the Mary Jane, beer, rum), but I really don't have any. I saw Yanely's delicious, naked body, saw my opportunity, heard "When We're

Dancing Close and Slow" on the stereo, said, "¡chingalo, rene!" and dove right the fuck in.

So now I found myself the object of derision in a damned robe that refused to close in the back.

"Wow," she said, sarcastically. "Syphilis and now gonorrhea. It's like you're trying to hit for the cycle."

Damn. That attractive, that intelligent, a single doctor who throws around baseball references. And she doesn't even want to touch my diseased ass with latex gloves.

"Not like I want to hit a home run," I said, deflated.

"Well, at least the infection's limited to the genitals. Your eyes don't seem to be infected."

My eyes? How the hell do you get gonorrhea of the eye…? Oh shit.

"Are you sure?" I asked, my voice cracking a little.

"Yes. I'm sure."

I was about as relieved as one can be in these situations.

"Should I give you the speech again?" she asked.

The (not-so) funny thing is that over the years, I'd developed a venereal wall of defense in my mind. I'd never had a desire to cheat on Samara, but there had been times when somebody would pique a bit of curiosity. And since I knew that infidelity was a process—that you didn't just slip and fall into a field of poom poom—that it was a journey that one took—you're curious, make eye contact, flirt, approach, fill the air with lies, flirt some more, deny to yourself and your target that your partner had never really ever existed, keep flirting, get the digits, contrive liaisons, etc.—I'd decided that I had to never take the first step. STIs (I think that's what they're called now) were a great deterrent for me. Who wants to bring back one of those? "Honey, I'm home!" I think that's what Samara had said to me. But that's another story. So, every time I saw an attractive woman, one who showed the least bit of interest in me, I'd picture her crotch a diseased pasture of oozing pustules of Chlamydia, HPV, herpes, HIV, and yes, ironically, gonorrhea and syphilis.

After Samara gave me a parting gift and thanked me for playing *The Price Is Right*, I worked long and hard to tear down that visual image I had of other women. I was going to be single and with pus-pregnant pussies popping in my head I was going to remain so for a mighty long time. It took months, obviously. It hovered on the edge of my head with Ina. I had a glimpse during my tango with Mayrav. It didn't so much as duck its ugly mug in with Yanely. And see where that got me?

"'For the wages of sin is death,'" Dr. Jenkins stated.

"'But the gift of God is eternal life through Jesus Christ our Lord,'" I continued for her.

She actually cracked a smile. I guess she didn't know a syphilitic brother could get all *Romans* on her ass. I was a Religion minor, for godsake.

"Well, just so you know."

"Seems like life won't let me forget."

Dr. Jenkins gave me a shot and a rainbow assortment of pills. I was on my way.

SUNDAY, NOVEMBER 20, 20—
1:42 P.M.

"Hello?"

"Uh, yeah ... Yanely?"

"Oh, Damian ... Uh, I meant to—"

"Yeah, well, I think you should probably go see a doctor."

"I was ... going to tell you to do the same ... actually."

MONDAY, NOVEMBER 21, 20—
2:19 A.M.

"So, why'd you break it off with her?"

"It wasn't like that, Kev. Rory's back in the picture."

"I don't think he's ever totally out of it."

"Apparently not."

"So now what?"

"Man, I'm just trying to piss in peace."

"What?"

"Nothing. Nothing at all."

"See, D, your problem is, you're looking for love when you *should* be out there looking for ass."

"I'm just trying to look for enough words to fill a book."

"What? I already gave you the first two sentences."

"And I will be forever grateful, brother man."

"No need to be sarcastic, punk. Anyway, you just need to get out there and get laid."

"You're right, Kev. I'm just *burning* with desire. I just need to quench this fire."

"Exactly. And once that's over, the words will just flow. You'll be able to write *thirty* booty novels. Or better yet, a *love* story. I decided—love's a much better sell. Chicks dig it."

"Hell, what do I know about that crap? Love is for beautiful people. Like you and Nandi. Maybe I should just hold off a couple weeks and write about your burgeoning love affair. How a playa goes straight with the love of a good woman."

"Sheeit. Put down the pipe, Damian. That shit ain't ever gonna happen."

"Why you gonna act like you don't like ole girl?"

"It ain't that. I mean, you know me. It's just that … you believe in auras?"

"I believe in ceftriaxone."

"Dude, when did Frank Gorshin die and make you the Riddler?"

"Sorry, I haven't smoked in awhile. I don't know how to think with a clear head. No, Kevin. I don't know if I believe in auras, or not."

"Well, let's act like you do. And see, me. I put out this, like 'stank motherfucker' vibe. Like I'm a playa. 'Cause, to be honest, that's what I be—qualms about the moniker aside. Actually, no. I'm not. I'm not trying to play anybody. I tell babes what I'm out for. If they want to try to make it about more, that's on them. But, because I emit this 'playa' aura, I attract babes who like stank motherfuckers. Ya know, the ones who are all about sex—'cause that's what I'm all about."

"Riddle me this…"

"C'mon now, you get it. Like, like attracts like. A good girl rolls to me, and she'll just get her heart broken. The older ones know I'm full of shit. The younger ones learn real quick."

"You cool with that?"

"Mostly. I mean, I ain't gonna change. I know that. I don't ever really wanna change. None of your 'love of a good woman' crap's ever gonna make me see the light, either."

"Just ask Yodit."

"That ain't right."

"Still."

"Anyway, your girl Nandi, she knew who I was the moment she laid eyes on me. She could sense my aura, dude. I mean, I wasn't even coming at her with my dick on my sleeve, so to speak. I could tell she was really smart. So, I played the reserved intellectual."

"Ha."

"Hey, I can do that. I'm a sensitive artist in pain, you know that?"

"Your torture is readily apparent, sure."

"So yeah, I didn't drop one, single line. And can the sarcasm. But not one line. Instead, we talked music history and theory, my vision behind the new band. How wonderful her tape was. She does have an amazing voice. You would've been proud of me, Damian. I never leered, didn't give that famous Kevin Byrd smile, never told her how beautiful she was, I knew how to play this one."

"And?"

"Dude, she just leaned toward me at one point, and said, 'You're full of shit, aren't you?'"

"Ha! She is cool."

"Yeah, right. And I said, 'Not about the music.' And it's true. Music's something I never bullshit about … not anymore."

"Well, there goes my beautiful people love story."

"You just need one of your own. You try computer dating, yet?"

"You know, I'm thinking being single might not be so bad."

"Screw that, bruh. You need to get back on that horse."

"Man, if that bitch throws me one more time, I'm likely to end up in a coma."

"Hell, at least have a little fun 'til it does. Try the on-line thing. And stop talking about me being beautiful. I'm getting a little worried."

DATE: Tuesday, November 22, 20— 12:29 P.M.
FROM: sambohannon@towpow....
TO: drcross@wintersoldiers....
SUBJECT: The Clap your hands, yall

HA! HA! HA! HA! HA! HA!

DATE: Tuesday, November 22, 20— 1:17 P.M.
FROM: clarissafranklin@yippeeyo....
TO: drcross@wintersoldiers....
SUBJECT: Thanksgiving Dinner

Dear Damian,

Your uncle and I are really looking forward to Deirdre and your coming for Thanksgiving. We have even prepared your old room.
Love,

Aunt Clarissa

TUESDAY, NOVEMBER 22, 20—
9:17 P.M.

All right. That's it. No more listening to Kevin. He has no clue what he's talking about (all right, the booty novel wasn't *that* bad of an idea—but God, "I'm in some ass right now"; what self-respecting Oprahphyte would see that and keep reading?). The on-line thing was a bad idea. OK, it wasn't a bad idea. It was actually a very good idea. Just not for me. Just not right now.

I just wasn't feeling right about it. I started feeling too much like a consumer, like I wanted to kick the tires and take 'er for a spin. I signed onto two sites and was immediately taken aback by how many attractive, single women were out there with high IQs and a lot more money than I could ever make. I was wondering why I'd never met them while I was out prowling the streets. All I could manage to find was gonorrhea.

But then, as I kept going, I started becoming more and more critical. Even snarky. Could I actually ever date a Baptist (I'm thinking Ina would say, "No.")? Why does cute Pacific Islander, Joy, darker than a lunar eclipse, only want to date white dudes? Why is Minerva, who seems perfect in every way, single at thirty-three? Why does "sexymary" have "Richard" as her real name? She doesn't even have an Adam's apple. Can *all* these women really like football? Should I start hanging out at the sports bar more often? Why does Dori have children—but not at home? Whassup wit' *dat*? Chanelle has beautiful eyes—but are they constantly plastered to her TV in the bathroom? The bathroom?! Why do you need a TV in the bathroom? What could possibly be that interesting? How can Sayira love heavy metal? *All* these sisters can't possibly have Native American ancestry. Not recently, anyway. But look at that good hair. Why would Nancy take a picture with five kids? You *say* they're not all yours, but ... Mimiglam, I think I love you, but they haven't built a condom strong enough for me to want to have another fling any time soon. I wish you were looking for more. There was never any "too tall," "too short," "too chunky," more than one "too skinny," and a lot of "but she ... but she ... but ... but ... but..."

You ass, when the hell did you become God's gift, the perfect genetic experiment with Denzel's good looks, Bruce Lee's body, Dave Chappelle's humor, and Stephen B. Hawking's genius? You're sitting up here, alone, in your bedroom, dissecting every woman into her parts (hair, lips, eyes, breasts, uterus...), performing dating autopsies without ever having met a single one of them. How would they dissect you? "How much money do you make? My God, that little?! What am I? The Salvation Army?!" "Look at the gut on him. I bet he can't even see his own penis." "You call that a penis?! There should really be another name for something that small. Like 'quark,' or something." "Ooooh, nothing at all like his photo. That extra dimension really *does* come in handy." "What? Was that a joke? And he's laughing. God, this bastard thinks he's Dave Chappelle, or something." You're too short, too fat, and too damned broke, Damian.

I started feeling really bad about myself. Like I really didn't have anything to offer these virtual women. Screw Kevin and his stupid ideas. What did he know about computer dating or dating, period? All he ever does is show up, and women are ready to do all kinds of splits for the man. That isn't dating. That ain't love. That's some *Mutual of Omaha Wild Kingdom*-type shit. Animal sex. Musk flying everywhere. That's not dating, not love. That's not what being with a woman is really like. That's Disneyland, and Kevin's just an engorged tourist. Like watching the Olympics. You see these amazing athletes and their incredible feats at their peaks without ever having to witness the four years of blood, sweat, tears, and injuries that got them there. And Kev just sits back, chomping on popcorn while his conquests pull Mary Lou Rettons off his Jack Johnson.

He's never had to suffer and struggle with a woman. Be a team. Has never had to deal with evil moods. Never had to live with her disappointment in him. He's never had to come home from work with too little money in his pocket and not nearly enough on his paycheck. He's never yelled and screamed and cried with her. When life's pressures were a little too much, when the frustrations fray her nerves. Hold her clammy hand as she told her parents that this was the man she loved. Weather their scorn storm. He's never seen her without her make-up or even her second tier of panties. He's never had to be there to watch her cramp and bleed. Or worry when the late period came way too early in her life. He's never had to wash the vomit from her hair and carry her to bed when she was too sick and weak to do it herself.

He's never had a woman do it for him, either. He's never had her humor him when he's told the same tired joke, the same exhausted story, for the umpteenth time. Or read his book until her eyes bled with all the violence. Never had her love his Steelers because she loved him and wear his oversized Franco Harris jersey—her legs, every bit of her, the most beautiful sight one could ever behold. He's never had that moment, that oh-so precious moment, just looking at her. Just looking. And everything is just perfect. Right. The sun, her hair, that cute little wrinkle in her forehead. And you can't take your eyes off her. Everything is right in the world, everything is perfect. Because you're with her and she's with you. And nothing can be better than this moment, right here, sitting at the kitchen table, eating your muesli. And you smile. And she sees you. And she smiles. Awkwardly. "What?" she asks. And you're so happy. Everything's so right. You just want to freeze this moment in your brain, your heart, every cell and neuron that has ever been or will ever be a part of you. You keep on smiling. "What is it, Damian?" And you simply chuckle. "Oh … nothing." You break your smile for another spoonful. Everything is aaaallllllll right.

Suddenly, I started feeling bad for Kevin.

WEDNESDAY, NOVEMBER 23, 20—
8:17 A.M.

Look, I am *not* an asshole. I am not one of those people who enjoys pissing others off or hurting them or even watching them squirm. I don't even like mild annoyance all that much. I'm not perfect, granted. I'm not one of those Jains, wearing a mask so I don't inhale and kill an insect or sweep in front of me so I don't accidentally step on the little buggers. I *can* hurt a fly. And I'll fuck up a cockroach. And I have hurt people in the past and will in the future. It's part of being human. But I don't do it on purpose. I don't revel in it. Hell, I feel guilty if I don't hold the door open for somebody with bags in their hands.

That's why this last hour hurt so much. I hurt my cousin. I don't know why DiDi did it. We both knew what was going to happen. It doesn't blunt the guilt I feel, though.

She woke me up just a little while ago before going to work and sat down next to me on my bed. I'd actually just fallen asleep.

"Mom told me she's called and emailed you."

I yawned, rubbed my eyes, and groaned, "She has."

"So?" Deirdre asked, expectantly. "Are you coming with me?"

Don't get me wrong. I love Aunt Clarissa to death. She's a beautiful woman, an angel. I owe her everything. Uncle Frank, on the other hand…

Uncle Frank is old school. Seventy-five years old with the wrinkles and temperament to show for it. A Korean War veteran who helped integrate "this man's army" and a life-long member of the NAACP. Nothing was ever easy for Uncle Frank.

And I think he thinks everything's been too easy for me (despite *overwhelming* evidence to the contrary). After my folks died and I'd moved in with them, he constantly let me know his displeasure. He was never actually cool with me. When I was a kid, Uncle Frank always looked like something had died when I was in the room. He used to call me "Sorry." And when he was unusually disgusted, he'd spell it out and add as many Rs as he deemed appropriate for the situation. I think it was his idea of toughening me up, or something. He thought the world was brutal for black folks and growing up during the Depression and WWII and Jim Crow, he just *knew* I was soft. He didn't like the fact that I drew all the time and read books. He hated that I didn't stick with football through high school. He didn't like the way I talked. All proper, and shit. He didn't think all those black folks had struggled and died for centuries so that I could draw superheroes and try to read Camus and talk like white folks, have white friends, and (horror of horrors) maybe date white girls. Maybe he was scared that maybe they had.

When I moved in at the tail end of my sophomore year, things had only gotten worse. Admittedly, I didn't try to make them any better. I was a head case. Come to think of it, maybe I should've been on anti-depressants. But that only would have made me weaker in Uncle Frank's eyes. But to have your moms die in a hospital and your father in prison within a month of each other is a lot to handle—especially for a sixteen-year-old. I was more withdrawn than ever, hardly ever leaving my room. Not even to go to school. I'd started smoking cigarettes and marijuana. Got into more than my fair share of fights. Almost got suspended twice.

Uncle Frank would have none of it. He yelled at me constantly, calling me "S-O-R-R-R-R-R-R-R-*R*-Y." He always bowed up on me, threatening to throw me out, kick my ass. He'd been in the Army, after all, fighting the North Koh-reans and Chinese, what chance did a little Negro like me have? Finally one night, I'd had enough and told him to do it, kick my ass. Since he couldn't do it to the North Koh-reans and Chinese and had to sue for peace. He shoved my head through a wall. I just laughed at him, picking chunks of plaster out of my throbbing hair. It wasn't nothing I ain't had before.

And after that, he knew I was tough. The only thing he could do was kick me out. Aunt Clarissa stopped him. I stayed. But it was tense. I finally felt at home. And wanted to leave. After that, I got my ass a job at Mickey Ds and volunteered to close every night. We barely saw each other after that. I graduated from high school, went to college, and have spent a total of, maybe, thirty-four hours in the Burgh ever since.

"Now, why would you go ask me something like that, DiDi?"

"Because my mother would really like to see you, Dami," she said, almost pleading.

I tilted my head and just stared at her.

"He's getting better," she defended. "He really is. I think he's actually started to accept the fact that I'm a lesbian. He even asks about Priti. And wants to meet her. Can you believe it? I think he's really starting to see the light."

"Yeah, yeah. You told me."

"And he actually asks after you."

This was really becoming too painful. I didn't want an olive branch. I'd burn the motherfucker if offered. There's just some hatred you can't let go, and you can really start to hate the person who tries to snatch it from you. I didn't want to hate DiDi. She's my cousin, my oldest friend, maybe even my best, why was she doing this to me?

"There is such a thing as redemption, ya know?" she proffered.

"I know, bu—"

"No, look. My dad asks about you. He's trying. He's old. And yes, he's sick. And frail. I don't know, maybe he's seen the errors of his ways. Maybe he knows he was never, ever fair with you—"

"Ha!"

"But listen—" she was actually tearing up "—no really, listen. You are the two men in my life I love most. You always have been. Can't you just try? Just this once? I can't promise perfection. Lord knows, Dad and I still have our problems. But he's trying. He really is. Can't you give him that? Can't you at least try?"

She stopped and inhaled. Her right hand jabbed at the tears in her eyes.

My stomach started cramping up. I wanted to put a reassuring hand on her shoulder. But I don't do those sorts of things. I just couldn't.

"I can't," I finally said.

"Why?" she cried.

"You know why, Deirdre."

She swallowed hard, composed herself. "I know, Damian. I know." She exhaled and chuckled briefly. "I can't seem to get anybody to go to Pittsburgh with me. Not you. Not Priti."

I hadn't realized. "Oh," I said. I couldn't stand seeing her like this. The room felt shrouded in guilt. "Look," I cringed, "can we shoot for Christmas?"

Her face instantly brightened. I knew I was going to regret this. "You promise?"

"Now, just because I say something doesn't make it a promise."

"I know," she said. "Do you promise?"

"Look, babe, it's not like folks can live outside of history. And your father and I have a hell of a history."

"Tomes. But you'll try, won't you?"

It was my turn to exhale. "I'll try. For Christmas."

"Good." She slapped me on the knee and stood. A new bounce in her step. "Your room. It smells … clean."

"I've stopped smoking."

"And I was gonna give you my stash. An early Christmas present."

"Give it to one of your battered women. They need it more than I do."

"True dat."

She started making her way out of my room.

"Hey, DiDi…"

"Yeah?"

"Sorry about Priti."

"No problem," she smiled. "She said the same thing. It's gonna be one hell of a Christmas."

4:21pm

Time for a change. Time to *Carpe Diem*, so to speak.

DATE: Thursday, November 24, 20— 4:21 P.M.
TO: sambohannon@towpow....
FROM: drcross@wintersoldiers....
SUBJECT: Re: The Clap your hands, yall

funny, sam. long time no see. how's that second divorce working for you? ;-)

damian

THURSDAY, NOVEMBER 24, 20—
6:17 P.M.

AAAAAAAAARRRRRRRRGGGGGGGGGGHHHHHH!!!!!!!!!!!!!!!!!

Every year, it's the same, damned thing!!! Cowboys! Lions! Cowboys! Lions! I hate you, National Football League and your gaw'damned deals with the devil! And this year, without all that turkey, collards, macaroni and cheese, ham, and sweet potatoes (damn, I'm hungry), I can't even get the Itis to save me from this eternal torment!

FRIDAY, NOVEMBER 25, 20—
7:13 P.M.

Now that the lovely Dr. Jenkins has given me a clean bill of health and a few more Bible quotes, the gonorrhea-free Damian Cross, author of *Winter Soldiers*, is ready to give his first celebrity endorsement:

"Fuck penicillin! I'm down with ceftriaxone, cefixime, ciprofloxacin, ofloxacin, Spectinomycin, cefuroxime Axotal, cefpodoxime proxetil, enoxacin, and erythromycins!"

Hell, if steroid-popping baseball players can hawk impotence, why can't writers pimp themselves out for VD?

And now that that's over, I think it's time for me to just be single. L-U-V only seems to give me S-T-Ds. As many flaws as my right hand has, it's never done *that* to me.

SATURDAY, NOVEMBER 26, 20—
3:57 A.M.

I wonder, if I would've known what my choices were going to be, which one I would have chosen for this weekend. At the time, it had only been between going to see Kevin's whack-ass fusion band (he was probably going to call it "Byrd in Flight," or something atrocious like that) or exorcising demons in Pittsburgh. Neither option all that delectable, to be honest (even though I do miss Aunt Clarissa's seven-cheese macaroni magic), but it was an easy choice to make. But if I'd known the drama I was going to be involved in tonight, I wonder which I would've chosen. Then again, somebody else's tragedy is always easier to watch than your own.

Night was settling in on a pleasantly dull day. I was lying around reading *Towelhead*, thinking that the author, Alicia Erian, was indeed cute but was she cuter than Deema Khatib, who I'd just watched in *Control Room* (it's been an Arab kinda day—I should've gone out for kebabs or at least listened to Nawal El Zoughby) and would either of them dethrone M.I.A. as my CURRENT CRUSH, when there was a knock on my door. I told whomever to come in. It was Hep with a CD in his hand. He was a bit dusty and disheveled. There'd been a lot of activity going on in their room that I'd been trying to ignore. It's been that way when it comes to Hep and Neville. Whether in love or abject hatred, they're painful to listen to.

"I'm just returning your Azteca CD," he stated, plainly. "I've had it for way too long."

"What did you think?" I asked, hopefully.

"I think I'll stick to Santana."

"Fair enough."

He handed me the CD and headed for the door. "I'm moving out, by the way."

"Oh, you and Neville decided to make the leap and own? I hope you didn't get one of those interest-only loans. I'm big on equity."

"No," he said, wavering a little. "*I'm* moving out."

I shot up in my bed. "Oh damn, what happened?"

"I don't want to talk about it."

"Fair enough."

I slumped back down in my bed and returned to my book. Hep returned to emptying the love nest. There was a bit of clanging and knocking about, but things were comparatively peaceful. Obviously, Neville was nowhere to be seen.

I was getting a little hungry, but I'm used to the hunger by now. While not quite on a diet, I am denying myself a lot of food until I can finally see over my stomach again. I was debating those kebabs, though, when Hep knocked again.

"I hate to ask, Damian, but I've got a lot of boxes. I was wondering if you could help me for a minute."

"Yeah, sure. I've got nothing better to do."

I absolutely deplore moving (who doesn't?). But I'm always willing to help since I usually need help when I move. Besides, Hep traveled light. Like me, all he really had were books and CDs—but a hell of a lot more clothes. And so much more fashionable than my rags. Maybe I should turn his queer eye on my pathetic ass. So, it only took about a half hour or so to load his Isuzu pickup with his stuff. He was offering pizza as we loaded up the last of the boxes when Neville's black Miata screeched up to us, headlights blaring.

"Oh shit," Hep gasped, his dark face ashen in the night, like he'd just seen the Savior, his Day of Reckoning upon him.

"What the hell do you think you're doing?" Neville roared, leaping out of the car and slamming the door behind him. Impeccably dressed, I might add.

Hep looked like he was shaking, trying to keep everything down. There might've even been tears in his eyes, but the glare from the headlights was tricky. He said, very calmly, "I told you what I'm doing, Neville."

Neville charged up to his lover, the box in Hep's arms providing a buffer. Nev was a few inches shorter, but he jabbed his finger at Hep to make up the difference. "Fuck that! You don't leave me! I leave you!"

"You left a long time ago."

"What the *fuck* is that supposed to mean?! What the hell is he talking about, Damian?"

I threw up my hands in surrender and started backing away.

"Where do you think you're going?" Neville screeched.

"Look, fellas, I really don't wanna be involved in this."

"Well, you involved now, motherfucker."

"Leave him alone, Neville."

"What? Why are you always defending him?" Neville straightened up and let out a laugh. "What? Is he yours now?! You sucking his dick, or something?!"

"I think we're jus—"

"Shut up, Damian!"

"That's not my style, Neville," Hep said, barely composed. "Now *is* it?"

Things went beyond ugly and were steamrolling straight to cataclysmic.

"Look, guys…" I pleaded.

"Aw, don't you start now," Neville threatened, rolling his neck.

"No! Don't *you* start!" Hep roared. "I gave you everything! Everything! And you threw it in my face! Fucking around on me! Don't act like you don't know what I'm talking about! Like *I'm* the fucking idiot!"

A devilish smirk spread across Neville's immaculate face. The bastard was actually proud of himself. "Are you done?"

"No."

Hep threw the box down. Books exploded onto the street. He rushed a terrified Neville. "No! Wait! It's Armani!" ole boy wailed before landing on the hood of his car with a thud. I stood shocked. Hep is truly someone who can't hurt a fly—but apparently he was more than adept at kicking human ass. He went at Neville like a demon possessed, speaking in tongues. "You son of a bitch…!!!" Neville screamed helplessly as fist upon fist smashed into his face.

I finally snapped out of it and pulled Hep off his boyfriend of four years. He was panting and heaving in my constricting arms. Neville whimpered and slid, boneless, off the Miata. He lay in a heap on the street among the books.

"C'mon, man," I said, into Hep's ear. "Let's get out of here."

"Yeah," Neville moaned, "get the fuck out of here, Damian. And take that niggerbitchfaggot with you."

Hep surged in my arms. I turned him around and pinned him to the tailgate of his truck. "Wow, all that in one man," I quipped. "You're one hell of a catch, Hep McNally."

"Fuck you," Neville flared.

Hep chuckled for the first time all day. "Yeah. Let's go."

I hadn't really intended on going with the man, but after that scene, what the hell was I to do? It wasn't like Hep was in any shape to drive. He was draining himself in an effort to not cry. I found myself driving to the Morningside Motel. We'd even left his books and Neville splayed out in the street.

Needless to say, after all that, life was no *House Party 1, 2, 3, 4,* or *5.* I parked in the motel parking lot and marched box after box past the receptionist. Wordless in each step. The room itself was dingy with decades of sex stains everywhere. I didn't have enough antibiotics left to risk even sitting down in the place.

"Some castle, hunh?" Hep finally chuckled when we were done moving in. He looked absolutely worn down—yet relieved. The worst was over for him. He looked down at his scraped knuckles. Now, all that was left was the healing. Nothing a little Bactine couldn't cure, right?

"What? Like Princess Di ain't never been in a joint like this?"

"I think she could afford better."

"True." I suddenly wanted to get out of there. I didn't know where to go, though. It wasn't like home was going to be any better right now with Neville there. Back in Pittsburgh, I'd be eating turkey sandwiches—if there were any dark meat left—or I could be picking plaster from my hair. It's hard to say.

"Did you want me to call you a cab, Damian?"

"No. That's all right. I could use the walk," I said, patting my belly.

He smiled. Then, something clicked in his head, and his face darkened, glum. "Do you know what the weird thing is?" he asked.

I knew he was going to tell me. There was no need to answer.

"I'm actually kind of happy. I know that's going to change. Any minute now. But for the moment, I couldn't be happier. Like the Israelites right after Pharaoh's army got swallowed up in the Red Sea."

"I hope it doesn't take you forty years to find the Promised Land."

I immediately regretted going for the cheap, Biblical joke. Hep's eyes started turning red and welling up. Damn.

"We used to be so happy, Damian. We really did. I know it's hard for you to believe because you only saw the end. But the beginning … it was glorious. We were inseparable. We couldn't get enough of each other. I used to just love parading him around. He's so goddamned beautiful. All the other men—and *women*—were so jealous. And he was all mine alone. I felt so lucky that he was. Like God gave me His very own angel."

"I used to feel the same way about Samara," I said, finally depressed. The weight of the day was becoming too much. I actually sat down in a ratty, sticky chair.

"Really?" His face lit up. He'd probably felt like he was talking to a wall before. But now that he knew we had some sort of common bond, I'm sure he looked forward to reaching out.

"I don't know," I continued, "I'm starting to think it's not such a good thing: to have one person feel so lucky to have the other. Like either both people have to feel that way—or neither. Because if one person feels like they're so lucky, he's probably *too* lucky. Like I thought it was too good to be true to be with a woman like Samara. So beautiful and intelligent, why was she with a poor, sad sack like me? Somewhere down the line, she must've started feeling the same way—and started resenting me for it."

"Yeah. Maybe Neville started feeling the same way about me. Maybe I fawned over him too much, maybe I was too needy. But I'd thought I'd found my soul mate. And the ultimate sex partner. If you could only imagine the sex between us…"

I have, I thought, remembering all the raucous sex romps they used to have in the room next to mine, and involuntarily shuddered.

"What? What is it, Damian?"

"Well," I started awkwardly, "well, you know…"

"What? If we were two women, you could see that, right?"

"And pay damn good money for the privilege," I added.

He chuckled, despite himself. "You're all right, Damian Cross."

"Thanks."

"I don't know, Damian. It's like people—we…" He inhaled deeply, pensive. "It's like we get into these patterns, these ruts. I don't know how it started with me and Neville, but … see, I used to get so jealous. I probably saw him flirting with someone one night and went ballistic. Neville was contrite afterwards, of course. And the make-up sex was absolutely *amazing*.

"It's been going on like that for years, though. The flirtations, the arguments, the sex. Can you believe it? Years? What would possess people to be like that? But you get in this rut, right? And it gets so deep you can hardly dig yourself out. Like you and not talking."

"What are you talking about?" I asked. I hadn't really expected to be a part of this conversation. He caught me off-guard. "I talk."

"Oh, you babble, you pontificate," Hep stated. "But you never talk about what's important to you. Like your internal world's closed off to the rest of us. And not in a 'Mysterious Stranger' sort of way. More like a wounded deer, or something."

I didn't know what to say.

"But yeah," he continued. "There must've been a day, a moment, when Neville woke up and saw himself in that rut. He probably wondered if that was all his life was going to be. All that arguing. Like, 'Why did I sign up for all this strife?' I often wondered the same thing. I just didn't know how to stop all the hate and just get to loving my man."

His shoulders slumped and started to heave. Something like pure misery bubbled up from his lips. I was hating the scene and myself for not being a totally liberated man. Hep was needing a friend, and I was uncomfortable with a man crying in front of me. Men *are* allowed to cry these days. But only out of empathy for someone else's pain or death. Or, like, if you win the Super Bowl, or something. But never for one's own suffering. Never in front of another dude. Unless you were full of bullet holes. I had to do something.

"Look, Hep," I piped up. "You're a great guy. I mean, shit, you're incredibly intelligent and you have one of the kindest, most giving hearts a human being can have this side of Mother Theresa. You have great tastes—maybe not in men—but at least in music. And fuck Neville. You're a great-looking guy. If I were gay, I'd fuck ya."

Hep laughed—like it was the funniest thing he'd ever heard. I didn't think it was *that* funny. What am I? Chopped steak?

"To be completely honest," I continued, breathlessly, "DiDi and I love you to death. And Neville's an asshole. I was kinda hoping we'd have gotten you in the divorce."

Hep continued laughing. I peeled myself off my seat and left him in a good mood. I knew it wouldn't last long. He's probably crying right now into a bottle of Jack—or more fitting his new environs, Mad Dog 20/20. But I did my best. The whole thing had gotten me a bit down.

When I got home, I instantly turned to pissed. I let myself in. Neville's door was closed. His stereo was loud and obnoxious, and he was screaming to Mary J. Blige. *Why not Aretha?* I thought, as I opened my bedroom door and turned on the light.

A hurricane had hit my room. Books and CDs were everywhere. Torn pages were strewn about. Shattered jewel cases lay splintered everywhere. Smashed CDs prismed fragmented light all over the place. I stood dumbfounded, a rage welling up in me I hadn't felt in a very long time. I heard a door open to my left and felt Neville emerge from his room.

"Do you like my new decorating job?" he asked, smugly. I refused to look at him. I could hear the smirk on his face. My room started turning red before my eyes. I tried my best to remain calm. "I think I have a flair, don't you?"

1, 2, 3, 4, 5, 6, 7, 8, 9, 10 ... 36, 37, 38 ... 52, 53, 54, 55...

"Well, don't ya?"

I squeezed my eyes as tightly as I could, and inhaled. "Look, Neville," I finally said, through clenched teeth, "I don't know what kind of martyr complex you have, but you're about to get your wish."

"I'm not afraid of you."

"It doesn't matter if you are or aren't."

It felt like forever ticked by. I could feel my muscles tensing, ready to pop. I could feel the boy sizing me up. Wondering if he could take me or not. I almost wanted him to try and see.

"Hmph."

I heard him slam his door, then his stomping along the floor. My muscles finally gave way. I fell against the wall and slid to a seat. I don't know how long I sat there, staring at the destruction Hep and Neville's relationship had wrought.

SUNDAY, NOVEMBER 27, 20—
1:11 A.M.

It took forever for me to get the taste for human blood out of my mouth. I wanted Neville dead. Dead, defiled, decimated. His ashes spread across Mt. Olympus. Luckily for him, he hasn't shown his cadaverous face around here, or else the crows would be plucking out his eyeballs this very minute. I mean, a man who snaps your *Black Album* CD in two deserves nothing less. If he would've touched my bootleg Prince and the Revolution *Paris 1986*, I would've drawn and quartered his monkey ass.

I'd had a lot of cleaning up to do. I now have to find a place that sells standard-sized jewel cases. There are a lot of books and CDs I'll ultimately have to replace. I've stopped asking myself why he would do such a thing. It was only giving me a headache. Though he was never a fan, I had no idea the man despised me this much. He probably doesn't. Neville just wanted to lash out, and I was just close enough to get sucker-punched.

I don't know exactly what to do about all this. I'm sure he won't be back for a long time—if ever. I'll have to ask DiDi when she gets back. If it were up to me, I'd beat him worse than Hep ever could. It wouldn't get my CDs and books back, though. And I'm not exactly sure how good I'd feel afterwards. I'm not really against violence, but I do hate it. It takes me back to a place I no longer want to be.

I was feeling about as calm as I could by the time night had rolled around. I'd cleaned most of the wreckage, and it felt good to have the house to myself. I wasn't much for company, anyway, and I was really dreading having to see Kevin's band rehearse. But I'd made a promise, and I was actually going to stick to it this time (and, I admit, I was a little curious about Nandi—the boy's been bragging on her skills for months now).

I was making pesto when the doorbell rang. It was Priti. She was looking good, though a little distracted.

"Hey," I said, confused, "you know DiDi's in Pittsburgh, right?"

"Yeah, can I come in?"

She quickly made her way past me.

"Uh, sure," I said, to her back. I sneaked a peek.

"What smells so good?"

"I'm making pesto. Come on."

We made our way to the kitchen. I looked at the water that never seems to boil and went back to the blender. She pulled up a stool—way too close to me—and sat down. I looked at her, but she didn't seem able to talk. I shrugged, annoyed at the intrusion, and hit Chop. Cheese, nuts, garlic, and basil melted under the blades' whirs. I waited impatiently for her to speak. But all I heard was the blender. Finally, I stopped the machine, dipped a spoon into the sauce, and pointed it at Priti. I didn't have to reach too far, though, and stepped back a little as she took the spoon and put the green paste to her lips. Has no one ever heard of "personal space"?

"That's really good, Damian. Thanks."

"Don't thank me. Thank garlic," I declared. "Like Don Cheadle, it just makes everything better. If I had the discipline to bake a cake, I'd put garlic in it."

"That's disgusting."

"And I'm repulsive. A match made in heaven."

Priti gave a slight chuckle and looked up at me with those big, black eyes of hers. There's a vortex in those eyes, and I had no clue what was going on behind them. I didn't want to know, and I didn't want to be sucked in. I just wanted to eat my pesto, listen to Kevin's crappy music, and call it a night.

"Can I tell you something, Damian?"

When the hell did I become everybody's father confessor? Maybe I should start selling indulgences.

"Yeah. Sure, Priti."

"Your cousin asked me to go to Pittsburgh with her. To meet her family," she said, with the gravity of Jupiter.

"Yeah, I know," I said, airily.

"I figured you did," she admitted. "You two are really close, aren't you? The thing is … the thing is, I think I'm in love with Deirdre."

My eyebrows shot up into my hairline. I shouldn't have been surprised.

It's just that everybody else's relationships seemed to be exploding around me. I wasn't prepared for happy news. The problem was Priti seemed to be on the verge of tears.

"I've never been happier in my entire life," she blubbered. Then wailed. Of course, the water started boiling. I looked at the crying woman and then the bubbling water. And that pesto smelled so damned good. Shit. With regret, I turned the water off.

"I'm sorry," she finally managed to say. She wiped at her doe eyes and cracked a broken smile. "I don't know what's gotten into me."

I didn't know what to say. When do I, really?

"It's just, I don't know. She asked me to go and meet her family. And I was so happy. But I freaked. I started thinking about taking Deirdre to meet *my* family, and I just fucking freaked."

"Why? Don't your folks know?"

Priti let out a bitter laugh.

"They're still trying to fix me up with Indian guys. I'm thirty-four years old, and they still bug me about getting married. You'd think they would've given up by now."

"But you've never told them? They've never figured it out?"

"You just don't understand."

She was right. My parents are dead.

"And it's not like I've never dated men," she continued. "I mean, I've always been a disappointment to them. Never did what they wanted me to do. They wanted me to be a doctor, lawyer, an engineer, maybe something with computers or finance. I go and study sociology and comparative literature. I get a Master's but no PhD. And I should've been married long ago."

There was nothing for me to say. I didn't know why she was talking to me about this. I didn't know why *everybody* was talking to me lately. But this was my cousin's girlfriend. I shouldn't have been hearing any of this. It was none of my business.

"Have you told DiDi any of this?" What I was referring to, I had no clue. I just felt the need to say something.

"No. I couldn't. She'd figure out what this is all about in a minute."

"What all what is about?"

"Look, Damian, my folks, they're very … conservative. Like I said, they're used to disappointment when it comes to me. But it only goes so far. They still want grandchildren. I think they could get over it if I brought home a white guy. They'd hate it. But they'd get over it. At least they'd get their grandchildren. But damn, I bring Deirdre home, an African-American woman…"

"Hey," I suddenly said. It was getting late. I had to go. And get away from all this, this … talk. "You wanna get out of here?"

"What?"

"I've got to go catch my friend's band rehearsal. You wanna go with?"

"But I thought you were getting ready to eat."

I was. I looked at my delicious pesto in the blender, the steam rising off the pot's still water, and the bag of freshly-made pasta I'd picked up from the Italian deli down the street and rolled my eyes.

Priti did go with. I guess she had nothing better to do. Even though, personally, I believe that self-pity *is* a worthy pursuit. On the way over, I filled the car with constant chatter about Kevin's music. How many instruments the boy plays, his squandered talent, the folks in his band. How he keeps saying he's going in new directions. Priti wasn't interested in the least. Her eyes were glazed straight ahead on the road as I drove. Every once in awhile, she'd nod or "Uh-huh" to act like she was paying attention. I knew she wanted to talk about something else. But I didn't want to hear about her and her parents and DiDi. As I said, it really was none of my business. This type of conversation was for best friends not your lover's cousin. I am all about boundaries—like the Maginot Line ... wait, the Germans just went around that one. And Priti seemed determined to go through mine. I felt this was totally inappropriate. Next thing you know, she'd start talking about what DiDi liked in bed.

The band's practice space was in a warehouse district that used to be the definition of urban blight. Crack, whores, crack whores, human feces, overgrown grass, and broken glass. It was the kind of place on-duty cops would go for blow jobs. But a few years back, developers marched in and turned the place into renovated lofts and a gated community. The blow jobs were moved across the street. A prominent black politician, who shall remain nameless, owns the building Kevin uses. She's a big fan of his—let's say—music and lets him use the space whenever he needs it. For a price, I'm sure.

When Priti and I arrived, the band was still warming up.

"It looks like a Benetton ad," Priti whispered.

There was Kev fiddling with his horns. There was this cat, Arturo, on trumpet. He used to be in a Latin ska band that was a lot of fun live but absolutely abysmal on disc. There was Tod, a heavily-inked, rainbow white dude, on bass. He was slapping that thing like he was Faye Dunaway in *Mommie Dearest*. Raheem was laying down a heavy beat on drums. There was this white chica on mini-Moog, Yamaha synthesizer, and Apple computer. I'd never seen her before. She was a firehouse redhead, and I was intrigued by all her hardware. What direction *was* Kevin going in? Junichiro was Mr. Bongo in the corner. Vikram "Skip Vindaloo" was on the ones and twos, scratching a mad itch on record. And there were two, scruffy white dudes on alto and tenor saxophones who were definitely IT by day.

"Yeah," I concurred. "Damned affirmative action forced the white folks in."

And there was Nandi, of course, guitar in one hand and cigarette in the other. I didn't even know she smoked. She was in deep concentration, staring millennia beyond the noise in this room. She was absolutely captivating being captivated like that. I couldn't keep my eyes off her.

"Glad you could finally make it."

"Wha—?"

"Hey! D!" Kev whistled and waved a hand in front of my face. I snapped out of it. Priti snickered. Kevin leered her way. "Who's this?"

"Oh," I said. "This is Priti. DiDi's *girlfriend*. Priti, Kevin."

He straightened up, gave her a very asexual nod, and turned my way. He was all smiles. Like he was excited, or something. I don't think I'd seen him this excited since *Low End Theory*. "I'm really glad you came, brother man."

"Sure, Kev. No problem."

"Riiiiiight," he chuckled. "Hope the floor's all right. We don't have any chairs."

"Do I have time to go to the bathroom?" Priti asked.

Kevin took her upstairs. I picked a side wall and sat down, watching musicians at work. I was always intrigued by moments like this, just before musicians went on. There always seemed to be a tangible electricity in the air that very few people can generate. Just musicians and athletes. You couldn't watch a painter about to work and feel this sort of energy. Nobody could be mesmerized by me as I prepared to sit at my laptop. Could you imagine an accountant at her desk, the loud speaker screeching, "Are you ready to reconciiiiiiiile?!!!" and thousands of people scream in anticipation? Nope. Only musicians and athletes.

Yep. I *am* jealous.

"I hear I'm beautiful."

I looked up into a peasant skirt, a "Vote for Pedro" T-shirt with two, perfectly pert breasts beneath, glowing golden-brown skin, a mesmerizing mouth, and smiling eyes. There was no denying Nandi's statement. I was both blushing and confused.

I gave the suavest "Hunh?!" you'd ever heard in your life.

"Kevin. He told me you think I'm beautiful."

Et tu, motherfucker? 'Scuse me while I take this knife out of my back, kidney, and forehead.

"That's a shame," she continued. I obviously couldn't say anything. "I think you're brilliant while you just think I'm beautiful—like I had anything to do with that." Nope, my mouth was still glued shut. "I wish there were something I *could* do about that."

Despite the regentrifyers, we were still in a dangerous neighborhood. I turned my back for *two* seconds, and somebody done stole my tongue. I couldn't say a damned thing. I could barely even open my mouth. Who needed the slobber, anyway? It didn't seem to bother her, though. She just kept on talking.

"So, who's your friend?"

"What? Priti? She's a … uh … she's a friend."

I only outted her to Kevin for her own protection. There was no need to do it twice. Nandi gave a little, self-satisfied smile. My neck was starting to hurt, looking up like I was. But I couldn't keep my eyes off the woman. I'm glad I have now vowed to remain single and that Kevin was trying to claim her, or else I could have made an (even bigger?) ass out of myself.

"Well, I hope you and your 'uh … friend' enjoy the show. Hopefully, I can display a little brilliance myself."

"I don't think I can handle both beauty *and* brilliance," I was finally able to joke.

"Let's hope you can," she smiled.

Nandi left me. Priti soon joined me. And the band settled down to play.

Sometimes, eating your own words can taste like a real shit sandwich. Other times, it can be a beautiful, medium rare filet mignon you can slice with a butter knife (or whatever the vegan equivalent is, Neville, you cocksucking—no offense—son of a bitch, don't let me *ever!* catch your punk ass, I swear to Go—breathe … breathe …).

Listening to Kevin Byrd's new band was definitely the latter. As I've said millions of times before, Kevin's music used to make Kenny G. sound like Kenny X (but if ever there was a slave name, "Gorelick" is definitely it). It was vapid. It was insipid, an insult to the id, as well as the ego and superego. It was the Muzak version of Muzak. It was tamer than a neutered amoeba. The kind of stuff that had you screaming in the middle of an elevator, praying for the Apocalypse.

But this … It was so much different, so much better. It was so much more than I expected from my boy since his album came out. There was jazz, there was hip-hop. They went round the world with their funk—hitting Stax, Brazil, Latin America, and Africa along the way. I was looking for the didgeridoo.

The redhead with her Apple provided some trippy atmospherics. And she knew how to groove with her mini-Moog. She wasn't the only one. Raheem and Tod dug trenches with their rhythms, and the horns bit harder than Mike Tyson. Nandi drove the song along with her guitar. Vik would scratch on his turntables, sometimes laying down dope beats of his own, other times just getting all Sun Ra-cosmic on our asses with the weirdest-ass scratch effects I've ever heard.

When they were at their jazziest was when Kevin would really shine. He can really blow (as opposed to his first album, which just blew). And he'd do it on alto or tenor to equally amazing effect. I forgot how well he could play. Priti gasped more than once. I could see the intrigue growing in her eyes. Arturo also blared on his trumpet. He and Kev had a couple of fun battles that had the rest of the band struggling to keep the song together, their wonder was so great. Kevin had them all on the floor when he and Vik "scratched" together. Kev on sousaphone, Vik on the decks.

I had to pick my jaw up off the floor more than once watching Nandi. She was really good with that guitar and really seemed to enjoy playing it. Her eyes beamed, she was constantly smiling, and couldn't stop dancing. There was joy in her every movement whether she was discoing down or offering up airy, jazz licks.

And when she sang ... my God ... it was like I was in the fifth grade again, having to put my hands on my lap to cover up an uncontrollable boner. She sang "Fried Neckbones and Some Homefries" in the most seductive, husky contralto I've ever heard in my life. Her eyes were closed as though in a trance and she dragged out every note into the microphone—not in that faux-chanteuse this-is-your-dick-I'm-mouthing way. It was this unconscious seduction, as though she were married to the song, and the rest of us didn't matter. She was glowing, sweat a fine mist all over her face, and I was hypnotized.

"She's beautiful," Priti whispered, breathlessly.

I nodded, not really paying attention to her.

"Kinda exotic-looking, isn't she?"

I turned to my wheat-colored companion and smirked.

"Friiiiiiiiiied neckbones," Nandi sang, "and some homefries."

The horns blared, and the band broke into a boogaloo. Nandi kinda blushed at herself and started playing her guitar and dancing around. They moved seamlessly into a funky samba that depended highly on her playing. She carried the song effortlessly, her peasant skirt swirling madly as she danced. Kevin jumped down, whipped out a big, black guiro (which, in my hyper-sexualized state, I momentarily thought was a dildo), started scraping it with a stick, and moved along until he was dancing with his lead singer. They were gyrating and playing together, that look of utter joy still on Nandi's face. My stomach actually started turning a little. Kev gave me a smug look, smiled, and winked. Why didn't he just piss on her, mark his territory, and get it over with? I already knew who was whose.

Nandi looked at us and twirled away from Kev. She spun until she was standing over Junichiro. He looked up at her and banged away like a beat demon. She kept dancing, signaling folks to solo. She finally finished her dance at Vindaloo, who looked at her with puppy-dog black eyes.

"It looks like you have competition," Priti whispered again. "He's a very pretty boy."

I gave her my best perturbed look.

"What?"

"That's a game I refuse to play," I declared, turning back to the performance. I knew Priti was looking incredulously at the side of my head.

Vikram started scratching frenetically. He laid down a scratch beat that he sped up and slowed down, jittering around with the fader like he was a junky in need of a fix. The rest of the band was cheering him on, heads nodding, arms bobbing up and down. Somewhere in the frenzy, he slowed the beat down again, and we could hear a woman moaning.

Priti bristled. "Amonkar," she gasped. I had no clue what she was talking about. It was just cool hearing this moaning with ole boy's ripped-vinyl beat. Junichiro screamed out in agreement and started banging away again. Vik nodded to him and slowed him down. He then looked at Raheem on drums. The brother added a little more bottom and then the hi hats. It took a moment, but then the three of them hit a groove.

It was mesmerizing. They were improvising, creating music out of the ether, before my very eyes. I was utterly captivated. I'd never seen anything like it.

Vik bobbed and swayed to and fro, heavy in the groove he'd established. He gestured for Nandi to return to the microphone. He beamed at her back the entire way as she complied. Poor bastard. He should know he's gonna lose that one. When she got there, she grabbed the mic and shrugged a question. Vik shrugged. *Do whatever,* he seemed to be saying. Confused, Nandi started chanting some voodoo shit. (No, seriously, I think they were Haitian chants; I heard "Legba" in there somewhere.) DJ Grandmaster Vikram Spicey D then gestured to the redhead, who immediately got on her laptop and Yamaha and injected some atmospherics. The air started swirling around us in a digital whirlwind. The DJ then nodded to Arturo and the mic. The trumpeter started rapping in Spanish. He could've been saying, "Kill all niggers," for all I know, but it sounded good. The next thing I knew we were all waist-deep in this funky Indo-African-Latino-rap funk that had me and Priti needing to dance. The horns joined in, quietly moaning in the background, calling-and-responding to Nandi.

The band was in its own world. Vik was beaming ear-to-ear, head bobbing madly in an utter trance with what he was creating. He started moaning himself, getting louder and louder—like a mad (Thelonious) Monk. Kev suddenly grabbed his mic, and rapped, "We hold these truths to be self-eviden—"

"Aw shit, nigga!" Vindaloo suddenly shouted.

Shocked, Raheem ripped a stick straight through his snare drum. "Fuck!"

He suddenly shot a look of utter contempt at Vikram. Everybody staring heatedly at their DJ. The boy started withering in the glare. He swallowed hard on something. "Uh … that's what I'm talkin' … 'bout?" he proffered, humiliated.

Practice was suddenly over.

I very quickly found myself in the Scotsman with Priti and Nandi. I was a bit disappointed. I wanted to talk to Kevin about his band. I was so hyped. I hadn't been this excited about music since *36 Chambers.* No, wait, make that *Black Star*. I wanted to rave and revel in the excitement. I'd wanted to finally exclaim over Kevin's talent like I've been waiting to do for these past fourteen years. But he couldn't make it. All he could do was smile smugly and say, "You liked it, didn't you?"

"Yeah," I smiled back.

After Nandi had suggested the Scotsman, he'd said he couldn't make it. "Gotta pay the rent." He bent to kiss Nandi, who deftly offered him a cheek. He took it to save face. Everybody saw it and sniggered. Then Junichiro offered his scruffy cheek with a coy flutter of the eyelashes. Soon, Kevin was giving everybody a kiss on the cheek. He then moved off to talk to a *very* repentant Vikram ("I blame MTV," Byrd had whispered to me just before he left, "got everybody thinkin' they're niggers. They don't know you gotta *earn* that shit.") and then, I guess, off to the landlord to settle his bill. Oh, the life of an artist.

So, I found myself in my old haunt with Nandi and Priti, Diane/Dakota serving us with hellafied attitude (even though, I do admit, she did look at me a little differently with my two companions—like maybe I wasn't leprous after all). I'd never been so disappointed in the company of two beautiful women.

I reconciled myself with the opportunity to talk about the band with Nandi, but Priti had other ideas. I had obviously failed in the confidant department, and she was busy lobbying Nandi for the position. I was quickly bored and wanted to get out of there. Occasionally, Nandi would flash a look of disappointment. And we started looking like two pathetic, caged animals praying to be put to sleep.

Priti didn't notice, though. She was in the land of woe and had applied for a green card. "But it's my parents," she droned on and on and on and on and … you get the idea.

I got up and moved to the internet jukebox. Priti had effectively killed my high. I needed some music, something like I'd heard tonight. That intoxicating world mix with heavy doses of jazz, funk, and hip-hop. The closest thing I could think of was Earth Wind & Fire, and suddenly disco beckoned me toward salvation. "Boogie Wonderland," "Le Freak," "Don't Leave Me This Way," "Love Hangover," "Love to Love You Baby." To hell with Priti, I was gonna have a good time if it killed me.

Unfortunately, I had to return to her and her solipsistic bitching and moaning. When the hell had I become so insensitive?

"Look," Nandi finally said, sucking on a Camel Light. "You've decided to live outside the pale. Didn't you expect there to be consequences? Did you just think you could be in an interracial, lesbian relationship and everybody would clasp hands, sing 'Kumbaya,' pull troops out of Iraq, and have world peace?"

"Well, there's really no need for hyperbole," Priti retorted.

"I actually like hyperbole," I volunteered. Priti flashed me an angry look. "It's funny."

"But my folks want me to marry someone like Vikram."

"Who? That nigger?" I laughed—alone. Hey, that was funny, too. Well … I guess you had to be there.

"They should've stayed in India then," Nandi stated, brusquely.

Daaaaaaamn.

"Excuse me." Priti was offended.

"No. Think about it. It's like your parents wanted to come to America, live the good life, whatever. But it comes at a cost, and we kids are the price of admission. They should hang a sign over the airport: 'Your kids *will* be American.' They want us to be good, little Indian girls or Chinese or whatever. But we're not. We're beautiful, fucked-up, watered-down Americans. They need to get over it.

"We're going to have black lesbian lovers, study the arts instead of medicine and law. We're gonna marry white guys or—heaven forbid—black guys. If you already speak English, we're probably not going to be bilingual. We're going to love rap and rock and MTV. We'll dress like whores and go to the club, get drunk and high, and we're going to sleep with whomever we choose."

She paused to take a breath, but she wasn't done. "It's like my father," she continued. "He's Chinese, right? From Jamaica. He comes here with his *black* wife because *his* parents refused to talk to *him* anymore. Everything he does is Jamaican, right? Curried goat, oxtails, peas and rice. He's got all these old ska 45s—"

"Really?" I squeaked. Oh, to get my hands on *those*.

"—yeah. Listens to ska, reggae. He thinks Bob Marley and Peter Tosh are two-thirds of the Holy Trinity. He even speaks patois.

"Anyway, so one day when I was like fourteen or something, he catches me after violin practice with my tongue down this white boy Darren's throat. When he tells me I can't see him anymore, I refused. Just said, 'No.

I'll see whomever I want.' He's pissed, right? I knew he wanted to beat me right there in the car. But all he can say is that a proper, Chinese girl does not refuse her father.

"Now, here's this guy who loves everything black and Jamaican, the food, the music, the language. The women, obviously. His people haven't seen China in like a century and he's going to come at me with this 'proper Chinese girl' bullshit?!"

Priti was enthralled. "So what did you do? Did you keep seeing this Darren boy?"

"No. He was a jerk," Nandi chuckled. "But I did see others. The worst was Lamar, though. Then my *mother* started giving me crap for seeing an American black and how disgusting and lazy and stupid they are and how we're so much better than that. What can you do?"

"Yeah. What?" Priti sighed.

Nandi glared at her and exhaled a puff of smoke. "Grow up."

WEDNESDAY, NOVEMBER 30, 20—
12:49 P.M.

"Nandi Huang," DiDi trumpeted, entering the room on her way to work.

It was way too early for me to be awake, but I'm trying to turn over a new leaf—if not several. I was sitting at the living/dining room table, eating my bowl of bran with apple slices on top. I was on my way to the gym and was dressed accordingly. Yep, fruit, fiber, and gym in the morning. My sacrifice to the god of Middle Age. I wish I could make it up to myself by having a burger and chili cheese fries for lunch. But I'll probably just have a light salad. Why didn't our parents warn us?

"Yeah," I chewed. "What about her?"

"You met her." She positively glowed.

"Obviously, I have."

"Was it cute?"

"The 'cute meet' only happens in the movies, DiDi."

"So, how did it happen?"

"I don't know. I was at WSQ with Ina an—wait. How do you know her?"

"Remember that lawyer who does pro bono stuff for the women at the shelter I was telling you about?"

I stopped to inhale, catching my cousin's breath for her. Then I groaned. "That's Nandi?"

DiDi sat down at the table across from me. I don't want to say she was giddy—I really don't—but she was. I hadn't seen that look since high school and knew I was in trouble.

"So, you like her, don't you?"

"Come to think of it," I started, facetiously, "from the first moment I saw her in the club, while I was trying to get into Ina's pants, I knew Nandi was the one I'm going to marry."

"Oh, you'll marry her."

"For the love of Jesus, Deirdre. Don't you have a woman to de-batter, or something?"

"That's not a word, Dami."

"Neither is 'Fuck you.'"

She ignored me. No big deal. I'm used to it.

"You ask her out, yet?"

"No. But I took a number. I'm right behind Kevin and Vikram—and about thirty thousand other niggers in the tri-state area."

"Why be like that, cousin? Those others don't have a chance in hell. Did I tell you how much she likes your writing?"

She hit my Achilles heel.

"Really?" I squeaked.

"Yeah. She thinks you're brilliant, or something. I told her it's only because of my editing skills."

"You would."

"Next time you see her, you should ask her out."

I thought about it for a moment. The next moment I started thinking about a lot of other things that were troubling me.

"I don't think so."

Kevin has that "Bitch" look I've been telling you about. DiDi has the "I'm-'bout-to-kick-your-ass" look. That's what she threw at me this morning. I ducked, but it still caught me square in the jaw.

"And why not?" she asked, the little authoritarian.

"I just—you know. I'm like … I just want to be single for awhile. Take it easy. 'Find myself,' I don't know. Finish my book."

"You're just afraid," she declared, haughtily. Like she *knows* me, or something.

"Of what?" I scoffed. "Of your being right?"

"Of falling in love."

I looked at her solemnly. I may have even generated a tear or two in my eye. "DiDi, please, if you really and truly cared…"

"Yes?"

"You'd put down the pipe."

THURSDAY, DECEMBER 1, 20—
2:09 A.M.

OK, I admit it. DiDi got me there. For a minute. I thought my decision to be single might actually have been cowardice. That I was just afraid to get back into the saddle after the year I've had. You've got to admit, the fillies have been stomping the shit out of this cowboy lately.

I thought it might've been depression. If you spend as much time as I do licking your wounds, you just end up becoming one, big two hundred-pound wound yourself.

I thought I was doing it because I'm not Kevin. Not beautiful. Like him and Nandi. People like them never have problems in finding partners. They just show up and folks trip over their own dicks and clits to be with them. Everything they say is utterly fascinating. They could talk about a pimple, and everybody's on the edge of their seats. We prols just bask in beautiful people's glow. We radiate in the privilege of their just looking at us. And if they wink or say anything to us we damn near combust. If they actually deign to have us on their arm, we actually do explode. And go all Hiroshima if we get to bone.

The rest of us, we have to work to find a mate. Study and pray that we're smart enough, earn enough money, develop a personality, try to be witty, clever, funny, actually become sensitive to the other's needs. Just to get syphilis, gonorrhea, and dumped for all our troubles.

It's not as though I'm hideous. I've been told I'm not a bad-looking guy (those were the actual words—not "attractive," never "beautiful," couldn't even manage a "handsome" or "comely"—no, "not a bad-looking guy" is the best I can ever do), gut aside. And, thanks to misogyny, I don't have to worry so much about letting myself go. But it's not like I cause traffic accidents when I go out on the streets, and I've never had to scream, "I am not an animal!"

Actually, though, I've come to realize that I really do enjoy my own company. I might even like myself. Well, I won't go that far. But without worrying about the VD and loneliness, I've had a really good time this week. I've been watching DVDs on the computer, catching up on my music reviews. Sat around looking pretentious at my favorite coffeehouse, Carpe Diem. I've gone to a couple Jamaican restaurants (listening to Nandi gave me a craving I can't seem to sate), saw a few movies. I've been reading like a fiend and writing like a maniac (I dumped a couple hundred pages on DiDi to read). My cousin even forced bitch-ass Neville to write me a $1,200 check, and I've been buying music left and right to replace the stuff he destroyed. I've been to the gym a bunch, where my trainer, Sista Olu, and her muscular dreads torture me with free weights, machines, jump ropes, and these damned rubber balls, all the while screaming at me like a damned Nazi. I even went to the museum and did the usual consumerist thing, glancing by all the works, giving my quick "Yea" or "Nay," never once pausing to contemplate a single piece. And tomorrow I'm going to Egon's bachelor party. I'm still tripping that his boy, Stefan, called me up to go. Everybody knows about the Blow Up. I guess I'm being offered an olive branch.

See, things are looking up. I've given up the Pursuit of the P, and now I have all this time to enjoy me. I just wish Nandi would stop popping into my head. I can't stand cockfights, and I definitely don't want to get in the ring with Kevin and Vikram to compete for milady's affections. Who's worth all that trouble?

FRIDAY, DECEMBER 2, 20—
1:44 p.m.

I don't know what it is about intelligent women…

Listening to The Kojo Nnamdi Show online with this German theology/robotic engineering professor. Listening to the woman pontificate about AI and God and am wondering just how wrong my wiring is. Because I am getting *horny*. I don't know why, but really intelligent women just get me hot under the waistband. I mean, damn. Any woman can either have or buy a nice pair of boobs; I'm no doctor, but I'm pretty sure they all have vaginas (though I did meet one without a belly button once); and they now have ass implants; but a polysyllabic siren talking over my head gives me a groinial tingle wantin' to be satisfied. I can't tell you how many female professors I've wanted to have scratch that itch. *I can't help it.*

Hell, I'm sure there's some deconstructionist/feminist psychoanalyst out there ready to lecture me on how I desire to subjugate the superior, female intellect with my superior, male physicality and that I've sublimated my misogynistic fear and impotence into pure sexual desire. Of course, I probably wouldn't hear a damned word she'd said, having been too busy picturing her naked. ;-)

SATURDAY, DECEMBER 3, 20—
5:15 p.m.

In all honesty, I don't know why Egon and I had that huge argument. I'm still confused as to why it's prevented us from talking all this time. I don't even remember what it was all about. I do remember it started over something silly—though I don't remember what exactly. Hell, it could've been over something as silly as Britney Spears. I probably came out on the pro side—'cause every brother deserves a trailer trash fantasy every once in awhile—and everything went all to hell.

I just remember it started a little after I'd come back from tour. Some time in May. Just before the Cataclysm. *Convicta et Combusta* had done fairly well before I'd left. Not commercially, of course. But critically. And people had begun talking about us around town. The papers had said I'd shown promise, and they'd just adored Samara in the lead. Egon wanted to follow it up with something else in the fall, and we'd gotten together to discuss it.

Egon was probably railing about the inanity of pop culture and how the downfall of Western civilization was epitomized by the popularity of Britney Spears. I'd said that everybody's been decrying the fall of the West for centuries and when the hell was it going to happen? I'm tired of waiting. "Besides," I'd more than likely said, "she's got a nice ass for a white girl."

Egon turned red and bled invective all over the place. He ranted against *Convicta et Combusta,* how the title was stupid and pretentious and drove people away from the box office. Who wanted to see a play they couldn't even spell? "Like *Equus*?" I'd interjected. "You leave Peter Shaffer out of this!" He went on to say how he didn't understand why Samara and I had gotten so much press when he'd gotten none. That the play wouldn't have been shit without his direction. He *intimated* that it was because of some kind of bullshit, PC, multicultural conspiracy and that he'd gotten snubbed because he was a white man. He *said* that his rewrite suggestions were what made the damned thing comprehensible. He charged me with biting Ionesco. "Ishmael Reed, motherfucker," I'd gently corrected. I mean, give credit where credit is due. And that Samara isn't all that talented, anyway. He *constantly* had to work with her to get it right. And her limited talent in no way compensated for her bad attitude. She was a prima donna *and* a bitch. And she'd get nowhere in the theater—maybe not even in life—and might as well be teaching preschoolers how to tie their shoes—if she didn't devour them first.

I don't know what I'd said in return. Probably something about his being a no-talent, no-dick, Eurocentric, white boy, who only loved *Pet Sounds,* Sartre, and Buñuel because some professor told him to, and that he was always overcompensating, abusing and misusing words from the thesaurus to hide the fact that he was actually kinda stupid and that he'd be out hustling blow jobs on Front Street if his pops hadn't given him this crappy theater company to save himself the embarrassment of having a loser son at the country club. Or something like that. Who knows? It's not important now (though now I can kinda see why we haven't been talking). I'd been invited to his bachelor party.

And I went. I was being a good sport. It was a little awkward at first and was bound to become a nightmare. But everything was as pleasant as could be expected at Ivy's, this little Malaysian spot across town.

The only black guy there, I was the fly in the buttermilk. And these were all bastards he'd gone to prep school with. They all had names like Stefan, Ian, Bradley, and Josh. They all joked about homoerotic adventures they'd had back in school. They found it funny. I thought it was a little creepy. I mean, who the hell thinks of heating up a potato in the microwave, cutting a hole in it, and fucking it? And why the hell did they pass it around? Who wants sloppy seconds on a russet?!

I hung around Stefan, 'cause he was the only other bastard I knew. He manages retirement funds or something, is married with one kid on the way, and has a huge McMansion in the burbs. But he used to hang around the theater sometimes and creep me out. The clean cut sumbitch with an MBA from Harvard with a love for faux Cuban cigars and martinis with Ketel One and rushes to see "DMB" whenever they're in town. Aaargh! Like people like him actually exist.

But he seemed all right tonight. Apparently, he never got to gang bang an Idaho and was never really a part of their reindeer games. So, we talked about my book and the tour and what I'm working on now; his fantastic job, his so-so wife, and this wonderful child due in May. It's going to be a boy, and he can't wait to teach the runt football. Unfortunately, Stefan's a Cowboys fan. No surprise there.

A little later on in the dinner, he sidled up close and started telling me how shocked everyone was that Egon and Pilar were actually getting married. Apparently, they had called the whole thing off back in May. He didn't know what the whole thing was about, but it was notorious and b-i-g (*God, even I groaned at that one, and I wrote it*). They didn't talk for months. Were even seeing other people. Then, out of nowhere, back in September, they'd gotten back together and put the wedding on again. Even moved it up. It originally wasn't supposed to happen until June. Now, they were having a holiday wedding in Rio. It was all a bit strange. But what could you do? Love's a real tricky motherfather sometimes.

Maybe that was the reason Egon and I had had that big blow up. Back in May. Maybe his life had been falling apart, and he needed to lash out. And if slavery movies have taught us anything, the uppity black guy always gets the whip. Little did I know at the time, my life was about to fall apart, too. We could've really used each other at the time. Instead, we were too busy being enemies. I looked at Egon with an odd sense of sympathy there at Ivy's. I tried joining in the fun but could only do it with alcohol. All my teenage masturbatory tales were of the sock-and-lotion variety. The folks were too poor to have me fucking around with the fruits and vegetables.

Everybody in the club was a little tipsy by the time we reached Studs 'N' Muffins. As soon as we walked in and I heard women squealing in delight, I knew I had to get ass-fucked drunk. One of those screams was Samara's

(I'd know it anywhere), as she was pulling her face away from a muscular brother's crotch. The Queen of the Cataclysm up to her old tricks.

"What the hell is she doing here?" I gasped.

Egon turned to me, gravely. "Sorry, Damian," he said. "I didn't want her here either, but she and Pilar became close over the summer. She's actually in the wedding party—if you can believe it. I bought her ticket just the other day."

"Wait," I said, my mind overloaded with questions. "Why am I looking at a bunch of naked dudes in a strip club?"

"This place is unisex," Stefan huffed, and pointed. Off to the left, there was a tiny stage where three women were dancing. I was a little relieved, a little confused. I just wanted to go home. "Egon and Pilar thought it would be romantic if they had their bachelor and bachelorette parties together."

"Yeah, isn't it great?" Egon asked, beaming ear-to-ear.

"Yeah!" I sarcastically gave two thumbs way up. *Freaky, little bastard.* When he started walking to the men's section, I gave his back the finger. Not only was I going to have to watch a bunch of naked men all night, but I was going to have to watch my ex trying to slurp dick in public. *Who could ask for anything more?*

As soon as I asked myself that question, I saw Nandi emerge from the ladies' room and join Pilar's party. I guess I should never have asked *that* question. How about this one, though? How small can a metropolitan area of over two million people be? How the hell do we all know each other?

"Are you all right?" Stefan asked. "You look like you're going to be sick."

"Give me time," I droned.

"Cool. It's not a party until someone vomits. Let's go get you a drink."

In all honesty, I can't remember anything about the sexual confusion I had supposedly suffered in my teens (after all, I wasn't confused—I knew exactly why I didn't get any back then), but I have never felt queerer than I did that night. I couldn't keep my eyes off the men. I was just riveted. I was forced to be. All the stages were in the middle of the club with the chairs and tables surrounding them. I couldn't turn my back if I wanted to (I'd just catch their reflections in the mirrored walls). And Studs 'N' Muffins was definitely for the ladies. There was only a handful of female strippers who were thrown in as an afterthought. The place was just crawling with hard-boiled, rippling, oily, naked men.

I couldn't help wondering how much they all worked out every day. And I just couldn't figure out how they kept themselves in a perpetual state of chub. Not *all* those penises could naturally be *that* long without *some* kind of medicinal aid. Did Viagra do that? Or was this all surgical? Inquiring minds want to know.

And then the female customers ... Hell, if we guys even *thought* about doing *half* the things these women were doing to the strippers, we'd be in the hospital getting our heads surgically removed from our own rectums. All the grabbing and kissing. I was flabbergasted. *Really, ladies, if you want to get dick-whipped in the face, don't you think you should do that in the privacy of your own homes?* I wanted to call in the Religious Right for some back-up, or something.

To make matters worse, Samara was showing her ass. She saw me, acknowledged my existence, and continued to act the fool. Her face was in the crotch of every dancer there. Just a-rubbin'. She was screaming the loudest, the most often, and throwing the most money around. She even danced with a few of the hard-ons.

I tried to distract myself with the few female strippers around, but pickins was slim. There was one brunette who was kinda cute—if you're into the sagging breasts and stretch marks of a teenage mother. Egon liked her, and we paid her to dance at our table way too many times. For some reason, she liked sitting next to me when others were dancing at our table. The yuppies looked at me jealously, but they weren't missing much. "Dakota" (told you that waitress just made the name up—nobody's actually *named* Dakota) kept talking about her two sons and how her boyfriend's an asshole, how he abuses her and always takes her money to feed his habit and how she finally left him a week ago and she's scared and do I want to go get high with her after she gets off of work? All I wanted to do was go home—though getting involved with a nineteen-year-old girl with a four- and two-year-old and an abusive boyfriend lurking in the shadows *was* tempting. Maybe this time I could get Chlamydia. I went to take a piss instead.

"You know," the middle-aged guy next to me in the stall, with a scruffy, blonde beard and a belly that forced him to do some long-distance pissing, said to me, "I just spent twelve hunnerd bucks in the VIP Room."

"Wow."

"And I didn't get nuthin' for it."

"Not even the steak dinner for $4.95?"

"Nope."

"You'd think they'd at least comp you that."

"You'd think."

"So, what exactly were you expecting?"

"Shit. For twelve hunnerd bucks, I was expectin' *something*. What the hell am I supposed to tell my wife?"

That you're a jackass.

"What?"

"I don't know, man."

I zipped up and walked out. Nandi was standing outside waiting for me. She was leaning against the doorway, sucking on a cigarette, looking sexier than any woman in the joint. I tried not to picture her naked … but it couldn't be helped, really.

"Are you trying to picture me naked?"

"No," I denied, blushing. "Why?"

"You just have this silly look on your face."

"I'm drunk."

She looked at me earnestly.

"OK, you caught me. I was picturing you naked. But I'm a guy. This is a strip club. I'd picture a nun naked in here right now. At least a young one, anyway. I was trying not to."

"Nuns, hunh?"

"It's a sickness, really. I should get help."

She smiled. All oiled up … red garter belt, red stockings. That smile. Those dimples. God, Damian. Maybe it *is* a sickness. Maybe a little Kenny G. in the background … Najee. Now I know I'm sick. Is Najee still around, by the way?

"You know, every time I see you, you're with another woman."

"It's a strip club, Nandi."

"What about that brunette?"

"God, with all these beefcakes around, you're paying attention to what I'm doing?"

"I'd be flattered, if I were you," she said, smiling coyly again, like she'd patented the expression. "And what about Priti? I know she's with your cousin, but I think she really likes you."

"Yeah. I've heard that before."

"And that mystery woman you ran off to see that one night? Yanely, was it?"

"Why did Kevin tell you about her?" I asked, defensively.

"I asked."

"Look," I said, a little heatedly, "did you come over here just to grill me about my private life?"

"No, I didn—"

"'Cause I'll tell you. That brunette just likes brothers. One of her kids is mixed. And I'm the only Negro in here whose dick ain't swingin' in the breeze. Priti's with DiDi. I *know* you know that story. And Yanely—I can't believe Kevin told you about her—Yanely just didn't work out. It was a mistake to begin with."

Why the hell was I telling her all this crap? It was none of her business. Besides, she was there when I met Yanely … oh yeah, she was there, wasn't she?

"I'm sorry," she apologized, touching my chest. "You were just looking like I was feeling—like you wanted to get out of here. Samara's been bad-mouthing you all night. And Pilar and a couple of her friends have all been saying what a great guy you are. And I wanted to talk to you. That's all."

I looked at her. I don't know what I was thinking.

"I'm sorry. I'm a little drunk, too. Can we talk about something else?"

I looked at her hand on my chest. She quickly withdrew it, but I wanted it there. I was more than a little drunk. I don't know why I'd gotten so angry. Too much alcohol in the bloodstream. Too much dick in the room. Too much Samara in the air. I just wanted to take that hand and run off into the night. *I'll fly away...*

"How do you know Pilar?" I finally asked.

"We went to Berkeley together. Law school."

"That's right. You're an attorney. You do work for my cousin's shelter."

"Well, I mainly do acquisitions and mergers. Contracts. Really boring stuff. I just do that other stuff on the side in the hopes of saving my soul."

"Well, this place," I gestured around the club, "is a good place to start."

She chuckled. "You know, Deirdre's been singing your praises for months now."

"Yours, too. She's been picturing herself as my matchmaker ever since we were kids. A quixotic task, if you ask me."

"What? She's never succeeded?"

"She thinks opposites attract. One time she set me up with this psycho who almost stabbed me."

Nandi laughed. It was infectious. Suddenly, "Lorena Bobbitt" Larissa actually seemed funny.

"I guess she likes our contrast: the devilish writer with the woman who sings like an angel."

I tried to play the last bit off like a joke. I don't know if it worked. But Nandi laughed again.

"I don't think cherubim sing contralto," she chuckled.

"No, seriously. You're really talented."

"Brilliant?" Nandi ventured.

A smile spread across my face. I couldn't stop it. "Wellllll, I wouldn't go *that* far."

It was her turn to beam. Her skin glowed a luminescent bronze, and she looked up at me with those almond eyes. I didn't want to be drawn in. My drunken mind kept scream/singing, *'Cause we're living ... single ...In a '90s kinda world, I'm glad I got my girls.* What?! Oh yeah. *I'm living the single, single, single ... life*. Always go with Cameo when you can't get the music out of your head.

Word up!

"Look," Nandi opened, nervously. "I've gotta go to Brazil for this wedding next week. But I was wondering, you know, when I got back … well, if we co—"

There was a sudden rush of air to my right. We both turned. I yelped. A tongue was rammed down my throat. And it didn't taste like tongue. I pulled away. Samara, of course.

I immediately tried to picture the horns, the cloven hooves, the pitch-forked tail, and two-pronged penis of Old Scratch. But I couldn't. It was Samara. The woman I had lived with and loved for seven years. She was in front of me, *with* me for the first time in months, tall and dark and beautiful, towering two inches over my 5'9" frame, her hair shimmering to her shoulders. I tried to remember all the bad times, but my drunken mind just couldn't. All I could think of was all the love, montaging before me like a bad romantic comedy.

But Nandi was there, too. And I had this funny taste in my mouth. This night was quickly becoming horrific.

"Hi, lover," Samara slurred.

"I think the term is actually '*jilted* lover.' But hell, let's be civil. Just call me 'ex-fiancé.'"

"Damian, please don't be like that," she pleaded, putting an affectionate hand on my arm. When the hell did I become so touchable? Stupid sueded shirt, why did I ever let that saleswoman talk me into buying it? She gave a cold eye to Nandi. "You're still here?"

Nandi threw her hands up in surrender and started slinking away.

"Nandi. Wait."

She gave a dismissive wave without even turning around. I just wanted her to finish her sentence. I turned back to my old love, who was smiling like she'd just eaten the pulsating heart out of a newborn's chest. "OK, you win, Samara," I conceded.

She wiped the blood from her mouth. "You know she's like some corporate attorney, or something," she said, disdainfully. "How pedestrian."

"She can also sing her ass off and ain't too bad on guitar. And she does pro bono work for DiDi's shelter."

"What? You fucking her?"

"No, she just rubs her face in my crotch and screams to high heaven every Saturday night. Pretty boring stuff. But the money's good."

You could see the steam rising from her eyes. But she quickly extinguished those fires with a disarming smile. I waited for her to say something, but she didn't seem able to get any words out. She was melting before my eyes, and before I knew it, there were tears in hers.

"Oh God, Damian. I miss you so much. I've been, I don't know, I've been lost without you. My life's such a mess. It's like, like, it's like I'm falling apart, or something. I need you so badly. I fucked up. I know that. But we all make mistakes, don't we? I mean, we all do. That's what being human is—right? Making mistakes and forgiving them? Can't you forgive me, Damian?"

Those were the words I'd wanted to hear seven months ago. Because seven months ago, I might've forgiven her. I probably would've taken my medicine, waited for the anger and itching to subside, and would've forgiven her. She would be my wife right now, and we'd still be planning our future together. Two hundred-some-odd days ago.

But now, in the middle of Studs 'N' Muffins, with genitalia flying everywhere, old Bon Jovi blaring from the speakers, the air reeking of cheap musk and beer, and this *fucked-up* taste in my mouth, I just wanted to ram those words back down Samara's throat. I inhaled deeply to remain calm. It seemed like every conversation tonight was doomed to fail, and I just wanted the world to shut up. "Hey, Sami," I finally said, "this isn't the time nor the place for this conversation. Can't you just go back to Pilar an' 'em, and have fun with the girls?"

"I've had enough." *You got* that *right.* "Some stripper just put Pilar's glasses up his ass and then put them back on her face."

"She'll be seeing E. coli for months."

"I'm too drunk to drive. Can't you take me home? I feel like I'm going to be sick."

You and me both, sister.

"I didn't drive," I stated, triumphant.

"That's OK. I did. But there's no way in hell I'm driving back. Why do I keep forgetting that tequila is the enemy?"

You have so many. How can you possibly keep them all straight?

"I don't really think that's a good idea," I said.

"My driving is an even worse one.... Ah, come on, Damian.... You know I'd—"

"All right, Samara. All right," I capitulated. "Just let me say goodbye to Egon."

She smiled. Of course she did, she'd beaten me yet again. "Good. I'll go get my purse."

We parted ways—again—only temporarily. I walked over to Egon and took a healthy gulp of somebody's beer. Finally, something that tasted good. I patted Egon on the shoulder.

"Hey! Egon!" Ian/Bradley/Josh shouted. "I think she likes you, man."

"Yeah, yeah." Egon pulled his face away from the brunette's gyrating ass.

"You think this one'll give you the clap, too?!"

Egon cringed. I paused. "Uh, hey ... look, man," I hesitated. "I gotta take Samara home. She's shit-faced."

"Be careful, Damian."

"I think I'm OK to drive."

"Hell, the cops would be doing you a favor if they arrest you tonight."

"Yeah ... well, sorry I can't be at the wedding next week."

"You should've been. It's all my fault, Damian. I'm really sorry."

He looked up at me with wet eyes. What is it with these people and alcohol? I need to start hanging out with the teetotaler set.

"We can talk about all that later. Congratulations. See you later. You're a lucky bastard to have a woman like Pilar."

"You don't know the half of it."

Those eyes again. Like he wanted to tell me the half, three-quarters, eight-sevenths of it right then and there. I slapped his shoulder and headed to the doorway. Samara was waiting there with a sloppy, drunk smile. Eyes half-open. She gave me the keys and a hug. I had to peel her off me and point her to the door. As she swerved along, I took one last look at Studs 'N' Muffins.

Nandi was nowhere to be seen.

"Damn," I said, as I turned to drive my drunken ex-fiancée home.

SUNDAY, DECEMBER 4, 20—
4:26 P.M.

"I knew there'd come a time in our relationship," Kevin opened, much to my regret. I have no clue why I always feel the need to answer the phone. "The time when I was gonna have to seriously bust your ass."

"What did I do now?" I groaned, my head throbbing.

I know what you're thinking. You're thinking, You spineless jellyfish, you did it, didn't you? You were driving her home and she gave you those come-hither-on-my-tits (sorry, I *was* just at a strip club) eyes, you had "So Happy Together" playing in your head, you started thinking of all the good times, *never* the Cataclysm, the good sex you used to have, got all misty, and fell for the okey-doke. You couldn't wait to jump into bed with her.

But it didn't happen like that.

I wish I could say she tried pulling that crap on me, and I got all Hamlet pimp-shit on her ass, and screamed, "Take thee to a nunnery, bitch!"

But it didn't happen like that, either.

"Just tell me what happened," Kev ordered.

Samara threw up a couple times in the Studs 'N' Muffins parking lot and passed out in the car. I rolled down the windows and drove her to our old apartment. I carried her all the way to what used to be our bed, stripped her down, and she said, "I love you, Damian." "I know, Samara," I replied, and kissed her on the forehead. I found a comforter, stripped to my boxers, and curled up on the futon in our old living room. And of course, I woke up with yet another huge hangover.

"Jesus. You're an idiot."

"I *thought* I was being a good Samaritan," I protested.

"All I know is, you've got this beautiful woman interested in your Quasimodo ass, and you keep leaving with someone else."

"OK. I'll give you Yanely. But Samara hardly counts."

"Your ex-*fiancée*?!"

"Could you keep it down?"

"It's just a weird habit you've fallen into. And what about Priti?"

"I think I'm gonna be sick."

"Good. I just don't understand you, man. Nandi likes you. You like her, and yet you keep fucking up. Going home with Samara?! Jesus. It's like you want to be miserable, or something."

"What I want is some aspirin."

"Just at least admit that you like the woman. At least tell me that."

"I haven't even admitted it to myself. And why are you and DiDi always on me about this woman all of a sudden?"

"Maybe we're just…"

"What?"

"You know what? Fuck this. I'm out."

MONDAY, DECEMBER 5, 20—

8:07 P.M.

After work, DiDi came into my room, sniffing. It's been like a huge weight lifted from our shoulders with Hep and Neville no longer around. The tension's gone, and I don't miss it one bit. Though I do wish Hep would come back. I do miss him, actually.

"Either you have one hell of an air freshener," she proclaimed, "or you really have quit smoking."

I looked her directly in her incredulity, and said, "I'm totally useless with the stuff. I needed to actually do something with myself."

"That reminds me." She pulled my pages from behind her back and sat down next to me. "I finished what you gave me so far."

"Yeah. What did you think?"

Now that Samara was no longer in the picture, I had to rely on DiDi to be my primary reader. It used to be her job for years, anyway. I was hoping she didn't mind it now. But by the wrinkles forming on her forehead, I could tell something was troubling her. It was only a first draft, but we artists always want to be unequivocally proclaimed genius no matter how rough the draft. We need the love. And we definitely didn't need any flak about taking our ex-fiancées home. I swallowed hard in anticipation.

"Well," she said, slowly. "It's not as hard to read as *Winter Soldiers*. I mean, you can follow it along pretty easily."

"I've learned my lesson."

"But the dialogue—well, it's a bit rough. I mean, awkward. I'm glad you don't have folks swearing as much."

"Awkward. Like, uh … how?"

I was feeling myself becoming defensive. I'd thought I'd outgrown that, but a part of you always takes criticism too personally. What could be more personal, really? It's like calling a mother's toddler a dickhead, or something.

"A little disjointed, is all."

I felt a little relieved. "Oh, that. I've grown bored with written language. Too smooth. I like the urgency of spoken language. I thought I'd write spoken for awhile."

There were question marks written all over her forehead, but she trudged on. "OK. But this hero of yours…"

"What about him?"

"Well," she exhaled, "well, it's like, I like the action. I mean, what happens to him. But it's like things are always happening *to* him. He never really takes any action himself."

"Oh, you don't like the passive hero."

"I don't know. He's sympathetic enough. I guess. But how can you feel but so much sympathy for a guy who always lets stuff happen to him?"

"What about when he got that disease?" I suggested. "He was acting then."

"But he was some place he shouldn't have been in the first place. And his boss man directed him there. It wasn't like he was really acting on his own. When is he gonna *act*, Damian?"

"I don't know, DiDi. I got this thing about powerlessness, and all these powers weighing down on us. Megalithic government, multinational corporations, data mining, and all types of media blaring at us all day, 'Buy! Buy! Buy!' Cameras filming us everywhere we go. And all the billions of people around us, the world getting smaller everyday. And all we can do is bear our load, hope our spouses don't leave us, our kids don't turn into junkies, and that we can retire before we go to the grave. It's like we wait quietly to lay our burden down and hope we can escape it all. But we can't. Even if you build a shack in the Montana wilderness and forage for your own food, eventually the Man is gonna nab ya."

"Yeah, but what about all that Joseph Campbell crap and the path of the hero you're always talking about?"

"That was Bob. I've never read the stuff."

"Really? … Anyway, I thought there was something like the boy becomes an apprentice, the mentor dies, and the boy becomes a man, right?"

"Pat Morita didn't die in *Karate Kid*. He was waxing on and waxing off even in the sequels."

"Yeah. But he was the original Arnold. You couldn't kill him off."

"Right."

"But that's the process, right?"

"Yeah. I think so."

"Then when is it going to happen, Damian? When does Ice become a man?"

DATE: Monday, December 5, 20— 9:53 P.M.
TO: drcross@wintersoldiers....
FROM: fela@africanopportunity....
SUBJECT: Investment Opportunity

Greetings Mr. Cross:

My name is Dr. Fela Ade Olatunji Abache, and I am the nephew of late Nigerian President Sani Abache. I am writing you because in my late uncle's will I was recently bequeathed $10 million USD in krugerands. I have exchanged them for their proper value in American dollars and need a temporary place to deposit the funds. If you could kindly provide me with your checking account information at secure.africanopportunity...., I will transfer the monies into your account and then move them to my Cayman account minus your fee of $50K USD...

DATE: Monday, December 5, 20— 11:07 P.M.
TO: drcross@wintersoldiers....
FROM: samhern@bcdi....
SUBJECT: So sorry

Damian,

I just wanted to apologize for how I acted on Saturday and to thank you for driving me home and tucking me in. You are always the perfect gentleman and such a sweetheart. I miss that about you. If it's not too much, when I get back from Brazil, can we get together? We can just have a coffee or a beer. I just miss you sometimes.
Love,

Samara

TUESDAY, DECEMBER 6, 20—
10:22 P.M.

Carpe Diem. I've been hanging out at this café now for the past couple weeks. Samara and I used to come here all the time when we had first started dating. I don't know why I'd decided to start frequenting the place again. I guess I've been finding myself on the verge of repeating old mistakes. Maybe I wanted to use this place as a launching pad.

It's a cool spot during the day, though. At night, there's a completely different vibe. But before the vampires emerge, you can really chill here. I've been taking my laptop, sipping my coffee, and looking appropriately pensive when somebody was looking. That's what we all do here—we without 9 to 5s.

There's an old, redheaded guy who's here every day, Robert. He's supposed to be some big-time poet, but all I ever see him do is sit comfortably in his scruff, staring mindlessly into space. But who can say where one finds their inspiration.

I find mine in Stella, the attractive half-Irish/half-Chinese (those Irish sure do get around—just ask my great-great granddaddy, right?) waitress who works the day shift. She has an incredibly lithe body with just a hint of ass and an ebullient personality that has all the guys rising to her occasion. She's a vamp, really. All the fellas love her, and she knows it. She works it. Hey, when you work for tips, you've gotta do whatever it takes. But it doesn't take much for Stella. A wink, a nod, a smile, and guys are digging into their wallets to buy her affections.

She started talking to me because I refused to talk to her. I didn't want to hitch a ride on the ship of fools salivating in her wake. The way those guys drooled made me ashamed to be a guy. I mean, how silly are we in front of an attractive woman? I wanted to act like I was not one of those.

"Nina Simone," she'd declared.

"What?" I asked, snapped out of my reverie.

Stella stood over me with a creamy smile. "You seemed to really be enjoying the music," she said. "I thought you might want to know who it is."

"Yeah. Right. *The Colpix Years*. I just love 'If You Knew.'"

"You never struck me as being that sentimental. I guess a guy who keeps to himself as much as you do would be, though."

I shrugged. "So, you a fan?"

"Yeah," she smiled. "I know it's a bit stereotypical to be a Nina Simone fan. Like I have inner depths or something. Or a mysterious sexuality."

"Do you?"

"Then it wouldn't be a mystery now, would it?"

She gave a coy smile. I knew it was intended to melt me. There was an awkward pause.

"I'd go Mel Tormé then. If you want to avoid stereotype."

"That old guy from *Night Court*?"

"*The Velvet Fog*. Yes. He had one of the smoothest voices ever," I informed. "Better yet, check out Johnny Hartman. If there's a God, then Johnny Hartman is His voice. Or at least God wishes he were."

"Johnny Hartman, hunh?"

Stella had actually written it down. After that, we'd talk every day I came into the place. She was young—maybe twenty-five—and was really getting into jazz vocalists. There's absolutely nothing about her that's resistible. Yet, I've been pretty cold toward her. I'll talk. I'm even interested in what she has to say. But my heart just isn't into it. I admit, I have Nandi on the brain. I don't know what my problem is. I just find myself troubled by so many things. Why would I invite somebody into the maelstrom of my mind? But I can't stop thinking about her.

I was sitting there this afternoon waiting for DiDi. She said she wanted to talk to me about something, but more than that, she wanted to take a long lunch for a change. The shelter can really drain her at times. I personally don't know how she survives all that pain and misery every day. I guess that's why she's studying for the GREs.

Stella was taking a break herself, sitting at my table and chatting about acting and getting her headshots. I was smiling stiffly at her travails. If I fell for another actress, I would personally take myself to the next Klan meeting and hand myself over. I did my best to act interested, while the few men present were staring enviously at us. I knew if I fucked around playing this cold act, she was gonna wind up asking me out, and I'd have to look up the Grand Wizard's number and make an appointment.

Suddenly, Johnny Hartman came on over the speakers. I smiled genuinely. She did the same, triumphantly, like she got me.

"You were like, so right about him," Stella purred. "His voice. You could just melt. Makes you want to have the slowest, most passionate sex of your life."

I know that was supposed to get a rise out of me. It didn't. But Nandi's entrance did. I'd already been looking at the door, waiting for my cousin. But when Nandi came in, I simply gawked. How could I not? She looked amazing in this suit-skirt thingee. OK, I admit it, from my brief foray into *Harper's Bazaar*-o World, I could tell you exactly what she was wearing. But please, let me hold onto this thin veneer of manhood I have left. Thank you....

It was Burberry, girl. I refused to look at the shoes. She had a nice briefcase, though. How much money does this woman make? Her hair shimmered ebony down to her shoulders, and she was wearing the telltale white, iPod earphones that'll get you jacked in New York. She seemed to really be into whatever she was listening to. That concentration haze of hers was simply magnetic.

I must've really been staring because I caught Stella turning to see what I was looking at. I heard a "Hmph," or something to that effect.

Nandi looked around and caught sight of me. She made her way to my table. Stella abruptly got up and made herself scarce. I could feel a discomforting heat from her departure. It competed against this damned inner glow I was feeling as Nandi sat down. She looked at Stella as she tugged the phones from her ears.

"Who's that?" she asked, nonchalantly.

"Stella," I said, defensively. "She works here."

"Hm."

"You're not going to start in on that again, are you?"

Why did I want to argue with this woman? Like I didn't know the answer. She screwed up her face in thought.

"I thought I apologized for that."

"Yeah. Of course. Yeah. You did. But I—well, I'm sorry about the other night. With Samara. Nothing's going on there—" *Shut up!* "—she was just drunk, and I took her home. But nothing happened—"

"It's really none of my business, Damian," she stated, icily.

"Yes. No—I mean, no, it's not. But well, shit. I just really wanted you to know that. That's all."

Time seemed frozen. She looked into my eyes. I squirmed. She smiled, and I relaxed. "Where's your cousin, by the way?"

"I don't know. I'm waiti—oh, shit."

"What?"

"Were you supposed to meet her here, or something?"

"Yeah. Why?"

"Damnit," I cursed. "Tell me something. Have you ever felt like your life were a bad sitcom?"

"No. My family's strictly melodrama."

"Well, welcome to UPN, girl." She gave me a questioning look. "DiDi. She's playing matchmaker again. I guess some habits are hard to break."

"Yeah. You told me something about that. Was there a knife involved?"

"Yes," I confirmed. "Hey look, I'm sorry. I'll kill DiDi when she gets home tonight. If you wanna go, that's perfectly acceptable. I won't be offended."

"No."

"No?"

"I took a half-day today—for *once*—and I'm flying to Rio tomorrow."

"Are you packed?"

"It takes me at least a week to pack. I started last month."

We both laughed until it crumbled to silence. Suddenly, we found ourselves looking at each other. We might've actually been blushing. Stella came by with a throat clearing (I don't think it really had anything to do with me; she just doesn't like competition—not really used to it, I guess) and took Nandi's order. After that little bit of awkwardness was over, I pointed to her iPod.

"What are you listening to?"

"Kate Bush."

"Kate Bush, hunh?"

"Yes," she said, archly, like I'd just attacked her. "I refuse to be a mediated Negress."

"A what?"

"A mediated Negress. Like I'm supposed to like certain things and not like others—dress, act, talk, *be* certain ways—to somehow prove my authenticity. So, yes. I *love* Kate Bush. I even like country music. Hank Williams and Sam Bush. I'm not ashamed. I've got nothing to prove. Hell, I even liked *Monster's Ball*."

I laughed.

"What? Oh. I'm sorry. I need to have at least one rant a day."

"No, no. That's OK." I eased back in my chair. "Well, you lost me with *Monster's Ball*. They'd never do that sex scene with a white woman. Though I'm sure people'd pay good money to watch Julia Roberts do anal. But damn, woman, I love Kate Bush."

"You do?" She was incredulous.

"Hell, back when I was a teenager—and earnest—I used to play 'Running Up That Hill' over and over again, singing with my eyes closed, maybe even squeezing out a tear or two."

"It must've been cute."

"Ain't nothin' cute about teenage angst."

But everything was cute and wonderful with Nandi this afternoon. I know when you first talk to a potential mate, you have the world in common. That's all part of the lust we mold to fit the other's genitals. But I couldn't help but feel a bond forming. And she was so intelligent, so warm, I was never once bored with the woman.

"You know, it's funny," she divulged, "I'm generally a shy person."

"I can't believe that."

"No. I am. I used to hate drawing attention to myself. I guess because I've always lived in my father's shadow. He's a big-time Economics professor at Case Western. Has even advised a couple presidents."

"I thought you were from Youngstown."

"That's where we live. He commutes—don't ask me why. He likes depressed economies, I think. He should've just stayed in Kingston for that."

Damn, imagining her with a Jamaican accent and that red garter belt from the other night's fantasy…

"What?"

I cleared my throat. "Oh, nothing."

"But on stage," she continued. "It's all different. It's like I'm another person. Like I'm actually a strong woman, or something. Like I can really take charge. It's inspired me, you know? I don't want people telling me what I can and cannot do. I don't know how. But I'm going to figure out a way. I'm almost thirty. It's time for me to go after what I want in life. At least that's … that's what I want to try to do, anyway."

"I'd hate to stand in your way," I joked.

Nandi looked at me, deadly serious. I could feel every molecule on my skin heating up to a sizzle. I looked away. Outside. The afternoon had grown dark and gray.

"Look at the time," I said, though I never wear a watch.

"What time is it?"

"I—don't know. I—I never wear a watch. But it's late. I need to get going. I have a cousin to kill."

We paid another waitress. Stella had apparently left awhile ago, and I hadn't even noticed. I walked Nandi to her Prius. All that *and* environmentally conscious. We stopped at her door. And the world stopped. It muted, expanded, contracted. All I could hear was a dull electric hum. And all I could see were those lips, those expectant eyes. I was being drawn to her by something outside myself, everything within me. I reached out … and landed a clumsy hand on her shoulder.

"Well, uh … you have a good trip," I stammered.

"Yeah ... Right … Of course. See you when I get back?"

"Of course, um. You know, I wouldn't miss the band for the world."

"The band … Right."

THURSDAY, DECEMBER 8, 20—
3:16 A.M.

Kev wanted me to listen to something. Apparently, he'd been recording the band's practices and has been splicing and dicing their work into something coherent, taking out all the stops and starts and re-editing all their stuff, composing new songs out of all the tape, Teo Macero-style [see Miles Davis' *On the Corner*].

I went over to his apartment with all its sheet music, computer and stereo equipment, musical instruments, albums, and CDs (really, and I thought I was a packrat), put my six-pack of Red Stripe in the barren fridge, and made a place for myself to sit.

We listened in silence for well over an hour. I really enjoyed it, and he seemed to be enjoying my enjoyment. But most of the time, he just sat with his eyes closed, bobbing his head hypnotically, the movement broken up occasionally by a smile or a wince. I knew he was listening on a completely different plane than I ever could, but what I heard I really liked.

Kevie Kev was truly outdoing himself. What I was listening to was something I've never really heard before (and I listen to a *lot* of music). It was like the entire world was being remixed into a jazz/funk/hip-hop mold. It's not like nobody had ever invented fusion before. Fusion is what music's all about. African rhythms meet the European marching band, and jazz is born. Dvořak had gypsy jungle fever and sampled their beats. The poms love American blues and doo wop, and we get the British invasion. Jamaicans love the same, and there you have ska and reggae. We get a Jamaican moving to the South Bronx with his dub plates and love of toasting and we get hip-hop culture. And DJs today plunder the world for the funkiest samples. It's how music works. So it's not like Kevin Byrd is reinventing the wheel.

But he is puttin' it on Dubs. It's just fascinating how it's all coming together. Jazz hasn't been this danceable since Herbie Hancock and his Headhunters. There's so much going on, yet it all seems so easy to understand. He's trying to move ya. And I couldn't stop my toes from tapping, my head from bobbing, and (if I had been standing) my booty from shaking.

"So, what do you think?" Kev finally asked, after the disc was done.

I put on my professorial music critic's mask. I was missing the pipe, though. "Well," I opened, "it is a bit rough in patches…"

"Yeah. I know," he admitted, a little disappointed. "It's still a work in progress."

"But damn, Kev. I really love it. It's like you're on some whole, other shit."

His face spread out into a smile. I couldn't help beaming myself. "Yeah. Isn't it, though? It's like, like I'm even surprising myself. Like I've got all these great musicians, Tod and Raheem and Arturo, Sarah and Vik. And like we're all pretty much on the same page. Maybe we've all been sorta thinkin' the same thing for years, and we're lucky to have found each other."

"And Nandi, she can really sing."

"Yeah. She's not so bad. She's got a lot of energy. I wonder what she can do on the violin. She refuses to bring it in. It's like some kind of Elektra thing with her Pops, or some shit."

"You really like her, don't you?" I ventured—afraid of the answer, despite myself. Neither possible answer was all that appetizing.

Kevin laughed long and hard. "You know, for such a smart guy, you sho' is eat up with stupid."

"What the hell are you talking about?"

The "Bitch" look.

"No. Seriously. What?"

"Why do you think I bailed on going to the Scotsman the other night?"

"To go screw Councilperson __________."

"Well … yeah," he admitted. "But I can do that any time. So why do you think?"

"Can't I just act stupid and you tell me? I've got a novel going on in my head. I don't have the space to think about anything else."

"Hey, you ever see that maxi pad commercial about women leaking?" he asked.

"You know I'm part of the cultural elite. I don't really watch television."

"Oh yeah, right. You throw in foreign words, too, to sound smart. Got it. Anyway, this commercial was talking about how women should wear pads all the time 'cause they're constantly leaking."

"And?"

"And I was thinking, how fucked up is that? So, you've got this shitting, pissing, farting, burping, bleeding, *leaking* mound of tits and ass who's always harping on you to take out the garbage, constantly telling you how wrong you are all the time. Who needs that shit?"

I do.

"You do," he pointed. "And Nandi might just be the one who'd be all that for you."

I was incredulous. "That's a bit fast. The woman hardly knows me."

"Look, man, I know you've been out of the game for awhile. But we're talking a single, childless woman entering her thirties. Play time's over. No more bad boys or going out with someone because you've never gone out with a mime before."

"Oh, so she's giving up and is ready to settle."

"Settling and settling down are two different things," he declared. "Though I guess the two do often meld."

"Exactly."

"No. What I think we're talking about here are pure, quality-of-sperm type issues now. Is this guy gonna be a good father, etc.? The romance, the rest of it, that 'spark.' That's just gravy. Time to get down to bi'nis."

"Well then, what about you?"

"Did you miss the *entire* point of my little tale there?"

"No. I get it. You're a misogynist."

"Exactly."

"And Niggaman Vikram?"

Kev scoffingly laughed. "That bitch is way too pretty. Put a sari on his ass, and *I'd* fuck him."

"He *is* pretty."

"Besides, he's not as smart as you, and our dear Nandi's a bit of a genius fucker. Though I personally think you've got her snowed. But at least you're not intimidated by an intelligent, successful woman. Someone who makes a hell of a lot more money than you do."

"How could I be?"

"Ain't that the truth? WIC recipients take in more than your broke ass."

"That's not fair. They get free health care."

"Still."

"True." I sat in silence for a moment, thinking. Then busted out laughing. "You had me goin' there for a second, Kev."

"What?"

"No. That was good. You almost had me there."

Kev gave a "Suit yourself" shrug. That took me back for a second. He couldn't possibly be telling the truth.

"Well," I sobered up, "it ain't like she ever said shit like that to me before."

"What do you want her to do? Throw her tits in your face, and scream, 'Fuck me, Damian! Fuck me!'"

"It'd be a start."

We both laughed.

"She could at least call," I said, glumly. My mood was suddenly changing.

"She's the woman. Not you."

"That's not what you've been saying all these years."

"Still. Some customs are hard to break."

I felt myself becoming ugly, going into a well-worn shell where it was dark and dank and reeked of my own death. I looked at Kevin and was suddenly despising him. Why was he pushing me? Why was Deirdre? And Nandi? Why couldn't they all just leave me alone? I've been here before, and I didn't want to be here again. But I couldn't think of a place I'd rather be.

"It's like you're hell bent on being miserable," Kevin sighed, I think, disgustedly.

"Maybe that's all I know," I shot back. "Have you ever thought of that?"

"Yeah … Damian. Yeah. I have."

WEDNESDAY, DECEMBER 14, 20—
6:52 P.M.

"Hello?"

"Damian?"

"Yeah? … Nandi?"

"Yeah. Hey, what are you up to?"

"Well, Kev gave me a disc of you guys's stuff, and it's inspired me to pursue my life-long, secret musical ambition."

"What's that?"

"The funk cowbell."

She laughed. It actually felt good to hear her. I'm glad she couldn't see the goofy smile on my face at that moment.

"Are you still in Rio?"

"Yeah. Have you ever been?"

"No. I've never left the country."

"We ought to remedy that."

We?

"So, what's up, Nandi?"

"Well, it's just that—well, I know you love music, and all, and I didn't know if you liked Brazilian music. I was thinking you did, but I didn't know."

"Uh, some of it. Like samba and bossa nova. I hate that MPB crap. It's like Muzak on Prozak. But they've got some old funk that's really cool. Why?"

"Have you ever heard of baile? It's like Miami bass—but Brazilian. It's a lot of fun."

"Ooooh, I've always wanted to hear 'Pop That Coochie' in Portuguese."

"It's a lot more fun when you don't understand what they're saying."

"The same with politicians. So, why'd you call?"

"Oh. No reason. Just to talk, I guess. I don't know. I gotta go, though. We're about to go have some Brazilian barbecue—though I guess that it's just barbecue down here. Then it's another night of dancing. This is the most exhausting wedding I've ever been a part of. And I've been in a lot lately."

"I'm jealous."

"You should be. Everybody's so *beautiful* down here. And they really know how to have a good time. Being an American sucks. Oh yeah. Samara says 'Hi.'"

"You're talking to *her*?"

What is that woman up to?

"What was that? I think you're breaking up."

"Uh, nothing."

"Yeah. Samara. She's a lot cooler sober. Kinda nice, actually. She has nothing but nice things to say about you now."

I laughed at that one.

"No, seriously. She told me how nice you were to drive her home that night. How kind you are. She makes you sound like a saint, Damian. I think when this wedding party gets back, every woman in it's gonna be calling you up for a date. Even the married ones."

"Well, I better get my BlackBerry ready."

"Yeah, you do that. I better get going. Keep practicing that cowbell. Bye."

DATE: Thursday, December 15, 20— 12:42 A.M.
TO: drcross@wintersoldiers....
FROM: jokefacekiller@22catch....
SUBJECT: Da Hoez

damian

do you have any pictures of these honeys? i'm kind of rooting for this nandi chick, but ina sounded kinda fine. is she? and how cute was this yanely babe? could nandi really be as beautiful as you portray her or is this all poetic license? it's so hard to tell. i say you throw some of the babes' pix up on your site and then put it to a vote. let the readers decide. but without the visuals, how are we supposed to know?

SATURDAY, DECEMBER 17, 20—
4:15 A.M.

Ladies, how to tell the penis size of a prospective partner in one, easy lesson:

"Damn, ole girl's kinda fine."

"Dakota?! Really?"

"Hell yeah, a tiny bod like that. It's like you could really do some real damage. Tear that ass *up*."

Mighty Mouse.

"You have *got* to be kidding. She has no ass."

"What? Oh, you need a woman with a big, *fat* ass, right? Like she needs a gurney just to walk down the street, or some shit."

"Naw. Nothing like that. But I do like curves. Something that tells me she's a woman."

Average Cat.

"Fuck that. Give me that gurney bitch. Hell, give me a seven-foot, three hundred-pound gorilla bitch with Rocky Mountain tits and a Himalayan ass, and I'd be spelunking *all* night long."

King Kong Motherfucker.

"What about you, Damian?"

"What?"

"What type of woman do you like?"

"Me? Well … uhhhhhh …"

MONDAY, DECEMBER 19, 20—
8:49 P.M.

I needed music. Yes, *need*. So, I went on down to *Soul on Wax*. I still had a bunch of Neville's money. In retrospect, he really didn't destroy as much stuff as I'd originally thought. I was finding it difficult to spend all the cash he gave me. I wasn't going to give it back. I ain't crazy now. I consider it my fee for not kicking his ass that night. Besides, do you know how much music's out there? I've got to buy it *all* before I die (minus rock, country, and classical, of course, but definitely including Tuva throat singing).

Mayrav greeted me from behind the counter as soon as I walked in. "Damian, hey. Your ears must've been burning."

"How's it going, Mayrav?" I asked, distracted.

"Now, is that any way to greet your African-American sister?"

I looked around apprehensively. No one had heard her. "Seriously, Mayrav, if the wrong person hears that, one day you're gonna catch a serious beat down."

She waved, dismissively, like she were seven feet tall instead of barely five. "Hey, when you're done, can I talk to you?"

"Sure. What about?"

"It's a bit private," she informed, to my curiosity.

"Sure. Whatever."

I can't tell you the joy it is for a poor music junkie like me to walk around in a CD shop with over a thousand dollars in my pocket. Before I became a critic, I used to have to constantly decide between eating and music. Ramen would always be there, but the extended CD of Jimi Hendrix's *Band of Gypsys* for $8.99 only came around once in a lifetime. I would sit up in my room dizzy from lack of food and the absolute Nirvana of listening to Jimi, Buddy Miles, and Billy Cox jamming away. It *is* the funkiest rock album in all Creation.

And now here I was—with all this music and all this money. And I didn't even have to buy used if I didn't want to. But old habits die hard. I hit the used bins first. And proceeded to lose my mind.

Marvin Gaye, Phoebe Snow, Full Force (?), Nina Simone, Billies Holiday and Eckstine, Wilson Pickett, Joe Bataan, Talking Heads, Kyoto Jazz Massive, Company Flow, Rakim, Rob Swift, Aretha, Azymuth, Beny Moré, Celia Cruz, Mad Professor, King Tubby, Lee "Scratch" Perry (in honor of Nandi's father) ... I thought my head was going to explode.

I kept running to the counter, dumping more and more CDs in front of Mayrav, her devilish smile growing wider to the point I thought she was going to need reconstructive surgery just to look normal again. I finally stopped, breathless, with DJ Rupture and all things King Britt. Mayrav looked absolutely ecstatic ("Support your local record store," that's my motto). She screwed up her face and held up Marvin Gaye's *Here, My Dear*.

"I distinctly remember your having this," she said.

[See THURSDAY, OCTOBER 11.]

I returned her grin. "Yeah," I confessed. "I have to replace that and a whole bunch of other stuff." Before she could ask, I answered, "Long story."

"Well, I'm glad you came here instead of Amazon."

She rang me up. It only came to some $900. I was proud of myself. I only spent $9.19 per disc. Old habits do die hard. She put all the CDs in a couple of boxes. Breathless, she looked up at me. "Could we go back to my office?"

I followed her. She seemed nervous, which made me more than a little apprehensive. She closed the door behind us and looked as though she were struggling to find the words. Her eyes combed the floor for them.

"What is it, Mayrav?" I finally asked, feeling trapped. Like I'd done something wrong.

"I'm gonna have a baby, Damian."

Wait a second! *Had* I done something wrong...? No, I distinctly remember leaving before I took the Nestea Plunge. Though I do remember leaving with a mighty mean thirst.

"Uh ... congratulations, Ms. Amou."

"I want you to be the father."

Stunned, I plopped down for a seat—which I missed, of course, crashing to the floor and smashing my head against her desk. "Always go for physical comedy." Along with that supporting local music stores thing, that's my favorite motto.

"Oooh, are you OK?"

She rushed toward me to put her hand on the back of my head. I instinctively jerked away. She stopped, her hand dangling in the air. She eventually withdrew it.

"Yeah. I'm OK. What the hell are you talking about? Unless you have the gestation period of a sperm whale, I can't be your baby daddy."

"No," she chuckled. "I *want* to have a baby. Sorry, I guess I didn't make that clear."

"No. You didn't."

"Well, I want to go in vitro, and I want you to be the father. I mean, the donor."

"Don't they have sperm banks for that?"

"What if I get a child molester's sperm? You're not a child molester, are you, Damian?"

"See, *these* are exactly the things we should know about each other before you have my kid."

"Well technically, it would be my baby."

"What? Like I wouldn't be involved?"

"You could if you wanted to be. But you wouldn't have to. I've got more money than I know what to do with. I can afford to raise the baby on my own."

"Oh hell no. If I'm having a baby, I'm *gonna* be involved."

What the hell was I saying? Mayrav looked encouraged. She was beaming. My heart started creeping up into my throat. I didn't know what to say.

"Look, Damian," she continued. "I'm thirty-eight years old."

"Really?!"

"Yeah. Why? How old did you think I was?"

"I don't know. Guess I never really thought about it."

"Right. And I'm running out of time. And it doesn't look like I'm getting married any time soon. I want to have a baby. That's all. I know it's selfish. I could adopt. But I want my own baby. Before it's too late."

"But why me? It doesn't make any sense."

"Sure it does. You're the sweetest guy I know. And probably the smartest. You're really talented and not a bad-looking guy. And if you want to be, I know you'll be an excellent father."

Sounds reasonable.

Oh, shut up.

"Yeah, but then you'll have this green-eyed-Armenian-Moroccan-black-Jewish-Catholic kid on your hands. Think of the stares."

"There are weirder combinations out there."

"Think of the guilt."

"That just comes with having a conscience."

The persecution complex … ? The paranoia? Somebody help me here.

See. This is exactly why I hate arguing with women. They always seem to have a retort for every objection. I lose every time. It's just not humanly possible. How do they do it? I need to buy myself a garage and start fiddling around with tools for situations like this.

"And it's not like the baby will be weird. Well, knowing us, maybe a little," she tittered. "But she will be this beautiful, immaculate gift. And she'll be ours."

My head started to throb, pulverizing any words in there into dust.

"And it's not even like we'd have to get married, or anything. Or even be particularly close. She would just be this gift we share."

"But what if you found someone? How would you explain it?"

"The truth?"

"I guess the same goes for the kid."

"Of course. Look, screw the nuclear family. It's a myth, anyway. Family's what you make it. It could be two people or two hundred. It doesn't matter. As long as the child's raised in a loving, supportive environment."

I exhaled, exhausted. "What would I have to do?"

"What you do every day …except in a cup."

"Funny," I breathed. "I do take Sundays off."

"Why don't you take some time to think about it? I know I just laid a bundle on your doorstep, so to speak. I just want to know you'll give it serious consideration. It would mean so much."

"Yeah. OK."

I picked myself up off the floor and made my way to the counter to pick up my boxes. They were damned heavy.

DATE: Monday, December 19, 20— 10:11 P.M.
TO: drcross@wintersoldiers....
FROM: jman@localrealtor....
SUBJECT: A cry for help

Damian,

I know this may seem out of the blue, but we met awhile ago at the Scotsman. It doesn't matter, though. I'm desperate. I've been having to watch this incredible Steeler season in the company of Browns fans. If you can only imagine the utter misery I've been going through, you'd come and watch the Steelers game with me at The End Zone Thursday night.

Jenna

DATE: Tuesday, December 20, 20— 12:44 A.M.
TO: jman@localrealtor....
FROM: drcross@wintersoldiers....
SUBJECT: RE: A cry for help

my goodness, woman. i had no idea the situation was so dire. no

> self-respecting human being should ever have to suffer browns fans. i'll be at the end zone on Thursday with terrible towel and other necessary armaments. we have to hold those barbarians off at the gate.

THURSDAY, DECEMBER 22, 20—
10:19 A.M.

I needed this party more than anything. I just had to get my mind off of Mayrav Amou. I've hardly gotten to enjoy my new CDs. I haven't really been writing, and what I have been writing has seemed a bit lame. Even Sista Olu's Germanic insults haven't really spurred me on like they used to at the gym.

I don't know. In all honesty, I don't even know why I'm contemplating it. Yet, part of me's really insulted that she would even consider me for a donor. Another—perhaps bigger—part is more than a little flattered. I mean, the woman knows a lot of dudes. She probably knows the entire music scene in town and probably large parts of scenes in other cities. She definitely knows half the arts scene around here. And who knows how many fools in the business world? And yet, she's asking me.

She thinks so much of me, she's willing to raise a biracial, green-eyed child and all the hassle that must entail—just because she likes my genetic makeup. That's a heavy trip, baby. Of course, she might have an unhealthy fixation with black culture (*Soul on Wax*, her calling herself "African-American"—joke or otherwise—even her email, boorman6girl, is a reference to *Putney Swope*, the greatest black comedy this side of *Blazing Saddles*—can I get an "Amen?!"), but so does the rest of America. That's what makes this country great.

I don't know what to do. I don't know what to think. I don't know what she's thinking. I even thought this might be some kind of drastic ploy to get me to marry her, but I had to laugh that one off. Who in their right mind would want to subject themselves to that? Definitely not Samara. I mean, genetically I might be an asset (which is undoubtedly doubtful), but financially I'm a huge liability. We writers don't make crap. Actually, if we could at least make that much, we could sell it for fertilizer.

So yeah, when Kevin called up asking me if I wanted to go to a party, I jumped at the chance. It was at this dude Miguel's house. He's a burgeoning backpack rap producer relatively new to the scene. I've heard some of his stuff. It's a little abstract (he's really into distorted samples), but pretty darn good. And definitely anti-bling. It promised to be a pretty artsy crowd, very intellectual. No hoochie mamas, Kristal, or bullets.

"Hey," I said, on the way, "your girl called from Brazil. Did you put her up to it?"

"I thought that's what you wanted," Kevin countered.

"No. I said she *can* call. I didn't say I wanted her *to* call."

"I hope you were at least civil."

"I'm a bourgie Negro. Of course I was civil. I ain't no gotdamned heathen."

"So, what's the problem?"

I couldn't think of one. At least not with her. I could think of millions for myself. So I remained silent.

"So, let me get this straight: you're all kinds of lonely, unattached as can be, and there's this beautiful, intelligent woman who's used to being pursued pursuing you, and *you're* playing hard to get."

"I ain't playin' shit, fool."

"Calm down, D. I'm just sayin—"

"What are you saying, Kev? What are you, DiDi, and Nandi—what are you playing at? I feel like I'm on an episode of *Punk'd* and Ashton Kutcher's gonna pop out at any second."

"You ever watch that show?"

"No. Why?"

"It just bugs me, is all. One, it *ain't* funny. And when you 'punk' someone, it means you make them back down from a fight without ever throwing a punch. Not make them the victim of a practical joke. I mean, if you're gonna appropriate our terms, at least appropriate appropriately."

I gave him a heated look as he drove on. He gave me a brief look and chuckled. "You know what she told me when I still thought I had a chance?" he asked, jovially.

"Of course I don't."

"She told me that she used to go out with jerks like me all the time. It was a force of personality thing. That forceful, egotistical shit. Said it reminded her of her father, and she couldn't resist. And just like Pops, we all ended up being dickheads."

"Wait, she told you she used to go out with guys like you?" I asked. "I thought that was a pick-up line, like 'I don't really know how to give a good blow job.'"

"And doesn't it just break your heart when they're actually telling the truth?"

"Sometimes, it just physically hurts. All teeth and vise grips."

We both laughed.

"Anyway, bruh," Kevin sighed, "she told me she was through with jokers like me. That she's now looking for a man of substance. And you ain't nothin' if you ain't a man of substance."

"Carbon and water, mostly."

"Whatever."

This Mayrav thing was really getting to me, and this Nandi affair was bugging me as well. What did people want from me? Oh yeah, my sperm apparently. But why couldn't they just leave me alone? To top it all off, I had to go to Pittsburgh in a few days, where *nobody* would be leaving me alone at all.

But I was determined to have a good time, which means I was halfway there. Miguel had the place decked out with cheesy Christmas decorations—replete with mistletoe and Mexican Santa. There was egg nog, thank God. So I knew what I was gonna be doing. He also had all kinds of Christmas music playing—from Bing Crosby and Nat King Cole to Jimi Hendrix and Mariah Carey to "Santa Claus Is a Black Man," "Santa Lost a Ho," and "Clint Frostwood."

We're eatin' CHALLAH! With salt and butta...

Folks were hip and happenin' and thought way too much. Being on the edge of culture is a precarious perch, and you had to really concentrate to stay on it. These people were even intense in their enjoyment. I floated in and out of different conversations, just happy to hear about anything other than ova. "Everybody says, 'Stay the course.' I say, 'Cut your losses.'" "I think every possible James Brown sample has been exhausted a million fold." "Have you thought about Stravinsky?" "I don't know. RJD2 or Prefuse 73." "What about Nac One?" "Screw the Fugees, if you ask me. It was all about the Digables." "A border is the only thing that stands between an IDP and a refugee." "Asians don't eat cheese." "You're kidding." "No. Think about it." "Who the hell wants to emulate William Gaddis?" "Who's ever read Marx all the way through?" "That's why I'm down with Maoism." "You can learn a lot from *Discovery Kids*. Not as much as from *TNBC*, of course. I mean, *Hang Time* was fucking genius." "Have you ever noticed that everything in life has already been summed up in a *Seinfeld* episode?" "I think if I ever had a chance to produce a film, I'd grab William Goldman and have him write a porno. I miss the days when they had plots." "The theater's dead, the novel's dead, cinema's dying, and TV never lived. The only media left are video games and commercials." "Then he told me he let Erica shove a wooden broomstick up his ass." "Did they use protection?"

I was really enjoying myself, free-agenting to different conversations. I didn't really know anybody there, but I didn't want to play the wallflower. It was a good way to pass the time. I did stay for one discussion, though. I bumped into this really cute, mocha-flavored honey in the kitchen. Belinda. She was an interior decorator in her mid-30s, I guessed. She had great child-bearing hips, a nice smile, and short, raven hair (if you haven't figured it out yet, I'm a sucker for black hair).

She could talk forever about interior design. And since I'd never given the subject a moment's thought, I could listen forever. Besides, if you saw her, you wouldn't be too eager to pull away any time soon either. Even if she were reading the dictionary. She went on about space manipulation, how to make a room look bigger or smaller, about color and atmosphere, and mood creation, the whole feng shui thing, and a whole bunch of other things I didn't understand. I stood rapt, quickly getting carried away in her enthusiasm.

"You sound like an artist," I volunteered.

"Yeah, my son thinks I should paint more," Belinda said, airily.

"Oh, you have a kid?"

Her shoulders shot up into her ears and her face folded in on itself. One, giant "Doh!" written all over her body. She quickly relaxed, like none of that just happened. "Yeah," she chuckled, uncomfortably. "Bradley."

Act interested, you idiot. "Really?" I said, voice going up an octave. "How old is he?"

"Fifteen," she exhaled.

Don't walk away, boy. I firmly planted my feet on the linoleum and tried acting like the thoughts going through my head weren't. *Fifteen?! Jesus. When did you have him? When you were in the womb? Fifteen-year-olds are such pricks. I know, I've been one. Could you imagine me with a fifteen-year-old stepson? Too bad. She's really cute, really nice, and it sounds like she's got some talent. Maybe if Belinda and Yanely could swap kids. That little Siobhan was such a sweetheart. If I weren't hell bent and determined to be single, I would've really liked her. Who am I kidding? Too bad about that kid.*

I'd always thought of myself as better than those words flashing before my eyes. Depressing to realize that I really am not. It takes a hell of a man to take on another man's responsibility. And in that moment, I realized I'd failed to measure up. *Should I ask her for her number, anyway? To make her (me?) feel better? Naw, that wouldn't be right.*

The conversation petered out after that, like watching somebody slowly bleed to death. Some time after talking about Bradley's father being an asshole and Bradley being the point guard for his high school basketball team, Nandi walked in. I tried to ignore her and resuscitate Belinda's and my chat by talking about the book tour and my new novel, but both were lost causes. Belinda saw my distraction and excused herself. Yet another reason for me to feel like a jerk.

I no longer wanted to be around. I wanted to go home (I do that a lot), but Kev was busy ushering his precious singer/guitarist around. I don't know why, but I was becoming irritated. Why couldn't I just get gone? I slithered off to a corner of the kitchen and watched the party party on.

After awhile, Kev bounded into the kitchen and dove into the refrigerator. I'd never seen him so happy. It looked like he could moonwalk on Uranus. He saw me in the shadows.

"Hey, come on, D. We're celebrating."

"What?"

"Miguel. After you said you liked the disc, I sent him over a copy. He's really geeked. Talking about producing a couple tracks. Even thinks he could get Roots Manuva to lay down a rhyme or two."

"No shit?"

"Yeah. I also Fed Exed a few copies over to the label. The creatives are really diggin' it. But who knows what the bean counters'll say. I am kinda eschewing my core audience. Fuck it. Come on. Let's toast."

"I don't know, Kev…"

"Bitch" look.

"Yeah. Aiight."

Kevin, Miguel, his girl, a few hangers-on, Nandi, and I toasted with Imperial. Afterwards, Miguel grabbed an acoustic guitar and gave another one to Kev. They sat down and started jamming and singing. I had no clue Kevin had such a nice voice. What couldn't that boy do? I was going to have to put an S on his chest. Somehow, I'd floated off to a corner with Nandi and immediately started feeling awkward.

"I don't think I've ever seen him so happy," I opened.

"Right," she smiled.

"No. Seriously. Look at him." We did. He and Miguel were roaring at the top of their lungs and laughing when their voices cracked. "It's like he's never produced music before."

"None that you ever approved of."

"What?" I looked at her. She'd gotten some sun down there. She was glowing red and beautiful. It took everything I had to pull my eyes away.

"He lives for your approval, Damian," she informed. "You're the only family he's got. It broke his heart when you hated his first album."

"I never said I hated it."

"You didn't have to."

I looked hard into the carbonation in my beer.

"But none of that matters now," she trumpeted. "You love his new stuff. And he's happy. He can't stop talking about it. 'Top o' the world, ma,' and all that."

"You two sure do talk a lot," I harrumphed.

"Of course we do. We're music partners—and friends."

"Hm."

We looked at each other. There were all kinds of words flying between us, but they were too loud for either of us to really hear. We both looked away.

"I bought you some music," she volunteered.

"Hunh?"

"Music. While I was down in Brazil. I bought a whole bunch for you. Well, Samara helped. She said she remembers your tastes."

"Do you know what Samara is to me?"

"Yeah. Your ex-fiancée. We've been over this. Samara and I talked a lot actually."

"I'm sure."

"Well, I bought it, anyway. No cowbell funk, but I did get that baile stuff I was telling you about. And Jorge Ben and Banda Black Rio, I liked the name. I also found this really cool, instrumental version of 'Rapper's Delight.'"

"Oh my God, Nandi. I could kiss you."

"How about tomorrow?"

"What?"

"How about I drop the stuff off tomorrow night?"

"Oh, um. I can't. I'm kinda busy tomorrow."

"Yeah, sure." She chuckled uncomfortably. "Just tell me when."

"Why don't we make it after Christmas? I'm going home—"

"To Pittsburgh?"

"Yeah. How did you know?"

"I talk to Deirdre, you know."

"Oh. Right. Well, yeah. To Pittsburgh."

"I've always wanted to see that city. I've only seen the airport. I know that place like the back of my hand."

"Well, you should drop by some time. I'll show you around."

"OK. So, after Christmas then?"

"Right. After Christmas."

"So, what are you up to now? Are you sticking around?"

"Naw. I've got a long day tomorrow. I think I'm just going to head on out."

"Oh … Well. After Christmas then."

"Sure. See ya, Nandi."

I chugged the rest of my beer and proceeded to walk home. Alone. In a bitter December wind.

What the hell is wrong with me?

Who the hell am I kidding?

I know exactly what's wrong with me.

SATURDAY, DECEMBER 24, 20—
2:49 A.M.

"Ya know, I hate it when people say all this crap about how football's all barbaric and a metaphor for war. They're a buncha effete jagoffs who never really looked into the sport. Or a buncha—I hate to say it—pussies, who were too scared to play it when they were kids."

"That's what me an' the boys used to joke in the locker room," I added, putting on my manly man voice.

"You played?"

"Just a little in high school. I sucked, though."

"So, you know what I mean then? I mean, sure it's violent. But it's not boxing. Violence is a byproduct of the sport, not the reason for it."

One couldn't help admiring Jenna. Not only because of her ability to pontificate about the intricate ballet that is football, which she did for the next fifteen minutes (how she loves the pulling guard), but hell, look at her. With her oversized Troy Polamalu jersey, white turtleneck, her blond hair swept up in a ponytail beneath her pink Steelers cap, and football intensity, she was every man's tomboy fantasy. All that and that cheerleader's body of hers. Damn. I was surprised I wasn't having to beat the fellas in The End Zone off with a stick. They were definitely circling, though, waiting for the moment the beer took hold of my bladder.

It was all a distraction, though. I knew who I wanted to be with. But I knew I wasn't going to be. It's what I do. What I used to do. I didn't know I'd fall back into this habit of surrounding myself with women I didn't really care about because I couldn't bear being around the one I truly did. Some of my old girlfriends were such distractions. Old habits seem to die hard, right? I thought this one was gone, but apparently I'd resurrected it somehow.

No matter. The Steelers were stomping the shit out of the Raiders. And I was really enjoying myself. Cheese sticks, cheese fries, the Steelers, and a beautiful woman. *Who could ask for anything more?* And Jenna was *really* into football. She was so full of facts and figures, I wanted to check for testicles. She even had a fantasy football team. She was so intense. Any time one of our boys would do something stupid, she would curse like a sailor (which was oddly endearing). At times I felt so bad for Big Ben. If he could only hear her, he'd be crying on the sidelines. And when they did something good, she'd yelp and jump up and hug me, which is what happened when Coclough intercepted the Raiders' alcoholic, racist quarterback for a touchdown.

"Ya know," we heard. "Sometimes I'm amazed that we African-Americans are such great athletes."

I released Jenna, and asked, "Why's that, Bob?"

"'Cause clearly, our ancestors are the ones who couldn't run fast enough."

I tried not to laugh. Bob sat down at our table and started eyeing us suspiciously. I knew what was going through his mind. He's nothing if not a cliché. "Bob Hancock," I opened. "This is Jenna Mankiewicz. Jenna. Bob Hancock."

They awkwardly shook hands. I knew this was gonna be a long second half.

"So, you a Stillers fan?" she asked.

"No," Bob declared, haughtily. "Football's a bit too barbaric for my tastes. Golf is more my game."

Jenna and I looked at each other and smirked. Bob noticed and was about to say something.

"So, how'd you know I was here?" I interrupted.

"DiDi told me."

Awkward pause. They replayed Monday night's colossal fumble at the goal line that lost it for the Redskins.

"Goddamned Clinton Portis!" she erupted (I guess he was on her fantasy team). "Hold onto the fucking ball, ya idiot!"

What a princess.

"He lost the game for me this week. Fucking asshole."

"So, what you up to, Hancock?"

"Wishing *Loving v. Virginia* had never been lost."

"What?" Jenna asked.

"It's the Supreme Court decision that made interracial marriage legal," I groaned. "Bob thinks we're miscegenatin'."

Jenna screwed up her face and looked at him as though he were a maggot-infested corpse. Bob smiled back at her like he was the Cossack general who'd raped and pillaged her folks' village back in Poland a century ago.

"Bob's not really racist," I offered. "Ever hear of Carlton Hancock?"

"The golfer? Yeah. He's great."

"My pops," Bob declared.

"Yeah," I continued. "Bob here's rich. He never had 'The Black Experience.'"

"What's that?" she asked.

"Ah, you know," Bob smiled, breezily, "growing up po', absentee father, dodging gangs and drugs while your older brother's in jail and your younger sister's pregnant with her third kid, collecting WIC, welfare, *and* social security."

"So, he makes up for it by hating whitey while living better than most whites could ever imagine. That reminds me, Bob, how's your stepmother?"

"Good one, Damian. Veronica's fine."

Jenna looked at Bob again with that maggot-corpse look. Bob shrugged, nonplussed.

"Oh," she said, meekly.

Well, that pretty much killed that afternoon. To believe I blew Nandi off for this. As soon as the game clock clicked :00, Jenna was outta there, effectively weirded-out. And we'd just clinched home field advantage throughout the playoffs. I was furious and simply stewed in my own vitriol. If it had been a white boy who'd sat down here spouting that crap, Bob would've been the first to punch a little black in his eye. Then again, if

Bob would've been white, I would've done it myself. Of course, the irony is, there are few white boys today who have the balls to sit down and say some shit like that.

"Is that black enough for ya?" Bob muttered, as she exited.

"What the hell's your problem, man?" I asked.

"You like her?"

"What?"

"Do you like this Jenna babe? I mean, she's more than cute ... for a white girl. You like her?"

"Like, am I ready to go and produce a bunch of tragic mulatto children? No." *Sorry, Mayrav.* "But yeah, she's cool. Or *was* cool until you started your *Loving* crap."

"Least I could do for the Cause."

"Man, you ain't never had a cause. You ain't foolin' nobody."

Bob looked at me—hard.

"Pops is cutting me off," he finally chimed in.

"What?"

"He said it's his Christmas present to me. My manhood. Says he's been supporting me for way too long. That I haven't done anything with that support. Just pissing around the planet, squandering his hard-earned money. He feels that he's worked too hard all these years for his son to end up being one of the laziest bastards he's ever known. Can you believe it?"

What I couldn't believe was that he'd come up in here acting all Huey P. Newton with Jenna and then expected sympathy from me because he was losing his J.P. Morgan sugar daddy.

Never gonna get it, never gonna get it!

"Well, what the hell do you expect, Bob?"

Carlton Hancock is a true, American hero. He was a poor, little Alabama boy during Jim Crow, caddying for all these rich, white folks. He ended up teaching himself golf, "borrowing" clubs whenever and wherever he could. He would've gotten in serious trouble if they'd ever caught him. And Birmingham was no place for a black boy to get in trouble in those days. But he did it. He taught himself how to play golf. And he became one of the best.

He taught himself everything and even scored a scholarship to Oberlin. He became a scholar and an athlete, graduating at the top of his class with a degree in biochemistry.

He joined the PGA and started touring, being the first black to play on most of the courses he played on. He even had the nerve to win a few times. But he lost so much in doing so. Whites and blacks scrutinized his every move. White folks kept talking about his "instincts" and "athleticism" and his "power"—like he was some kind of goddamned mindless gorilla out there in the rough. Black folks thought he was a sell-out because "niggas don't play no golf." And he damned near lost his life on several occasions. Being out on the greens with black skin put a red bull's eye on your chest.

"Right," Bob conceded, "my Dad's a hero. Do you know how hard it is to be the son of a great man?" *Frankly, no.* "Always to be compared to someone the entire *world* looks up to? When you do right, it can never be right enough. And when you do wrong, it's the worst thing that's ever happened in the history of humanity. No matter what you do, you're a disappointment.

"And I am. I am a disappointment. I've always known it. I think I just declared myself a writer because it was the furthest thing from golf and biochemistry I could think of. But the writing ... the Black Power shit ... Hell, I went to Exeter. I'm such a *poseur*. What the hell am I supposed to do now, Day?"

"Oh. I don't know. Get a job, get paid too little, struggle to pay your bills—see how the other ninety percent lives."

Hancock chuckled. "Yeah, I guess the aristocracy should never ask the peasants for sympathy, hunh?"

"No. But they constantly do. Or else we'd never have had the Republican Party."

"A jobbie job," Bob speculated.

"Yeah. You better hurry up and get you one."

"Well, first I'm going to Ireland. Belfast. For Christmas."

"Wow, you're really stressing out over this, aren't you?" I asked, sarcastically.

"Ya know, I've always been a bit of an IRA sympathizer ... oppressed peoples of the world, and all that. I thought it'd be cool to see them in their natural habitat."

"I don't know, Hancock. I'd be careful. I think even Aristotle called them insane. 'Fearing neither flood nor earthquake,' or some shit. Think about it, twenty-three hundred years of crazy motherfuckers. I'd watch my ass, if I were you."

"What? Me worry?"

11:40 P.M.

Shot through the heart,
And you're to blame...

I must confess, I've never been an immigrant. Hell, I've never even left the country. I've never had to deal with la Migra, language barriers, Jerry Springer, or other immigrant issues. I've never had to figure out which parts of my native identity to abandon and which American parts to adopt. I simply don't get it.

Like of all the things America has to offer—chop suey, chimichangas, Lawrence Welk—why the hell did Priti Patel choose hair bands? While she was drowning in the melting pot, why didn't she reach for the hip-hop preserver? It had saved me.

It would've made the drive to Pittsburgh a *lot* shorter. All three of us could've been snaking, cabbage patching, and Trooping through the Allegheny mountains. Instead, DiDi and I had to find our happy places (which for me is *Schoolhouse Rock*) while guitars wailed, androgynous white dudes screeched bloody murder, and Priti banged her head, blaring, "Isn't this great?"

Yes, I'm a Bill

Yes, I'm only a Bill…

"Sure is, Priti!" I yelled.

It was just past Irwin when I decided that I could never love a woman who loved the Whitesnake.

But the cacophony was only a small part of the chaos in my head. Bad memories upon worse were bouncing around in my skull, giving me a migraine. I wanted to scream, cry, vomit, to turn around and go back home. Why had I agreed to go back to Pittsburgh? Why voluntarily be conscious for your own nightmare? This was like feasting on your own corpse, and I was steadily becoming nauseous.

"Are you OK?" DiDi asked, while I drove.

"I'll be fine," I groaned.

She put a reassuring hand on my forearm, as Priti screamed, *"Welcome to the jungle! It gets worse here every day!"*

Ultimately though, I'm quite proud of the way I've conducted myself today. I didn't lose my shit once. There were a few moments where I came close, but I always somehow maintained decorum.

Everybody was on edge, anyway. Priti was doing her best not to be a nervous wreck—that was probably why she was screaming the Scorpions up and down the Eastern seaboard. DiDi had invested so much in getting us to come, this thing was so important to her, you could tell she was going to lose it at any moment if anything went wrong. We knew Uncle Frank was going to be crawling out of his skin the entire time. And Aunt Clarissa was going to be constantly poised in the starting blocks, ready to dash out any fires. Nobody needed me to act the fool.

The three of us arrived late. Christmas Eve dinner (which used to be a big deal in our family) was already waiting for us when we got there. Since Uncle Frank has had his strokes, my aunt has become a multi-culti vegetarian gourmet. DiDi begged for no Indian fare—out of deference to Priti. Her mom was confused and disappointed and made Chinese instead.

Uncle Frank was looking old and tired—and really fragile. In his seventies, I suddenly wanted to do some carbon dating to ascertain his exact age. Because he looked centuries older than I had remembered him. It seemed like it had taken a lot out of him just to come and open the door for us. He barely had enough strength to erect himself and shake my hand. He used to revel in crushing it but now didn't have the energy. I almost felt sorry for the bastard and summoned a bit of sympathy for the guy until I saw the spackled section of wall where my head had once been.

"Hello, son."

"Hello, Uncle Frank."

DiDi and Priti quickly followed me beyond the door. I felt Uncle Frank's strength return to his hand, and I had to free myself from his clutch. He tried to hide his discomfort but was as rigid as a board. I couldn't help smiling.

"Hi, Daddy," DiDi greeted, and gave him a kiss on his stunned cheek. "Mom!"

Aunt Clarissa emerged from the kitchen with an apron on. She beamed at the sight of us, looking as beautiful as ever—though a lot grayer. She rushed over and hugged and kissed DiDi and me. Then she swept over to Priti and gathered her in her arms. Priti was tense at first, chuckled awkwardly, then melted into Aunt Clarissa's arms. My mother's sister always seemed to have that effect on people.

We settled into a fine dinner of noodles, vegetables, and tofu. What I really wanted was an Italian hoagie engorged with artery-blocking salami, ham, pepperoni, and Swiss cheese, but what can you do? Her veggie spring rolls weren't half-bad.

We filled the time with empty, getting-to-know-you chatter. I stayed pretty quiet. So, there were no major blow-ups. Uncle Frank seemed to be handling his lesbian daughter and her lover fairly well, but it did seem to exhaust him. Aunt Clarissa seemed to be her usual, loving self—perhaps a little *too* loving—but she didn't seem to be strained by the effort. Unlike Uncle Frank, who looked like he'd just put in OT at Dachau.

After dinner, the women moved off into the kitchen to clean up. A bit atavistic, but when in Rome, right? They really seemed to be enjoying each other's company. Priti looked visibly relaxed, and Aunt Clarissa seemed to really take to the woman. But it used to seem like she simply adored my father—so you never know. DiDi looked like most of the weight of the world had been lifted from her shoulders.

The old man and I just sat in the living room staring at each other beneath all the female laughter. After forever, he ushered me downstairs. To his bar. When we were kids, DiDi and I used to sneak down there and look at all his *Playboys*. In retrospect, I now realize that she enjoyed them as much as and for the exact, same reasons I did. That sneaky bastard.

It was an old school bar area with faux wood paneling on the walls, a large mirror, and tan leather stools. The old black velvet paintings were gone, but the "Nothing's Better Than a Tight Pussy" license plate with the *Fritz the Cat* feminized feline drunk off her furry ass was still there.

"Have a seat, boy," he ordered.

I obeyed while he moved behind the bar. He grabbed a remote, pressed a button, and Frankie Beverly and Maze started playing.

"Bourbon or scotch?" he asked.

"I've never known the difference."

He exhaled in disgust, "S-O-R-R-R-R-R-R-R-Y" flashing across his dark forehead. He produced two glasses, filled them with ice, and then poured the bourbon-or-scotch. He handed me a glass.

"So, what's with this Priti woman?"

"I don't know, Uncle Frank. She's cool. Really smart, pretty nice."

"Is she gonna hurt my daughter?" he huffed. It was really paining him to even be considering this whole situation. It's not like DiDi ever lied to them about being a lesbian. But her father has been lying to himself all these years. Like the truth could never possibly exist. Nobody knew if he could handle it now that it stared him plainly in his face. I'm not sure he knew. But he was soldiering on. He was a Korean War vet, after all.

"I don't know," I admitted. "I doubt it. But it's possible. They seem really happy, Uncle Frank."

He put a frail hand on his chest. His shirt billowed out from the pressure. He really had lost a lot of weight.

"Good."

"Why don't you have a seat?" I offered.

He moved around the bar and did. We were now sitting closer to each other than we'd ever done in our lives. Our legs accidentally touched. He put a hand on my knee. I flinched; but he kept it there.

"That's really good to hear," he said. "Nothing means more to me in this world than that girl's happiness."

"I know."

Why won't he move that damned hand?

"I know I've been a bit tough on her over the years," he declared. "Probably too tough." He looked into my eyes and cleared his throat. "This world, Damian. It's so different than the world I started out in. All this change—it can be hard on an old fool like me sometimes. And sometimes, you don't know you did shit wrong until it's too late. I'm just hoping it's not too late, son. I *did* try my best. You understand that. Don't you, son?"

"Yeah. Sure," I lied. "I do… Really."

He smiled broadly. "Good. Now how 'bout you? You've got another book coming?"

"Yessir."

"Good. We're so proud of you, Damian. Your Aunt Clarissa and I. We're your biggest fans."

Probably my only fans, I thought.

"It damn near broke our hearts when we found out about you and Samara."

"Found out what?!"

He backed up, apprehensively. Finally, my knee was free. "That you broke off the engagement, of course."

"Oh. Yeah. That."

"Do you ever talk to her?"

"No. There's ... there's really nothing to say."

"Seven years. You two were together seven years, right? That's an awfully long time for kids your age. Are you sure you can't patch things up, son? You've invested so much in that woman."

"Um. Ya know, I really don't think that'll be happening."

"Why not?"

Because she cheated on me and gave me syphilis! You imperious old coot!!!

"We ... we had a lot of problems, Uncle Frank."

"Boy, relationships *are* problems. That's what happens when two people try to negotiate this world as a single unit. Do you think your aunt and I haven't had our problems?"

Syphilis?! ... No, no. I don't want to know.

"My parents had tons of 'em," I said, defiantly flippant.

Uncle Frank shot straight up in his stool and glared at me. Some of that old rage returning. "That was different, boy," he hissed. "You damn well know that."

"Sorry."

He relaxed a bit. "See, that's the problem with you kids today. Everything's so easy for you with your microwaves and Tivos and the internet. You think everything in life is supposed to be easy. If your VCR breaks down, you just get another one. If your boss gives you too much flak, you go out and get another job. Or you start your own company, and the government gives you money. But it's all an illusion, boy. Life isn't really like that. People aren't toasters. If you want a relationship to work, you have got to work at it. You can't just go off, get a divorce, and get yourself a new toaster. I mean, you kids are getting divorces more than any other generation because you don't understand work like we did."

I wanted to tell him that it was the "Greatest Generation" who started the divorce craze right after the war and it was the Baby Boomers who'd turned it into an institution and that our generation, if you exclude the Bible Belt and their getting married at eighteen and divorced at twenty, twenty-five, and thirty-two, was quite stable in our marriages. But I didn't.

I was tired of being a smart-ass around the old guy. He seemed to really be trying. The least I could do was give peace a shot.

"There are just some things that are impossible to work out, Uncle Frank. Trust me."

"I don't know—" *What?* The *Franklin Franklin doesn't know something?!* "—Maybe you're right—" *Holy shit! I, Damian Rene Cross, might actually be right?! Were those trumpets I heard? What are those four guys doing on horseback?!* "—I'll tell you something though, son. And you *are* my son—" *Hey, I'm too much in shock to be arguing with you right now* "—There's nothing like death staring you in the face to tell you what a fool you've been. All the mistakes I've made with you, with your aunt, and your cousin, with so many people. I *have* been a damned fool. I don't want you to make the same mistake. I could've lost Clarissa so many times. And she's a good woman, the best woman I've ever known. I'm truly blessed to have found her and to have *kept* her—despite myself.

"You're probably right. There probably are things you and that girl couldn't work out. I don't know. That's between you and her. I don't even know if she's a good woman. We never got to meet her. It doesn't matter. I just want you to know, there aren't that many good women out there. And next time you find one, if you do find one, you snatch her up, boy, and you *love* her and you cherish her, cherish that love. Because that love is a gift. It's the greatest gift two people can give to each other. Remember that, Damian. And don't let me ever see you let it go."

There were actually tears in the old man's eyes, and I could feel my own pupils heating up. We both took huge gulps from our drinks before we did something stupid like cry and/or hug each other.

SUNDAY, DECEMBER 25, 20—
2:22 P.M.

I must confess, I don't really have any good associations with Christmas. As a kid, Dad was always drunk, Mom scared, and I was perpetually terrified. Admittedly, with Aunt Clarissa and Uncle Frank, the holidays were much, much better, but by then, I was too far gone to enjoy much of anything. Samara was never really into Christmas either. We'd exchange gifts, have sex, and go see a movie. That was about as Feliz as my Navidad ever got.

I wasn't expecting much of anything this morning, and things went pretty much as expected. We woke up and had breakfast casserole. DiDi was all into it, which was kinda freaky. I mean, I've been having moments where I've reverted back to the brooding seventeen-year-old who used to live here. But I've been fairly successful in reining that punk in. But my cousin, she jumped straight back to the third grade, or something. She was all enthusiastic, hopping around and squealing, fidgeting under the Christmas tree. It was all quite unseemly. I truly felt sorry for ole girl.

After breakfast, we exchanged presents. The aunt and unc got me a sweater. For sixteen years now, I've asked for nothing but music and have gotten nothing but sweaters. Can someone please explain that?

There was a phone call, which I assumed was Aunt Glay, who actually isn't our aunt but our fourth or fifth cousin or our first cousin-thirty times removed, I've never been able to figure out how that all worked. She's whatever your mother's mother's cousin is. Anyway, she calls every Christmas. But it wasn't her because I wasn't asked to the phone. It must've been one of DiDi's friends because she was. With the interruption, Priti called her folks to wish them a merry Christmas. I was a little confused at that, but my head damn near exploded when she asked DiDi to the phone and they ended up talking for some ten minutes.

We finished with the presents, nibbled on some fruit and raw vegetables, and the four of them went off to church (they didn't even bother asking me—things were definitely changing), while I learned what it meant to be regular. I ended up talking to Aunt Glay alone. Ninety-three and still going strong. Bless her heart. All in all, a very pleasant morning. And still not one major blow-up.

MONDAY, DECEMBER 26, 20—
12:10 A.M.

Ha! Ha! I did it! I motherfucking did it! I kept my head! Only one more day to go!

11:12 P.M.

Yep. You guessed it. I spoke too soon. The blow-up did happen after all. Not quite Nagasaki. More like a dirty bomb in Dubuque. I guess I'll ultimately have to admit it was my fault, so … it was my fault. I just lost it. No excuse for it. Why bother? Sometimes, you've just got to own your fuck-ups.

It all started with that mystery phone call Christmas morning. It had been Nandi, calling from her folks' home in Youngstown. Apparently, DiDi (ever the meddler) had asked her to stop by today since she had to come to Pittsburgh anyway to catch her flight back home. She'd called my cousin to see if it was still OK. DiDi had said it was.

She arrived some time late afternoon, saying, "Happy Boxing Day," with a small bag in her hand.

We stared at her blankly.

"You know," she ventured, with an awkwardly dimpled smile. "The day after Christmas when the lords and ladies of England give their servants their Christmas boxes. Their gifts. They were probably just re-gifting, but you get the idea."

We were still pretty dumbfounded.

"I don't know," she shrugged. "My folks used to say it was big in Jamaica."

After that bit of discomfort, Nandi regathered herself, gave me the CDs she brought back from Brazil, and proceeded to dazzle my aunt and uncle. And it didn't take long for them to fall in love. I don't blame them, really. She was absolutely marvelous.

I learned a lot about Nandi Huang today. She's from Youngstown, and her dad's a big-time economics professor at Case Western Reserve (which I knew). Her mother's an accountant (which I didn't). She has an older sister living in Belgium. She went to Berkeley all the way through law school because her father had heard it was the Harvard for Asians and she just had to go. Her dad also made her take up violin from the time she was four, and it was a *huge* family tragedy when she switched to guitar at fifteen. Uncle Frank fell in love with her when she said that she loved old Stax records because she could never really get into middle-class, integrationist Motown—though she does recognize the latter's greatness. You could occasionally see the old man physically wishing he were forty years younger.

But he wasn't the only one smitten with the woman. Aunt Clarissa oohed and ahhed like ole girl was walking a tight rope across Niagara Falls. DiDi, of course, kept singing Nandi's praises, telling the folks all the good work Ms. Huang has done for the shelter. "And to believe she's actually a corporate attorney," my cousin added. "Ooh, really," my aunt admired. "Mostly mergers and acquisitions," Nandi admitted. "Pretty boring, but it pays the bills, right?" "Nothing wrong with paying bills," you-know-who declared. "Is there, son?" "No, Uncle Frank," I whined. Even Priti got into the act, winking and nodding an "I told you so" the entire time. And Nandi, sensing her success, would constantly look my way and smile. Of course, I smiled back—despite myself—because I *am* smitten. I admit it. But, God. It was so obvious to everyone in that house that she was being interviewed for a position in the family. And it was equally obvious from everybody's raves that she had gotten the job. She could have easily taken my place. Then everybody would've been happy. After all, they all seemed to forget that *I* was the one, in theory, who made the hiring decisions.

In the middle of this orgy of adoration, I pulled my cousin aside to the kitchen.

"What the hell do you think you're doing, Deirdre?" I seethed. I had to keep my voice down, though it really didn't take a genius to figure out what was going on.

"What do you mean?" she asked, coyly, like an idiot savant.

"Why is she here?"

"What? It's Boxing Day. The lady had to give her servant his gift."

"Funny."

I was tensing to boil.

"Why do you always have to fight it, Damian?" she asked. "There's maybe one person in this entire house who doesn't love you. And I'm talking to him."

She left me with that. I had no clue what to do. I rejoined the good time, but I was not enjoying myself. I was becoming resentful at their cloying behavior. I was a lot of things. What I mainly was was that diffident seventeen-year-old again. I didn't want to be. I just didn't know how to be different. I would have done anything to just grab that woman and take her away from it all—to jump on a plane, a train, a Haitian raft, and gone anywhere, it didn't matter, as long as I was with her. And just hold her. And give her all the love I'd never been able to give myself. And bask in the glow of it all until the Earth swallowed us both into dust.

But I couldn't. All I could do was feel my nerves fray in agitation. My family was being nicer to Nandi than they'd ever been to me. They weren't even this happy when I got my first novel published. What the hell did this woman have? And why was everyone conspiring against me to have her in my life? Kevin won't shut up about her. We all know where DiDi stands—directly above, yanking my chains, making me dance like Pinocchio. And Priti, why was she being so encouraging? She was the one who was supposed to be interviewed today, and now they were all acting like she was an in-law. Did they all forget that she was half of an interracial, *lesbian* relationship? Where's the disgust? What happened to the Old World outrage? And all that supposed sweetness sober Samara was saying about me in Brazil? When did she start hitting the pipe?!

Why do all these people want me to be with Nandi? When did they all start wanting me to be happy? Didn't they all realize that I am perfectly content with being miserable? Why are they trying to fuck it all up?

Apparently. I was out to show *them*.

Boxing Day dinner (if there ever were such a thing) was the fantastic, artery-clogging leftovers of Christmas dinner (which does exist). "Hell," Uncle Frank had proclaimed, "I ain't planning on dying anytime soon, but what's the point of living if I gotta eat tofu all the time? I didn't integrate the Army and fight a war for *that*." Collards with ham hock, that immaculate macaroni and cheese and cheese and cheese (add four more cheeses), black eyed peas (a week too soon, I might add), corn bread, cheese bread, ham, turkey, and a roast. I got the Itis just looking at it all. Uncle Frank and Aunt Clarissa sat at the heads of the table. DiDi and Priti were together. And I, of course, was sitting next to Queen Nandi.

I was on edge, but everything seemed to be going well. The prayer was said, the food was passed, and nothing but chewing and clanging could be heard. It was that good—even the second time around. I thought I was actually going to survive myself. I was wrong. My aunt started looking all happy at all of us. Her wearying gaze settled on me. I started squirming in the scrutiny.

"Ah, Damian," she sighed. Everybody started looking at me. "Your mother, my sister. She would've been so proud."

I bristled. DiDi darted nervous eyes across the room.

"Mom, maybe this isn't—"

"What, Deirdre? Harriet would've been. Look at the boy—" *No. Please. Don't.* "—so handsome and intelligent. And a *novelist*. You're everything your mother ever wanted for you."

I could feel Nandi's eyes on me, sense her smile.

"Yes, Clarissa, we're all proud of Damian," Uncle Frank concurred, nervously.

What?!

My aunt started choking up. "She sacrificed so much for you, Damian Rene. It's just a shame she couldn'—"

"Clarissa."

"What is it, Frank? It's just a shame, is all. A shame you can't choose who you fall in love with."

"What?!" I erupted, knowing before I said it, I was going to regret what I was about to say. "That's total bull—"

"Damian!"

"No, Uncle Frank. It is. People choose who they fall in love with every day. That's what we do. We decide who we date, who we'll continue dating. Who we'll marry and have kids with. Every day we wake up we choose whether or not we're gonna stay with the person we wake up with. Every, fucking day!"

"Boy!"

"Folks just don't want that responsibility, so they say stupid shit like, 'You can't choose who you fall in love with.' But my mother! She chose that shit! Every day! She didn't have to stay! She could've walked away … she could've—she could've run. But she … but sh … she chose … she … chose … oh my … God."

I was stunned by my own words. I stood, shaking. Aunt Clarissa was balling, and I had done that to her. On fucking Boxing Day. DiDi's eyes were pouring into her napkin. Nandi and Priti were stunned. Uncle Frank was reverberating with rage. His skeletal hand was balled into a fist. He was ready to put my head into the wall again.

"Oh my God," I croaked. "I'm so sorry. I … I …"

I rushed out of there, and collapsed on the front porch to shiver in the frigid, Boxing Day air. And I wasn't even cold.

I don't know how long I sat out there, wishing I had the physical dexterity to kick myself in the head. What an idiot. I'd just been looking for an excuse to blow up. I saw my chance and took it. I didn't realize that was what I was doing, but it was. I wished to hell I didn't have to be that way. I didn't have to be. But I was. And I ruined a perfectly wonderful holiday.

Nandi came out in her coat and sat down next to me. I didn't even look at her. I wanted her to go away and to hold me in her arms at the same time. We sat there for awhile. Finally, she said, "Do you want to talk about it?"

"No. Not particularly."

More silence.

"Do you want to talk about your booty novel?"

I looked at her. She was smiling. She looked like an angel.

"You know, I tried to write one," I confessed. "Actually, two. But I just couldn't do it. I'm a misfit, Nandi. And only misfits seem to identify with me. To try to appeal to the mainstream—the soccer mom with white-picket children and a minivan—that would be an exercise in utter futility."

"Good." She positively glowed. "You know you can talk to me, Damian, don't you?"

"No. I don't. But I appreciate that."

That silence again. More awkward than ever.

"Why are you here, Nandi?"

"I told you I'd always wanted to see Pittsburgh. You said to come by after Christmas and you'd show me around." She smiled. "It's after Christmas."

I laughed. "Right. Boxing Day," I sighed. "All right then."

I grabbed her hand and drove her up to Mt. Washington, which is the top of a huge mountain (which is all my hometown is, "The Capital of Appalachia," as my old friend, Ron, used to say) that overlooks "Dahntahn Picksburgh." I took her to one of the overlooks, and we settled against the railing.

There was very little traffic along the rivers, but the city burned brightly in Christmas colors. The Highmark Building had an enormous, electronic wreath. PPG Place had green and red lights blinking atop their glass minarets. Everything looked so calm and peaceful in the winter breeze.

"This is cool," Nandi marveled. "You can really forget your troubles up here."

"What kind of troubles do you have?" I chuckled. "Everybody—me, included—seem to think you're perfect."

"God," she sighed, looking up at me with magnets in her eyes. "I had to tell my parents that I was going to quit my job to go on tour with the band."

"You are?"

"I never liked being a corporate attorney, anyway. Never wanted to be one. It was my father's idea. And I'm tired of doing what he wants me to do."

"I had no idea."

"You definitely have no idea what havoc my announcement caused. My parents have been all over me. I just had to get out of there. See what a normal family was like during the holidays."

"Well, I'm glad I didn't disappoint." I laughed bitterly. "So you really find this place cool?"

She looked down and marveled. "Oh my God, yes."

I looked down on the city, and all I could see was pain. I saw the first grade principal who put me in the dumb track despite my 1— IQ. The fifth grade teacher who consistently failed me to the point that I had to correct my own tests, and then she'd give me an A on the test but steady Fs on my report card for my bad attitude. The guidance counselor who made me repeat Algebra and Earth Science when I transferred to high school, even though I'd gotten straight As the year before with the exact, same books. There were the white kids who hated me because I was black and the black kids 'cause I was "white" (as dark as I am). All the fights. And the white kids who caught me one day and threw rocks at me until I bled. The cops who'd stop me in my own neighborhood though they knew perfectly well where I lived. The girls who refused to date me. I saw my mother, my father, Uncle Frank, and the inside of drywall. I waded alone in everybody's scorn. All those people who hated me because … because? … because I was born at the wrong place in the wrong time…?!

"Could that have been it?" I gasped.

"What?"

I looked at Nandi. I can't describe all the emotions that were boiling within me. She smiled up at me. I pulled her close to me and kissed her. I felt myself drain—only to be filled with happiness. Relief.

"What was that for?" she asked, breathlessly.

"I was just thinking about how good the perogies are in this town."

"What?"

"Nothing."

I pulled her close to me, and we turned, together, gazing down at my hometown.

TUESDAY, DECEMBER 27, 20—
10:59 P.M.

"I'm sorry, Aunt Clarissa."

It was late in the morning, and DiDi, Priti, and I were about to leave. My aunt was in the kitchen, busy not making us a plate, but a vat, of food to go. Uncle Frank was hanging out at the VFW. I knew he had to be pissed—not like I blame him ... this time—to go there. He hated those guys—yet another place he had to integrate.

Aunt Clarissa looked at me with a smile and a tear in her eyes. "I know, son."

"I just don't know what came over me."

"The truth."

We both swallowed hard on that one and didn't know what to do with ourselves. The truth is something we Franklins have a hard time with. Just another burden to bear silently.

"Damian, you know I love you, don't you?"

"Yes, ma'am."

"Your uncle does, too. Nobody wants to see you in pain. And it hurts us to see you like this. We're not stupid, Damian. We know why. We've always known. But look, son, you're a thirty-two-year-old man now. You've got to, you've got to let all that pain—you've got to let it go."

"Ma'am?"

"The pain, it's eating away at you. You've got all this, this misery inside, and it's going to kill you. That's the problem with our people—the decent ones, anyway—we have all this anger and pain and we keep it there, bottled up. We're constantly suffering in silence. Like we *need* to own it. And we die young and suffer hypertension, have heart attacks and see the Lord way before He's ready to see us. Look at your uncle. For over eighty years he's been angry. He's been miserable. A real bastard sometimes—"*Amen, sister* "—He's lucky he's lasted this long. It took him his third stroke before he realized just how lucky he is.

"And he's been so much better, son. Not perfect. But better. Do you see how he's taken to Priti? He actually *likes* her. The old Frank would've shot her on sight. And he didn't put your head through the wall last night. Because now he understands. He understood before, he just couldn't do anything about it. But now. He knows he's failed you. You went through what you went through—" *Say it! Why won't you say it?!* "—and he couldn't be what you needed. He didn't know how to be. But at least he can *try* now. Can you recognize that, Damian?"

"Yes, ma'am," I gulped. "I think I can."

"And can you at least try to let some of that anger go?" she continued. "You have so much going for you right now, son. And that Nandi, she's such a beautiful girl, and she really likes you. Do you know how fortunate you are? Just give yourself a chance to be happy. Then you can be a miserable, old man like that fool uncle of yours."

She smiled at me. I smiled back. I really do love my aunt.

"And don't you ever let me catch you cursing like that in my house again."

She cuffed me in the back of the head.

"Knucklehead."

"Hey, have you ever noticed how old people are always wantin' to drop pearls of wisdom on your ass?" I asked, driving the three of us back home. No metal bands now. Wu Tang and Stevie Wonder only. "Like time automatically bestows sagacity on even the biggest idiot. I say, once a jackass always a jackass."

"Can't we listen to Def Leppard?" Priti asked.

"No," DiDi and I said, simultaneously.

"Jinx," we laughed.

"That reminds me, Damian," my cousin opened, looking at me from the passenger seat. "Mom thinks Priti and I should move in together."

"Really?" I was shocked. "That's cool."

"So, I'm moving out."

"Oh."

"Well, I did really well on my GREs."

"Did I know that?"

"No," she answered. "I didn't want to tell you until I decided what to do. But yeah, I aced them. And well, Nandi keeps talking about how great Berkeley is, and they have a Master's/PhD program in International Development I'm really interested in. So, if I get in, Priti and I are moving out there together."

I looked in the rearview mirror. Priti was beaming. There was a tinge of anxiety in her eyes, but she looked genuinely happy. I was trying to put selfishness aside and be happy for them. But DiDi is *my* cousin, damnit.

"Your aunt also thinks that I should get pregnant and that you should be the donor," said Priti.

I almost slammed on the brakes. At eighty-seven mph, *nobody* would be getting my sperm. Unless they scraped it off the steering wheel.

"The lengths that woman will go through to have grandchildren," I sighed.

"I hope this moving out thing doesn't put you out. We just want to see if we can stand each other before moving all the way out to California."

"But you two basically live together now."

"Yeah," Priti concurred. "But it's a lot different when a drawer becomes an entire dresser."

"And she squeezes the toothpaste from the middle."

FRIDAY, DECEMBER 30, 20—
9:10 P.M.

I had wanted nothing more than to put in some disgustingly filthy, old school porn like *Edward Penishands* or *Mad Jack Beyond Thunder Bone*, hear that horrendous dialogue—"Yeah, you like that, bitch, don't you?"—look at monster cocks slamming into needle-bruised thighs, wack off into a cup three times, gift-wrap it for Mayrav, and say, "Merry Christmas, baby."

But I just couldn't. Theoretically, I had absolutely no problem with her proposition. I was actually kinda flattered. She seemed to really need me, and I really didn't want to fail her. And I've *never* had a problem with masturbation.

It's just that deep down where I suppose my heart is I've always wanted to be a father. A real father. I want to change diapers and have the brats piss in my face. I want to take my boy to soccer practice and my girl to football. I want to be uncool and embarrass them in my Birkenstocks and black socks and my pants hoisted way above my belly button. I want to scare the shit out of twelve-year-old punks trying to date my daughter. And I *really* want to say things like, "You call that music?! Why, back in my day, *nobody* played instruments, and *we* rapped about things that mattered. Like bitches and hos."

And I want a partner. A wife. A person who will go through the pains and triumphs with me. The frustrations and joy. So that we could look back on those trying times together and wrap each other in our arms and smile triumphantly at each other as the rug rats walk down the gangplank and gather up their diplomas, and say, "Yeah. We did it."

I just couldn't cum in a cup and call it a day.

So, I went down to *Soul on Wax* to deliver the bad news. It took a lot out of me to summon up the courage. I hate letting people down, yet that's all I've been able to do lately (why have I not called Nandi?). I almost gave the specimens just so I wouldn't have to see Mayrav's eyes dull green with disappointment.

When I got there, though, the woman looked happier than I had ever seen her. She was behind the counter, all cuddly with some dude who looked way too familiar. Stuart, that smug Aryan bastard. I hadn't seen him in years, and he was looking *old*. I guess self-adulation takes a lot out of you. He had a proprietary arm around her waist, as my girl screeched, "Damian!"

"Mayrav. Stuart."

"Damian."

"Look!" Ms. Amou thrust out her left hand. The glare from the rock damn near blinded me. I may have hissed like a holy-watered vampire. It's hard to say. "We're engaged."

"What?" I gasped, utterly confused. Stuart ran a satisfied hand through his salting blond hair and smiled victoriously down at me.

"We're engaged," he declared, smugly.

"Yeah," she agreed. "We got to talking over Christmas. I told him about—you know, our plans. And well, then we started talking about us again, and it was like when we first met. No, even better. I mean, we really do love each other, Damian."

"Yep," he said. I mean, here was a guy who was so pretentious that he would quote Wittgenstein while we were talking Van Halen, and the best he could come up with was "Yep." Bitch.

"And then he did it. He proposed. *Finally*. We're getting married in March. You're invited, of course," she rattled on, breathless.

I stood dumbfounded while they smooched. After several seconds of revenge fantasies flashing before my eyes, Stuart pulled away from his fiancée and gave me a cold, blue stare.

"So, Damian. I don't think we'll be needing your … package. I think I can deliver."

SATURDAY, DECEMBER 31, 20—
11:59 P.M.

Happy New Year, you pathetic piece of motherfucker.

SUNDAY, JANUARY 1, 20—
1:19 P.M.

"Happy New Year, bitch!"

"Right back atcha, Kev."

"Where was you at last night?"

"Home. Why? What was last night?"

"You know, if I weren't afraid of breaking my hand over your thick skull or you actually getting a lucky shot in and splitting my lip, I'd come over there right now and punch you right in the eye. Then maybe you could see straight."

"I thought the tradition was black eyed *peas*."

"Screw them. They *never* shoulda got that singer. And screw you. You know who I was hanging out with last night at Triple Six?"

"Beelzebub?"

"No. Nandi. And she was with Vikram."

"…"

"I mean, damn, you should've seen ole boy in action. He just rolls up to the woman after practice and lays some real pimp shit on her. Like, 'We're going out New Year's Eve, and none a that "friends" shit. But a real date.' And she just says, 'Yes,' like a deer in the headlights, or something. Can you believe that shit? Raheem's still kicking himself. He's been wantin' to do that for months. But he likes you too much. He didn't want to fuck up your game. But Vik—he don't give a shit. And he's about to take your woman, D."

"He can fucking have her."

"Aw Jesus, Damian. I made it up."

"What?"

"I made it up. In that booty novel I'm writing for you, that's what would've happened. You would've been so pissed, so overwhelmed with jealousy and love, you'd've been spurred to action and would've had to run to the church and break up the wedding, or something."

"That's cheesy and derivative, Kevin Byrd. I think you have a future in Hollywood." I paused. "Is she all right?"

"Jesus, you're pathetic. If you're thinking she has a gun to her head or is drinking herself to oblivion, no. Nobody's worth all that. But you can definitely tell she's distracted. Practice was abysmal. You're fucking up my music, boy."

"Sorry."

"Just tell me what you did."

"Wait. Did you see her last night?"

"No. She was probably just as lonely and pathetic as you were. Though she *really* doesn't have to be. Now. What did you do?"

"I said, 'I can't.'"

"You what?"

"I said, 'I can't.' I don't know. I was going through a lot of shit that night. I freaked. Everything was so fucked up. So right. I don't know. I might've even been happy. I just said, 'I can't. I … I … you know, I've got this book an—'"

"Stop right there."

"What?"

"I know what you're gonna say. I've heard it all before. And I—I … I just don't want to hear it anymore. Sorry, Damian."

"What are you tal—?"

Click!

TUESDAY, JANUARY 10, 20—
3:14 A.M.

"Hey, whaddup, D? Ain't seen you in a coon's age."

"We ever figure out who the coon was?"

"Naw. Let's just say it's Clarence Thomas and call it a day. Can you come over?"

"Sure, Kev. What's wrong?"

"Nothing. Everything. I don't want to talk about it."

"Sure, bruh. I'll be right over."

OK, I understand that last part might have been a little confusing, but I know my boy. Whenever he doesn't want to talk, he really needs to. Whatever was said before was already water under the bridge. So, I rushed over there. And when I arrived I could see that he was having a bad day. He was a wreck. The sun was setting, and neither of us realized at that moment how bad his night was going to be.

"What is it, man?" I asked, moving some sheet music to sit down.

"Been writing that booty novel?" he deflected, staring off into a place I was nowhere near.

"Naw. Straight-up science fiction. Well, nothing's too straight where I'm concerned."

"Got that right," he agreed. "Got any weed?"

"Quit. The only thing I've been doing right lately. That and the gym."

"You do look slimmer."

"So, what i—?"

"Fuck this. I need to get drunk."

"But you don't get dr—"

"Damian!"

We headed straight for the Scotsman. I drove. Breaking all kinds of traffic laws.

His label was threatening to drop him, he finally confessed over his third Red Stripe. The suits didn't think his new direction was worth the investment.

"I don't have a big enough name for them to be 'indulging my hubris,'" he informed, bitterly.

"It's so good. It'll sell."

"Not if they don't want it to. You know that."

It's true. As a music critic, I've seen really good acts get dropped from their labels as their album was just coming out. I've seen labels shelve really good albums by marquee names because they didn't like it—for whatever reason. I've seen damned good artists get no support and wither and die while total schlock sold millions. Hell, I knew some rock brothers who got torn apart by their label because the label only wanted the lead singer—only to drop his ass a minute later—and then sued the whole bunch of them. A multibillion-dollar, multinational corporation suing a bunch of penniless kids for every dollar they made for the next five years. I knew exactly what Kevin was up against.

"Well then, why don't you make the crappiest crap you can think of, call it *Booty Music*, and make millions?"

"No. Never. Not again."

It went on like that for hours, Kevin getting steadily drunker as we looked the dark specter of his future straight in the eye, when the Ghost of Romance Past strode in. Yodit. His Eritrean love. She was tall and proud, beautiful with her scorched-desert glow, high cheekbones, and silken hair. The moment she walked into the Scotsman, everybody instinctively knew Beauty had arrived and were irresistibly drawn to her. She took in all the attention and absolutely basked in it. The impish-looking brother next to her in Armani found his scrawny chest puffing in the adulation. *That's right, bitches,* he seemed to be gloating, *she's with me.*

Kevin saw her and started trembling.

"Hey, let's get out of here."

"No. I'm cool, D. I'm aiight."

He swallowed hard on his beer as she took a booth with the midge by the door. The bar was pretty empty, so it wasn't long before she noticed us, smiled strychnine sweetness our way, and waved. Kevin nodded. The little guy saw what was going on and leaned forward to take hold of Yodit's slender fingers. She smiled again and stroked his cheek.

"Seriously, we can go."

"Please, Damian. Shut the fuck up."

Byrd flew out of his chair and went in the opposite direction to the bathroom. Yodit noticed and smiled. I returned it awkwardly and drank my beer. Finished it. Started drinking another one. Damn near finished it when Kevin came wobbling out of the bathroom. His gait was determined, yet sloppy. He wiped a furious hand across his mouth and stormed right past me. I wanted to stop him but was too late. By the time I'd gotten up, he was already at their booth. I sat impotently back down.

A few words I couldn't hear were exchanged. Kevin jerked his head toward the door. Yodit got up. Mighty Mite tried to interdict, but Kev stared him down. He looked a mess, but Yodit floated gracefully out of the bar. Armani Boy gave me a questioning glare. I shrugged my shoulders in defeat.

Q: What the fuck's going on here?

A: You know how Snoop Dogg always used to say, "I don't lah' dem hos"? See, for him, that's just a character he plays. He's got a wife and kids and even coaches Little League (what I wouldn't give to be at their victory parties). And his wife got him to stop producing pornos with Larry Flynt, and that's money! Only love can come between a man and his Mammon.

For Kevin Byrd, though, that no-ho-loving policy has pretty much held true ever since I've known him. Like me, his folks screwed him up pretty badly. His father was a fairly petty criminal and drug addict who was never around. He still doesn't know if his old man's alive or dead. He doesn't want to know.

His mother's alive. He wishes he didn't know that, though. She has followed every drug trend since the '70s. Marijuana, heroin, crack, meth. She's been strung out longer than liberalism's been dead. She's abandoned him, beaten him, cursed him out, and has sponged money off of him. She's even pimped herself out before his very young eyes. All the while, never providing for him, never caring, never even coming close to loving him, blaming *him* for the abysmal state *she* was in.

If it weren't for his grandmother, who knows what Kevin would be right now? She took him in when her daughter so obviously failed. She was the one who made sure he had food, clothing, and shelter. She was the one who encouraged him to be the incredible talent he is today.

But his Moms. He can never let go of that hate. He came close. With Yodit. She always came to see him play back when he was nobody. There were a lot of women who did that back then as well. There still are. But he was totally smitten with her.

For awhile, they were inseparable. I mean, I'd never seen him so happy. They went everywhere together. He even wrote songs about her, for godsake. And they were actually *good*. I don't know what happened. He never talks about it. But as the months wore on and the happier he got, he seemed to start stepping out more. It was hardly noticeable at first. There will always be women around the Byrd man. He's beautiful. It can't be helped. We had all just assumed he was blowing them all off like he had been for months.

But then certain women kept showing up at different gigs. And they seemed to be more and more intimate with the man. Yodit never missed a show, and she definitely didn't miss what was going on. She would break down and cry after the show as he spent more and more time backstage, from which she was strictly barred. When he'd finally emerge, he would be so loving and endearing, even I would fall in love just listening to the brother.

It was bizarre. Absolutely perverse. You could tell in some sick, twisted way, he truly did love that woman, cuddling up to her smelling of another. But it couldn't last. He was breaking her in two, and he knew it. He cared, but he'd be laughing all the while when he was doing it. Finally, she left him, shattered. He immediately gave up be-bop and went straight to fusion.

I don't know if ole boy got all that with my shrug, but it didn't matter. Yodit was soon back. Alone. She swept past her booth and headed directly toward me. She didn't look happy. Wrecked, actually. Though completely composed. I couldn't help tensing up. She gave me an icy smile that chilled my testicles.

"You better go get your friend," she said smoothly, and quickly rejoined the fly Fly.

I settled up quickly and rushed outside. I looked everywhere and couldn't find him. Finally, I went back to the Tercel. Kevin was slumped over on the ground. A pool of vomit congealed in front of him.

"Kevin?"

"Why'd she show up today?" he moaned. "I haven't seen her in over a year, and she has to show up today. That kinda crap only happens in bad movies."

"Or mediocre novels," I proffered.

"AAAAARRRRRRGGHHHHHHH!!!"

Vomit splashed everywhere.

As I walk through this world

Nothing can stop the Duke of Earl

He threw up a few more times. I waited a few minutes to see if the coast would ever be clear. I guess it never is in these situations. I just had to go for it.

"Do you think you can stand?"

"Yeah, sure," he slurred.

He staggered, crashed into the car, and slid back to the ground. I stepped over the gastric lake and stooped to pick him up. I leaned him against the car, struggled to open the door with one hand, and folded him into the car.

I broke a bunch of traffic laws again and somehow managed to get him to his apartment before he spewed in my car. I sat him down on top of a bunch of magazines, found a trash can, emptied it onto the floor, and set it beside him. I didn't know what to do with myself. I wanted to go home (as always) but felt that I shouldn't.

"Why couldn't I have loved her?" he whined. "Properly? Like a normal person? Why couldn't I do it, D? I wanted to—more than anything. I just couldn't. Why is that?"

"I don't know, Kev. Maybe you just have too many options."

"No. No. That's not it." He belched, grabbed his mouth, and shot toward the trash can—missing it *drastically*. He settled back into his chair, his eyes plastered shut. "No," he slurred on, "that's not it at all. I'm a prick. That's it. All us 'playas' are. We act like we love women. And everybody goes along with the lie. We love *fucking* women. But that ain't love. Not at all."

"Yeah ... well..."

"It's so fucked up. The shit that goes through my head. And I should know better. I *do* know better. I just can't stop myself."

Then I saw something I'd never seen in the man in the fourteen years I've known him. Tears. He started blubbering and actually cried. I ... I couldn't believe it. I sat there. Stunned.

"But why Yodit? I wanted to be the world to her. I tried. I really did. I loved her so much, Damian. The best I possibly could. But why wasn't it enough?"

He literally wailed. I shuttered. I definitely wanted out of there. But Kev is my boy, my best friend. My brother. I unsteadily walked toward him and knelt down beside his chair.

"Uh, come on, man," I ventured, but the bastard wouldn't stop crying. I reached a leaden arm for him. He swatted it away with a grunt. "You fucked up. It happens."

He roared. "Don't you fuck up, too, Damian!"

"I won't, Kevin," I promised. "I won't."

I reached for him again. He swatted me away again. I tried again, and he went at me. I tried deflecting the flurry of blows, but he caught me in the chest. "Bitch," I yelped. I don't know how he even saw me through the tears. I grabbed him, and he amazingly relented. He started heaving and sobbing into my chest.

"Man, you remember back in the day," he chuckled, "when all it took was a glass of grape Kool Aid to make us happy?"

"Naw, man. I really don't."

WEDNESDAY, JANUARY 11, 20—
4:45 P.M.

"D?"

"Yeah, Kev."

"About the other night..."

"Yeah, man. Don't worry about it."

"... All right. Cool."

SUNDAY, JANUARY 15, 20—
8:35 P.M.

The Steelers simply refuse to beat the Patriots. Home field advantage throughout the playoffs, yet again. And they lose. Yet again. 35-24.

THURSDAY, JANUARY 19, 20—
5:50 A.M.

And what was I going to lose with this meeting? Whatever it was, it wasn't going to be pretty. But I went, anyway. I never could refuse Samara. Even after she cheated on me and gave me syphilis, *I* was the one who wanted to work things out. I hate to admit it, but *she* was the one who broke it off. She just couldn't … I don't know … not anymore, she'd said.

So I met her. At Carpe Diem. Stella, of course, was being her usual, flirtatious self as Norah Jones somnambulated through the speakers. I saw Samara walk in, and the air caught in my throat. I will always love this woman. She looked so beautiful, striking against the gray sky outside. She seemed wrapped in a shroud of sadness that suffocated her like a second skin. But it didn't stop those old feelings from tugging at my heart. I wanted to reach out. She sat down across from me with a wan smile, and I kept my hands to myself. Stella walked away.

We made civil, small talk for awhile. There were so many things I wanted to ask, so many epithets I wanted to shout. But all I could do was sit there, small, in my seat. Finally, with a grave look that reminded me of the day I got my test results, she said, "I just wanted to apologize, Damian?"

"For what?"

Stupid question.

She swallowed hard. "For everything."

"It's OK, Samara. I—"

"No, it's not," she protested. She looked down and played nervously with her coffee mug. She suddenly looked up, eyes rimming red. I had to remind myself that she *is* an actress. Contrition's just one of her tools. I wasn't going to fall for *that* again. "I took … I took your ability to be loved. I took that from you. And I apologize."

"What the hell are you talking about, Samara?" I flared, growing angry.

"When we first met," she began. "You were so fragile, so hurt. And I was so drawn to you. You had such a, such a wonderful spirit. And well, *I* wanted to be the one to heal it."

"I feel like I'm in a French film all of a sudden."

"Stop that, Damian. Don't lash out at m—"

"What?!"

"I'm trying to do something here. Say something." She exhaled. "Please let me say it."

I closed my eyes and tried my best to relax. "Go ahead, Samara," I wheezed, already exhausted.

"You were just so *hurt*," she repeated. "It was like, like so many things happened around you, to you, you felt they were your fault. Like you were somehow an evil person, or something. But you're not, Damian. You're the sweetest, kindest person I know—"

"Yet, you—"

"Please let me finish."

I threw my hands up in surrender.

"And it was so hard loving you in the beginning. It was so *frustrating*. I think that's part of the reason we argued so much sometimes. Not all of it. I'm just impatient. I want things *now*. I wanted to love you, but you wouldn't let me. Those people you grew up with, your folks, they hurt you so badly, you felt you didn't deserve love."

"What are y—?"

"You didn't, did you?"

I didn't want to, but I suddenly thought of Christy, that freaky, little blond I slept with for a couple months in college. She terrified me sometimes. She was the first woman who ever asked me what I liked in bed. I couldn't handle it. I'd never been asked. I'd never even thought about it before. As though my own pleasure was somehow … *wrong*.

I started to think how I used to flinch whenever somebody would try to touch me. I even used to do it with Samara for the first year or so. How I'm flinching again now. And then I thought of my father beating the shit out of me and then beating the shit out of Mom when she tried defending me. Or when he was drunk. Or 'cause she didn't know her place. Or just because…

"What are y—" I stammered. "Why are you doing this to me? What are you getting at, Samara?"

"I—Damian, it took so long. To get you to love yourself, to get you to feel that it was all right for me to love you. It was a lot of work. And then I screwed up. I can be hateful at times. I'll admit that. But that's the worst thing I've ever done in my life. Taking that away from you. And to this day, I don't know why. Maybe I have some of the same issues…. No. I know I do."

My chest was constricting, and my eyes were burning. I had to get out of there. Fast.

"It was Egon, wasn't it?" I nearly shouted. "That's why he and I had that big blow up over some bullshit, wasn't it? That bullshit was you."

"Don't, Damian."

I shot up out of my seat, threw down a couple bucks, and gathered up my laptop. Samara grabbed my arm. Her eyes were bleeding tears…. Actresses. Before she could say another word, I tore out of there.

MONDAY, JANUARY 23, 20—
2:49 P.M.

"What up, Brer Rabbit?"

"Just ran right smack into the Tar Baby."

"Damn, and you thought you couldn't get no blacker, Day."

"Ain't that the truth. So, what's going on, Bob? Where are you now? I know not looking for a job."

"You know me. Still in Belfast."

"That good, hunh? You finally jump the fence and married you an Irish lass?"

"I sure could use one right about now. But I couldn't do anything with her—even if I wanted to."

"Why? What's up? You sure do sound happy."

"Dude, they got me so doped up, you'd think I was Whitney Houston *and* Bobby Brown combined."

"What happened, man? You're worrying me."

"Ha! You wouldn't believe how fucked up I am. Couple black eyes, some smashed teeth. Broken clavicle, five fractured ribs, some fucked up vertebrae, broke my left leg. Even had a concussion. Hell, I was out cold for *weeks*, boy."

"What the hell, man? What did you do?"

"That's what everyone keeps askin'. But I don't think I did a damned thing. Swear ... to ... God."

"So, what happened?"

"I don't know, bruh. I was chillin' up on Falls Road. Ya know, that place that used to be split in half between Catholics and Protestants. In this joint called the Beehive. I don't know, I think it was an IRA spot."

"Crazy bitch."

"I've been in worse spots. Shit, I've been to Rwanda! Anyway, it's not like I wasn't careful. I *did* stick out like a sore thumb, though. I mean, folks were cold staring. But there were a lot of cool folks there, too. Fools were buyin' me drinks left and right. Beer and whiskey flowing. Really chatting a brother up. I had a group of fellas around me, just having a really good time. Next thing I know, though, I was in the hospital, kid. All kinds of fucked-up. In traction, and shit. All these tubes flowing out of me. Ever piss from a tube, Damian?"

"Can't say I have. What the hell were you doing, Bob? You didn't start with that *Blazing Saddles* 'We'll take the niggers and the chinks, but we don't want the Irish' shit, did you?"

"Ha! Nope. But I should've, I guess. I told you, man, everybody keeps asking me that. You wouldn't believe what'll start a fight over here. Next time I come up here. I'm gettin' me a kilt and a cow bone and goin' to town."

"Sounds like you need an AK-47."

"Yeah. Probably."

"So, like what starts a fight?"

"*Everything*. Like, they keep asking, 'Were you talking to some guy's woman? Were you *looking* at some guy's woman?' And I'm like, if you're so goddamned insecure, lock the bitch up or get a penis extension, something. Then it was like, 'Did you unknowingly take somebody's seat? Did somebody take somebody else's seat, or your seat, and you asked him to move?'"

"Are you kidding me?"

"Naw, that's like raping somebody's sister up here, I shit you not. And it gets more and more ridiculous. I tell you, these Irish, they're like the most generous, most hospitable psychopaths on the planet. I think it really boiled down to the fact that I was breathing."

"They don't like their niggers breathing in Ireland?"

"Apparently not, brother man. They actually arrested the dudes who did this, and I ain't never seen them in my *life*, boy. Never said Word One to the bitches. They just saw me in the pub and couldn't stand me. Didn't say shit to me, never bowed up, nothing. No confrontation whatsoever. Apparently, it's bad form over here. Proper etiquette is to just sucker punch a motherfucker and then jump him. I mean, these six paddies just rolled up on me, cold cocked me in the back of the head, and proceeded to stomp the shit out of my black ass."

"So, you gonna be all right, Bob?"

"Yeah. I might have a limp, but I'll play it off as a pimp strut. I always wanted one of those, anyway."

"I'm sorry, man."

"Ah, don't be, Day. I'm a star."

"What?"

"Once they found out I was American and the son of *the* Carlton Hancock, there were all kindsa news articles, and shit. Editorials. 'Are We Racist?' Crap like that. As though they don't know. There have been profiles on the horrible treatment of immigrants, you wouldn't believe it. That's why they arrested those fools. There was actually a public outcry. I've been interviewed in the papers, radio, on the Internet. I even made it onto BBC and ITN."

"Well, obviously they picked the wrong nigga to fuck with."

"Ha! No kidding. It's like getting my ass kicked was the most important thing I've done in my life. Like I really think I've advanced the Cause, can you believe it? And now, folks are fallin' all over themselves to be nice.

I probably could have that Irish lass now, but they just took the calosthemy bag out yesterday. Anyway, you need to come and visit me."

"Uhhh … Bob, you know I love you, right?"

"Naw, not here, bitch. Dad's getting me transferred to London. I've got a few surgeries coming. And with all this attention, I got a few job offers to write for some papers down there. Race relations through an African-American's eyes, crap like that. Is that black enough for ya?"

"Hancock, that's just crazy."

"What's crazier is I used to be an IRA supporter. I've actually given Sinn Fein money. Now, ain't that about a bitch?"

TUESDAY, JANUARY 24, 20—
4:15 A.M.

The lies we tell ourselves, the way our minds bend our memories so we can go on living with ourselves. I can suddenly see them. Too clearly. I see Bob looking at himself in a morphine stupor. It took him years to finally realize he was nothing but a dilettante revolutionary, a *poseur* (his French pronunciation—not mine), as he told me at The End Zone. Now being beaten senseless was going to make him "conscious." If he plays that role, he'll one day forget how disingenuous he truly used to be.

But I'm no better. I can see my lies staring back at me. I'm thinking of Mayrav and the first time I'd met Stuart. It was at Cast Iron, one of many bars I used to hang out at that are no longer around. Initially, I'd thought it was a chance meeting, but it had soon become apparent that they'd been talking. I knew who Stuart was by then. Mayrav and I had been sleeping together for a couple months. The sex was intermittent at best, as though we were both bored with each other but inertia kept us going.

Stuart just somehow strolled into the bar and eventually sat at our table. I had thought it was happy accident, but now I can see the intricate staging that had been involved. I immediately knew his intentions. We were talking about Van Halen. I was in the David Lee Roth camp. Mayrav, Sammy Hagar (why I'll never know). Stuart, the aesthete, had no clue what we were talking about, but it didn't stop him from talking.

"Why, isn't this simply a matter of personal proclivities?"

"No," I said, heatedly, "Sammy Hagar is a corny motherfucker."

"Well, I wouldn't know anything about that. I strictly listen to classical music."

I rolled my eyes. "Then why say anything at all?" I asked.

"A philosopher who is not taking part in discussions is like a boxer who never goes into the ring," he declared, pompously.

"That's Wittgenstein, isn't it?"

Stuart looked down his long, aquiline nose at me, trying to hide his surprise. I knew what that fool was up to. He wanted a cockfight. There we were, two guys competing over one woman. We didn't have any feathers to puff up. We definitely weren't going to come to blows—he would've lost. And it would definitely have been impolite to compare penis sizes at the bar. But he was determined to best me. He just *knew* his brain was bigger than mine. "You know of him?" he huffed.

"Ludwig Josef Johann Wittgenstein, Austrian-born philosopher, protégé to Bertrand Russell. Author of *Tractatus* and *Philosophical Investigations*. Major influence on logical positivism. In the Austro-Hungarian army during World War I, became the most decorated warrior/philosopher since Socrates?"

"So, you do know of him?"

"Naw, I don't know anything about that nigga."

Mayrav erupted in laughter. I left soon thereafter. I refuse to get into cockfights. If she wanted to choose Stuart's goy ass over mine, she could have it.

We didn't see each other for months. Over the years though, she'd pop back into my life, and we'd hang out quite a bit. We never had sex again (I don't think Samara would've been cool with that), but we would see a lot of each other. And she'd always be heartbroken over some foolishness Stuart had done. And then, sooner or later, he'd appear. He'd be more fervent in his love than he had been previously. Mayrav, of course, would disappear again from my life. At one point, the vanishing act had lasted a couple years. I'd wanted to blame Samara, but I've been wanting to blame her for everything this past year. She was partially to blame. She would give me a lot of grief over Mayrav. But it's not totally her fault. These past couple years Mayrav and Stuart had been in love. And when they weren't, I seemed to magically appear in October. We messed around once, then I was asked to be a father to her child, and then Stuart reappeared with a ring that cost some Sierra Leonean kid an arm and a leg."

And I can see other women. Sophomore year. Keisha. How we'd been sleeping together for months and then she wanted to be serious, to actually stop the creeping and declare our coupled status in broad daylight. And I ran straight to Christy, who lived on the same floor, because we both knew there'd be no declarations there. And I ran from Steffi when things got too serious with her. And I ran from … forget it. You get the picture. I just ran. Only Samara was able to hobble me. And the woman who is oh-so-wrong was right about that. She *did* fight me. And I fought back. I ran and she caught up to me, pulled out the lariat, and hog-tied my ass. Why did she do that? It couldn't have been easy. It just doesn't make any sense. And why do I run now? It's not like I'm an Olympic sprinter with a Nike contract, or something. I'm thirty-two. Isn't it about time I retire?

9:20 p.m.

"Hello … Nandi?"

"Oh … Damian …"

On the frozen tundra of Lambeau Field…

"Uh … hey. I never thanked you—properly, that is—for those CDs. Those ones from Brazil. I really liked them."

"…"

"So, uh—well, what are you up to?"

"Right now? Wondering if I'd chosen the wrong battle. Because I still can't figure out how I lost."

"Uhhh…."

"Did you know my name means 'Patience?'"

"I thought Nandi was a Zulu queen."

"She was. But it took her forever to ascend to the throne. Who has that kind of time?"

"Look, Nandi. I'm sorry I haven—"

"The book, right?"

"Right. The book. Yeah. I'm sorry. But ya know, can we get together and talk?"

"We *could* have."

"Oh. Right."

"…"

"…"

"Jesus, Damian. Is that it?"

"No. But you sa—"

"Forget that. Look, we're going to go see Goapele in concert Friday night. But we're meeting at the Scotsman first. So, be there. Around eight. We can talk then. I can't believe I'm doing this. Fighting for what I want, my ass."

THURSDAY, JANUARY 26, 20—
10:55 p.m.

I was crawling out of my skin and feasting on the scraps. I needed to talk to somebody. Bad. But no one was around. DiDi was busy building her love nest with Priti. Kevin and I haven't really been talking since he broke down before me. We were both a little embarrassed. Besides, he's been busy putting the final touches on the band's upcoming tour. And they've been practicing a lot. I knew Nandi didn't want to talk to me. And it would've been a little awkward to talk about her *to* her. Bob was bedridden in Belfast. And Malik would only annoy me with his marriage troubles. There's just a time to call it quits.

So I rolled to The Ease On Inn—sorry, Morningside Hotel. Hep was a little confused by my urgent call, but he told me to come over, anyway. He looked thinner. And not necessarily in a good way. Like he'd been through some shit. But he was smiling a lot. I think Hep is happy. He'd finally shed Neville from his mortal coil. He hugged me when I entered. It took some effort, but I let him do it.

"You're right," I said, sitting down on my favorite stained chair. "I don't talk."

"What?"

"You said I don't talk. About what's important to me. You're right. I don't. I don't do a lot of things, Hep. I really don't. I write. That's about it."

"And you're not too bad at that."

"Thank you," I said, distracted by my own thoughts. "And you were right about ruts. I'm in one now. I think I've always been in one. It's like … it's like … most people, you see, most people, they gravitate to the things that make them happy, right? TV, sex, whatever. Me? I run from it. *I* run towards misery."

"Why?"

"What?"

"Why? Why do you run toward misery?"

I slumped down in the chair, and said meekly, "I think it's all I've ever known, Hep."

"Damian. I'm so sorry."

Hep was seated on his bed across from me. The room was really small, and we were really close. He reached a sympathetic hand my way. I flinched.

"Don't."

"Oh. Right." He straightened up.

"No, it's not that," I rushed. "I don't like being touched. It's one of my … ruts. I want to get out of it like—this woman. Nandi. She's the most incredible woman I've ever met. And this sounds juvenile, but I really like her. And all I want to do is be with her. But all I *can* do is run away. That's all I ever do. Run away. But I don't want to. Not this time. I didn't the other times. But *really* not this time. And I don't know what to do."

"Don't."

"What?"

"Whatever you do—don't. Don't run away."

"It's not that simple, Hep."

"Ya know, sometimes it actually is. You know what you're doing wrong. So, don't do that."

I looked at him with "stupor" written all over my face.

"All right, look," he opened. "If you weren't you, what would you do?"

"Does that even make sense?"

"I thought adults were able to think in abstractions."

"OK. I don't know. Totally outside myself.... I guess I'd be Eric Benet. Shit, tagging Halle Berry and still gettin' some on the side.... If that ain't hebben, I don't know what is. Though I'd hope I'd make better music."

"Damian."

"All right. I don't know. I wish I could be totally corny. Romantic, whatever. Make some kind of grand gesture. Climb Everest, swim the Channel, slay a dragon. Fight for the hand of the woman I love," I laughed.

"God, that is corny," he whispered, then spoke up, "There you go then."

"What?"

"Fight for the hand of the woman you love. Or maybe you should just ask her out on a proper date."

SATURDAY, JANUARY 28, 20—
11:42 P.M.

She slapped. He smashed. I snapped.

The next thing I knew, I was staring numbly ahead in an adrenaline haze. The road was whipping by me. I turned my head. Nandi was driving, crying in the dark. My right hand was throbbing madly. I winced in pain. A cell phone rang.

"Could you get that, Damian?" she croaked.

"Hello?"

"Damian. Shit. Thank God."

"What's going on, Kev?"

"Shit. Fucking chaos, bruh. Cops are everywhere. Ambulances."

"Really?"

"Yeah, man. They're takin' dude to the hospital. Johnny Law won't let anybody leave. Don't worry, nobody's talking. That bitch got what he deserved. Vikram was squawkin', though, about justice, and shit. But I told him I'd Partition his ass if he said anything."

"Taking over for Bob, are you?"

"Hey, you my boy … Damian? Damian?"

"Yeah?"

"Shit. Put Nandi on the phone."

I reached over, confused. Damn, my hand hurt. "Here," I winced.

She took the phone in a desperate grip and slammed it to her ear. "Yeah

... Yeah ... I know ... No ... I think he's in some kind of shock or something ... Yeah. Right ... OK. Shit!"

She threw down the phone and jerked the wheel. Tires screeched somewhere. Horns blared.

"Shit! Kevin says the cops are looking for you!"

"Oh my God, is it finally my turn?"

Somebody laughed.

"Malik!" Nandi yelled.

"What? That's funny."

What was Malik doing here? I was pissed off at him, the annoying bastard. We had been drinking at the Scotsman. I was nervous as hell, ready to fight for milady's hand—or some such nonsense. But Nandi wasn't there yet. Malik was. Kevin. So were Raheem and Vikram. We were all waiting for the queen to go and see Goapele. Vikram kept looking at me like he wanted me to kick his ass. I guess my disappearance had given him hope with Nandi. But now that I was back, the pretty boy seemed to really be sizing me up. Constantly making snide comments. It was driving me up the wall. It took a lot out of me to not get ethnic. I got up and walked around a lot.

Malik had finally caught me in his favorite conference room, the men's room. I should really learn to stop using urinals. He caught me once again with my dick in my hand.

"I fucked up," he declared, desperately.

"Aw Jesus, Malik."

"I didn't do anything," he quickly amended.

I groaned.

"I tried. I was really close. Donna and I went out after work for a couple drinks. We've been doing that a lot lately. Judy was out of town visiting her folks."

"Can you make a long story short?" I asked, zipping up. "I wanna wrap this thing up."

"Allrightallrightallright. So, we're having a real good time, right? She was having problems with some dude, and I was doing the confidant thing. We go back to my house—just to hang. But she was lookin' so good, bruh. I mean, damn. I couldn't resist. I made my move."

I groaned again.

"And she just pulled back. Like real shocked, and shit. Like it was the worst thing a man could've ever done. Like Auschwitz never happened.

"So, she starts yelling at me, calling me all kinds of names. And I was like, 'But you're so this and so that ... and that, admit it, you really like me, too.' And she admitted that she did. She really *does* like me, Damian. Because she thought I was really special. Not like other guys. And she wanted me. But when I made my move, it proved that I'm just like all the rest. Ain't that some shit?"

I didn't have an answer.

"What do you think I should do?" he asked. "Should I apologize to Donna? Should I tell Judy?"

I chuckled incredulously and got the hell out of there without washing my hands.

"What the hell are you doing here, Malik?" I asked, in Nandi's Prius.

"I'm a big guy. I was the only bastard who could pull you off that fool."

"What fool?"

"Stop it, Damian," Nandi bellowed. "You're scaring me. Should we take him to the hospital?"

"No. If somebody talks, the cops will probably look there soon enough."

"What cops? Where did this blood come from?"

"Oh God."

"You really don't remember, do you, Dame?"

"No. I don't."

"Jesus," Malik sighed, from the back seat. "You beat the hell out of some white boy. Apparently put him in the hospital."

"That's not what I had in mind," I whispered.

"Yeah," he continued. "It was weird. We were all finishing up. Nandi *finally* got there—"

"I got tied up at the office!"

"Anyway, we were about to move onto the concert. This couple was arguing over at the next table."

"Really?"

"Yeah. Then ole girl, she screams, gets up, and smacks the bastard. He roars, shoots up, and decks her square in the mouth. She goes sprawling. Everybody's stunned—but you. You went all *Action Jackson*. Jumped right the fuck up and went for the guy's throat. I mean, you were really choking the fucker, smashing him in the grill. 'I want my two dollars!' Shit like that. We were all too scared to move. You were just smashing the shit out of the bastard. Slamming his head against the ground, everything. Hell, you were beatin' that white boy so bad, I couldn't get 'What's Love Got to Do with It?' outta my head."

I laughed.

"It's not funny, Damian," Nandi admonished.

"No … I guess it's not," I admitted. My hand was blowing up like a balloon and shaking violently.

"I wouldn't worry about it. You're a regular. Nobody's gonna rat you out. Besides, as I said, that pussy-ass motherfucker got what he deserved.

Hittin' a goddamned woman like that. I'm just pissed I didn't get to him first."

Nandi dropped Malik off. He gave me a pound, and Nandi and I were off. It was a quiet, tense ride. I didn't know what to say. She evidently didn't want to talk. I don't know what had gotten into me. It must've scared the woman. Eventually, she parked. I had no clue where we were. I looked dumbly at her. She stared at me with the reddest eyes the night had ever seen.

"Come on, Damian," she finally managed to say.

We got out of the car. She led me to the end of the block. There was a large, wooden fence. She pushed aside a few slats and squeezed through. I stood still. "Come on."

I eked my way past. Thank God for the gym and Sista Olu. The place was dark and choking with weeds. She scampered down a path, and I followed, thinking *Blair Witch Project* the entire time. Finally, we reached a chain link fence, which she deftly hopped over. I could barely manage with my left hand. My right hurt too much. But I ultimately made it over. There were more weeds and trees until I saw a concrete mountain.

"Here we are," she announced, and started climbing.

It was an urban graveyard. There were acres of discarded concrete slabs, monstrous clay, concrete, and metal pipes, rebar jutting out from every opening. Nandi nimbly climbed up the largest industrial hillock, grabbing footholds unconsciously and pushing herself onward and upward. "Are you coming?"

It took awhile. I only had the one hand. But I eventually made it, panting and sweating. She smiled warmly at me and sat down. I sat down next to her. Straight ahead, there was another high fence and the highway zooming by.

"Cool, isn't it?" she said.

"In a *Blade Runner*, post-apocalyptic way."

"Do you want to talk about it, Damian?"

"No. Not really."

"You know you can talk to me?"

"N—Yes. Yes, I do."

I fell silent. She looked intently ahead, and sighed. "It's like," she opened. "Like, we live in cities, right, but we don't know what they're made of. Their inner workings. What a complex system a city really is. We just drive on the streets and walk the sidewalks, never realizing that we hardly ever actually touch the ground. Beneath our feet isn't earth. There's this amazing labyrinth of sewers and cables, pipes and wiring. There's this huge city, just buzzing beneath us unbeknownst to a single soul. And this stuff here is what it uses to work. Sort of like people. All the things going on beneath the surface, and we're totally oblivious."

I looked around and saw nothing but detritus. But what can you do? She's an artist.

"I'm really sorry I haven't called."

"I know. The book," she sighed. "I guess I understand."

"It's not that. It's …"

"What?"

Her eyes bore into me. I shied away from their intensity. And swallowed hard.

I asked, "You ever hear of those really romantic stories where this really old couple's been together for, like, a millennium? And finally one of them dies, the other one's so heart-stricken, realizing they can't go on without their other half, and dies a few months later?"

"Yeah," she said, confused. I think I was scaring her. "Of course."

"Well, that's like my parents. They died a week apart. Except … except …" I was drowning in my own words. It was hard to breathe. "Except it wasn't like that, Nandi. It was … it was a fucking nightmare. He used to beat the shit out of her, ya know. Beat the shit out of her, out of me. He'd yell and scream. He'd kick her in the gut, punch her in the face, pull her hair. He didn't give a fuck. He'd threaten her with irons or boiling water, whatever was close at hand. He even smashed her in the head with a beer bottle. I saw it. Right in front of my fucking eyes. I was, what, nine or ten? And he did it. There was glass and blood everywhere. And he would just laugh. She was crying, and he'd laugh. Like he was proud of himself. Like he'd done something to fucking be proud of."

"God, Damian." She reached for me.

"No. Wait. No, she went to the hospital…" I was crying now. I couldn't help it. I couldn't stop it. "She went so many times. I lost count. And then one time, when I was seventeen, she never came back. The fucker had killed her. His steak was too rare, and he just carved her up. Like my mother—my *mother*, Nandi—like she was some kind of fucking pig, a fucking piece of meat."

I exhaled tremulously. "And I wa—I wa—they arrested the bastard. And he died in prison a week later. They said it was suicide. Like that fuck could ever feel guilt over what he'd done to her. I hope the brothers raped him with the knife he'd used on my mother. Ha!"

I laughed and swiped at my damp cheeks. "I'm sorry. I'm never like this."

"No," she groaned. "Don't be."

"It's just … it was so—I'm so, so fucked-up, Nandi. I forgot that for awhile, with Samara, but I am. I don't know what kind of man you, you imagine me to be," I gasped. "But I'm not him. I don't know if I ever could be."

She looked at me. I could barely see her, but I knew she was there.

She reached beneath my hair and touched the back of my neck. I tried to get away, disappear. She held on tighter and pulled me closer. I was in her hands. Her cheek slid into mine, our tears mingling.

I've never had a breakfast meeting with attorneys. How weird, but what would you expect after the night I'd just had. I had some things to work out. I didn't think my guy would be up to it. He's an entertainment lawyer, after all. But go with what you got, that's what I always say. The four of us shook hands and sat down to coffee, fruit, and beignets. It promised to be a long morning.

"OK," my lawyer opened. "My client, Damian Rene Cross, first wants to make it clear that last night's display was indeed an aberration. He does not actually have a violent temper, and, while he has had physical altercations in the past, he had never lost his mental faculties like that before."

Nandi leaned over and whispered into her lawyer's ear. She was looking immaculate in her J.J. *Good Times* "Dyn-O-Mite!" T-shirt. I was still in last night's clothes. She finished, and her lawyer nodded gravely. "Ms. Huang is in complete understanding with the underlying causes of last night's incident. We see no problem."

"Good. My client also realizes that he *does* have self-esteem issues and is willing to work on it. He is even willing to seek counseling, if necessary—though you can't tell anyone. Apparently, 'black folks don't do that shit.' Sorry, African-Americans."

"Understood. My client has similar issues, as well as a bit of an Elektra Complex—if you don't mind my saying, Nandi. She *has* sought counseling over the issue and feels that she has made significant progress."

"That's good to hear. You may have also noticed that Mr. Cross has no real sense of style. Now that he is over thirty and steadily losing 'the beauty of youth,' as he is wont to say, he realizes that this must indeed change. He will most definitely seek your client's counsel in this area."

"Idiot," her lawyer hissed.

"I know, I know," I conceded.

"I adamantly advised against it," my lawyer stated. "But I guess love makes you do absolutely ridiculous things. Any other areas we need to cover?"

"Toothpaste?"

"From the bottom."

"Toilet seat?"

"Mr. Cross puts down the seat *and* the lid."

Nandi nodded her head approvingly.

"Does Mr. Cross like sports?"

"He must needs watch his Steelers. His words, not mine."

"Oooh, that's a sticky one."

"This is a deal-breaker, Hank, you goddamned Cowboys fan."

"Is it my fault the Eagles suck?"

"Gentlemen!"

Nandi separated the two and conferred with her lawyer for a moment.

"OK. But he will have to learn to appreciate gymnastics and figure skating."

"Subjective sports!" I erupted. "With corrupt judges! You've *got* to be kidding!" But then I looked at her. *What am I? An idiot?* "All right, no promises. But I'll try. Michelle Kwan is kinda cute."

"All right then. Hygiene and general cleanliness."

"Mr. Cross does groom himself every day, but he is a bit of a slob."

"So is Ms. Huang. That is something they can negotiate without our help. One last thing. Your client must promise to never write about my client in his fiction."

"That's easy. He's a science fiction writer."

I cleared my throat.

"Oh yeah. Right. What if he uses aliases and fudges some of the details?"

There was a long silence. Nandi finally nodded.

"All right, but don't be surprised, Mr. Cross, if you find yourself the subject of a song or two."

"No references to penis size or lack of sexual prowess."

"Done."

OK, it didn't *exactly* happen like that. But we did spend a lot of time at breakfast warning each other. Duly noted. I think I can do this.

MONDAY, FEBRUARY 13, 20—
3:47 P.M.

"Hey, Kev."

"What's going on, slugger? Where you been these past few weeks?"

"Well, you know how it T-I-is."

"No. I don't. But that's cool. If you're glowing half as much as Nandi is, I know you one happy motherfucker."

"Guilty as charged."

"Thank God nobody ever talked."

"Thank God the bastard got out of the hospital."

"Diane/Dakota told me the fool convinced his old lady to get back together."

"Of course."

"Guess what? The label dropped my black ass."

"Sorry, man."

"Don't be. They told me to change, or else. I told them to go fuck themselves."

"No. You didn't."

"Hell no I didn't. Even attacking Pearl Harbor wasn't *that* stupid. But it did feel good to claim creative differences. Made me feel like a real artist. Hell, D, somebody's gonna pick us up. My agent's already fielding offers. And Vik is with Bomb Hip-Hop. By the time the tour's over, we'll have a deal. So, why'd you call, Damian?"

"You ever notice how happiness is always a montage?"

"What?"

"In movies, romances and shit. Boy meets girl, boy gets girl, boy loses girl, boy gets girl back. All of that is painfully documented. But the happiness part—when the couple's madly in love—that's always a montage."

"Why's that, Shakespeare?"

"Because pain and conflict are compelling. And while we all strive to be happy, it's pretty boring stuff. If you made a movie or wrote a book about two people happy in love, it'd be an excruciatingly boring experience."

"So what you're saying is, you and Nandi, you're living a montage?"

"Roll 'em!"

THURSDAY, FEBRUARY 16, 20—
9:49 A.M.

MONTAGE:
MUSIC: Johnny Hartman's "The More I See You"
A crowded NIGHT CLUB.
The DJ is waving his arm rhythmically from side to side.
DANCERS are also waving their arms in the same fashion.
DAMIAN and NANDI are doing same, mouthing, "Hey! Ho!"
NANDI jumps into DAMIAN's arms. They kiss.

An ICE SKATING RINK.
CHILDREN are skating hand-in-hand with their parents.

DAMIAN is struggling on his skates. NANDI skates swiftly by, playfully poking him in the sides. DAMIAN teeters and falls. He looks up, comically shaking his fist like an old man.

NANDI is skating backwards, laughing at him, until she skates into a wall and falls.

DAMIAN winces.
NANDI looks up, laughing.

DAMIAN laughs.

DAMIAN and NANDI are sitting together at the kitchen table over plates of pasta.

DEIRDRE and PRITI are doing the same.

The four of them are laughing at the kitchen table over a large meal.

DAMIAN and NANDI, chuckling, stop to kiss.

DEIRDRE and PRITI look on adoringly and kiss each other as well.

In the kitchen, later, DAMIAN is washing dishes and NANDI is clearing the table.

DAMIAN stops and looks to her.

She stops, looking coy.

He smiles and approaches.

She smiles and approaches.

They slide onto the table, kissing passionately.

A framed PHOTOGRAPH of a young NANDI with her parents; the FATHER looking stern; the MOTHER conflicted; NANDI sad. NANDI's hand clears it off the desk and puts it in a box.

NANDI stands with the box at her desk. The office is empty. She picks it up and solemnly exits.

PEOPLE in the hallway give her sad looks as she leaves.

Outside, DAMIAN waits anxiously in his TERCEL.

NANDI exits the building with a hangdogged expression.

DAMIAN looks tense.

NANDI suddenly drops the box, thrusts her hands victoriously in the air, and dances ecstatically.

DAMIAN laughs hysterically, slamming his cast on the steering wheel.

Lotus sex complete, NANDI collapses on DAMIAN's chest.

DAMIAN
Nandi?

NANDI
(breathlessly)
Yes, Damian?

DAMIAN
I was wondering if you'd like to go
to Mexico. After the tour. I've got these
tickets and thought you might deserve
the break.

NANDI
God, Damian. That's so sweet.

She kisses him enthusiastically.

DATE: Tuesday, February 18, 20— 5:01 p.m.
TO: Cheryl@slagleassociates....
FROM: drcross@wintersoldiers....
SUBJECT: Ice, Ice, Baby

cheryl,

here's the novel, _ice_, a pretty crappy title, but i've never been any good at that kind of thing. sorry, but it's pure science fiction. much to my own chagrin, i realized that i could never be jennifer weiner.

SATURDAY, FEBRUARY 18, 20—
10:52 P.M.

Or Julia Childs, for that matter. Of course, the cast didn't help matters any. But I was determined to make this cake. Tomorrow's Nandi's thirtieth birthday and the night of Yemaya Blue's (the band's new name) big debut concert. Then it's off to their month-long East Coast tour. I'm going to be along for some of it and miss my woman like hell already for when I won't be there. I wanted this meal to be special. And the cake was going to be the perfect cap to the evening's meal I had planned. I had a wonderful time with it. I enjoy cooking again. I'm enjoying everything lately. I'm one goofy-ass fool in love. But why red velvet cake? Who eats that?

As you may remember, I have a real tough time following directions. That's why I never bake [see **THURSDAY, SEPTEMBER 27**]. But y'all would've been proud of me. Uncle Frank wouldn't have recognized me. I used *exactly* two eggs—even scraped the mucus out of the shell to be certain. I used the knife to scrape the excess flour from this thing called a … measuring cup? I threw in exactly one and a half ounces of red food coloring. When the recipe called for beating gradually, I beat gradually. And beat well when I was ordered to. I even sprinkled in soda and vinegar—which sounded pretty disgusting. I had to seriously fight the urge to throw in a clove of garlic. It really does make everything better. I had no clue pans came in inches, but I used a three-eighth-inch one and baked at three hundred fifty degrees (no more—no less) for *precisely* thirty minutes.

The cake didn't turn out too bad (though the kitchen was a disaster area). Nandi actually liked it. She has no clue how proud I am of myself. She liked the entire meal, actually. Nobody had ever made five courses for her before. It was the best pre-birthday she has ever had. Man, I felt that I could do anything. My next task is to figure out how to write a grammatically correct sentence.

SUNDAY, FEBRUARY 19, 20—
11:52 p.m.

The more I see you, the more I want you
Somehow this feeling just grows and grows
With every sigh I become more mad about you
More lost without you and so it goes…

The Banana was absolutely electric. Boogie woogie woogie. Filled to capacity, brimming over with anticipation. Word spread quickly about Yemaya Blue. Kevin and Skip Vindaloo have a lot of fans in the area. People still affectionately remember Arturo's old Latin ska band, and Miguel's been hyping how excited he is to be involved. People couldn't wait to see what these idiots had up their sleeves.

I had been there all night. I wanted to be there for my boy and my woman. I wanted to be there for every minute of her birthday. I stayed off in the corner with a book, though, snugly out of the way. I hate it when people interrupted my writing, and I didn't want to be underfoot. But I was there, watching them set up and practice and generally piss around. Besides, I'm always fascinated with sound checks.

I love just being around Nandi. I love everything about her. She's simply wonderful. So fragile and strong. So intelligent and determined. She makes me laugh, and, most importantly, she makes me smile. I've caught myself more than once just staring at her with the silliest grin on my face. I hope she'll never catch me. I just want to revel in her.

I sat transfixed just before the concert. Nandi was staring off into space, contemplating the ether. Her ritual cigarette smoldered in her hand. She always smoked one before she performed. I asked her what she was thinking when she did that, and she said she didn't know. Who wouldn't love that?

When the lights went down and Raheem banged that drum slowly, the crowd erupted. I was right along with them, screaming my head off. DiDi and Priti stared at me and giggled. I didn't care. Yanely was there, too, with her baby daddy, Rory, the WASPafarian. We exchanged an awkward nod of acknowledgement. Ina refused to come. She no longer listens to secular music. And it wasn't like I wanted Mayrav anywhere near me. I was still pissed at her—when I thought about it. Which was less and less often. But Hep was there with this tiny Dominican brother, prettier than Prince. He'll never learn. Speaking of which, Bob was there with his *wife*, Judy. They were in an adolescent lovey-dovey, kissy-face mood that might've been endearing—if I knew absolutely nothing about those two.

Yemaya Blue was simply wonderful. Some of Kev's older fans quickly left the joint. I think they were expecting his old, fusion stylee. When they heard that wild world/hip-hop/jazz mix, I'm sure it was pure noise to their ears. But those who stayed got a show they wouldn't soon forget.

The band was much tighter than when I'd taken Priti to their practice. They had really gelled. Vikram was scratching like mad, creating beats out of wax and melding perfectly with Raheem and Tod on bass. That drummer was too funky, and had everybody dancing. Tod was off his nut and just went insane on his solos—like he was Flea on crack. Sarah really grooved on her keys and was trip-hopping with her laptop. Arturo blared on his trumpet. He and his horn section punched harder than Ike Turner. When he rapped, you could hear people cursing out in Spanish. But in a good way, I think.

Kevin was his usual, brilliant self. He was all over the place, dancing, playing, singing. I think I saw four or five different horns in his hands. He floored the crowd with his sousaphone "scratching." You could hear "Go, motherfucker!" sprouting up all over the place, which I know is a compliment. He also played guitar and even got on the floor and jammed with Junichiro on the bongos. The percussionist was especially hot tonight, showing out for his wife, Brianna, who looked even more marvelous than I'd remembered—motherhood seemed like it was really good for her.

But she was nothing compared to my girl … damn. She was absolutely captivating. She looked so *happy* up there. I just wanted to cry, I was so happy for her. She was so *proud*. She should've been. Her guitar playing was spectacular, and her voice immaculate. She had the crowd eating out of her hand. "She's so good." "Damn, that girl can *sang*." Some of the women within earshot marveled at how beautiful she is. And brothers were like, "Damn! Who dat?" I was dancing on the ceiling (that's right, I'm so goddamned corny and proud of it, I'll happily throw around the Lionel Richie references). I wanted to tap everyone on the shoulder, and say, "She's with me!" I almost screamed it from the rafters when the music slowed down, Kev picked up an electric guitar, and Nandi got her acoustic.

Sarah started playing strings on her Yamaha synthesizer. They sounded vaguely familiar. Tod thrummed a familiar bass line. Kevin plucked out a melody I knew by heart.

"Oh my God," I gasped.

Nandi started strumming intently. She moved up to the microphone, glowing in her own perspiration. Her eyes were closed, and she looked as though she were in a trance. She sang so sweetly, "Those schoolgirl days…"

"'To Sir with Love?'" DiDi asked, looking oddly at me.

I smiled broadly. How did she know…? I know it's cheesy, but it *is* one of my favorite songs. I love the movie, I love Sidney Poitier, hell, I love Lulu. How did she…? She only heard me … that night—when my urine started burning. That's right. I put it on on the jukebox. How the hell did she remember that?

I searched for Yanely in the crowd. She was already looking at me with an uncomfortable smile. I don't think I'll tell Nandi that part of the story. She'd never sing it again. Who was Yanely, anyway? It was all about that beautiful woman on stage singing directly to me, *for* me, in front of all these people. I screamed my love, hands thrust high in the air.

She opened her eyes and looked down at me. I did some retarded move that would've shamed me under any other circumstance. She chuckled, then belted.

"If you wanted the sky
I would write across the sky
In letters
That would soar a thousand feet high
To Sir with love."

When she finished, the crowd screeched. I was the loudest among them. I think they loved the retro kitsch. I loved her. Nandi looked down at me and winked. I actually blushed.

"I think your cousin's in love," Priti teased, smiling.

"Because that knucklehead finally listened to me," DiDi triumphed.

"Funny, Deirdre."

They laughed at me. I shrugged. *Like I care.*

Nandi and Kevin turned their backs on the crowd. They seemed to be conferring. Suddenly, Kev threw his hands up in surrender. Tod suddenly went epileptic on the bass. The crowd erupted again. He eventually slowed, and then the band started singing, "We want the funk! Gotta have that funk!"

The Banana exploded. People dancing on the walls and shouting along. Nandi looked down at me and thrust a cowbell and drumstick my way. She urged me up on stage with her eyes. I stood frozen. I looked at Kevin. He gave me a new look, the "Go ahead, bitch" look with a giant smile.

I couldn't contain myself. I jumped up on the stage. "We want the funk! Gotta have that funk!" I took the bell and stick from Nandi. "You're brilliant!" I screamed.

"What?!"

"I said, 'You're brilliant!'"

She laughed heartily and kissed me on the mouth in front of all those people. Me. The crowd "ooh"ed like I'd just told Fonzie to sit on it.

"Gotta have that funk!"

It was a bit awkward with the cast on my hand. I had to cradle the cowbell in the crook of my arm but then started banging away like a true Funketeer. George Clinton would've been proud. "We want the funk! Gotta have that funk!"

"On funk cowbell!" Nandi announced. "Damian Cross!"

The club reverberated with applause, cheers, and whistles. They had no clue what they were cheering. I didn't care. I couldn't stop smiling if I wanted to. No writer ever feels anything like this. I was a giggling ass.

"We want the funk! Gotta have that funk!"

I beamed in every direction. Vikram was scowling at me, ripping his records like they just killed his family. I turned to Kevin. He gave me the finger, laughing the entire time. My finger was broken, so I stuck out my tongue. I then looked at Nandi with tears in my eyes. They felt so different. So good. She looked back at me, and laughed with her all.

"We want the funk! Gotta have that funk!"

Damn, I thought. *If this is what being loved by Nandi is like, I could love this woman forever.*

Thanks

I could fill a book thanking all the people who have helped me throughout my life. So, I'll try to be as brief as possible. First, I have to thank my wife, Angie, who has made this book a complete work of fiction—it's been a pretty good decade, eh?; all the friends, family, and friends' family who housed me, fed me, and made me feel loved throughout the first book tour; the brave souls who read and actually enjoyed *Sunshine Patriots*; my agent, Bob Mecoy; Iwan Bagus for the photos; Soko Hirayama for the cover design; my web guy and little brother, Gerald Mohamed; Julian Thompson for being a sounding board throughout and keeping me sane; Karen Baumgaertner for her efforts; and to all my intrepid test readers for their invaluable input: Karima Barrow, Freda Brédy, Jenn Curry, Erica Dholoo, Grant Harris, Blanka Homolova, Jilo, Byron Johnson, Jacqueline Johnson, Dona Jones, Josetta Jones, Ahnya Mendes, Terri Onstad, Paul Rohlfing, Shelley Wade, and Cord Williams. If I've forgotten anyone, please forgive. You know I ain't quite right, anyway.

Printed in the United States
73686LV00003B/97